TROUBLESHOOTER

By
Rod Lindsey

Editor, Margot Ayer.

Cover art, Megan Rackleff.

The author would like to acknowledge the U.S.
Marshals Service, U.S. Army Rangers, and the "army"
of professional nude dancers working out there every
day. Errors in descriptions of U.S. Marshal Service
protocol or action involving Rangers in Vietnam are
entirely the fault of the author and he begs forgiveness.

ISBN – 978-0-615-61244-7

For Nita

Without you, I wouldn't be.

Chapter 1

"Marshal! Hey there…marr-*shaaall*!" Steven Mays called
from an abandoned hunter's cabin barely visible in the darkness
up ahead. Mays was an escapee on the run. Had a reputation
as a meth-head, a smalltime dealer. Right now he was a wild
card, nervous and unpredictable. And the panicky tone of his
voice suggested to U.S. Marshal Ezra Hooten that he was
seriously pumped-up, high on methamphetamine or who knows
what, adrenaline nudging things up a notch or two. Mays was
pushing himself to the edge. Hoot had seen this sort of thing
before – it seldom ended well, and he figured he would be
seeing the proof of that very soon. Hopefully soon enough.

"You still out there, lawman?" Mays hollered in a
taunting way, raw disdain dripping from the word, *lawman*.
And then almost immediately he added, "I'm gettin' tired a-
waitin' old man. So bring it on if you're gonna."

His challenge hanging unanswered for only a second or
two, Mays continued, sounding like he was on the verge of full-
fledged panic, "Yeah, I know you're still out there. I seen your
spooky white head sneakin' 'round in the dark. Heard you
scratchin' in the brush. Soundin' like a fat rat in a woodpile."

A half-moment later, impatience trumping any instinct
for caution, Mays hollered again, "Guess what…I like t'shoot
rats!"

A wild shot into the ferns a few feet away on Hoot's
right followed. And then another much closer. There were a
few brief moments of silence. Tense silence. Not the peaceful
sort at all. Then Mays said, "How're those two badge-wearin'
buddies-a-yours, Marshal? They dead?"

Incessantly damp here in the old-growth woods of the
Olympic rainforest, the distinctive aroma of gun smoke

1

lingered in low spots between ferns and cedars, giving the dense woods a battleground aroma. For Hoot it was an all-too familiar smell. The devil's back yard on the fourth of July. He looked up at gargantuan trees and darkness beyond. It was a moonless night – getting foggy – well after midnight and getting later second by nerve-wracking second.

Giving his right temple a quick massage to unconsciously fend off a looming headache, Hoot glanced off to the left, near where he knew his partner's body lay dead in the darkness. A highway patrolman lying seriously wounded down in the draw, Hoot had burned up ten precious minutes slithering up the slope of a brushy embankment while under sporadic gunfire. He was making one last attempt to gain an advantage on Steven Mays and his pal, Melvin Keen, holed-up escapees from Twin Rivers – escapees who were not known to be armed until they had opened fire without warning.

Not that it would have made any difference for Hoot to know that Mays and his cohort were armed. He had been treating every shithead he tracked as armed and dangerous all the nearly forty years he'd been a marshal. Go in heavy or don't go in was the golden rule that he lived by. Simple. This being true, it still hadn't kept the action against these two from blowing up in everyone's face an hour-and-a-half ago – bullets flying instead of the lengthy standoff or quick arrest that Hoot and his team had expected.

The first responding backup officer had been the now-wounded trooper. Should have waited for a full contingent of backup before making our move. Should have waited for a chopper, Hoot thought, while in the back of his mind he was hearing his boss, Senior Deputy Horner, say the exact same thing. Hoot was the Deputy in Charge of this operation – sometimes called among marshals the DIC or *DICK*, an appropriate acronym, he thought, for a position that had backfired on him before – and the decision to take action had been his. An uphill assault at dusk. Trying to beat the deepening darkness that had so quickly cloaked the woods like a heavy blanket. His call. His mistake. Wasn't the first.

Even though Hoot was as subject to second-guessing himself as anyone, he would never admit it in a million years because if there was one lasting lesson he had learned in his brief time on earth, it was that it's pointless to ponder what *might* have happened. Still he wondered; am I getting sloppy here in the twilight years of my imperfect career, the more colorful parts of my reputation starting to stick, starting to define me? Am I really a shoot-first Wild-West sort of marshal stuck in the wrong century, a squinty gunslinger barely one notch above a bounty hunter on the food chain? Am I willing to risk the lives of others to quickly wrap up the sideshows and get back to the main event?

Okay…so maybe there have been plenty of days when these would have been flip-of-the-coin questions, but today is not one of them. I'm no gunslinger, Hoot thought, not really – mountains of evidence to the contrary. I'm just quick to cut the bullshit and do things in a very direct manner.

Stilling his thoughts, Hoot listened with all the concentration he could muster. Just beyond the ever-ringing tinnitus in his head he could hear Mays rustling around inside the cabin, mumbling unanswered curses at his partner. The cabin had only one entrance, the one facing Hoot. With another furtive glance toward the darkness off to his left, Hoot considered how much better it would be to have a partner ready for action over there instead of the lifeless body of a young deputy marshal lying in the underbrush – Hoot's latest partner; his third partner in five years to die in the line of duty. How's *that* for some kind of a record…

Hardly noticeable. Just one more smudge on the old Permanent Record, Hoot thought. The Permanent Record that inevitably influenced every fuckin thing in a man's life while never *never* telling the whole story. Nooselike, the Permanent Record around Hoot's neck had been growing tighter year by year, his entire adult life. "My buddies are doing fine!" Hoot hollered back, lying. Thoughts he was having about the man in the cabin were foreboding, the likelihood of him surrendering getting closer to nil with every passing minute.

Crouching, knees aching, Hoot crawled around a Jurassic-size fern, giving a very large clump of thorny blackberry brambles a wide berth. He added; "They're just

3

taking a coffee break! Got some fresh Krispy Kremes…you want one?"

No reply came back, the cabin hunkering quietly in the dark for the moment.

Hindsight kept telling Hoot they should have waited, but hindsight will hang you every time, Hoot knew, and the situation at the moment didn't allow for it. Bad deal all around was what this situation had become, but there would be plenty of time to ponder that later. Not to mention mountains of paperwork. Computer work. Debriefings. Depositions complete with labeled diagrams and photographs. Another goddamned condolence letter to write to another partner's widow – one copy filed away in a folder full of condolence letters written over the years. Virtual heaps of responsibility to live with. Self-recriminations that he would be unable to let go of, eventually attempting to drown them in alcohol.

With a wry smile, it occurred to Hoot that the whole concept of 'later' was basically a big headache waiting to happen. Sad truth is that I've been packing a growing load of shit my whole life, he thought, and I'm simply tired of it. Topping off the shitload recently was Senior Deputy Horner, always lingering in the background, one eye on me since the day I landed in Seattle. Horner with his relentless agenda to get my attitude plumbed-up before I slide into retirement, Hoot thought.

Another wild shot from the cabin took a splintery bite out of a cedar not two feet away from Hoot's head. Another miss, but Mays had figured out Hoot's general location, the little red laser dot wandering so close, he was bound to get lucky eventually.

Just pile it on, Hoot thought. No problem – I can take it. Assuming I get out of here with my head still on, that is. There was certainly no guarantee about that outcome at the moment. And no time to worry about it.

All that Hoot dared allow himself to worry about right now was the field dressing that he had applied to the wounded trooper's gut, imagining that it was leaking blood faster than a duct tape patch on a dimestore air mattress.

4

Backup and medical aid was another half-hour away. Maybe more. Bad guys holding the high ground. No available cell phone service out here so deep into the rainy backside of hell. And, adding a little spice to the situation, there was no way to get back to the vehicles and their long-range two-way radios without significant exposure across open ground. The trooper had gone down trying to do exactly that, leaving no way to send word any farther than you could yell it. Real bad deal. Oh yeah…

Goddamned hick hoodlums, he thought, always eager to make a desperate last stand somewhere out in the sticks. Hoot had seen more than enough deep-in-the-trees-and-undergrowth action in the jungles of Vietnam back in his Army days. Had learned since to prefer urban showdowns, the action going down where backup was nearby. Where a man had resources at his disposal. Where there were civilized bars with happy hours.

"How 'bout your pal Melvin Keen, Mays? Would he like a doughnut, too?" Hoot added, pretty sure that he'd hit Mays' erstwhile cellmate square in the sweet spot during the big exchange, and hopeful the two escapees didn't have Kevlar protection to go with their high-caliber firearms and laser scopes. This was not to suggest that standard-issue vests had done such a great job of protecting his partner lying dead in the bushes or the patrolman lying wounded back down the hill. Bad guys had the latest goodies these days, taking advantage, apparently including Teflon-coated rounds in this case.

Hoot wondered where the hell a pair of recently-escaped shitheads got all this gear. *Craigslist* for cons? He looked around and noticed that the fog seemed to be thickening a little. Could be a small advantage. Only one he had at the moment.

"Whatsamatter? Did Mel check out on you, Mays?" Hoot called.

"Yeah. 'Fraid so. Looks like he's all done," Mays said. Sounding stressed. Sounding breathless. Possibly wounded. Mumbles, grunts, and shuffling sounds came from inside the cabin.

"Some partner, huh?" Hoot said.

"That's alright. I don't need him. Didn't like him much, anyhow."

The woods went as quiet as woods ever get for a few seconds while a breath of breeze high up in the tree branches moved the fog ever so slightly. Gave it a spiritual aura and made Hoot think of his first love, Donna Messenger. Made him think that her spirit was, as always, keeping an eye on him. And that thought caused Hoot a moment of angst remembering Norman Carpenter, the onetime friend who had married Donna and then murdered her less than a year after the I-do's.

Norman. The ex-best-friend who'd escaped on Hoot's watch. Norman was the real *Main Event* as far as Hoot was concerned.

Norman – the rotten bastard!

Hoot turning himself into a laughingstock tracking him year after year. Norman was the fugitive he really should be apprehending right now instead of sneaking around in these god-awful wet woods after a couple of worthless creeps who'd just taken the life of a good man. Maybe two good men if the patrolman didn't get help soon.

Disgusted, Hoot felt wrung out. Weary from marking time. From chasing fools. Mostly he was damned weary of chasing a psychopathic ex-friend and never catching him. Always waiting for him to stick his head up. Always ready to put him down as soon as he did.

Listening and looking with sharpened senses, Hoot heard some kind of owl hooting a ways off, sounding like a forest pager calling Hoot's name and dropping the *t*. No sound of distant sirens rushing to the scene. No *whup-whup-whup* of a chopper with a spotlight hovering overhead, just the constant drip-drip-dripping of ever-wet trees.

"How 'bout you, old man? You down to sneakin' 'round out there all by yer one-n-only, now?" Steven Mays called out, breaking the moist silence with a bark of laughter that sounded to Hoot exactly like a crazed hyena he'd seen in a grandkid's Disney cartoon.

"Yeah, that's what I think," Mays said. "Yer the last lawman standin'…"

A cougar or some other wild creature screamed in the distance as if answering Mays' crazyman laugh. Maybe the scream was in protest of Mays' dark sense of humor.

Or simply a new noise from the owl's repertoire.

"Sounds like some kinda big-ass cat comin' after you, marshal. Maybe comin' after me too," Mays offered. "Weird, huh? Yer buddies on *break* an' all. Here I was thinkin' that me an' you were the last two big bad cats still playin' in these woods."

"You're right," Hoot called back, bending and stretching slightly to relieve his lower back. "Truth's finally out. It's just me and you left, now. And I say fuckit! I'm ready to put away my toys if you are. Call it quits and go home."

More hyena-like laughter issued from the cabin. "No way, lawman! I know you aint got the balls t'come up here an' a-rest me all by yerself, so whaddya say we just get good an' comfy 'til the cavalry comes..

"*If* it comes," Mays added, heavy on the *if*.

"We could do that, sure," Hoot answered, shifting his position to a better vantage point, his knees starting to give him some real hell after all this time in the cold and damp. "But I feel I should warn you that you mean absolutely nothing to me, Mays. Honest to God, you're just another sorry shithead wading around in the deep end of the shitpot. That's it. Nobody special.

"You're not the infamous bad guy I came to this ever-wet corner of the country to catch. You see Mays…there's no extra credit in it for me for catching a two-bit outlaw like you. None at all. No front page headlines with my name spelled right. No passing Go and collecting two hundred dollars. No deep sense of accomplishment. Nothing!

"What's more – and this is important, Mays, so listen up! I'm getting too old for this shit. It's way past my bedtime so I'm tired, and I'm in an extra-shitty mood 'cause I'm hungry and I have low blood sugar. The way I figure it, I've played more than fair with you. Been as patient as I know how to be. So as far as I'm concerned, your time is up. Meaning if you

7

don't throw down and surrender right fuckin now, I'm gonna come up there and kill you…"

This last bit was the kind of comment, Hoot knew, that can easily fall into the 'Famous Last Words' category. But, as his father had so often said: there was no stuffing it back in his mouth now that it was out. And it was not an idle threat.

The way Hoot saw it, his butt was already pressed up good and tight against Senior Deputy Horner's ass reamer over this whole deal going south. Hoot just hadn't felt the bite from it yet. And he knew from plenty of previous experience with Horner and his ilk that, at this point, he'd only be wagering a small amount of additional butt-flesh by playing hardball from here on out.

Mays' response was another wild shot into a tree trunk a few feet to Hoot's left, very near the spot he had just vacated. The muzzle flash showing Hoot exactly where Steven Mays was located inside the shadowy cabin.

Okay. Hardball it is, then…

Hoot recalled how all those long years ago when Corporal Norman Wayne Carpenter first became known as *Creeper*, Sergeant Ezra Monroe Hooten also had a Special Ops handle. Best shot in the battalion, they had called him *Troubleshooter* back then, and he had a reputation for cool fearlessness under fire to go with that handle.

Fearlessness – what a laugh. There was no such thing in Hoot's experience. In his case, it was all just a bunch of jungle-jive left over from Vietnam that he'd never been able to shake. He'd always thought it amazing, the way a man's bad-ass reputation can grow from something no more heroic than a desperate fool in a tight spot going through the motions necessary to save his own skin. And yet he'd seen it happen. Been there. Done that.

And now, here he was again. Alone in a tight spot just like back in 'Nam.

Yep…it's time to end this foolishness, Hoot thought.

It's *past* time. To hell with the consequences.

From nowhere, a tune began to play in the back of Hoot's mind. A goofy riff bouncing off the walls of the old inner sanctum. It was one of those persistent tunes that he knew would not go away. And that was okay – it was comforting, actually. He'd always done this; conjure some nonsensical jingle-like soundtrack in his head whenever he was stressed. Hoot's ex-wife, Linda, used to say a person would have to know Ezra Hooten prettydamned well to know this; that he was even capable of experiencing stress.

And no one did. Not anymore.

Hoot set his assault rifle aside and checked the clips and chambers on his 9mm Glock 19 and the .25cal Beretta that he carried for backup. Both were loaded and cocked. Safety's off. He took a moment to park his fear in the numb zone at the back of his mind; then he stood and started squeezing off rounds from both pistols while walking straight uphill through the thorny underbrush toward his objective.

Nine shots from the Berretta and sixteen from the Glock.

The soundtrack playing in his head approaching a crescendo, the stark gunshots became a backbeat to his determined stride, *Bam! Bam! Bam!*

His one-track concentration blocking out everything but the kill and the shortest way to it, Hoot picked up the pace. He'd be risking a crippling fall in the dark except that instinct mapped the path ahead the way it had always done whenever the shit got close to the fan.

Halfway to his objective Hoot had started to whistle along with his goofy inner tune. It was just a wheezy hissing sound through his teeth, really. He'd never learned to whistle properly, all songbirdy, like his father could. But it sounded as sweet and spot-on as the first chair flute in a madhouse orchestra to him. An orchestra of death. Celebrating the art of violence at full volume. Pure insanity...

Only a few panicky return shots were fired from the cabin.

This was Hoot's first real taste of the Olympic Peninsula, the rainforest part of Washington State, and thus far he didn't care for it. It was the middle of November.

Chapter 2

You're smoking too much pot, Norman Carpenter told himself. That's because you're stuck in this cheapass Seattle motel waiting for a phone call that's taking its own sweet time coming. Certain people wanting to cut a certain old man out of the smut and dope business in the Emerald City. People thinking it's time to grow the business. Time to take on new partners the old man wouldn't approve of. People looking for a freelancer and setting up the hit. Calling *Creeper* to do the job because using in-house talent could start a stink that might linger.

Norman paced across worn and faded carpet from the window to the bathroom door and back to the window, mini-surges of vertigo lurked behind his eyeballs making the turns a little bit challenging. He was thinking: No, I'm not smoking too much pot. I'm smoking just enough. Exactly enough.

He looked down at the floor, at the so-called *carpet*; detecting a faint whiff of commercial cleaning solution, loathe to speculating how much unsanitary detritus must've become permanently pressed into the fibers to make them so stiff and smooth. He looked up. Stared through gauzy curtains and streaky window glass at a little slice of Highway 99. Traffic going past lickety-split in both directions. Everybody having important business to tend to.

Yes. It was this place that was making him impatient, Norman decided. This filthy, unwholesome place. That and the simple fact that Norman Carpenter considered himself, by nature, a man of action. And experience.

He sat down on the edge of a mattress that was about as stiff and unyielding as a sheet of plywood, reloaded his bong and lighted it, cleaned his horn-rimmed glasses, replaced them on his nose, and looked at the silent phone. Had to be a landline. No cells allowed, he thought, the wisdom of that simple old-timer's precaution more valid than ever here in the so-called information age, everybody having access to information about everybody else, the new definition of *wireless* being *easy to steal*. Hence, he was tethered to the goddamned thing.

The gaudy yellow corner of a Denny's sign located next door to a Christmas tree lot beckoned to him from across the highway. Norman thought how an afternoon breakfast would be tasty. Call it second breakfast. Or third. Easy to lose count. He took another hit off the bong. Being patient. Superstitious that he'd miss his call the instant he left the room.

The only call he was hearing was the call of Denny's sizzling bacon. Almost smelling it. Denny's restaurants were generally pretty clean.

He looked at the phone, thinking: Fuckit. If I miss it I miss it. The man can phone back later...

Yeah. But you said you'd be here.

He took another bong hit. Holding the moist smoke in, letting it expand, feeling the buzz build behind his eyebrows and knowing that all this unfocused waiting was causing him to get shitface stoned.

That was okay. Norman could handle being stoned.

Eventually the phone rang and the sound of it was like a hot javelin being stabbed through his brain from ear to ear. It rang several times while Norman took a moment to organize his wits before answering. Then he picked it up, saying, "Yeah?" and a voice he recognized told him; "Tonight. Ten o'clock. Room number forty-six-oh-one. A suite at Westin. Got it? Number forty-six-oh-one."

"Yeah. I got it. Ten o'clock. The Westin."

"Don't be late. The door'll be unlocked. You walk in and take care of business. Nothing to it." The voice on the line sounded like he thought he was a real somebody. Sounded like he was boxing Norman's ears and getting the job done.

"No problem. I'll be there," Norman said. "Will the old man be alone?"

"There'll be a party girl with him. No bodyguards."

Norman imagined that she would be young and stupid. Probably one of the dancers from The Club. A new one. Getting broke in.

11

"And the girl?" Norman asked.

"Girl? What girl?" the voice said.

Then he added, "Stop at The Club on your way out of town."

***

On December 11th Tukwila police issued a routine press release reporting that twenty-six year old Angela Hunter was missing. Both Seattle newspapers mentioned it. The local television stations did not. The newspapers reported how the pickup truck that Angela was driving had been found abandoned at Southcenter Mall where she had reportedly gone earlier in the day to do some Christmas shopping. Gifts were in the cab. Angela's husband, Lester, hardly the worrisome type, had called the police when she failed to come home by dinnertime, saying: "Bitch never goes anywhere by herself. Left the kids with my sister. Fucking crazy women. Both of 'em."

The newspapers wasted no ink on Les' comments. But they did make note of the fact that Angela is the mother of two children, a girl aged five and a boy aged eight who were currently under the care of their aunt, insinuating the possibility of foul play as surely no mother could possibly abandon her young children during the holiday season without soon turning up dead in a back alley – stay tuned for more. Both articles also mentioned the police were requesting that anyone having information regarding the whereabouts of Mrs. Hunter contact them immediately…

At least this was the way Angela Hunter's imaginary scenario played out. A semi-silent movie in her mind – audience of one. A thin smile cracked her lips as she thought: Anyone having information?

How likely is *that*? Anyone who might've been in a position to actually know something about my situation never cared enough to find it out in the first place. The whole scenario is bogus – I'll probably have to turn myself in as a missing person for Les to even realize I'm gone.

Waiting near the Holiday Carousel at Westlake Park in the heart of Seattle, Angela believed it was the hand of fate that had brought her here from Southcenter on a Metro bus. Loki playing the role of fate and casting her into the holiday hullabaloo; a place where people buzzed with festive spirit while children whirled past on gaily-painted horses and beasts, the calliope sound of it all reverberating into so much screech and clatter in Angela's ears.

Children, Angela worried, feeling a stab of guilt that pierced straight into her heart. A slight numbness crept into her lips, fingers fidgety. She consoled herself that her kids would be fine with their favorite aunt until she got back. Just fine…

Keeping a tenacious grip on that idea, Angela was holding a Bon Voyage gift to herself – a small box of Godiva chocolates – with both hands, her backpack hanging from her shoulder by one strap. She felt lost in this crowd and more than a bit fearful. Doubts trying to nudge determination aside.

Oh God…what have I done? What am I *doing*?

It was late in the afternoon. The sky cloudy and getting dark. The air moist and chilled. City lights blazed as if vainly trying to hold the darkness at bay. The big Starbucks coffee kiosk behind her doing a brisk business, Angela watched impatient traffic struggling up the street in a nerve-wracking crawl and she briefly wondered how many of those cars and trucks really needed to be out and about. How many were just taking up space. How many, if any, were going her way.

Nearby carolers sang of hope and devotion. At the corner Angela observed one man clutching a bible and feverishly preaching of damnation while twenty paces away another preached of salvation. A third man begged for charity with a cardboard sign reading; "Homeless. Please help. Wife and two kids. Thank you, God Bless!" Across the street well-groomed Percheron draft horses were hitched to festive holiday cabriolets loaded with passengers. They were queued up, waiting with their well-groomed drivers for a chance to forge into the endless traffic mill.

Jingle bells were ringing outside the nearby store and mall entrances, the noise of them coming from every direction at once and challenging Angela's ability to hold a thought. The air was so heavily laced with the aroma of curbside coffee and sugary treats it was almost nauseating to breathe.

13

In the middle of it all stood Angela. Scared and confused – closing in on freaked-out. And waiting on fate.

Angela believed that you can argue the existence or non-existence of fate forever and never win the argument. She and her sister had given it their best shot the last time they were together – they were always at each other about *something*, it seemed. But one thing you can be certain of is that fate will arrive on schedule if it is coming at all. And so did her new best friend. At precisely four o'clock she came walking across Third Avenue. Smiling and friendly as if she and Angela were reunited best friends.

"Wanna latte?" the woman asked with a quick hug, her fragrant warm breath making little puffs of steam in the chilled air. "A Grande Americano sounds good to me. I'm gonna get one for the road."

"No. I'm okay."

"Not a big coffee drinker…huh? I'll get you a hot chai tea, anyhow. My treat. You'll love it."

Angela reconsidered, said, "Yeah. That sounds good."

Suddenly it sounded very good indeed. She'd heard of hot chai tea – never had one before, but was willing to accept that it was delicious. Angela had blundered into this journey knowing mostly nothing about almost everything, scared to death about leaving her kids for even a little while, and unsure how she was going to get where she needed to go to do what she felt she had to do on the less than two-hundred dollars she had in her backpack.

But she'd had faith that somehow everything would work out. And now someone had arrived and taken charge. Someone who knew what was delicious. Someone who knew what to do. Angela's sense of relief turning profound, she realized that she was hungry, said, "I think I'd like a muffin, also."

"Yeah. Good idea," the woman said. "Blueberry sounds good, don't ya think?"

Angela's new friend was a boyish-looking woman of uncertain age, small in size, but huge with self-assurance, she had short-cropped platinum blonde hair, hazel eyes, and a broad smile that radiated charisma. She wore dark nondescript baggy clothes and not a trace of makeup. But she also wore sizeable diamond stud earrings and at least eight rings of apparently significant value decorated her fingers and thumbs. She had said her name was Liz. "Not really. But that's what I call myself," she explained. "It's one of my professional names. And I like it a lot better than my real name. I'm a nude dancer, by the way."

"Seriously?"

Liz grinned. "And an artist…"

Earlier, when Liz had sat down on the bench next to Angela at Southcenter Mall, it seemed that the virtues Calm and Reason sat down with her, and Angela immediately felt a kindred spirit had arrived, a decent human being who'd noticed that another human being was hurting and bothered to stop and offer help in the form of a clean tissue and a few kind words. After a few silent moments had Liz said, "Looks like you have some things to do. Shopping maybe? Maybe need to make your mind up about some things?"

"Actually, my mind is made up," Angela answered. "It's just that I haven't felt quite *right* recently. It's almost like I don't even recognize myself anymore," thinking; I'm sure Mom would walk across hot coals to second that little confession in a heartbeat. She dabbed her eyes and cheeks and nose with the tissue, said, "I do have some things to do – that's true. Mostly, I need to get an important part of my life back. Make amends. I need to go somewhere. Back home. First I have to make some phone calls – then I have to get away. I have to get out of Seattle before I lose my nerve." She had never expressed these feelings in so many words before and felt a profound sense of liberation at having spoken them, liberation accompanied by a fresh flood of tears.

"Sounds like a big step to me. Gutsy," Liz said. "Look…it just happens that I'm leaving for Spokane in a couple of hours. I'm driving, and wouldn't mind some company for the trip. If Spokane happens to be on your way and you want to ride along, meet me by the carousel at Westlake Park at four o'clock."

Liz had walked away as quickly and mysteriously as she'd arrived. And now she was back as promised, buying hot

15

drinks and muffins and taking charge. Even if only for the moment, she was a huge relief to Angela.

Angela gratefully took her chai tea. Gave the box of Godiva chocolates to the homeless man with the wife and two kids, and followed Liz a few blocks to a parking garage and her car. It was an enormous thing, a dusty-pink Cadillac Sedan deVille with enough room inside to host a Tupperware party on wheels.

When they left Seattle the sky was pitch dark and a deep chill was settling in. Angela saw several jet airliners through the Cadillac's moon roof, each plane full of passengers as anxious as she, no doubt. They followed one behind another on glide paths heading south toward SeaTac airport. Down below them ferryboats glided across the dark expanse of Elliot Bay on watery cushions of churning light. Arterials and secondary streets were clogged with cars and busses and trucks scrambling in every direction.

Everyone hurrying to get somewhere else, Angela was simply eager to leave while her nerve held. Tall downtown buildings lit from top to bottom; the whole city was shining, a gigantic urban diamond determined to remain unforgotten – and she silently promised not to, then turned to look ahead.

***

Norman Carpenter stood at one of the floor-to ceiling windows in suite 4601 on the top floor of The Westin. He looked at the city outside as if he were watching a movie at the Cinerama. 3-D. Widescreen. And impressive as hell. But not real.

He knew that his old friend and blood-brother, marshal Ezra Hooten, a.k.a. *Hoot*, a.k.a. *Troubleshooter*, was somewhere out there in the hubbub. He could *feel* him, so close. And confident that he would leave no fingerprints behind, no hairs, no shoe tracks that could be tracked, scarce forensic evidence of any kind to show that he had been the one taking care of business here other than *style*; he also knew that what he was about to do would draw marshal Hoot out like pus from a festering wound. Because Hoot would recognize the style. He would instinctively feel Norman's hand in it. He was cursed that way. They both were.

Norman closed his eyes for a second and then re-opened them, seeing that his own reflection in the glass – dark, pony-tailed hair salted with streaks of gray at the temples, smooth grafted skin on his right cheek and jaw line, severe eyebrows, blotchy skin coloration, missing ear lobe – had become transformed into an image of his white-haired old friend Hoot when they were both in Vietnam. He searched his mind, looking further back, and replayed a memory of himself and Hoot as fifteen-year-old boys. Wearing breechcloths in spite of merciless teasing from others – especially the younger kids – they were entering a low lodge made of logs with a mud-and-straw roof and a cowhide door, his mother's sweat lodge. Inside, smoke was clinging to the ceiling. It was so close and hot inside that even here and now in The Westin a droplet of sweat ran into the corner of Norman's eye and popped the illusion.

Patience, Shooter my old friend, he thought.

It's almost time.

Can you feel it? I can. And I'm ready.

The sitting room that was reflected behind Norman was quiet and dark except for a cone of light coming from a bedroom off to one side. He could see the party girl standing at the backlit bar behind him. She looked to be sixteen going on thirty-six. Stark naked. Short. Brunette. With big silicone-enhanced hooters and wearing an expression that said, pay first – *then* play. Helping herself to champagne and caviar from a room service cart, her eyes never left Norman's eyes watching her in the glass.

"Hey! Baby! You wanna grab that bottle of Dom, bring it in here?" a voice from the bedroom called out. It was the old man. Good as dead already, but not knowing it.

The girl knew it.

Standing there naked with her Barbiedoll titties, skin as smooth and taut as Visqueen stretched over volleyballs, nipples like medallions. Her reflection in the window glass somehow making her seem even more naked than when she had first appeared, she was looking at Norman and munching Russian fish eggs with a silver spoon. She knew it and she didn't care.

Cold-hearted little kitten, Norman thought.

"I'll let you play with my big Bazooka some more," the bedroom voice called in a teasing tone.

"I'm gonna take a shower," the girl called back, her eyes still glued on Norman's reflection in the window. Jaded, unafraid eyes telling him to go ahead and take care of his business with the old man. Telling him the two of them could do a little business of their own afterward if the price was right.

"Hash me out a nice fat line, Mister Nick. We can play when I'm all squeaky clean," she said, walking barefoot across lush carpet to the bedroom, the bathroom beyond. A slow and lascivious strut. Leaving Norman alone with the view.

Norman looked into the windows of neighboring buildings. Nothing nearby as tall at The Westin. And he saw nobody looking back. He watched the ferries out in the bay. Traffic looking like toys in the streets below. Tiny people. All this was part of a world he walked through every day without allowing too much of it to stick.

Pretty soon Norman heard the shower running in the bathroom and he saw a reflection in the window of the old man coming out of the bedroom. Heard him grumbling, "Lazy bitch." Turned around to face him while reaching for the snubbie Smith and Wesson .38 revolver that was tucked under the waistband of his trousers at the small of his back.

Always a revolver. Or a knife. No spent casings to clean up before leaving.

Mister Nick noticed Norman at the window and stopped about two feet short of reaching the coveted bottle of Dom Perignon sticking out of an ice bucket.

Sorry bastard. Norman watched him stop and stand there with his hotel robe hanging open. His chest sunken and pasty. His belly round. His wrinkly fuckstick dangling from a patch of gray pubic hair like a sad old sausage, the spice all gone.

"Who're you?" Mister Nick demanded.

"Well, I'm not room service," Norman replied. Raising the pistol. Taking aim at the center of the old man's sunken chest. "And I'm sure as hell not here to play with your big Bazooka…"

Chapter 3

It was a quarter past midnight and Norman took a moment to
appreciate how the street was almost completely quiet. Very
little traffic in South Everett at this time of night on a Sunday
night. Nothing going on because it was a working-class
neighborhood, the hard-working denizens all tucked in for their
hard-earned Z's.

That was good. Even though it was late for most folks,
it was still early for punks who might be heading out to look for
mischief. That was good, too, Norman thought, taking a long
hit on very potent joint, muffled bronchial spasms insuring that
the smoke was fully absorbed. He closed and locked the door
of his rattletrap white 1982 Ford Econoline, the words *Wonder
Wand Carpet Cleaning* painted on the side. He would wait.

Hiding in a small clearing between treelike
rhododendron bushes behind The Office tavern, dressed in
black from head to foot, Norman carefully snubbed out the joint
– preserving the remaining roach in a lidded aluminum tube –
and then stood perfectly still and quiet. He was watching the
comings and goings of guys who seemed to be regulars. Guys
probably straight off the Boeing second-shift line, still wearing
their ID badges. Stopping in for a few after work before going
home. To a pissed-off wife, most likely. To surly kids up way
past their bedtimes. To warmed-up meatloaf and mashed
potatoes. Late-nite television.

Invisible, Norman could easily wait in shadows like this
for endless hours at a time. This was different from waiting for
a phone to ring. This was *focused* waiting. It was one facet of
a set of skills that he'd shown natural talent for and been well-
trained by the U.S. Army to do expertly forty-five years ago –
skills that, once learned, you don't forget – a skill set Norman
had learned to do so well, in fact, that he'd eventually been
deemed "too brutal" and reassigned. Then discharged after he
was wounded. A load of shrapnel in the ass. Burns on his face

and chest. That he was a trained *brutal* killer being set loose on the streets of America was apparently of no immediate concern to anyone whose business it may have been to be concerned. The post-trauma therapy offered by the VA both voluntary and idiotic.

Too brutal for war? Imagine that...

Norman had never quite figured that one out.

There was also the business with Donna, the Homecoming Queen and his old buddy Hoot. Never figured that one out, either.

Talk about brutal! *That* had turned into an old-fashioned fuckup all around. No denying it. No making it better. Norman's whole damned life would've been danced to a more pleasant tune if he'd been able to control the devil inside where Donna was concerned. If he'd had enough sense to stay away from his best friend's girlfriend in the first place. Hadn't been so quick to take advantage of her college-girl liberal attitudes about sex and drugs and her surprisingly masochistic ideas of fun – places a guy like him shouldn't go without expecting some blood to flow.

Certainly there had been many times since that fateful day in '83 when he excused himself from incarceration that he'd had to do things he was not proud of. Things he did just to make ends meet. Using certain skills for cash. Often consorting with some of society's more sordid elements. The whole time staying low while staying on the run. But waiting in the shrubbery to kick the shit out of a common street punk was simply too low and demoralizing for Norman to think about. He was too old for this crap. It was depressing – hardly work offering the rush and satisfaction that he knew the real deal did.

Popping the old man in Seattle. Now, *that* was more like it. Had some buzz. The look in Mister Nick's eyes when he realized he was looking at the last thing he was ever going to see. The way Barbietits had treated him like Superfly afterward. She died happy – Norman believed that. And now look at how I've fallen. Look at what I've become. An ordinary street thug, he thought. Hired muscle.

21

Certainly, he was not standing proud in the same league where he had started – in Vietnam, in Covert Ops. Except they didn't like calling it that back then. Those men without rank in casual attire. The same men who took one look at his record and then decided to pass when he was discharged from active duty.

It was their loss, really, Norman thought.

On the record, Norman's job in combat was straight-up L.R.P. – Long Range Patrol. Some of this work lent itself to the dark and secretive side of what eventually became the Green Berets, and ultimately Covert Ops run by Military Intelligence with strings pulled by the CIA. He had been a sniper, so called.

Norman had never liked that word, *sniper*. But he liked the way it worked: one target…one shot…one dead. Clean and simple. Usually a two-man team, spotter and shooter, would set up a sniper position on a selected target. Hoot was usually the shooter because he never missed. Norman was usually the spotter because his reputation was that he could disappear behind a single tree leaf whenever he wished.

They also played around with one-man, shooter-only positions for hits in close proximity – this Norman had excelled at. Soon enough he became the preferred guy for up-close work. No hiding in a fucking tree for Norman, for *Creeper*. No long shots using a scope powerful enough to count a target's nose hairs three clicks away.

Norman had never had the slightest qualms about getting close enough to his targets to touch them as they were going down. Close enough to use a knife. Close enough to count coup. He was unique that way. Thought of it as the way of his Sioux heart even though he was no more Sioux than any other American kid raised on a steady diet of TV westerns in the early sixties. His actual tribal affiliation was *Kootenai*. A fucking fisheater, if you could ever get him to admit it.

Norman was thinking that his second 'Nam tour was where the real action had been, the real kick. He probably would have re-upped for a third tour if they'd just left him alone. But certain high-ranking bastards in military attire took offense at his yen for close work, at his inclination to revamp long-shot missions into up-close ones, at certain details of his kills. Those other *non*-ranking bastards – the ones in civvies; the ones he *really* worked for – didn't seem to have a problem with Creeper's ways but also didn't have the balls to stand up for their creation once unloosed. Fuckers took back his third stripe after a particularly creative LRP effort had resulted in Gook body parts hanging from tree limbs like Christmas ornaments.

Grotesque, they called it. Scrambled to put a lid on it. As if it was the first time this sort of thing had happened and they could stop it before it grew.

Reassigned to the 4th Air Cav, Norman became a goddamned helicopter gunship door gunner. M-2, Ma Deuce twin .50-caliber machine guns. Something else he had shown a natural talent for, but there was no pride in it. The kind of work best done stoned…which he had done. And sure as shit he got hit. Fragged and burned when the chopper went down. Damned near all the chopper jocks got it eventually. It was safer in Covert Ops.

Slightly shaking his head, remembering those days, Norman never understood how the hell anyone could think the six-hundred-rounds-per-minute death he rained down from his gunner's post on the bad guys, their women and children, their dogs and cats and chickens and anything else that had a heartbeat was less brutal than a cold-blooded hit on a selected target. It was a fucking chopped suey mess by comparison. Never made a bit of sense to Norman. Still didn't.

Nearly an hour passed in the rhododendrons and Norman didn't move other than to shift his weight slightly. Finally, the punk he was waiting for walked out of The Office tavern with two buddies, all three walking into the parking lot and straight toward Norman. They were wearing gang-style clothing and dreadlocks in their hair, their attitudes preceding them. If they actually belonged to a gang, Norman suspected the three of them were the whole of it.

As soon as he saw them Norman had to stifle a flashflood of rambunctious thoughts about how this punk was definitely not worth the extra grand he was being paid to teach him what he should already know. Thinking that it didn't make sense to bust up a guy who owed you money. How the hell is he supposed to pay if he can't work? Can't hustle?

Spend a little effort up front, Norman thought. Qualify the people you give credit to and save yourself a shitload of grief in the end.

"Got a little something extra I need done," the man at The Club had said. Passing Norman the envelope containing his payment but not turning loose. All glam and attitude. Acting proud of what he had made happen. He was the Big Man now. His ship was about to come in. Strippers clinging to him like refugees to a raft.

"I don't do that kind of work," Norman had answered.

"You do when you've just been paid fifteen-large for a job worth ten." Gesturing with the envelope. "There's an extra bill inside for this little favor."

Only because you can't ask your own people to do it, Norman had thought. You being a complete chickenshit from the big pawnshop diamond studs in your Hollywood wop earlobes, to your bogus electric suntan, right down to the fake alligator boots on your Hollywood wop feet.

Sure, Norman knew the old man had been West Coast Family. Making the chickenshit West Coast Family. Making him *protected*…to a degree yet to be determined. He also knew the chickenshit's people would be nervous when the news got around. Nobody would want to take sides too early. People playing the wait-n-see game. Worried that the chickenshit might have offed the wrong uncle. Besides, the job was worth twenty, he thought. Not fifteen. You got it done for fifteen because certain people behind you have class and connections. Not because of anything you, personally, bring to the game.

The *ultimate* game, the *big momma* of all games, Norman thought.

The big game is evil, no doubt. Norman had long understood that those who played are evil people to one degree or another – himself included. Everyone on a fast track to hell. And, win or lose, it makes no real difference in the end because the big game endures. It's strife. It's war. It has always been here and will always be here.

24

Norman firmly believed that if the population of the earth were reduced to only two men, those two men would find something to fight over, something each would manipulate and attempt to kill the other for. Everyone knows this – fundamentally, it has always been this way. Always will be.

This, in a nutshell, was the nature of the game as Norman knew it, as he had known it since even before he had the words to describe it. He knew that the game endures because young men love it as if it were the ultimate expression of hot sex itself. Old men have long profited from it, while women have a more pragmatic view because they get to clean up the mess and fret over it.

Still it endures. Always it endures. And everyone knows that the true worth of any game has little to do with the game itself, but lies in the value of what is put at risk in playing it. The chickenshit played recklessly simply because his risk had always been hedged by others – Norman wondered if he even realized that he had cashed-in the best insurance policy the game would ever extend him when he offed the old man.

"You have your own people for this kind of thing," Norman had answered, wanting the chickenshit to back off.

But he wouldn't. Big man was on a roll. "I prefer to use outside talent at the moment," he said. "You do this for me an' we're square. Just scare the guy's all I want. Break some stuff on your way back to my favorite uncle in Spokane, but leave 'em alive."

You mean leave a pissed-off *witness* alive, Norman had thought.

It was too late to back out now. He was in bed with this chickenshit and his people. The only way out was to kill him. Kill a few others the way he had done in Oregon. Make it anonymous. Make everything all nice and quiet the way it should be. Clean. The idea had merit. He'd have to think about it...later.

Fuckit, Norman decided. I think too much for my own good, sometimes. No more. From here on I do my job and that's all I do. *Why* and *who* aren't part of it.

He carefully took off his glasses and put them in a secure pocket. Removed his dentures and put them in another

25

pocket – the front teeth he lost when the chopper went down, when he picked up a butt cheek full of shrapnel, burn scars on his neck and chest that inevitably had chicks and doctors alike asking what had caused it all.

He checked for any traffic in the parking lot or on the street, saw none, and waited for the punks to step a little closer.

The tallest punk was the closest, adjusting his ball cap worn half sideways a' la mode, working his hip-hop stride like it was a goddamned aerobic exercise program he was being paid to promote.

Next was the tough punk, the one Norman was here to educate. This one regarded the others with intense indifference, saying, "Somebody gimme a fuckin cigarette…"

A short, heavyset punk was bringing up the rear, hustling to give the tough punk a cigarette and lighting another for himself.

A whirl of darkness came into their midst from the shrubbery. No warning.

Norman smashed the tall punk's nose and upper lip with a single blow using the palm of his hand. And then he spun around and cracked the short punk's cheekbone with a roundhouse kick that sent his just-lighted cigarette flying. He turned lastly to the tough punk and saw that he'd somehow managed to open a butterfly knife, brandishing it wildly. Norman disarmed him by shattering both bones above his wrist with a quick chop. A flathand punch to the face loosened several teeth and shoved the cigarette to the back of the tough punk's throat. He stumbled and Norman followed him to the ground, landing with one knee in his chest, his own knife in play, a one-handed grip locked onto the punk's neck, thumb pressed into the soft place just above his voice box.

Now the tough punk was choking on the not-quite swallowed cigarette and the pressure from Norman's thumb, his useless right hand twitching at an odd angle to his arm. The tall punk lay whimpering somewhere near the rhododendrons. And the heavyset punk was on his knees in the parking lot gravel, searching wildly around for the knife that had gone flying.

Norman stabbed his own knife into the ground next to tough punk's ear, reached inside the kid's mouth, and said,

"Give it up, kid. You ever hear that cigarettes are bad for you?"

Removing most of the crushed fag, he flipped it aside. Then he continued, "Now, I want you to look behind me at your fat friend. Make him understand that if he makes another fucking move for that knife, I'll beat him to it and cut his dick off with it. Feed it to you. Okay?"

The tough punk was turning blue but he managed a nod. A glance at his buddy.

Norman was disgusted. Disgusted with these three punks. Disgusted with the situation. Disgusted with himself for being part of the situation. It would have been easier to just kill the three of them and walk away. He was a hitman. Not a bill collector. Nor a leg breaker. Notwithstanding court documentation to the contrary, the fact remained that Norman Wayne Carpenter was a cold-blooded *professional* – not a cold-blooded *murderer*. A clear distinction between the two in Norman's mind. And he definitely was not muscle for hire by the pound…not *meat*.

Norman took a deep breath. Getting a grip. Trying to polish some tarnish off his pride at having backslid to doing this sordid work. Big-kid babysitting is what this was. He certainly wouldn't want Shooter to get wind of it. "I hope that's only bone bits and snot and not some of my employer's cocaine I see floating in the blood from your nose," he said to the punk under his knee. "Because you owe my employer some pretty serious money and I'd hate to think you're dumb enough to blow the fucking product up your fartsniffer before you've paid for it. So, here's the deal…you *will* pay what you owe. *All* of it. By tomorrow. Nobody cares how you do it. Nobody cares how many sisters you have to pimp as whores. How many friends and relatives you have to bleed. Whose testicles you have to hock or what bank you have to rob. Just that you do it. On time."

Tough punk's eyes fluttered, his mouth working without making any sound the way a fish out of water will suck pointlessly for life. He was close to being asphyxiated.

"Let me also tell you this," Norman continued. His voice slow. Controlled. Self-conscious of enunciating his s-

27

words, speaking without his front teeth, "I'm taking a little souvenir for my trouble." One-handed, he grabbed his knife and cut a single dreadlock from the choking punk's head including the quarter-size bit of flesh the hairs had grown from, held it up and said, "Notice that little piece of skin there with the hair roots in it? That's what makes this a *scalp*. Meaning you've just been scalped…get it?

"Now, here's the rest of the deal…if I have to come back later and kill you I'll be very disappointed I didn't go ahead and do it now. Save myself the trip. That happens, I swear to you by all the gods and good luck charms I've *ever* considered holy that I'll make it hurt like you can't even fucking imagine. You got that?"

The tough punk barely nodded his head, eyes rolling up in their sockets.

"Remember it." Norman said. He rose to leave, releasing his chokehold, and the tough punk sucked in a long gasp of air. Coughing. Puking up cigarette bits and gingerly touching his bloody head with the hand that wasn't hanging limp, disbelief on his face.

Looking down at the fallen trio Norman almost felt sorry for them. This had often been a problem for him – sometimes he was just too goddamned compassionate.

He fished in his pocket, found his teeth and unobtrusively slipped them back into his mouth. Put his glasses on. He didn't want to feel sorry for them, these punks. They had it coming. And it was a cheap lesson.

Norman put away his knife, picked up the dropped butterfly knife and handed it to the heavyset punk who was still kneeling in the parking lot gravel, said, "Looks like your friend has a broken wrist and a bloody head. You should take him to a hospital."

Chapter 4

"I have to make a quick stop at a place called The Club in North Seattle on our way out of town," Liz explained to Angela. "Do a little favor for my boss in Spokane. You'll be able to get a taste of what nude dancing is all about while we're there. But keep in mind that Goodtime Charlie's, the club where I work in Spokane, has a far better atmosphere than this Club has or will ever have."

Atmosphere? The very idea that atmosphere could be of major concern in a nude club struck Angela as funny. Once inside The Club she could see the word *atmosphere* seemed to mean the same thing as *dark*. When she was a kid Angela had gone with her parents and brother and sister on a family vacation to Branson Missouri: It was one of the few times her father could get away from his development and contracting business, and they took a tour of Marvel Cave while there. Deep underground, about halfway through the tour, the guide turned off all the lights so that you could experience genuine total darkness. The darkness inside The Club seemed only a degree or two lighter than Marvel Cave's total darkness to Angela. Everything in the place was black or red, chrome or mirrored, and the music emanating from the DJ's booth was being delivered from invisible ceiling-mounted speakers at deafening levels, seeming to further compress the claustrophobic darkness of the place. She stumbled over two chairs and a customer en route to the bar where she stopped, clutched the padded leather bar railing, and let her eyes adjust.

With Liz's help, Angela finally found a seat in the center of a sofa-like bench that ran the full length of the back wall. There were eight small round bistro tables spaced along its length and a continuous mirror ran along the wall above it. A heavily-tattooed waitress in a black mini dress with a plunging neckline came and took Angela's drink order, bending down to listen and exposing shadowy cleavage all the way to the Mississippi Delta had there been enough light to see that far. What immediately caught Angela's attention were all the barely-clad women – dancers who were not currently on stage – prowling the floor of The Club like some primitive tribe of lust-driven carnivores.

Maybe it was the two lines of coke that Liz had shared with her in the car before walking in the door. Or maybe it was just because this whole sex-world environment was new to her – illicit, and thus fascinating. Whatever it was, Angela found herself completely spellbound, sitting in the middle of the most amazing spectacle she'd ever seen, and that included two Ringling Brothers' Traveling Circus shows under their Big Top canvas tents, one of the last Ice Capades tours in Kansas City, and Garth Brooks in concert at the Tacoma Dome.

There were two spotlighted stages, each with a woman dancing, both of them naked or nearly so. Brass poles reached to the ceiling at the corners of these stages and the dancers performed amazing acrobatics on them. Hanging upside down by clamping the pole between their thighs while both hands were engaged removing their bras, and flying off the edge of the stage only to circle back while clinging to the pole by one hand and a cocked knee seemed to be compulsory maneuvers.

Full-length mirrors backed both stages. The dancers paraded before them and pressed themselves against them, doubling their images, playing pussy hide-n-peek with customers in the front rows. Angela noticed that many of the dancers engaged their audience by flirting with a special chosen one or several at a time using overstated eye contact. Others seemed to be completely off in another world when onstage, someplace where the customers vanished and nothing remained but themselves and their reflected image in the mirror.

That idea appealed to Angela – being completely exposed and yet invisible – though she was certain she lacked the courage to do such a thing herself. Simultaneously bold and chickenshit too.

Make them *look* for you. Make them call *ally-ally in free*, she thought, remembering the summer evenings of her youth. Playing hide-n-seek with neighborhood kids until it was indecently late. Angela was almost always the last one in.

"I gotta run to the back office," Liz said, reappearing after an unexplained absence. "Take care of some business with the bossman. I'll be a few minutes."

"No problem. I'll wait here," Angela said, smiling like that was all in the world she had to do, thinking that the coke must be kicking-in bigtime, feeling the tingly beginnings of a euphoric sensation entirely unknown to her before now. "I think I've crossed over a line to somewhere I've never been before. No going back to the Land of Innocence for this girl."

And yet the whole scene seemed perfectly normal. Somehow...*right*. It was like she could feel something sticking its horned head up deep inside herself. Something very wicked that had been residing unnoticed inside her skin her whole life – living *with* her – a long-planted seed that was just now germinating.

"Watch this next dancer," Liz said. "I know her. She's good."

A small Asian woman came onstage wearing a miniskirt so tiny it was little more than a leather band around her itty-bitty bottom and a tee shirt that didn't quite cover the underside curve of her nearly-flat breasts. Looking so small and so young under the red and blue stage spotlighting, she cast the illusion of a little girl playing very naughty dress-up. A thirty-year-old little girl. She strutted back and forth in the most severe platform high heels Angela had ever seen, parading around the stage with an apparent subliminal connection to the music that accompanied her at an eardrum-pummeling volume.

Using the pole and mirrors to maximum effect, the dancer up on stage was soon stripped completely naked save for her wicked shoes. Skin as smooth and unblemished as cream in a saucer. No tattoos. Shoulder-length jet-black hair with bangs and a single blonde streak. Her pert little breasts were capped with marble-like nipples. Her straight black pubic hair had been shaved into a narrow Mohawk. The entrance to her own tiny Marvel Cave clearly on display between slender thighs, she danced with her eyes locked on Angela, her apparent chosen one.

31

It was the first time in Angela's life she could remember seeing an Asian woman naked and she found the experience utterly exotic. The blatant flirting...electric.

Just before disappearing into the back of the club for what turned out to be a very long time instead of the few minutes promised, Liz snuggled close to Angela, winked at the Asian woman on stage, and said, "Kiss me quick before I lose you forever."

Lose me? Was that an implied flirt, Angela wondered?

Yes, it was. She was suddenly quite sure of it as Liz's soft lips found hers.

Breathlessly breaking the kiss, Angela's internal clock seemed to have stopped ticking. And then *all* time stopped. She could feel the cocaine drawing a shy smile across her face in the darkened club while her blush – thankfully unseen – was turning up the heat and heading north.

***

It was after midnight and Angela was asleep when Liz's car skidded off the road. U2 was on the stereo, Bono singing plaintively about looking for something that couldn't be found.

"Wake up, Girl," Liz said, opening the driver's door to a frigid blast of air thick with whirling snowflakes. "I gotta pee. And we're stuck in a snow bank."

She disappeared out into the snowy maelstrom for an instant, and then was back. "Hey! You want the last of my Americano? It's cold, but still good."

"No," Angela answered with a big yawn. "Not really."

Liz stood just outside the open driver's door. She tossed the last dregs of her Grande triple-shot Americano in the snow, quickly unfastened her cargo pants, yanked them down and squatted over the cup. "Flash the headlights and honk the horn if you see someone coming," she said, finishing her business. Then she tossed the cup aside.

Liz's dusty-rose '92 Cadillac had once belonged to a Mary Kay salesperson. She'd explained to Angela how she saw it in a used car lot and instantly fell in love with it, thought it was a fitting automobile for a professional nude dancer. Said

32

the first thing she did was scrape off the Mary Kay decal in the rear window and replace it with the word *Slutmobile* in large hand-lettered gold leaf script, making it perfect. And now the Slutmobile was stuck on the median side of eastbound Highway 2 near Stevens Pass, snow up to the floorboards.

Liz reached in and turned on the emergency flashers. A tiny cloud of sweet-smelling caffeine-tainted fog wafted up from not three feet away and Angela had to laugh. "If you were just going to toss it right there in the snow, why'd you need the cup?"

"Neatness counts. Didn't want to risk getting any on my boots."

Zipping up her pants, Liz climbed back inside the car, said, "Check it out. These are genuine Harley-Davidson boots."

"You'd think they would be pee-proof, then. Wouldn't you?"

"You're very funny," Liz snickered. "Really. You are."

The two women were passing the time smoking a joint that Liz had dug out of the cavernous Slutmobile glove box, giggling, and imagining every sort of marketing twist on Harley-Davidson's pee-proof boots when a flashing yellow light came up from behind them. It was a highway department snowplow on duty, trying to keep pace with the snowfall, keeping the pass open.

"Yea! Our hero has arrived." Liz said. Dashed out of the car and into the snow again to greet the arrival of their salvation. She was gone several minutes and then returned with the snowplow driver in tow. "This is Chuck," she said, pushing a middle-aged man into the Caddy's back seat and climbing in after him, dusting the snowflakes out of her hair with her fingertips. "And, he's gonna help us. Aren't ya, Chucky?"

Angela turned and looked into the back seat. The snowplow's yellow light was flashing through the rear window, filling the car with surreal amber strobes. And Liz was digging into the fly of Chuck's insulated coveralls, layers of buttons and zippers giving way while U2 played on, Bono singing with considerable feeling on the stereo.

Chuck's pink-headed cock was revealed for a nanosecond in the flashing amber strobes. And then it disappeared into Liz's mouth.

Angela was stunned by what she saw even as her imagination went supersonic. Openmouthed and mute, her eyes became fixed on the scene. Unable to look away and unsure that she really wanted to. Mortified, she recalled her husband Les's aversion to anything beyond basic missionary-style sexual intercourse. Doggy-style from behind – but still in the 'correct' hole – being the epitome of kink for him. Everything else being *perverted*.

The yellow light kept flashing.

The music on the stereo kept playing. With feeling.

And Liz kept sucking.

Suddenly Chuck's eyes went wild. The fleshy shaft of his cock would appear for a moment and then disappear again. His arms and legs started flailing, boots kicking the front seat.

Liz looked up at Angela. Holding Chuck's glistening business firmly clenched in her fist, she said, "Just relax, big boy. This will be over soon. I know what I'm doing." She winked at Angela and went back to work on Chuck.

The amber light seemed to be flashing faster and faster. U2 was reaching a bass-driven climax.

And so was the snowplow driver. He reached out and grabbed Angela's hand, his eyes fastening onto hers; drawing her in and making her an active part of what was happening. His grip getting tighter and tighter, he suddenly began to mumble something about his dear mother and the Lord Jesus.

Then he went limp and groaned.

Liz sat up, tidying the corners of her mouth with her fingertips. She gave Chuck a cheerful slap on his padded thigh, said, "Okay, Chucky…time for *you* to go to work."

***

Ten miles down the road, laughing until on the verge of hysterics, Liz was saying; "Hope you didn't mind that business with Chucky. Saved myself sixty bucks back there. Though truthfully, a hundred is pretty much bottom dollar for a blowjob these days…so maybe I came out about even-steven and Chuck got a deal. Can you believe it? Fuckin' guy wanted sixty bucks to drag a couple of helpless women out of the snow. Said it was the standard rate."

"Whatever happened to good old-fashioned Boy Scout chivalry?" Angela replied, realizing she was riding with the gutsiest gal she'd ever known. Wondering if all nude dancers were like that. Gutsy. And blatantly…happily…*whorish*?

"Must have changed Be Prepared to Be Prosperous I guess." Liz answered with a closing giggle.

Angela gave her new friend a quick look. Stifled an impulse to mention that she had once been a pretty good cock sucker, herself. At least she'd thought she was pretty good back in her private Catholic high school days. Before Les made it clear he thought it was dirty, verging on throwing up on her behalf after she swallowed every drop on their second date. She had sometimes wondered during the intervening years how differently things might've turned out if Les had only craved oral sex half as much as every other boy she had gone out with. Instead of pushing her to *do it right*. Getting her pregnant by their fifth or sixth date.

Nine years and two kids later…

Angela said, "Toward the end I believe that Chuck the Snowplow Driver wanted to share his little treat with both of us."

Liz answered with a challenging glance, "Come here and you can still have your share." She pulled Angela close and kissed her mouth for the second time. Hard and sensuous. Tongue-to-tongue. Sharing the unmistakable taste of semen.

Tearing away and returning her glance back to the road, Liz's eyes flashed with a serpentine sparkle. Angela blushed at that sparkle. Not at the scene she had witnessed between Liz and the snowplow driver. Not even at the scorching kiss or the shared taste of semen on her tongue. But that brief *glance* had left her feeling flustered and short of breath. Just thinking about it deepened her spreading blush from rose to crimson, made her feel hot in places that had been lukewarm for a long time. Inside the dark corridors of Angela's libido doors long closed and mostly forgotten were swinging open on rusted hinges. Mysterious and delectable places waited behind them.

Turning sober, Liz said, "I don't know about you, girlfriend, but I could stand to freshen up instead of pushing through to Spokane tonight. We could get a cheap room in Wenatchee. My old stomping grounds."

Liz described the town of Wenatchee to Angela saying it was nothing but a wide spot hunkering on the banks of the Columbia River, surrounded by apple and peach orchards – the town full of the dorks who owned them and the illegals who worked them. God's country, she said, to those who claim to love it. Having graduated from high school there and knowing what a graveyard it truly was under the homey veneer, she was not one of those claiming to love it. Said there were lots of taverns, gas stations, and quick marts. Fresh fruit out the ass when in season. One-star motels and restaurants along the highways. Diddlysquat for a teenage girl to do.

"You have family here?" Angela asked, riding down from the mountains toward Wenatchee's main drag off Highway 2 and seeing the town all lit up with dated thirty-year-old Christmas decorations fastened to light poles on both sides of the street, looking to her exactly as Liz had described it. "Desperately dustbowl-glam," she'd said, the nude dancer and artist having a nonchalant, visual way with words that made her seem casual yet still angst-driven.

"Some," Liz answered. "And a couple of old high school friends. Don't worry; we're not stopping for social calls, this time of night."

Liz checked them in at the Big River Inn and then they went to a restaurant called *Martha's* for sustenance, the enormous sign in the parking lot promising the best cherry pie this side of *George*, Washington.

It was very late, or very early depending on your point of view. The bitter-cold wee hours before the sun crawled up out of the Idaho panhandle to shine on the huge breadbasket that was the middle of Washington State. And they ate like a pair of hungry wolverines, hardly talking until the food was nearly gone, more coffee and tea on the way. Then Angela asked, "What made you decide to help me out?"

36

"Seemed like the right thing to do at the time," Liz answered, eating the last French fry with a big glob of ketchup cantilevered on the end. "Was it?"

"Yes. I think so. And if I didn't say so before…thanks. I definitely needed some help. Guess I was coming a little unglued at the mall. And then, poof! There you were. Like you were my guardian angel or something."

"Hey girl, don't even try to make me out as one of those answer-to-my-prayers kinda people." Liz opened a fresh pack of cigarettes and offered one, saying, "I swear I'll dump you right here if you do."

Angela declined the cigarette, said, "So our meeting was just a random coincidence?"

"I don't know about that. Don't really believe in coincidences where people-meeting-people is concerned. But I do know that I'm no goddamned angel. Guardian or otherwise. Trust me, if it's an angel you need you'd better keep looking."

Undaunted, Angela gazed out the frosty window. The parking lot was full of big rigs. Some just arriving. Some leaving. Most were simply parked and idling their diesel engines. Remembering Liz with the snowplow driver, Angela imagined all kinds of illicit business going on in some of the sleeper cabs, ordinary sleeping going on in others. No way of telling one from the other.

"I'll do that. Keep on looking," she said.

Chapter 5

U.S. Marshal Ezra Monroe Hooten almost always spoke in softly measured tones with an undercurrent of urgency in his voice as if self-conscious about imposing himself, yet wanting to be clearly understood the first time. Tall, slender, and exceptionally pale, with straight white hair. Big hands with long and graceful-looking fingers. He had been mistaken for a florist a couple of times and an undertaker once. He had been accused of being a preacher and even a vampire. But he was seldom pegged as a hardboiled lawman until people looked him in the eyes. Unflinching, cool, powder-blue eyes usually hiding from the sun's hateful rays behind dark glasses.

The eyes always give you away, he knew.

Looking into the eyes of Searl Bishop while waiting to transfer him from the federal courthouse in Seattle, where Bishop had just testified in a racketeering trial, back to Twin Rivers in Monroe where he was serving three-to-five years for receiving stolen property, Hoot saw nothing but trouble looking back. Ornery little peckerhead, he thought, pegging him as one of those jailhouse rats always looking for trouble and always finding it. Searl Bishop's sheet suggested to Hoot that he was about as mean-spirited as the devil's own three-legged mutt, and apparently as stupid, but he'd said something that caught Hoot's attention.

"*Creeper*," was what he had said to another handcuffed peckerhead standing nearby. He was talking about somebody. A hired gun.

"What about this Creeper?" Hoot wanted to know, his gut recognizing that he might be getting a lucky break. A break that he'd been waiting over six months in Seattle for. Knowing without doubt that it would pop up like a babe in a birthday cake if he simply waited. Stayed sharp. And here it was. Fresh word of the only fugitive who really mattered to him, some serious history between them.

38

"Hey, man, I already gave my testimony," Searl Bishop said.

"Not about *this* guy, you didn't."

"So? What...you offerin' me a new deal?"

Hoot stepped closer, pushed his shades down on his nose and put his pale blues on Searl Bishop. On him and through him all the way down to whatever little nugget of self-preservation and good sense was hunkering deep down inside. He said in a near-whisper, "New deal? Sure." He took one of Searl Bishop's cuffed hands in his as if to seal a pact, squeezed hard, and said, "How many of these fingers you still wanna be able to use back at The Rivers? Got somebody to feed you there? Wipe your ass?"

Searl Bishop backed away. "Easy, marshal! No big! All I know's what I heard in the bull pen, waitin' for trial. Just a rumor's all."

"A rumor? Tell me. Rumor about what?"

"'Bout some guy people call *Creeper*. Came over from Spokane t'do wet work for a connected pussyvendor who didn't like Nick Petosa. I don't even know the guy. But he's supposed t' be a real badass. People say he's the one took out ol' Nick."

"From Spokane? You sure?"

"Yeah...no shit. That's what I heard. Crazy, huh? Like Seattle don't have 'nough talent for that kinda work already."

Hoot stepped away, replacing his sunglasses and nodding his head. His halo of white hair giving him the look of a pale white angel – the avenging sort.

"Spokane?" he repeated. "No shit, you say."

"*Gospel*."

Just as I suspected, Hoot thought with a lupine smile. Watch out Spokane, here I come...

***

"You're telling me this ghost you've been chasing for...what...twenty-eight years now...is hiding in *Spokane*?" Senior Deputy Horner said to Hoot through an unmasked sneer.

39

"You made the same claim over three months ago. Remember? And a month before that. The Spokane office couldn't find a trace of him either time."

"*They* won't find him. *I* can," Hoot said.

"We've had this conversation before."

"I have a new lead."

"So you say. You overheard a conversation about the hit on Nick Petosa at The Westin and you think it was your guy did it. Ran off to Spokane afterward."

"Yes. That's right. It was Norman Carpenter who killed the old man. I went to the morgue and saw the body. I know it was him. I can feel it."

"You really choke on *sir* when you address me, don't you, Hooten?"

"No sir. Not that I've noticed."

"If I recall correctly, before Spokane it was Kalispell, Montana – it was a *feeling* you had then, too. About Kalispell. About him being there. In fact, deputy marshal Hooten, your personnel file shows that you've had similar feelings about Kalispell at least a dozen times in the past ten years alone. Helena office went through the drill every time and never found a trace of your guy. And in Bend, Oregon; same thing – Fort Bragg, California before that. Does that sound correct so far?"

"Mainly Spokane and Kalispell. He comes and goes there. It's where he was raised. Last I heard his mother is still alive and living on the Flathead reservation near Kalispell. He goes to see her."

"Twenty-eight years on the lam…and a momma's boy the whole time. Very touching."

"I have vacation time I need to use. I could do that, if you prefer," Hoot suggested. "Go to Spokane, to Kalispell…"

"Forget it," senior deputy Horner said. "No way am I going to let you run off on a goddamned vigilante manhunt. No. I want to keep a tight leash on your scrawny neck until it's safely retired. You can cash in your vacation time then. Do whatever you want.

"Meanwhile, I just finished reviewing your report on Mays' and Keen's *capture* and certain details elude me. What I want to know is how the hell Stephen Mays managed to catch eleven slugs resisting arrest. I'm just trying to imagine it. Keen was dead. Your partner was dead. Your Highway Patrol backup was seriously wounded – completely out of action. And you decide to storm the hideout…alone…

"Just you and Mays out there in the woods…

"In the fucking piss-ass drizzly *dark* of the woods, no less…

"I honestly can't quite see it; the urgency of taking that cabin without waiting for additional backup. Admittedly late backup, but even without communications you knew help was imminent."

"The trooper needed medical attention."

"But *eleven* slugs? Eleven of *your* fucking slugs…the man just refused to give up, did he?"

"You really think my neck is scrawny, sir?" Hoot said with emphasis on the *sir*.

"Shut the fuck up and listen, Hooten! Only reason you're getting a letter of commendation instead of sitting behind bars awaiting investigation of the incident is because the highway patrolman survived to file a report corroborating yours. *And* the minor fact that none of those eleven slugs were in Mays's back. Only reason I'm keeping you on active status instead of parking your ass on indefinite admin leave is because we're shorthanded around here and Northwest Region HQ would ask questions. Only reason I'm sending you to Spokane is because I can't stand to look at your pale white face anymore. Furthermore, Spokane is even more shorthanded than we are. But don't forget, you're being assigned *to* Warrants and Court Support and *off* Fugitive Apprehension. Unless your guy actually shows up over there."

"Yes *sir*. I understand."

"One more thing," senior deputy Horner said as Hoot was about to leave: "I'm assigning you a new partner. It would be in everyone's best interest if this one lived long enough to see you retire."

* * *

Hoot pulled into a well-established joint called Papa Mia's Italian Restaurant and Sports Bar on Pacific Highway South for dinner. He had noticed this cozy-looking dive before but never stopped. Tonight he was looking for something loaded with carbs and calories, comfort food to help him bounce back from Horner's ass chewing. He might even order a side dish of extra cholesterol. No need to get in a big hurry. Plenty of time for a smoky martini or three before dinner.

An hour later, his innards busy slamdancing his dinner and adult beverages into submission, Hoot decided that the linguini with clam sauce had been a pretty good choice even if a little richer than his current state of indigestion might've preferred. A replay game of the Seattle Seahawks versus some pitifully lesser team was showing on the big screen in the bar and he watched the final quarter in a distracted mood. Hoot passed on the spumoni for dessert. Instead he had a double espresso that didn't like him nearly as much as he liked it. He chased the coffee with a couple more smoky martinis and a handful of antacid tablets. Then he tapped the screen on his iPhone to look at Creeper's most recent tweet on Twitter once more – as if expecting this time to see coordinates pinpointing the device it had been sent from.

Some girls are born trash and they die trash was all it said – a typically cryptic note from Creeper.

Leaving Papa Mia's, he stopped at a Quick Mart up the road for a fresh pack of cigarettes and some chewing gum. Hoot bought his cigarettes a pack at a time, unwilling to succumb to the more thrifty approach of buying cartons to support his addiction because a tiny holdout of hope residing deep inside him truly believed that each pack *could* be the last.

Hoot recalled how, in his impervious and unflappable youth, he had survived his breakup with Donna and made it through two tours in 'Nam without smoking a single cigarette. Didn't light up the first time until detective Thomas Hamm of the Pleasanton Police – *Homicide Division*, such as it was – met him at The Rafters, a popular crab and lobster house in nearby Comstock Maine. Told him that, as suspected, Donna's drowning was no accident. Told him they'd found the blunt object that had dented her skull *before* she sucked enough lake water into her lungs to stop her heart – a two-foot-long ironworker's sleever bar with traces of her blood on it and Norman's prints all over it. Said they had found it in Norman's tool kit at work.

Arrogant fuck hadn't even tried to get rid of the goddamned murder weapon!

This was two years before Hoot gave up commercial fishing to become a marshal – two years of legal wrangling, tribal defense lawyers having procedural convulsions, trying to drag ethnic discrimination into the mix, prosecutors having their issues, waiting for a conviction, for appeals, the whole time Hoot growing convinced that Norman would somehow beat the rap. He remembered sitting at The Rafters' bar all that afternoon, smoking like a forest fire out of control, smoking as if he had sucked them down all his life, getting headachy as hell and dwelling on the news he'd just learned. He recalled that he started drinking the hard stuff with real purpose that day, too. Patrick, the bartender, giving him the bushy eyebrow treatment but saying nothing. Keeping 'em coming.

Evidently a natural for every vice he tried after that, Hoot had cut back on his drinking these past couple years until it wasn't really a problem anymore. More specifically: he didn't live in a bottle anymore. Still, once you have a drinking problem you never really lose it. At least not in the eyes of others. But Hoot hadn't missed work, been sick, helped close a joint at two AM, or failed to find his way back home in a couple of years. In his book that meant the problem was fixed. Old habits *can* be killed, though sometimes they die awfully hard. Still, push-come-to-shove Hoot could hold his liquor better than anyone should the need arise. One of my more well-honed talents, *sir*, he told Horner in his imagination, his mind still working in replay mode. Those old days were just around the corner. Unreachable except in memory.

Shortly before Norman's last appeal came back denied, Hoot threw his father a curveball and gave up commercial long-line fishing – just like that. Like the family business meant nothing to him. Joined the U.S. Marshals. He told his disappointed dad that he wanted to be in a position to keep an eye on his old friend and shoot him in the head if he so much as looked sideways. Dad did not approve. Said Norman was sick and there was nothing Hoot could do about that. Hoot's younger brother Eric was unsure about the kink Hoot's decision would put in the family fishing empire.

"I know him, Dad," Hoot had said. "Norman feels no remorse for what he did. Remorse doesn't apply to him. Give him half a chance and he'll be gone."

That was almost thirty-seven years ago, when Hoot joined the Marshals. Thirty-seven years! And now Hoot prided himself that he hadn't smoked in an agency vehicle in more than a year. Silly, he was so close to giving up cigarettes altogether he didn't know why he didn't simply quit. He didn't really like them anymore. Wasn't sure he ever had actually *liked* them. Maybe he just wasn't ready to jump on that wagon. In the meantime his chewing gum consumption had gone up considerably. Chewing gum had become his new crutch. Some days he leaned on it hard. How lame...he'd turned into a Juicy Fruit junkie! Sometimes he caught himself chewing gum and smoking a cigarette at the same time and was completely vexed when it happened, was actually embarrassed that he might be seen.

Hoot had actually quit smoking once. Gave up the cigs for almost three weeks. But then Justice assigned him to Waco just in time for the fiery shootout with the Davidians and he started again after the second day there.

Bad time to quit smoking.

He'd tried to blame Waco for his divorce too, even though he had known it was coming for a long time. He was ready to quit again on September 10th, 2001. Had the patch attached and everything, and then sucked down a record number of cigs in the three weeks following the 11th. Middle of the fourth week, his father died.

There never seemed to be a good time to quit. It was disappointing.

No big deal. Hoot routinely let himself down. Let everyone down who'd ever cared about him, too. A master of disappointment is how he'd come to regard himself here on the cusp of retirement. Beginning with the way he had let Donna slip through his fingers. Let her marry a man Hoot knew to be deranged. Then there was Linda and the fact that Hoot had turned out to be such a lousy husband and father. There were other issues running close behind, but on honest reflection, the one topping the list was the undeniable fact that *he* was the one responsible for Norman Carpenter's escape. Creeper had played him like a cheap fiddle. Walked away from a routine prisoner medical transfer. A transfer when Hoot was the DIC and he blew it. End of story. No excuses.

That was the one big mistake of Hoot's life. The one that wouldn't allow him to let the past lie and move on. It just wouldn't let go – probably because he didn't want it to. Sadly, he had come to believe that he could retire in peace if he could just walk up to Norman Carpenter and shoot him dead. If he could only believe in his heart that Donna had not died hating him...

Hoot was pretty sure that when his father was still alive he'd ultimately become ashamed of his oldest son. Ezra Hooten...destined to inherit the family fishing fleet, turning aside from family to pursue the devil's spawn. Hoot knew that the unbearable load of guilt he bore for what happened to Donna was why. He just couldn't let it go

"You should forget about Donna Messenger and take better care of Linda. Linda's a good woman," his father had said countless times including the day before he died.

Of course, the ol' man couldn't quite fathom the full depth of the fact that it was Norman's *escape* that had his son tweaked – *on top* of how responsible Hoot felt for driving Donna away. Practically insisting she hitch her wagon to Norman's. Leave him to find his own lonely destiny without strings attached. Hoot had cut her loose, and in doing so it was as if he'd buckled her into a cheap seat on a crashing plane – it would've been better if he had.

"I can wait if you want," Donna said at their final parting, "'till you're ready."

"Don't," he told her. Why he'd said that was something Hoot had long since given up trying to understand.

A single word described Hoot's parting with Donna...*thoughtless*. *Don't*, was all that he had said to her. No explanation offered; just the lame cop-out that college wasn't

45

for him after all. He was going to fish for a living. It was the family business. It had always been in the cards and college couldn't teach him how to fish.

And then, later, when Hoot came back from 'Nam and Donna was Norman's wife, all he could think was how much he, himself, had changed. Hoot feared that the horrors he'd seen and been a part of in Vietnam had left him unfit and undeserving of her. Never once extending that thought to include how Norman was even more undeserving when the tables were turned.

Don't. How many times afterward had he wished he could stuff that single ill-considered comment back in his mouth and swallow it whole? Countless times. No matter if he choked to death on it.

Then came Linda. Hoot knew that he had not deserved Linda. And she certainly didn't deserve him, the worry and disappointments that came along with him. He had picked up some bad habits by the time Linda came into his life and she'd picked up the crazy notion that she could fix him. Give her credit for trying. Best part of all that was the kids. Give her credit for them turning out with their heads on straight, too – he was too busy chasing bad guys to have much time left for family…

There was a state liquor store next door to the Quick Mart. Hoot went in and purchased a bottle of Glenlivet single-malt scotch. Sometimes he liked to drink scotch neat and he preferred a decent single-malt. And he preferred to drink alone nowadays. Less likely to be drawn into the deep end of the pond that way. Easier to make a clean break altogether when the time was right.

Eventually the time would be right.

Maybe after he quit the cigs.

Chapter 6

The parking lot was crawling with King County cops and CSI personnel when Hoot arrived home at the Citadel Luxury Apartments complex near SeaTac airport. He pulled into his assigned parking spot and saw senior deputy Horner walking over to the car before he even got his seatbelt unfastened.

Determined strides. Horner was a natural-born alpha male if ever there was one.

"Where you been, Hooten? It was practically yesterday already, when you left my office," Horner said, looking in the rolled-down driver-side window and casting a hard glance at the bottle of Glenlivet clutched in Hoot's fist. "Party time, is it?"

"Yeah. If I'd known management was coming, I'd have bought a cheaper bottle."

Their conversation went briefly on hold for the noise of a departing jet from nearby SeaTac airport, and then senior deputy Horner said, "Leave that here, smartass. Let's take a little walk."

"Me? *Smart*ass? I hardly have any ass left, boss, after you got done with it."

Horner scowled. Started walking.

"Tell me," Hoot said, scrambling to exit the car and catch up, taking in the busy crime scene with long glances as he walked. With another jibe at his boss, he said, "All this is about that off-duty parking ticket from a coupla weeks ago…right? If you want I can take care of that before I leave for Spokane."

They navigated a logjam of official vehicles crammed between parking shelters to arrive at the dumpster corral just off the end of Hoot's apartment building. A team from the county coroner's office had removed a body from one of the big green bins and placed it on a gurney.

47

"I want you to take a look at this," senior deputy Horner said, unzipping the black body bag." Inside was a woman – or a body that had once been a living female. Nude. She was less than fresh.

"You see how she's been severely worked over with a knife?" Horner said. "Not just stab wounds. See how her breast implants appear to have been...*drained*?"

What Hoot noticed with a hard slap of sobriety was the way this woman's skin had been flayed in places. Lots of places. *And* she had been scalped before being tossed into the dumpster – a patch of flesh and hair the size of a large coin was missing.

Some girls are born trash and they die trash, Hoot immediately thought, remembering Norman's last taunting tweet.

"This look like your guy's handiwork?" Horner asked.

The question momentarily blindsided Hoot. Standing mute, he looked at the body on the gurney and felt his head spin as if he'd never seen this sort of gruesome thing before. Yet he had. Exactly this sort of thing. Too many times.

Resolute, Hoot stood resisting a strong urge to turn and walk away...forever. He was just so goddamned *tired* of it. Right down to the bone. It had become the worst imaginable curse – a lifetime spent chasing an old friend turned psychopath, Hoot playing by the rules as much as he was able while Norman just kept on being *Creeper*.

How hard could it be to just say fuckit and forget all about Norman Carpenter, he wondered. Go ahead and retire? Go fishing?

"Yes," Hoot answered his boss after another moment's reflection. "It does."

"Alright then," senior deputy Horner said. "What we've got so far...CSI team's preliminary investigation suggests that this unfortunate young woman was the same one present in the room at The Westin when Nick Petosa was killed. We'll know for sure soon as DNA results are back and fingerprints are confirmed.

"Now here's the kicker," Horner said. "*I'm* here instead of being at home enjoying dinner with my loving family because *I* indicated an interest in Mister Petosa's demise on *your* behalf. I did that because *you* made a major fucking point of insisting your guy is the one who offed old Nick. And now the simple fact that this young cadaver turned up in *your* garbage dumpster leads me to think you may actually be onto something this time, Hooten."

And they die trash. Hoot could almost hear Norman's voice saying the words like an impromptu mantra, spirit-world drums pounding in his head. He couldn't tear his eyes away from the body on the gurney. He had seen this sort of madness so many times before...first time in 'Nam.

It was definitely Creeper's work. He was sure of it.

"Listen up, Hooten," the senior deputy said. "You get your scrawny white ass sober. Get it to Spokane or wherever the hell the trail leads you and DO NOT let this *Creeper* fucker slip through your fingers again! I want to see his sick hide nailed to the fucking barn door. And I want to see it there soon..."

Hoot was starting to feel very sober, indeed.

***

Lying in bed. Wide awake. The body from the dumpster still fresh in his mind, Hoot remembered a particular time when he and Norman were on recon together. This was the first time Hoot had seen with his own eyes evidence of the madness that had claimed his friend. It was late in 1968, after the infamous Tết Offensive earlier that year, after the Powers that Be had had time to figure out the details of their gargantuan strategic fuckup. Hoot and Norman's mission was to observe Viet Cong activity along the Laotian border and gather eyes-on intel. They were assessing damage from stepped-up U.S. bombing of roads, paths, and waterways that had recently become famous as the *Ho Chi Minh Trail* – the supply line that had made the Tết Offensive possible. They were working largely on the illegal-to-be-there Laotian side of the border if anyone was watching too closely.

By the time Hoot got in-country the Vietnam War had become the media's war. This was inevitable simply because the media controlled the public – and thus Congress via popular opinion of said public – and Congress controlled the budget for planes and bombs and every damn thing else. Vietnam was the first war to be broadcast *live* on TV straight into the homes of middle-class Americans. Voting Americans were bombarded with biased coverage of an unpopular war – unpopular largely because of the nightly news coverage including a constantly-growing body count. Awful yet compelling, it was war as entertainment. Every semi-cognizant American was vested in it, yet all the strings attached to it seemed to lead to someone basking in an elected post far from the sweltering jungle.

Hoot recalled the pre-op briefing when the CO told them that Charlie's movement of men and supplies on the Ho Chi Minh Trail through Laos and Cambodia had reached an intolerable level. Said the trail was what had made the Tết Offensive possible. It was the first time Hoot heard the GI slang term *Ho Chi Minh Trail* used officially. The CO said increased Air Force bombing runs seemed to be helping the problem, but the bombs were currently falling at a rate that was exhausting the maximum monthly ordnance allotment while VC activity continued to increase. In order to nudge Congress toward allocating more money for more bombs, they needed proof of the enemy's escalating sneakybastard use of the trail that would stand up to American media scrutiny. Three teams of LRP sniper-spotters would be deployed. Their mission was to find that proof.

After Hoot and Norman had been six days in the jungle, keeping eyes on a network of paths that were parts of the trail they had surprisingly little to report. Past noon on the sixth day, slithering, moving soundlessly, Norman pulled back to Hoot's position. It was sweltering hot, both Hoot and Norman camouflaged to appear part of the vegetation, both stinking like moist muck and caked-on shit. As his partner got close Hoot sincerely hoped that his caked-on shit smelled better than Norman's did.

Voice held low Norman said, "There's squat going on in this sector. Last two days and nights all I've seen moving are bugs and snakes."

"They know we're here," Hoot said, his voice barely a murmur. "They don't know exactly where or they'd have come to get us by now. But they know we're here."

Norman nodded his head in agreement. "No bombs falling in this sector for a week – it's like putting up a 'We're Here!' sign. They won't risk showing themselves until they're sure we've left. We should move west. Intel shows another route farther from the river."

"Our orders are to recon *this* route. We could get our asses bombed if we move. Interfere with another team. Get shot by one of our own."

"This route's cold."

A bird cried and both men froze for a second, motionless and silent. Then Norman said, "You ready to pack it up?"

Hoot had looked to his left, upjungle, said, "Look how they've already repaired the trail from last week's B52 carpet-run. How do they *do* that so fast? They hiding heavy machinery somewhere out here? Are we looking at it and not seeing it?

"And don't forget the river – we wanna catch them using the river if we can."

"We can't go. Not yet."

Norman agreed, "Good enough. I know the fuckers are here. I can *feel* them."

Hoot knew all about his friend's instincts and he respected them. Knew since one particular experience in Norman's mother's sweat lodge that he possessed a few unexplainable instincts of his own, though he wouldn't rely on them the way he would rely on Norman's. Still, he said, "They can feel us, too."

"What if we move but stay in the zone? You set up a new position about a click north. I'll go west a couple clicks. Take a quick look at that other route."

"No good. Puts us too far apart to watch each other's back," Hoot said.

"Won't matter if we're the only two monkeys in the jungle. We'll meet at your new place, twenty-one hundred hours tomorrow. Decide then to stay or go," Norman said, and then was gone as silently as he had arrived.

That was…what…forty-four years ago? Hoot thought, rolling over again, trying to shut off his brain and get some real sleep.

Seeing 4:00 AM illuminated on his bedside clock, he decided to give up and get up. He made coffee.

Goddamned jungle dreams, he thought. Hoot hated them.

All that happened before I had any idea of the monster Norman would become. We had trust between us then. Friendship. Even if there had been clues all along; Norman's ever-there anger, his utter disregard for dogs or other pets – not to mention his utter disregard for *people*. Later, the violence that Norman brought down on Donna Messenger had been impossible for Hoot to imagine at the time. But it came to him ever since in headachy nightmares, robbing him of sleep already too precious.

Funny thing was…Hoot couldn't even see Donna clearly in his mind anymore. The Donna he'd loved had become a faded once-vivid memory. Fuzzy snapshots, at best, of the way she was all the years of their friendship before the injuries Norman inflicted on her. Then afterward…her head! Her scalp! Her battered face, her broken wrists! *That* lingering image of Donna's broken body was foremost in the closetful of haunts that tormented Hoot with relentless tenacity. He was more aware of Donna as an ethereal *presence* now, unable to conjure an image of her as easily as in years before, though no less needful to do so. These days, she wavered. It was maddening, the way he couldn't be sure if his recollection of the undamaged Donna was accurate anymore, yet details of what Norman had done to her remained vivid as if etched on his very soul.

If Hoot couldn't remember how she looked, he could still remember the way she was. A friend since the first day of first grade, Donna was always the one in charge. Not bossy, precisely. Just very aware that the choice was obvious, making him aware of it, too. Always taking the initiative. And cute as hell. Even if he didn't remember every detail of her appearance anymore, the overall impression was lasting.

Donna would be avenged. She was *not* a victim. Hoot would not allow that. Hands balled into fists, he reaffirmed his longstanding oath that, whatever it took, he would see Donna's spirit rest easy. He fell asleep on the sofa just before his coffee finished dripping.

***

Hoot realized that his friendship with Norman reached its critical mass on the Ho Chi Minh trail that summer of 1968. Looking back, especially after that experience, at all the opportunities Hoot had had to kill *Creeper*, just leave his body in the underbrush.

One more for the evening body count.

Hindsight...ain't it perfect!

That night, Hoot's immediate reaction when he heard a single shot from the east was to check his wristwatch. It had been oh-four twenty-eight hours – almost 4:30 in the morning. Still dark. And drizzly. He'd been catching a light nap. That's all the sleep a sniper ever gets in the jungle. Light naps. But there was a distant shot and he was awake and alert in an instant.

He quickly checked his perimeter for any sign of disturbance. There was nothing. His Claymore booby traps were untouched.

Too distant to be certain, the sound faint, Hoot thought the single shot he'd heard was the sharp *crack* of an XM-21 sniper rifle. *Norman's* M-21, no doubt. Other teams shouldn't be anywhere near enough to hear. A single shot suggested that Norman had made a sniper hit.

Better be goddamned Ho Chi Minh himself to risk revealing your position without me there to back you up, Hoot thought.

All quiet in his part of the jungle. Hoot shifted his position to concentrate his field of fire in Norman's direction, ready to cover his friend's expected retreat. Long minutes passed, and then he heard a distant burst of gunfire. Again

53

faint. But this time he was certain that he heard Viet Cong AK-47 full-auto fire mixed in with the distinctive M-21 fire. Definitely from Norman's approximate position – a bad sign.

Assuming that Norman had taken out a selected target with that first single shot, protocol was for him to immediately retreat to a pre-selected secondary position, then to Hoot. The burst suggested that Norman's selected target had some pissed-off friends who'd made both of his established positions and he was fighting his way out instead of slipping away.

Crap! Hoot thought. I *knew* we were too far apart!

Still, Norman would lead his pursers toward Hoot's position. Protocol was for Hoot to wait. Reset his Claymores and wait. The ambush would come to him.

Hoot was doing exactly that a half hour later – *waiting* – when he heard another distant burst of fire. The explosion of a Claymore. Too distant to tell for sure what was what but *something* was sure as hell going down in Norman's neighborhood, and it didn't sound good.

Then, like a tickle in the back of his mind, Hoot could *see* Norman in deep serious shit. He was wounded.

Fuck protocol! he thought, grabbing his gear.

Hang in there, Creeper. Shooter's coming…

***

"Yeah, you hang in there, you fucker…Shooter's coming," Hoot said aloud, locking memories of Vietnam *and* the body from the dumpster away behind one of those unmarked doors in the back of his mind, getting up from the sofa and heading for the bathroom. "And when I get there, all hell's gonna break loose."

Hoot seldom looked at himself in a mirror except every ten days or so when he would shave his sparse outcropping of silver and blonde whiskers. Today was that day, and the reflection he saw was not pleasing. Bloodshot eyes looked back at thinning hair – amazing the way his hair *thinned* without receding, each hair seeming to grow thinner and more transparent, turning invisible now that it had turned gray – or, rather, *white*. Skin so fair it would blister and threaten to burst into all-consuming flames before it would tan in the summer sun. Nearly indiscernible eyebrows. Pale blue eyes. Gaunt cheeks. Always thin, between the army and commercial fishing Hoot had laid on muscle that, once toned, now lay in slack ropes across his torso, his shoulders and back, and along his arms. And, yes…he really did have a scrawny neck.

Hoot remembered a movie that he'd seen back in the seventies; The Man Who Fell to Earth, with David Bowie as the alien. Good God…he looked like an *old* alien! He smiled. It felt good to be hot on Norman's trail again.

Last time Hoot had been this close to capturing Norman was five years ago in Sacramento. And that had ended badly. A laundry owned by a Korean man and his wife was supposedly robbed. Five years ago and Sacramento PD *still* had it on their books as a robbery-turned-hate crime!

Hoot knew better. The robbery was a cover to hide a cold-blooded murder. He had personally investigated and found out the Koreans were making and selling meth, crowding in on the local good ol' boys. He suspected the robbery was a sham to cover up a professional hit. Returning business to normal without too much headline news.

And Hoot knew that Norman had done it. In one of his creative moods. Hoot had seen the crime scene. The bodies. The flays. Scalps. Ears. Fingers. It was Norman's work. And Norman was no common thief. Meaning he must have staged the robbery as a ruse. Norman playing games. Showing off and having fun.

Sometimes it seemed to Hoot that his old friend and blood-brother Norman had had a run of good luck far beyond normal reckoning – as if something supernatural actually did control Norman's destiny as Norman had always insisted it did.

But Hoot knew the actual shockingly dull truth – and this was simply that nothing other than plain dumb luck kept Norman going. Thinking that he was protected by a whole tribe of ancestral spirits he referred to as his *Spirit Guides*, Norman was reckless.

And his day would come. It was coming soon.

Chapter 7

Summer of 1967. Pleasanton, Maine. It was two weeks after
high school graduation. Temperature and humidity racing to
set new records. Crickets making a ruckus in the wee hours.
The smell of new-mown grass. Eighteen-year-old Ezra Hooten
was convinced that life was good, the best part still ahead.

The Rolling Stones were hot that year but The Doors
were the new bad boys on the airwaves in Pleasanton. The
Beatles had met the Maharishi, turning transcendental.
Donovan was divine. It was get-high music. Hoot and Norman
Carpenter, Donna Messenger, the whole gang gobbled it up like
Dairy Queen. The soundtrack to their eager lives.

Gas was thirty-four cents a gallon – twenty-nine when
there was a so-called 'gas war' going on and it seemed like
there was always a gas war. There was no such thing as
unleaded. Regular and Ethyl were your choices. You could
cruise all Friday night on two bucks. There was nothing else to
do. Saturday night Hoot would pack everyone into his '55
Chevy coupe; Norman, Donna, Irene Karns and Gilbert Roscoe,
and they'd go to the drive-in movies. Norm, Hoot, and Donna
– receiver, quarterback, and captain of the cheerleaders in the
front seat. Gil and Irene – tagalongs in the back. Always the
same.

Then Norman got drafted and no one pretended
surprise, knowing how he was jinxed, his whole life a shitty
deal from the get-go. They were at the Crest Drive-in south of
town. Watching *The Dirty Dozen* featuring a stern and
determined Lee Marvin, Norman said he knew he would most
likely not be coming back, said Vietnam was a faraway hole
swallowing up guys like him without remorse. Norman looked
at Hoot. Hoot looked at Donna and she looked away. In the
back seat Irene sobbed, and Gil cussed a blue streak.

"Your grades are probably good enough. You're smart
– too smart to study and that's your problem. But you can still

56

enroll at UM," Donna said. Community College if your folks can't afford the U."

"Won't work," Norman answered.

"Maybe you could get a scholarship through your mother's tribe?"

"I don't think it works that way," Norman said. "Even if Mom conjured-up a scholarship, I'd have to be enrolled already to get a deferment. It's too late. I've been *selected.*" He looked at her. Looked at Hoot. Said, "You guys keep a smartseat warm for me. I'll catch up after I've killed my share of Gooks. Go to college on Uncle Sam."

A big going-away party was being held down at Cougar Park. Norman full of bravado about the whole thing. Donna putting on a brave face...badly. Hoot was introspective as hell. Gil went on his usual rant about Harley-Davidsons compared to piece-of-shit Hondas and Kawasuckies, offering to fight anyone who disagreed – his only two passions being Harleys and football, Irene more of a pastime than a passion to him.

Hoot looked over at Donna with eyes recently opened by the rounding of third base and sliding into home the evening of senior prom. She stood by the bonfire with a group of girlfriends. Smiling. Talking. Wearing a University of Maine sweatshirt that clung to her breasts with noticeable tenacity. They were vivacious, proud, fun-loving breasts practically begging for attention. And every male within range yearned to answer. Especially Hoot and Norman, the proverbial friends who had vied for Donna's attention since junior high, Donna unable to decide between them.

Hoot stole Norman away from the bonfire crowd and they walked along the river.

"Bummer that we have to cancel our big trip," Norman said. "I think you and Gil should go ahead without me." He was talking about a pipedream they'd nursed throughout high school; Norman, Hoot, and Gil, all three of them buying motorcycles after graduation and making a cross-country trip to California before the rest of their lives grabbed them by the balls.

"Fuckit," Hoot answered, "I can't really afford a bike and college too. And without you along I'd probably strangle

Gil to death. Can't you just imagine the two of us camped out on the side of the road somewhere; Gil on one of his endless rants. What if he started farting? I'd have to kill him. Have to hide the body. Explain to his folks."

Norman grunted his understanding. "Only one thing I'm sorry about," he said, tossing a pebble into the ever-passing water with a distant *plunk*! "I let you beat me to the draw, asking Donna to the prom."

"Yeah...so I'm the quarterback and she's Homecoming Queen. It had to be."

Norman glanced toward the bonfire, said, "You and Donna already *did* it, didn't you," and after a moment Hoot nodded.

"Figures," Norman said. "You fucker. You guys'll be married and have a half-dozen brats by the time I get back...*if* I get back."

"Don't say that anymore!" Hoot warned. "Don't even think it."

"I'll tell you what I'm thinking," Norman answered. "If I do get back in one piece I'll steal her away from you. *That's* what I'm thinking. So enjoy it while you have it, buddy, 'cause it ain't gonna last..."

***

It turned out that Norman didn't have to steal Donna away at all. She and Hoot broke up before the end of their first semester at the U. Their dreams for the future – the nice house on the inlet, a happy family including two happy children, his engineering career, or maybe a fleet of long-line commercial fishing boats with the kids' and grandkids' names painted across their sterns – all of it, gone. Norman got back from the jungle a full year before Hoot and there was Donna, practically waiting for him with open arms.

Seemed to Hoot that all that was a lifetime ago.

Hell, it was...

And now he had no nice house. No happy wife. No *life* to speak of. His life was a merry-go-round of recalcitrant assholes who thought the whole justice system was designed to be fucked with.

In truth, Hoot had fucked with the system quite a lot, himself, from time to time, in order to stay on Norman's trail – a trail that would sometimes go cold for a year or more at a stretch. Consequently, Hoot's Personnel Record file was filled with as many minuses as pluses. Maybe *more* minuses, he wasn't sure. And, of course, there were all the dead partners...

Hoot had followed one district transfer with another and another for his whole career. Always chasing Norman. Never putting down roots or building close relationships that could lead to promotions. And now he was the oldest U.S. Marshal in his pay grade. Still humping it, day in and day out in the field. Living on the road for all practical purposes. Presently calling home the sprawling, homogenized, uniquely characterless Citadel *Luxury* Apartments on the flight path to SeaTac.

***

Driving the I-90 Interstate to Spokane, Hoot told his new partner about Horner's mandate. Told selected tidbits about himself in terse snippets of small talk; that his apartment would have a view of Mt. Rainer if he climbed up on the roof and stood on his tiptoes, and *luxury* – as applied to the Citadel Luxury Apartments – meant that covered parking and air conditioning were included. Then, under admittedly-skillful and determined interrogation for a rookie, Hoot told how he planned to retire on his sixty-fifth birthday. How he was going to buy himself a nice new fifth-wheel camper, a new F350 Ford pickup to tow it with, and spend a few years touring the scenic back roads of America.

Hoot's new partner, a second-year rookie deputy named Marcus, was the blackest black man Hoot had ever met in his life. And then there was Hoot...

...Hoot suspected that he and Marcus must be the blackest and whitest marshals in the U.S. Marshals Service. Paired together we look like a fucking recruiting poster touting service diversity, he thought.

59

Marcus had a first name...*Leon*, but said he didn't like it much because he was named after an uncle he detested. Told Hoot he didn't mind when it got dropped. "Kind of like I've got two first names, anyhow."

"Try calling me *Ezra* and see what gets dropped," Hoot grumbled.

"So why are we driving to Spokane in the dark instead of flying over later in the morning?"

"Budget."

Marcus gave Hoot a measured glance that clearly said *bullshit* without using the word. They were just cresting Snoqualmie Pass and it was snowing, Marcus' look suggesting that anyone choosing to drive in this weather was certifiably nuts.

"I don't sleep much," Hoot added. "And I'm not crazy about flying. Figured we might as well get moving even though we're in no hurry. Give us time to get used to each other.

"Remember, the man we're after was ready to leave Spokane the day he arrived. Count on it. But he won't until he gets a whiff of me. And he hasn't...yet. Though I imagine he's expecting me so we have to move carefully."

Miles later, Marcus said that he had been recruited straight out of Stanford where he graduated in the top ten percent of his class and this was not particularly surprising news to Hoot. He said that prior to being recruited into the U.S. Marshal's Service; he had worked in the Stanford college payroll office to fulfill the work portion of his work-study financial aid package.

Said he met his wife there. A woman too good for him who was now self-employed as a court reporter in Seattle. They had recently purchased a nice home in a nice Seattle neighborhood that had them mortgaged to their eyeteeth.

"No kids yet. But we plan for two," Marcus said.

He said he'd been a newspaper delivery boy throughout high school. Saving every dime for college because his parents were worried he wasn't athletic enough for a big-dollar scholarship, Hoot thinking that Marcus' parents must be proud of him after all that worry.

Marcus said he had also worked preparing pizzas. About a million pizzas. And you couldn't get him to eat one on a bet anymore. "That's it," he said, "no other work experience of any kind," and Hoot thought it showed.

Green to the gills. Certain to make the trip to Spokane a true learning experience for both of us. Only an hour on the road so far and he already knew more about Leon Marcus than he'd known about any of his previous partners or even his ex-wife before marrying her – a thought that Hoot found as amusing as it was disturbing.

"So, what'd *you* do before becoming a U.S. Marshal?" Marcus asked, apparently angling for a little more reciprocity in the conversation, and Hoot answered, deadpan as dirt, "Nothing my mother would've been proud to know about."

Marcus watched a half-mile of new snow pass by in silence and then tried again; "You've been chasing this guy…this *Creeper*…for how long?" he asked.

"Long time. Off and on," Hoot replied. Kept on driving.

With a sidelong glance, Hoot finally took mercy on his new partner, not wanting to be guilty of shutting the guy out until after he'd dodged a few bullets and proved his longevity, adding; "He's a record holder, Creeper is. A *Top Ten Longest on the Lam* record holder. Number three or four, I think, depending on how many others have cashed-in their chips recently – I don't keep track anymore. He escaped in 1983 while being transferred from a hospital visit for a skin graft in Kansas City back to Leavenworth prison. I requested the duty and got it. Was DIC.

"Norman – *Creeper* – escaped during the transfer, and I got the stink-eye from the top of the chain of command all the way down to the lowest rookie as if I'd set the whole thing up. There are still marshals who believe I was in on Norman Carpenter's escape. Or at least responsible for it. And they have a point; Creeper knew me so well, it made it easy for him to slip away.

"I followed his trail from Kansas into southern Missouri. To Colorado where he played hell with a Denver crack factory. You may remember hearing about that one during one of your kindergarten recesses. Media called it the Rocky Mountain Mafia murders – it was Creeper's work. And then throughout the Southwest, Arizona primarily. If the Cowboy Mafia was there, so was Creeper.

"In fact, if you're interested in a particularly gruesome read, look up an incident called 'The Sun Mountain Business' in '89. A supposedly respectable businessman and a state senator were found butchered. Pieces of them hanging from about five acres of prickly pear cactus – that was one of Creeper's more creative moments. Off his meds that time, I suspect. Next he took a little side trip to Boise where a well-known local televangelist with an unwholesome interest in young boys vanished without a trace. So did Norman. Showed up the following year in San Diego. Then he traveled up the I-5 corridor leaving a trail of corpses from LA all the way to Portland, Oregon.

"That's how I ended up here in the Northwest. Waiting around for him to stick his head up again. The guy moves around a lot. Lives like a bum mostly, but he's smart, artistic, and fairly computer savvy for an old con – self taught. He stays off the radar as much as possible, but he's probably one of the busiest hitman anywhere in the world outside a terrorist training camp. You can't be that busy without making a blip now and then no matter how careful you are."

"What happened in Portland?"

"Simple, really. My old buddy took another front-page-headline hit contract and then immediately disappeared. Again. Something he does very well.

"Disappeared along with a handful of especially nasty coke dealers he put out of business down in Salem. Local ATF out of Portland wanted to send him a thank you note. He's a merciless killer. Two cokeheads turned up as dead as Julius Caesar in a dumpster within a week of Creeper coming to town. Remains of a third one floated to the surface of a mountain reservoir outside of Bend Oregon about a month later.

"Fourth guy is still unaccounted for," Hoot said, remembering the postcard that was forwarded to him. An aerial picture of the Mt. Bachelor ski area near Bend on the front, the words: *Saw you in Sacramento. You're starting to look your age. Me too. Keep up the good work, Norm*, written in a familiar scrawl on the back. It had been mailed from Seattle. Hoot didn't mention the card to Marcus. Nor any of the other cards from Creeper he had collected over the years. The phone calls. The chat room messages.

Hoot said; "That was over six months ago. Some people believed that Creeper also got popped in the Salem deal. Thought he was dead. They were certain of it. Others said it was his last gig and he retired afterward. They were equally certain. Both were wrong.

"The moral? Never trust what people say. People don't know shit. Obviously."

"Retired?" Marcus inquired. "Like he got in his thirty years – or *cadavers* in his case – and now he draws a pension. Goes fishing a lot. Like the way a teacher or a cop retires?"

Hoot grunted a snicker at Marcus' attempted humor. "I didn't mean to paint a pretty picture of the hitman lifestyle. It's been my experience that most pros retire to lethal injections, or the noose, or the electric chair depending on the state they're executed in. Or to life sentences. Few are any good at saving money. Fewer still live long enough in that business for it to matter."

"But it could happen, don't you think? A hitman comes to realize how hard he's pushing his luck, gets superstitious and kicks back to a quieter life. Maybe finds an honest line of work."

"No. Guys like him never quit. Believe me about that."

"Some have, surely…we don't hear about them, and they fall off the grid."

Hoot, his pale blue eyes naked without his shades, looked over at Marcus and remembered reading that internet-based legitimate businesses were popular among ex-cons, said, "I suppose it is possible. But none I personally know of have done it. And definitely not Norman Carpenter. Not *Creeper*. He would've been better off to leave the country twenty-eight years ago, become a merc in some third-world war zone. And he's smart enough to know that. But he has tenacious roots – or likes to think he has. A twisted sense of loyalty. And *I* wouldn't be there for him to fuck with.

"That's a lot of it. He still thinks we're *connected* somehow. Part of some mystic American Indian bullshit that his mother got him started on."

Marcus said, "I heard that you two were old friends before you were a marshal."

"Yeah," Hoot answered. "I knew him – I *know* him, you could say. We were friends when we were kids. I'd say I know him well enough to know that he sure as hell isn't retired."

Marcus said, "I heard that you served together in Covert Ops in Vietnam. Heard that he calls you up sometimes. Leaves messages. Sends cards."

"Where'd you hear all this?"

"Rumors. You know…people talk. Other marshals. FBI guys. Cops. Your reputation is that you're an old-school surrender-or-die-type gunslinger."

"No shit? I had no idea…"

"I heard that you were a sharpshooter in Covert Ops. A sniper. And that you once shot a lit cigarette out of a man's hand at three-hundred meters just to give him a scare."

"What'd I just tell you about paying attention to what people say?"

"Is it true? About the cigarette at three-hundred meters?"

"These people, these rumormongers, any of them mention how damned near every partner I've ever had has ended up getting shot? Some of them fatally? *Including* my last partner?"

"It might've come up once or twice."

Yeah. You bet your dark chocolate-colored ass it came up, Hoot thought. The superstitious scuttlebutt going around about me is thicker than Grandma's turtle stew and I distinctly remember being unable to swallow that crap. Rumors about what a dangerous partner I am. About how I'm fixated on one case to the detriment of everything and everyone else around me. About bullets flying wherever I go.

Hoot took a long glance at his new partner and said, "You do your job. I'll do mine. We watch each other's back. And we'll get along just fine."

A few silent miles followed. Then Marcus offered, "Maybe you should downsize your plans." His face deadpan except for the gleam in his eyes. "About retirement, I mean. Cash in right now and hit the road in a used VW Microbus instead of towing a new fifth-wheel behind a new pickup."

"Don't think I haven't considered doing exactly that," Hoot answered, starting to like his new partner a little, a thin smile cracking his lips, thinking, Hell, if I don't cut back on the drinking and give up smoking I probably won't live long enough to get all the way back home to Maine, anyhow.

Hoot remembered a few years ago telling a previous partner that the sooner he died the happier he'd be. What he'd meant to say was the sooner he *retired* but it came out all wrong. "No truer words," the partner had replied before Hoot could recover his wits. He later wondered about the obvious subliminal implications of the slip.

Just thinking about ex-partners had a sobering effect on Hoot. Made him long for a wholly different life, a life he had never personally experienced but nonetheless knew existed. Maybe his father's life. Or his younger brother's. A life with roots. With family. With a home. With friends and co-workers who didn't get shot before you got a chance to know them.

"Funny what a man will call home," Hoot said. "I figure in my lifetime I've spent more time standing in front of public urinals with my dick in my hand than I've spent in the pleasant seaside town of Pleasanton Maine. Still, that's home to me for whatever it's worth."

And recently Hoot wanted nothing more than to reacquaint himself with it – briefly, at least, to see if it still fit him at all. He yearned to put fresh flowers on a certain gravesite. Depressed him to think about it.

Problem was that the job had hit a new all-time low. Not that he expected much from it anymore. The job sucked. That wasn't new. Once the idealism that gets a person into law enforcement in the first place wears off what's left is a nasty job – fact of life. It was just that every asshole he tracked down and returned to justice brought him closer and closer to the bottom of the shitpot. His life had become an endless parade of assholes.

And still that one remained – Norman Carpenter – the one who had to be put away before Hoot could go home with a clear conscience. *Then* he could retire.

Did that make Hoot a dangerous partner, his determination to clean up this one lingering mess before he parked his bony butt in a La-Z-Boy? It was heavy, the feeling that he was treading on his last chance. This trip to Spokane.

It had quit snowing, the road getting icy now. Hoot and Marcus stopped at a freeway truck stop for gas and coffee, a bathroom break, and then they headed east again, another hour to go. The rising sun was soon in their eyes, Hoot's expression veiled behind the curtain of his sunglasses, the polarized lenses quickly turning darker and darker.

Driving into the glare, Hoot thought about a time long ago in a place so alien it could have been a different world in a different galaxy. *He* was different then. Filthy. Stinking. Decked-out in jungle camo to the nines and heading out on another LRP mission, warning Norman – *Creeper* – that he seemed to be getting awfully close to his handle, that he was getting way too fuckin creepy. Always wanting to use the knife. Get in close instead of taking the long shot. He remembered Norman saying that he wanted to *see* them and remember them in his mind's eye, the targets. Always wanting to touch them.

Yes…the signs had always been there. Even when they were teenage kids. Norman would spend summers with his mom and stepfather in Montana and come back all creeped-out, his dad and stepmother in Pleasanton offering little better in the way of positive influences. Hoot also remembered spending the summer vacation after junior high school on the rez with Norman at his mother's place – turned fifteen with a blood-brother ceremony in Norman's mother's sweat lodge. In the nude, no less…talk about an eye-opening experience! A textbook environment for an abusive home life, some might later suggest. Not that Hoot ever suspected that Norman had been *physically* abused – no, it was more like abuse by example. And what examples he had! Jesus, how does a kid outgrow influences like those? No wonder Norman was different. He never had a chance; you look at the whole picture.

Yet no one seemed to notice.

Would Donna still be alive if anyone had bothered to notice?

If *he*, Ezra Hooten, had bothered to notice? Or, having noticed...*done* something.

Hoot slowed the Ford Five Hundred down to sixty-five from eighty-five, said to Marcus; "That cigarette you heard about? The one I shot out of a man's hand at three-hundred meters? It was a mistake. All of it. A mission that went totally sideways. The guy was an ARVN officer, supposedly on our side, but he was a suspected Viet Cong double-agent. And he lost a couple of fingers in the deal. Never did come to God."

Marcus, looking over, said nothing.

"Just wanted to set the record straight," Hoot continued, driving on. "I know my sheet isn't exactly pristine."

After a couple more quiet miles he said; "So, I take it that you heard my last partner was shot dead just last month? It's true. Happened the week before Thanksgiving. A routine capture that went to hell in a heartbeat.

"I'd been hanging around in the Seattle office, serving a few warrants, waiting for my old buddy Creeper to pop up again. Knowing he would. Meanwhile, a couple of shitheads decided to take a walk from Twin Rivers and I was the lucky bastard who drew the assignment to go get 'em. My partner – Edmonds was his name, Peter Edmonds – was a young guy, like you. I didn't get a chance to really know the man. Didn't even have any fuckin idea what his wife's name was until I sat down to write her a goddamned condolence letter."

"*My* wife's name is Eva," Marcus said.

Chapter 8

Norman Carpenter sat in a booth in Martha's Restaurant in Wenatchee, Washington. He was finishing a #2 Breakfast Special before hitting the road again. Pancakes so large they hung off the edge of the platter. Sausage links and scrambled eggs on another platter. The food was not exactly gourmet but it was plentiful. And that was okay. Norman didn't care if the food was less than five-star as long as the restaurant was clean, and Martha's was about as clean as you could expect a highway eatery to be. He watched two women enter with immediate interest, arm-in-arm like a couple of lesbian lovers, a couple of blondes, and he was surprised to see that he knew the spiky-haired one – Liz was her name. Hell, she lived in the same fucking apartment house in Spokane that he did!

Small world. But not for long – after the high-visibility job in Seattle Norman knew he'd have to be moving on. And soon, no doubt. His old pal Hoot was likely to stick his snowy white head up any day now. This was something of a shame as Norman had come to like it in Spokane. But moving on was a necessary sacrifice to the lifestyle. Staying low meant staying *mobile*. Spokane had been a useful place to disappear to and tend to his growing, web-based, graphic design business, CatScratch Graphics, and it had enough street work with area smut and drug peddlers to keep a little extra cash coming in. He would miss it.

The apartment was a good deal thanks to Vincent P – free rent in exchange for being on call for occasional bill collection work; it even came with a certified babe living downstairs. *Two* babes now Norman guessed by the lovey-dovey look he was seeing on Liz and her friend's face across the dining room. Best of all, Spokane was halfway between his mom's place on the Flathead Reservation in Montana and Seattle where there was always plenty of street work if he needed it.

It was just that he had really *felt* Hoot's presence in Seattle this last time. Felt his old blood-brother's attention turning his way as surely as if he'd seen him with his own eyes. And that made Spokane a bit too close to Seattle for comfort because Norman knew that Hoot could feel him, too, even if the hardheaded old coot didn't have a clue how to dial it in. How to use it. Nonetheless, Hoot being one of those dogged, never-give-up lawman types, Norman knew his old friend would soon be taking a hard look at Spokane.

Laying down his fork and reaching into his lap for his napkin, Norman took his own hard look at the two lesbians. Liz was a good-looking woman, no denying. But Norman's eye was irresistibly drawn to her friend. There was something refreshing about this other woman. Something *familiar*. And innocent.

Innocence was impossible, of course, if she was with Liz. Liz, he knew, worked at Goodtime Charlie's just outside of Spokane, the titty bar Vincent P owned. The same Vincent P who'd recommended Norman to a cousin to take out the old man in Seattle.

Supersmall world. Way too much a coincidence, seeing Liz like this, he thought, our paths converging in the middle of nowhere right after I finish a job. Norman didn't like it. Didn't like Liz, either. Even if she was a babe.

Stuck up bitch, that Liz. A poser. Playing the fey intellectual. Putting on airs of the *artiste* around the apartment while putting out for a buck at Vincent P's place the whole time. She had looked right at him when she walked into the restaurant, then walked on by without the slightest sign of recognition in her eyes. Without a word.

A gal like that, a professional slut, a so-called *dancer* at Goodtime Charlie's, guys checking them out every day, she probably wouldn't recognize *any* of them with their dicks tucked away and the lights turned on, Norman thought, taking an absentminded sip of coffee…

Of course, I have one of those forgettable faces. Too fucking ugly to remember. Lucky me. That's it…Liz probably didn't even notice me, Norman thought, taking off his glasses and giving them a halfhearted wipe with his napkin.

But the other one sitting with Liz reminded him of...of...

Could it *be*?

She reminded him of...Oh *shit*!

Replacing his glasses, Norman suddenly realized the other woman was the spitting image of Donna, his dead wife! The one person linking him forever with Shooter.

Talk about a bad omen! He didn't like this at all...

He covered the check with cash and walked out of Martha's without looking back.

***

1964, the summer they both turned fifteen, Hoot and Norman decided they were 'best friends' and Hoot spent his summer vacation on the Flathead Indian Reservation in Montana with Norman. It was the weirdest summer of Hoot's life, still new to his friendship with Norman.

Soon as they arrived, Norman's mother, Inez Feather – insisting Hoot call her Inez, absolutely *not* Miz. Feather or certainly not Mrs. Carpenter, but *Inez* with emphasis on the *nez* – wanted the boys to join her in the sweat lodge to cleanse their spiritual backsides before running off in quest of saddle sores and mischief.

"Should have warned you about that," Norman said. "Mom is big on getting naked and sitting in the sweat lodge, beating drums and communing with the spiritual world."

"*Naked*? You're shittin me...right?" Hoot responded.

"Don't worry. It's not so embarrassing when everyone else is naked, too."

"What do you mean *every*one?"

"Members of the tribe. Guests. Like you. It's okay. It's dark in there..."

Not dark enough, Hoot soon found out.

"What happened to the chief?" a girl, maybe a couple years younger than Norman and Hoot, was asking as they entered. Though dark in the back corners, there was plenty of light radiating from the fire pit in the center of the lodge for Hoot to

70

clearly see the girl; she was short and round, with puffy buds where potentially-pendulous breasts would someday appear indicating that her hormones were busy at work even as she spoke. The fatty flesh at the conjunction of her thighs was bare, brown, and seemed to smile up at Hoot when she sat down and crossed her legs.

Inez, looking like one of those bare-naked butt-ugly natives that Hoot had seen featured in certain issues of *National Geographic* magazine, beat her hide-covered drum with a flourish and answered, "He died in 1904 on the Colville Indian reservation here in Washington. The same reservation my father was from. Actually, my father was taken before the chief when he was born – it was a great honor. I remember many stories about Chief Joseph that my mother and grandfather told. There is a monument to him beside the road in Nespelem Washington, a crumbling pile of stones with a fading wooden sign that gives little hint of the greatness of the man."

"That's a sad story," the short girl said.

"Wouldn't be an American Indian story if it weren't sad."

There were fifteen people crowded together in the sweat lodge, breechcloths and blanket wraps left at the door. Hoot knew this number to be a fact, counting heads over and over to keep from staring at the fully-developed breasts and furry little triangular pelt clearly displayed by the sixteen or seventeen-year-old girl who was standing and acting as raconteur, telling the story of Chief Joseph. This girl, a natural raven-haired beauty with skin the color of cinnamon, frequently looked to Norman's mother for assistance, her glance bouncing off Hoot sitting next to Inez when she did.

They continued like this. Everyone naked as newborns and beating drums with apparent randomness. Some recounting stories. The bed of hot coals in the middle of the sweat lodge with smoke trailing out through a hole in the ceiling. Hoot repeatedly stealing glances at the teenage beauty on the other side of the coals while trying to conceal the physical evidence of his growing interest with an awkward posture.

"My grandfather was a powerful and honored shaman in his day," Inez said, beating her drum as she spoke. "His knowledge of things both spiritual and worldly was very great. He told me about a time before his time, when The People could not locate buffalo, so they asked my grandfather's teacher and mentor, Bear Track, for help.

"Bear Track gathered all the young men together and he took his drum and beat it and sang, making everyone join him in the song. After singing a while, he said, 'The Piegan tribe has made strong medicine and keep the buffalo away. I will break their medicine and make the buffalo come. In four days the buffalo will arrive, and you will see many of them.' And it happened; just exactly as he had said it would..."

Hoot began to feel a little dizzy, either from the smoke, the magic of the drums, or the eye strain of trying to take in every possible detail of the naked beauty seated across from him without staring.

"Do you ever see the future, Hoot?" Inez interrupted, breaking the spell that had hold of Hoot's young libido. Her distinctly creased face was close to his, her coal-black eyes staring into his blue ones.

"Uh...I don't know. Only in my dreams, sometimes...I think," Hoot stammered, surprised, and not pleased to be included in this exchange. "I'm not sure."

"Yes, of course, in your dreams," Inez said. "That's where the second sight works best. It's not so unusual, really, though most people don't know what to make of it."

"Shamans do," the naked beauty said.

"If they're any good they do!" Inez answered with a laugh and more drum flourishes. "And others, if they are willing to try."

Still looking at Hoot with the intensity of a raptor, she said, "I detect a hint of talent in you, young *Hoot*." Then she continued, "The Great Shamans were *very* good at it. My grandfather was very good. My fondest memories are of him telling me stories about the history of the People. Not just histories of the Flatheads and other Salish people. He told me the stories of many Western tribes. And of their betrayal by the

Whites. About that, he told me that it had been inevitable. Easily foreseen by all the shamans. But no less a tragedy."

"Aren't things better for Indians now, after all these years?" the short girl asked.

"Are they?" Inez Feather asked.

Norman, who was seated next to Hoot and apparently unaffected by the beauty across from them, spoke up, said, "How different would it be if Chief Joseph had made it to Canada?"

"That's a bad question," Inez answered, putting her drum aside. "It suggests a greater importance to what we do in this life than there actually is. Or worse, that we can somehow go back and correct our mistakes. Chief Joseph was a very great man, but even he was a minor player in the greater picture. He knew that all we can do is walk the path we're on. When a crossroad comes along we choose, or a choice is made for us. And then we walk *that* path. At every turn, at every step, the path is a new one. The reason we can't go back is because the path that brought us here no longer exists."

Those words; *the path that brought us here no longer exists*, settled in Hoot's mind, thankfully taking a bit of pressure off his loins. They were words he remembered often, his whole life.

Chapter 9

Three years before, when Norman was twelve-years-old, his
father drove him cross-country from the Rez in Montana to
Pleasanton Maine – environments about as opposite each other
as they could be. Said the trip would take three or four days.
Said they would have a great time. He also said it would be an
adventure; "Just us two guys." Joseph Carpenter taking his turn
at full custody, bringing his son to Pleasanton to live with him
and Eileen, the wife who had replaced Inez. A cozy family.

The mode of transportation for the trip was Joe's 1958
Oldsmobile Dynamic Eighty-eight station wagon. Rear fender
fins with Buck Rogers-style rocket taillights. Two-tone red and
white paint job where it wasn't pocked with rust. Chrome
galore inside and out. It was fitted with a strap-on rooftop
luggage rack and it hunkered low to the pavement, loaded down
with shit both inside and up top; shit for the trip; shit that Joe
had left behind when he fled the reservation five years before
and yearned to have it near at hand again; Norman's shit that
Norman's mother sent with him to have in Maine; and two
dozen cases of unstamped Canadian whiskey bought from a
Reservation smuggler. Almost a thousand pounds of bottled
booze. Joe planned to sell the whiskey in Pleasanton. Cover
the expense of the trip.

Even loaded so heavily the Eighty-eight was capable of
cruising at eighty-eight miles per hour, feed it enough fuel.
"It's why they call em that…Olds Eighty-*eight*!" Norman's
father insisted, and he held the speedometer pegged at that
speed most of the way.

"A man can go a long way on a package of wieners and
a bag of chips" was one of Norman's father's many profound
pearls of manly wisdom, and he seemed determined to prove it.
They avoided stopping at restaurants as much as possible, and
they slept in the car.

"Couple-a guys on the road. We can just pull over and pee. Take care of our *other* business when we stop for gas" was another manly pearl well proven along the way.

The trip would have taken five days but required six because of the whiskey. Because of it Joseph Carpenter was unable to cross the border into Canada and take advantage of the shorter route from Minneapolis to Montreal, then down to Portland. Instead, he took the long way through Chicago and around the bottom of Lake Michigan and Lake Erie. Six long days of driving and four short nights of sleeping in the car. One night in a roadside cabin after Joe offered a ride to a beatnik girl at a truck stop somewhere west of Sioux City Iowa. Six days of constant cigarettes. Windows rolled down. Windburn. Mounting body odor. A neverending quest for something to listen to on the radio and mostly finding the ever-popular group harmony sound. Occasionally some doo wop to break the monotony. *Arthur Godfrey Time* and the oh-so appropriate *Traveling Man* by Ricky Nelson.

Norman was demoted to being squeezed in with the sleeping bags, pillows, and sundry clothing in the back seat of the Olds, and could attest without a doubt that the beatnik girl smelled worse than either he or his father. But she was entertaining, at least, talking non-stop about everything under the sun. And her braless torso – halfheartedly concealed under a man's sleeveless tee shirt – kept Joe Carpenter's eyes wide open the next four-hundred miles even if not one-hundred percent on the road. She went her own way sometime during their uneventful night together at a Cozy Roadside Inn near Chicago...

"Wanna get something to eat?" she had asked.

"We have wieners," Joe said.

"I know. We ate some on the road, remember?"

"We have more."

"You're kidding."

"Plenty of beer and chips to go with."

"Well...okay then. Whyn't you two go ahead and start without me," she said.

Norman grinned, his barely-teenage young eyes practically crossed by the sight of two shapely breasts

75

struggling with various degrees of success to wriggle free from smelly captivity through oversized arm openings. He said, "Don't worry. We'll save some for you, in case you change your mind."

"You guys mind if I grab the first shower?" the girl inquired, nipping the wieners-for-dinner conversation before it could gain traction. "It's been awhile."

She took a very long shower. Exhausted, both Joe and Norman fell sound asleep while she was in there.

The sound of water splashing like a waterfall. A naked nymph, wet and singing just beyond the thin warped veneer of the bathroom door. Norman saw her in his dreams. Pink pointy nipples playing peek-a-boo behind a curtain of long and tangled sun-bleached hair. Dark-blonde fuzz in her armpits and down...*there*.

She was gone the next morning.

Norman woke with a stiffy. So did Joe, even though he tried to hide it. Joe said it was just plain good luck the tittyshaker didn't steal anything. Not even his billfold, fat with four twenties. Even all the whiskey was still accounted for.

They continued on until, finally, after one last twelve-hour day on the road largely spent pegged at eighty-eight miles-per-hour, they arrived in Pleasanton the day before school started. Sixth grade.

Eileen drove Norman to school that first morning. Obviously eager to get him out of the house after only one short night. Hinting to Joe that they needed to talk...*right away*. Hinting that certain events had transpired during his two week absence and they needed to be discussed...*privately*.

This was the morning of the day that Norman first met Hoot and Donna.

A long and winding road traveled to a falsely auspicious beginning.

***

School in Maine was another universe compared to school on the Rez. Norman was ready to just say *fuckit* by lunchtime that first day and head back to where he came from. He did, in fact, say fuckit several times that first day, earning some quick reprimands from teachers and clandestine looks from other students.

Ezra Hooten was one of those other students giving the new kid a look. "I remember seeing you out at Cape Porpoise last summer," he said after class was finally out, Norman waiting for Eileen to pick him up. "You were standing on the breakwater rocks, trying to spear fish."

"Yeah. I remember. I was back here then. Visiting my old man and his new wife. Listening to them talk about custody – talking about moving me here like I wasn't even in the fucking room. You didn't watch for very long or you would have seen me get one."

"Spear a fish? With a *stick*?"

"Yeah…with a stick. A sharp one. People do it all the time where I come from. You don't fucking believe me?"

"So, where are you from that people spear fish with sticks?"

"Montana. The Flathead Indian Reservation. My mother lives there. Those fucking Flatheads spear spawning salmon with sticks all the time. Stand on scaffolds over rivers and catch them in nets with long handles, too."

"Yeah. I've seen pictures of that in National Geographic or somewhere. Didn't know it was something that your people still do."

"*They* do. Something *they* do," Norman said through lips curled in distaste. "The Flatheads are fishermen. *I* don't. *I'm* Sioux. The Sioux are hunters. And warriors…"

"If you're Sioux, how is it that your mother is Flathead and your father is white?" Ezra Hooten asked.

Norman stuffed his hands in his pockets and looked away, refusing to justify such a stupid question from a ghostly-pale white boy with an answer. Wishing he could just go away from this place, he looked at a girl walking toward them. A very pretty girl. She was smiling. She walked up to Ezra Hooten and said, "Hiya, Hoot." Taking his hand in hers, she asked, "Who's your friend?"

"Hi, Donna" Hoot said. "This is Norman. He's in my homeroom class. New in town. From Montana."

"*Hoot?*" Norman repeated, refusing to let Donna's smile fluster him. "Like an owl? The fuck kind of a name is Hoot?"

"It's short for Hooten…my last name. My friends call me Hoot."

"Sounds like a bullshit Native name, like Talking Owl, or Farting Fox. Are you Indian?"

"I dunno. Could be, I guess. I'm a Boy Scout, Order of the Arrow…*that's* Indian."

"The fuck it is!" Norman said, taking the high ground. "It's just a bunch of dumb fucking white kids playing with breechcloths."

"You sure say *fuck* a lot," Hoot said.

"So? That a problem for you…*Hoot?*"

"Nope. Don't mean *fuck*all to me. How 'bout you, Donna?"

Donna just kept smiling, holding Hoot's hand while quietly melting Norman's young heart. Thus began a long and complicated three-way relationship…

***

Early in 1972 Norman asked Hoot to be his best man when he married Donna. Planned the wedding date for Hoot's next R-and-R rotation stateside from 'Nam. "I'm sorry, but I don't think so," Hoot said. An awkward conversation. Hoot explaining how things had become a bigger mess than usual along the Laotian border, the brass, as usual, thinking that something big was brewing. Locals caught in the middle with the VC were losing their warm-n-fuzzy feelings for GI's.

By this time some of the things that Hoot had seen and done in-country had left him unwilling to look in a mirror. Unable to sleep. Last thing in the world he wanted was to look Donna in the eyes and wish her luck in her married life with Norman. The *You Coward* letter she had written to him after their breakup had said about all that could be said on the subject. Donna, his girlfriend since before middle school, since grade school…hell, practically since birth, calling a spade a spade after he came to the realization that they were "two neutrons speeding off on separate trajectories" as he told her.

That was such obvious bullshit. And he was ashamed for saying it. But now, truthfully, he was not the same person she had known. Not even close.

Told her *don't* when she offered to wait for him.

Elaborating on the neutron theory, "Neutrons don't wait," he said. "They fly off on their own. They collide with other neutrons. They explode."

How could he possibly say *congratulations*, eat wedding cake, and make suggestive champagne toasts after dropping such a load of shit, after such a cold slap?

"I really don't think I'm up for spending time with my old man. With Mom and Sis and my brother. With friends," Hoot told Norman, and it was not a lie. Not entirely. "Think I'll take my R-n-R in Hawaii instead of coming home."

Norman had called him a coward, too. He was right about that, he and Donna.

"Just be glad you're gone from here," Hoot said via an American Red Cross Forward Base Area Phone, words crawling at a snail's pace through land lines and cables, saying *over* at the end of each sentence to avoid long pauses and talkovers. "Donna is the best, *over*. You're a very lucky man, *over*. Have a good wedding...*over*."

Chapter 10

Angela waited in the middle of the queen-size bed in room 123 at the Big River Inn in Wenatchee Washington. Blanket and bedspread thrown aside, sheet up to her chin.

She was nervous. Aroused by the sight of Liz walking naked toward the bed from the bathroom. Thinking that Liz was a very beautiful woman in the *classic beauty* sense of the word even though there was nothing specific about her that Angela would ordinarily think of as *classic*. She looked taller without her baggy boyish clothing. Her neck made a sensuous line curving gracefully into narrow shoulders, then downward to her breasts. Simply stunning breasts, they were much larger than Angela's and capped with nipples that looked firm enough to hurt someone – a significant contrast to Angela's. Even after nursing two children Angela's nipples had remained disappointingly tiny; although feeling hot enough at the moment they could easily burn holes in the sheet, she thought.

So many differences between them. In contrast to Angela's pale round tummy Liz's stomach looked muscular, as if it was accustomed to hard work. Wide hips tapered into athletic legs. Pronounced tan lines highlighted her breasts and backside, suggesting a good amount of time recently spent in a tropical locale wearing an exceptionally lewd bathing suit. But the most remarkable thing about her was her pubic hair – an unbelievably thick mat of precisely coiffed curly blonde fur rising up from the meeting place between her thighs, spreading with uniform thickness from hip bone to hip bone and halfway to her navel.

Liz walked over to the bed, took Angela's hand and placed it on her pubis, pushing her fingers deep into the furry thicket. Hair as dense as sheep's wool, and surprisingly soft. Once touched it begged to be caressed, drawing Angela's fingers into its warmth. "Welcome to the Sherwood Forest of pussies," she said, and then leaned down and kissed Angela's mouth, her lips warm, and as soft as melting wax.

***

Norman drove out to Goodtime Charlie's as soon as he got back to Spokane.

Technically, he knew, Goodtime Charlie's was located two blocks within the city limits of Stateline Idaho, though it was considered a Spokane club by most of the patrons, the distinction blurred years ago when Spokane had two or three Go-Go clubs and Stateline had an honest-to-God *topless* joint – Goodtime Charlie's.

Back then, there were still a couple of semi-legal old fashioned whorehouses in operation a few miles farther east in Wallace, places where silver miners, loggers, truck drivers and other men with needs could go for relief. Later, when the Go-Go joints all went topless, Goodtime Charlie's in Stateline went all-nude.

"Gotta stay ahead of the suckers," Charlie Nightingale, the original owner, was famous for saying. He was also known for saying that time will eventually change *all* things – including vice – not always for the better.

Norman knew all there was to know about the nude dancing scene in the Northwest since he was nine years old; Goodtime Charlie's as much a part of his youth as Dairy Queen to most kids. After his parents' divorce – the middle years when he spent the school year with his father and stepmother in Maine – he spent summers spent with his mother on the reservation in Montana. He remembered riding along with his uncle on his mother's side, Max Feather. Uncle Max driving to Spokane from Polson on business and spending an hour at a certain house in Wallace, Idaho. Norman having cookies and hot chocolate with flowery-smelling, scantily-clad women downstairs while Uncle Max took care of business upstairs. Soon it became a couple hours at Goodtime Charlie's in Stateline, Norman waiting for Uncle Max in the game room of a Mexican joint up the highway. These later forays were usually followed by a quick run to the Lazy Daisy Motel with a dancer between shifts – the Lazy Daisy, an appropriately-named establishment where Norman fondly remembered eating popcorn and playing eightball for quarters with the night clerk on a worn pool table in the lobby.

Uncle Max let him come along to Goodtime Charlie's when he was fourteen and looked older. Paid a redheaded, bucktoothed, grandmotherly dancer named Mary fifty dollars to pop his cherry for his fourteenth birthday. "Don't worry, Sweetie," she had said. "My little Itsy knows what to do," wrapping her legs around his thighs and drawing him in.

Happy Birthday, Norman…

Back in Pleasanton, Norman told Hoot about the birthday fuck, and Hoot was so startled by the detailed report – in which the bucktoothed, grandmotherly whore was transformed into a nubile young beauty offering her first trick to a boy nearly her own age – he stuttered, "She d-d-did w-*what!*"

According to Uncle Max Feather the whole adult male entertainment scene in Spokane and the Idaho panhandle had started falling apart by then. This was a time at the cusp of smut for the masses, the heyday of drive-in-movie parking lots littered with condoms and peepshow voyeurism. Playboy magazine. Long before the internet – before anyone could imagine the world of free porn that was coming just around the corner. A man had to go out and find his fun in those days.

Uncle Max said that what really happened was the independent Idaho silver mines started closing down. Almost overnight miners became a vanishing breed, and there just weren't enough other regular customers to keep the whorehouses in business like before. Some of the Idaho whores hung around until local politicians needing a fresh horn to toot campaigned on a *clean 'em up for good* promise and won.

The few working girls left by the time Norman got his birthday present; those not interested in becoming *dancers* at Goodtime Charlie's or elsewhere were ready to retire anyhow. It pissed Uncle Max off when all the old whores began vanishing. "Hell, I helped break some of those gals in," he said, and Norman knew it was the truth. A few years later

Uncle Max slapped his knee and laughed when he saw how the old whorehouses were being dragged out of obscurity, cleaned up like grandpa's doughboy uniform and reopened as legitimate historical icons. Tourist attractions, they now sold their whore's tokens as souvenirs for the same amount the originals had fetched when a man could redeem them for a romp.

Nowadays, men like Norman's uncle could get a fraction of the kick at Goodtime Charlie's for ten times the money or more. Going home faithful for the most part. Disease-free usually. Broke and frustrated always. Uncle Max called it a fucking shame with emphasis on *fucking*. Soon enough the politicians decided to clean up the nude dancing business, too, and suddenly Uncle Max Feather had all sorts of convoluted new laws and codes to bitch about. Most of the new laws and codes were designed to protect the smut business and keep it exclusive, not to protect the community from its influence, he said, sounding like a man running for tribal council – which he was.

One particularly brilliant piece of legislation revoked liquor licenses for all the area nude clubs, the purported idea being to drive them out of business by depriving them of their customer base. The actual result was that they simply quit serving liquor and the minimum age limit for patrons dropped from twenty-one-years-old to eighteen – *sixteen* in Idaho. The minimum legal age of dancers also dropped. A whole new customer base was more than delighted to pay $10 at the door and $5 for a soft drink as long as they could enjoy the totally nude charms of a genuine teenage girl up close in a darkened place. And, as an added bonus, almost overnight high school-age kids had something new to do.

Norman first met Goodtime Charlie's current manager/part owner, Vincent P, when he returned to his mother's place in Kalispell while on leave from Vietnam and made a little jaunt to Spokane to have a look around. A dozen years later, lying low from the Donna mess back in Maine, he did his first freelance gig for Vincent P; resulting in a local prosecutor mysteriously vanishing…and staying gone. Stubborn man.

It was his first hits as a *civilian contractor*, the way he thought of it, and proudly. The case had remained on the FBI's unsolved list all this time. Norman still kept a treasured bit of dried scalp hidden away from that one – part of a collection of scalps comprising the bulk of his professional hits plus a few treasured tokens from Vietnam.

To Norman's profound approval and relief, nothing much had changed at Goodtime Charlie's in the years since that first bit of business – except the place had been remodeled. Paint, mirrors, and furniture, mostly. Lit-up at night, with the parking lot full, it looked upscale and prosperous. And it was, considering what it was.

There were now two small stages instead of one big one, a front stage halfway along the wall from the entrance and a rear stage deep in the back, everything not chrome plated or mirrored was painted black, and the sound system could crush bricks. The dancers were a hodgepodge of women in every body type from very thin to very round, from very tall to very short, some were all leg, some all boob, some all butt. They ranged from nearly beautiful to almost ugly – most being definitely *plain* if seen in natural light – wearing outfits consisting of very little to considerably less.

One at a time the dancers broke off from prowling the floor to take turns cavorting and parading with lurid coyness across the main stage, remorselessly undressing until completely nude while accompanied by music somewhat but not completely buffered by the one-way mirrored glass window in Vincent P's office wall. The DJ, a chubby fellow cloistered on a raised platform at the end of the bar, introduced each dancer, hawking her features and charms in excited tones similar to the style of announcement used at Monster Truck Rallies.

Vincent P looked prosperous. Savvy and wiser. He said to Norman, "Mister *C*…glad you're back from Sin City! My nephew was very impressed with you. The work you did."

"Your nephew is an idiot." Norman said. "Fucker took advantage of my connection to you. He exposed me. And for *what*?"

"Yeah. That Everett thing afterward – I heard. Was bullshit. 'Course, I had nothin to do with it."

"Won't surprise me if I'm going back to do your nephew inside of a year," Norman said, looking out at the club floor. "I only mention this because I wouldn't want it to be a problem between us, should it come up later…"

It was early in the day, more working girls than customers scattered in the cavernous darkness. One dancer, up on the back stage showing off everything she owned, was looking toward the office glass as if she could tell that Norman was there, daring him. He watched her like he'd watch copulating cats. Older gals working this time of day. Most of them looking bored, slouching around with their shaved pussies and flaccid asses. A nude club open this time of day…the morning customers weren't picky; many of them were retired and would probably confess that they only hoped to achieve one more boner before they croaked.

Vincent P dropped a conspicuous envelope on his desk, said, "No worries. It's been a good year. A little bonus for the work you've done for me. Merry fuckin Christmas."

"I'm going to lay low awhile," Norman told Vincent. "Go visit my mother. Maybe take a vacation."

"When?"

"Next week. Week after. I'll let you know. You need me, send a text message. You know the code. I'll call back on a land line. If I don't answer within two days, I'm not going to."

"As it happens, I do have something coming up," Vincent said. "In Vancouver."

"Canada? Can't help you, there. I don't cross any borders. Don't even have a current passport."

"This thing…it can wait till after the spring thaw. I know a way. Using certain back roads through the mountains."

Norman knew people who knew back ways Vincent P couldn't even imagine. He said, "I don't know. That business with your nephew left me feeling extra cautious."

"Understandable. You go ahead. See Mom. Give her my regards for the holidays," Vincent said, betraying no emotion. "We'll talk later. Get you a clean passport."

The dancer on stage wasn't putting much effort into it. Overdone makeup. The soft purple lighting making her look like a loitering Kewpie doll – step right up, gentlemen, get a boner and your weight guessed! Norman wondered if Liz would be bringing her new friend around to get naked and dance. Show it all off. He thought he might have to stop back in for that, if it happened. He remembered the friend's innocent-looking face from the glimpse he got at the restaurant in Wenatchee. Looking like a little girl out in the big bad world for the very first time. Looking like the young Donna Messenger's long-lost twin if not her outright fucking ghost.

Strange, her showing up right out of the blue…

Norman picked up the envelope, said to Vincent P, "Happy fucking Hanukkah."

Chapter 11

Snow flurries blowing down from Okanogan country
challenged the two women in the rose-colored Cadillac driving
east from Wenatchee all morning, but they figured it was still
too warm for anything to stick in Spokane. It made the road
wet and slippery as snot, but the Caddy just hunkered down and
pushed through, leaving a churning jetstream of surface water
and snowflakes stretched out behind. From Coulee City all the
way to Wilbur pheasants were scratching for grain along the
shoulders of the highway, taking to wing or ducking for cover
when vehicles passed. Hunters, decked-out in camo caps and
orange vests, craned their necks and swerved their pickup
trucks while gawking at the birds, shotguns hanging in their
rear window racks. Blathering weathermen on the radio agreed
that a cold front was moving in. Christmas was looming.

Liz's apartment was on the main floor of a converted
story-and-a-half clapboard house on Spokane's South Hill,
second from the corner on Arthur Street. It was kind of a
dump, but the price was right, Liz explained, telling Angela
how it was owned by the same guy who owned the club where
she worked. Behind the house there was a cramped parking
space in the narrow grassless back yard. She parked her huge
car next to an ugly and unused-looking old wooden motorboat
hunkering on a rusted trailer with flat tires.

"Welcome to Casa Pervie," she said with a grand
gesture toward the house, "where the denizens are all perverts
of one sort or another."

Once inside Angela immediately saw the most striking
feature of the apartment: the walls throughout were covered
with an outrageous collection of paintings and sketches,
colorful and bold, large and small, framed and unframed, all
signed *Liz*, a scrawl in the bottom right corner.

"Wow...you weren't kidding – you really are an artist!"

"Yeah. Crazy, innit? I do all this to stay sane," Liz said, waving a hand at the artwork on the walls, turning on a baseboard heater with a tap of her boot. "I dance to pay the bills."

"I don't know if I could do that," Angela said.

"Draw? Or dance?" Liz said.

Angela's reply was an exaggerated frown.

"Sure you could, if you wanted to. In fact, you might wanna think about giving it a try. You need money. Cute as you are, young-looking as you are, you could make a small fortune in no time. Unless, of course, you've got something else in mind?"

"I know how to finish concrete."

"Say again?"

"Concrete. *Cement*. I know how to finish it. You know…make it smooth. My daddy was a construction contractor and used to let me help out when I was a kid. My older brother got to run the skill saw and build stuff whether he wanted to or not. And mostly he didn't. My younger sister was a precious little princess and didn't do very much of anything which was exactly what she wanted to do. What I liked to do was finish concrete. I'm pretty good at it, too. Or at least I used to be."

"Sounds hard – pun intended. I just don't know if there is a whole lot of that kind of work around here in the wintertime."

"Probably not."

"Look, I know that what I do wouldn't exactly fill your daddy with pride, but I'll bet I spend a lot less time on my knees than any concrete finisher and get paid a lot more for it. And, before you have to ask…I'm not a whore. At least *I* don't see it that way. Others may disagree."

"I didn't mean it like that," Angela said, "I don't actually see anything wrong with it. Nude dancing. If that's what you want to do…"

"Oh there's *plenty* wrong with it – I promise," Liz said. "Fact is a person would have to pick quite a large amount of bug shit out of the ground pepper to find anything remotely

88

redeeming about it. It's definitely a walk on the wild side at the very least."

"Wild side?" Angela echoed. "Truthfully, I've been feeling my wild side recently. Getting crazy urges and ideas. I don't know from where. I just don't think *I* possess the nerve to parade around naked in front of a bunch of strange men is all I meant."

Liz answered, "Believe me, there isn't a nude dancer alive who didn't say exactly that right up to the minute she went on stage the first time. Some still tell themselves that every day after years in the business, and they go right up there and strut their stuff anyhow. Besides, the strutting around naked part just gets the customer's attention. It's the attention that gets you the money."

Angela wandered throughout the apartment, looking at the art. *It's the attention that gets you the money* taking up residence in her mind, pushing aside lingering doubts about where she was and how to get to where she wanted to go like so many dust bunnies into dark corners.

Liz's art looked both strange and familiar, something about it making Angela feel for the first time in a long time that there was hope for her becoming her true self again – even if she was becoming a completely different self at the same time. She was captivated by a large painting of a female torso that was molting, growing new feathers, thinking: that's me…I'm molting. All this is part of a big journey, and I'm only stopping here on the way to there. I'll get there one way or another.

Liz's method didn't seem so awful at the moment.

The house's living room was a remodeled version of the original and made up the bulk of Liz's apartment. It had a big window that looked out on a tree-lined street. A covered front porch with no access to the apartment from the porch since the original entry parlor had been remodeled to make a private front entrance leading directly upstairs to an attic apartment. A door from the living room led into the original downstairs bedroom. This room belonged to Liz's housemate, Emilio, whom she described as a gay Mexican chef at one of Spokane's finest ethnic cuisine establishments. She also mentioned that he had the biggest cock she'd ever seen on a man.

89

"*Monstrous* thing!" she said. "And beautiful...sculptural – I think I'll cast it in plaster one day. Wait'll you see it, big as a three-pound summer sausage and limp as a noodle. I walk around here half-naked half the time and it's never even lifted its head to say Hi. And it's a good thing, too. That man's cock would scare the bejeesus out of most women if it ever got really hard and stood at attention. Including me. It's no wonder the man's gay, poor thing. Except he hasn't always been gay, apparently; he has a wife and a bunch of kids back in Mexico. Maybe he's just gay as a way of being faithful until they can come here."

"You said, wait'll I *see* it?"

"Yeah. Emilio's got a phobia about small places, so he leaves the door open when he takes a bath."

"Uh-huh. I see..."

"Don't worry about Emilio. He's harmless. Friendly as a puppy. And he's cute in a Mexican puppy dog sort of way, too. You'll like him. He should be home around midnight tonight. But the guy upstairs, Nathan Cook, takes a little getting used to. He's the *real* pervie around here, I'm sure of it. Supposedly he's a graphic designer – looks down his computer-rendered nose at traditional-medium artwork like mine, I suppose. I don't really know. We haven't talked much. But I know men, and I can just tell that something isn't right about that one. And for a guy who works at home he seems to be gone a lot, drives a butt-ugly van advertising a carpet cleaning service, so what he actually does for a living is anybody's guess. Good thing is that when he is here he mostly hangs out in his apartment upstairs and doesn't bother us first-floor types."

Liz smiled. Peeling off her jacket, she hung it on the back of one of the kitchen chairs. "Question is," she teased, "where're you gonna sleep tonight? With me or with Monsterdick?"

Color raced into Angela's cheeks faster than fireworks on the Forth of July. "The old me would be looking for a way out of here about now," she said, dropping her backpack on the kitchen table. Removing her trench coat and unbuttoning her blouse, she walked into Liz's waiting embrace.

90

The blouse fell from Angela's shoulders. Her bra followed it to the floor.

Liz's fingers, hot enough to be on fire, burned pathways up both of Angela's bare arms, fell smoldering across her collarbone and then down her torso, finally caressing her soft breasts with an artist's attention to detail. Liz buried her nose in Angela's hair, said, "Wanna take a hot bath together in a tub old enough to be your grandma's while we wait for the apartment to warm up?"

***

Norman Carpenter, *Nathan Cook* to the few people he associated with in Spokane, had watched the two women arrive from a good vantage point in his kitchen, the window tucked up in the shadow under the peaked eave at the rear of the house on Arthur Street. Liz parking her obnoxious automobile in her assigned spot. Getting out and showing her new girlfriend what's what. Norman took a good long look at the girlfriend, confirming what he had noticed when he first saw her in Wenatchee. Unbelievably…*yes*, she looked just like his dead wife, Donna. *Exactly* like her. Could be Donna's living ghost. Looking as closely through the window glass as he dared, it was hard for Norman to peg her age, but he thought a couple years older than Donna was when she jerked his chain the last and final time. But it was definitely Donna no matter her age. Made his pulse quicken just to look at her.

A ghost…Donna's ghost! Norman thought. A skinwalker!

He stepped back from the window, closing the blinds, feeling the small hairs on his neck rise. He would get a better look soon enough.

Meanwhile, he was hungry. Nothing like tending to a good appetite to take the edge off a man's heebie-jeebies, Norman thought. He dug around in a kitchen cabinet, found bread and enough honey-roasted extra-crunchy peanut butter for half a sandwich. Some blackberry jam in the fridge. He opened a beer to go with the sandwich, and returned with his lunch to the table by the window.

91

The small drop-leaf table was covered with organized stacks of papers and notes including some unopened mail in a tray. In one corner was a tin containing a packet of rolling papers and a tiny resin-encrusted pair of scissors used to clip bits off of high-potency sativa buds to roll into joints. Another tin contained his roaches. A blown-glass bong that he used exclusively to smoke dissected roaches took the place of honor that a flower arrangement in a vase might otherwise claim in the center of the table. An antique ceramic humidor containing a stash of fresh bud stood by. In another corner was a holster containing the weapon he thought of as the *big bastard* – a loaded .45-caliber P220 Sig Sauer pistol similar to the Colt he'd favored in 'Nam.

Along the table's narrow end stood a fourteen-inch-tall bronze *Venus de Milo* figurine lamp with a beaded red velvet shade, a cell phone plugged into a charger, a selection of jump drives, and his computer.

He sat down, placed the .38-caliber snubbie Smith and Wesson he'd used to kill old Nick P next to the other pistol, took a big bite of the sandwich, and reached for his pistol cleaning kit. Norman was not the kind of hitman you read about or see in the movies, always in a hurry to throw away a perfectly good weapon just because he'd used it. But he did believe in cleanliness. In his weaponry as in his life. A clean weapon is a reliable weapon – Basic Boot Camp 101.

A half-hour later, the sandwich and beer were gone and both pistols were cleaned and oiled. Those business chores done, Norman turned on the computer, thinking it was time to get informed and 'shop some photos. CatScratch Graphics was the legitimate side of Norman's life – if he could be said to have such a thing – freelance graphic design for clients anywhere in the world via the internet. Business conducted incognito from a virtual office; that, and legalized medical marijuana – who could've guessed?

A self-taught techie, Norman's computer was his one true love, the consumption of marijuana having advanced from *love* to *necessity* some years ago. An indispensible tool to a graphic designer, his current computer was less than a year old, a Mac G-5 tower with 20 gigabytes of RAM, and a massive quad-core Intel processor. It was the object of a constant and endless search for the latest upgrade – soft and hardware. Featured a large flat-screen monitor. Cordless mouse and keyboard. A VSL-plus cable modem. It was also hard-cabled to his old computer, which now served as a file backup for his growing collection of Photoshop files, a proxy driver, and for archiving the video monitoring system that he had covertly installed throughout the whole house. Exterior mini-cameras covered the front porch and rear entry; one in the staircase leading up to his apartment; one in the basement; a servo-gimbaled high-def color cam concealed inside the return air duct high in the wall of Liz's bedroom and another micro-mini hidden in one of the molding rosettes over the tub in her bathroom.

He clicked the video monitoring system to activate the cam in Liz's bedroom, adjusted the angle and zoom to center on her bed, and then sat back saying, "Excellent. This is going to be worth waiting for."

Norman was pleased that Liz had a new lesbian lover, even if her new lover was actually *his* old lover reincarnated. Not that Norman approved of lesbianism per se. Far from it. He just felt that women were somewhat cleaner if they abstained from heterosexual intercourse. Not much, but some. Enough to make a difference.

This belief was driven home by Norman's memory of Donna, his deceased wife. The *real* Donna and not some bogus skinwalking ghost come to haunt him. What an unexpected slut Donna had turned out to be when Norman came home from 'Nam. Running around with her love-and-peace hippy attitude, her patchouli-scented tits and loose skirts. Preaching *free love* all the fucking time. It wore thin.

Yes. The real Donna should've become a lesbian instead of a common slut, he thought. He could have forgiven her that. So much cleaner…

Norman possessed no similar laissez-faire attitude for Liz's supposedly homosexual housemate, Emilio. Could hardly stand to look at the man. Nonetheless, after pausing to enjoy several steamy realtime minutes of the two women bathing each other, he scrolled farther back into archived footage until he found a similar scene of Emilio alone in the same tub. The mini-cam's wide angle security-quality view wasn't the best for detail, but Norman could clearly see his Mexican neighbor soaping up his penis. This was truly revolting to Norman. Yet fascinating. Emilio using the washcloth in long determined strokes. Taking his time with the soap. His unbelievable erection growing in length and girth with every stroke.

Fucking freak faggot! Goddamned thing is as big as my forearm, Norman thought. He clicked off before the inevitable climax. Enough of that...

Scrolling back to real time again he returned to Liz and Donna's clone enjoying a leisurely rub-a-dub in the old tub. Zoomed in to study the new girl as well as possible given the grainy black-and-white image. They were soaping themselves and each other – *thoroughly*. Especially between their thighs, exercising a pretext of wholesome cleanliness. To Norman it seemed an awkward bathtub ballet of vulgar familiarity.

A corner of Norman's mind was surprised that this Donna specter would even register on video. *Was* she actually spectral, a ghost moving about in the material plane as he suspected she must be? Or was she flesh and blood. Was it possible that she was a genuine reincarnation of his dead wife instead of an empty skinwalker? He searched his mind for details of Donna. Every detail that he could recall. And he was certain that what he saw on the screen compared exactly to what was forever stored in his mind's eye.

Too exactly. The shape of the new girl's breasts was precisely the same as Donna's. The curve of her neck the same. The high cheekbones that always made her look on the verge of smiling. The fullness of her lips. All *identical* to Donna's features and therefore completely impossible...

This was surely a haunting! It was totally unexpected. And therefore the experience was doubly troubling to Norman's superstitious nature.

After all this time...why now?

He hurried to shut the image off as if he were hexing it away. Told himself he would wait for a better look from the high-def camera in the bedroom.

Donna...he thought. Where did it all go wrong?

94

Norman had not had sex that he hadn't paid for in almost forty years, one of the truly bitchy parts of the lifestyle he lived – the whole gig a far cry from any glamorized Hollywood hitman mythos. But then, his entire life, as he remembered it, had never been remotely close to the Sears catalog picture-perfect existence that so many ordinary people seemed to take for granted, as if these other normal lives were always out there for the taking, waiting and accessible.

This, he knew, was simply not true. He would happily give his left nut for a taste of *normal*. One *normal* relationship…was that so much to ask for?

Relationships…Norman had no practical experience with any other than the damaged variety. His marriage to Donna after returning stateside from 'Nam had been brief. A real fuckup from start to finish. "Women have a remarkable talent for turning themselves into truly disgusting creatures," Norman once told Donna. "*Girls* aren't so bad," he said, "but *women?*" This conversation had occurred shortly after their marriage, and it may have been one of their deeper conversational exchanges.

Norman believed that the younger the woman was the less likely she was to be possessed of disgusting and irreversible traits. The nature of feminine innocence so ephemeral that merely contemplating it risked tarnishing it. Tarnished, the value of that innocence diminished and withered faster than a hothouse rose.

Norman also believed, regarding feminine innocence, that it could not be trusted if it existed at all, that image is everything. One had to be careful. To ravage the innocence of a young woman was to destroy the root of her beauty. And once *that* was destroyed…what good was she then?

Best to put her out of her misery.

Opening his internet link via two proxies, Norman tried a couple of free public access forums, and left messages: 'Shooter. Go to Twitter. Creep,' then he exited those boards and typed in Twitter.com, confirming that Troubleshooter was still listed as one of his followers.

The recent business with Nick Petosa, followed so closely by the appearance of Donna's ghost, was causing the *hide* instinct to flash like a red warning light in the back of Norman's mind, making him feel the urge to move again in the worst way. And it would have to be soon. It also made him feel the need to communicate with his old friend, Hoot...*Trouble*shooter. Might as well. If he knew Hoot – and he *did* – then he had to assume that 'Shooter would be percolating like a garage sale coffeepot right about now. Boiling over and ready to blow after the business with Nick Petosa happening practically in his lap.

Shooter's bloodhound nose on the scent, his instinct would know beyond a doubt it was Creeper's work. The old Troubleshooter could be a formidable adversary, Norman thought, if only he'd get his head out of his ass. If only he truly believed in the blood bond between us. If only he used the connection...

Hoot's loss...

Nonetheless, the bond existed. He and Hoot were one and the same.

Had been since both were boys. Same blood. Same heart. Same spirit.

And if Donna's ghost had come back from the grave for one – well then she must have come for both.

Chapter 12

Late in the fall of 1964 was the third and last time a Pleasanton PD squad car left the neighborhood with Norman's father cuffed and sullen in the back, while Norman's stepmother, Eileen, waited inside the house for someone to give a genuine shit. Waited for the newly-formed so-called *Domestic Unit* officer to finish her asinine paperwork that was unlikely to ever change a goddamned thing and leave so that she could pop a 'lude and stop shaking.

Norman was fifteen and he knew all about the pills. He knew about the red ones. The blue ones. The yellow. He knew about the grass, too. The ever-present speed – white cross and black beauties. And then there was the booze that always seemed to set everything off. He knew about his father's girlfriends. Both of them. The pistol hidden away in a shoebox – there was nothing he didn't know.

"You aren't like that, Normie," Eileen said. "Just 'cause your daddy's that way don't make you the same."

Damned straight about that, Mamasita, Norman thought, knowing his old man was a loser and he wasn't about to follow down that road. Knowing his stepmother's concern was genuine but thin, the way Norman understood it; his part to play in the Pleasanton Maine family drama was the role of *dependent child* on the monthly welfare check, the arrangement remarkably similar at the other end of his life in Montana. It was all the same.

Norman could see that Eileen had a new shiner – not her first – just starting to swell shut; and it was going to be a real humdinger as Norman's mother, Inez, would have said. Eileen also had a cut over her eyebrow that the DU officer said needed stitches.

"You want me to drive you to the clinic?" Norman asked after all the uniforms finally cleared out. "Get that looked at?"

"You aren't old enough to drive," Eileen said.

"Forget I asked," Norman said even though he'd been driving every summer at his mother's place on the rez for the past three years – *four*, counting off-road excursions. He slung his jacket over his shoulder, said, "I'm going out. Don't sweat dinner."

"Where you going?"

"Hoot's place."

The cut over his stepmother's eye looked like a bad one, shaping up to be another ugly reminder that would last forever. Scars seen and unseen. But would she ever learn to simply keep her mouth shut?

Probably not.

"Don't forget to eat," she said.

***

The Spokane U.S. Marshal's office was currently operating in one-boss, two-peon mode with three other marshals either on medical leave or vacation, and both of the marshals on duty were tied up in district court for the morning. Bob Wilson, the senior deputy marshal manning the office was affable in spite of the workload.

"Everyone just calls me Wilson," he said. Not too many years younger than Hoot, hair thinning into salt and pepper strands, eyes squinting in the middle of a lined, sunburned face below a pale forehead, Wilson was quick to warn the two Seattle men about Patricia Peyton, SAIC.

"She's the hen in charge of the FBI coop in these parts. The whole federal show around here is hers," he said. "You'll be working under her purview…and I do mean *under*! Peyton is mighty young at thirty-eight to be a Special Agent in Charge and she doesn't mind working twenty hours a day to stay one. The woman looks for toes to step on and finds plenty. You can be sure she saw yours coming long before you got this side of Snoqualmie Pass. And don't plan on being shown to her office until late this afternoon – she'll be in court all morning. You won't be able to take the first step on your manhunt 'till she says *go*, so I hope you didn't leave Seattle early to get here early."

Ignoring a glance from Marcus, Hoot said, "Thanks for the warning. You got some work needs done? Maybe some warrants you need served while we're waiting?"

"Bet your ass I do. You can see we're a little short-handed around here."

At a meeting much later, special agent Peyton was exactly the sort of boss senior deputy marshal Wilson had described her to be. Professionalism taken to the wall. Affirmative action with a capital *A*. Actually, Hoot thought that Peyton had a lot in common with senior deputy Horner in Seattle.

"Must be one of those latent-DNA things, genetic markers that doom certain unfortunate individuals to lives of hardcore leadership in law enforcement," he later told Marcus. She was a natural redhead with a well-crafted stern demeanor, her whole attitude packed tightly around a tall gaunt frame and tucked neatly into a properly starched uniform. Single as God's own Adam before Eve, she had reined herself into a stoic, crime-fighting lifestyle. Thus, free from the everyday passions that ignited others, Patricia Peyton was free to burn hers on the job.

The guys called her *Bosslady* and she was okay with that. Even had a name plaque on her desk that read, Patricia (Bosslady) Peyton, S.A.I.C., a gift from the regional director in Seattle. FBI agents working under her were usually quick to warn others that the normal visible indicators of mood were completely absent from their boss, as were most other outward signs that might reveal a hint of personality – but she took a long look at the two U.S. Marshals, old *superwhite* Hoot and young *ultrablack* Marcus, standing side by side in her Spokane office and laughed out loud, exclaiming; "You guys gotta be kidding! Quick, someone bring a camera."

"We're very serious, Mum," Marcus said.

"As is the man we're looking for," Hoot added. "Norman Carpenter. Escaped while in transit from a surgical center back to his cell in Leavenworth almost thirty years ago, leaving a trail of bodies throughout the West ever since."

There were two file folders lying in the center of agent Peyton's desk. The top one was tagged 'N. Carpenter' and she flipped it open. An outdated fax photo of Norman was attached to the inside flap. "So I see," she said, turning a few pages. "Subject of one of the longest-running escapee files in the U.S. Marshals' archives. Seattle office informs me he may be the one put a wiseguy out of his misery at The Westin Sunday night." She leafed through several pages of photographs. Said with an almost undetectable wince quickly held in check, "Wiseguy's girlfriend too, apparently. I understand that you saw the girlfriend's body?"

"I did."

She tossed a photograph across her desk, said, "And you think the guy who did this was your guy on the lam?"

"Could be. Looked to me like his work."

"You say that because of the...it says here, 'approximately ten-centimeter patch of *scalp* cut from the victim's head?'"

"And other signs." Hoot handed the photograph back.

"This Norman Carpenter...you've been on his trail how long?"

"A long goddamned time, Agent Peyton," Hoot answered, Patricia Peyton's stonewall stare beginning to wear on his patience, a mischievous corner of his mind desperately wanting to turn to Marcus and say "Special agent Dee-Pee-In-Charge needs to know! So I'll just tell her...

"I got a lucky tip," he said instead. "Gives me reason to believe he's currently holed-up here, in Spokane."

"The way I understand it, *Marshal* Hooten; you and your new partner, Marcus, here are in Spokane to run errands for Bob Wilson until your man is confirmed to be here. Is that correct."

"He's here," Hoot said.

"I understand that's what you believe. You say you know your man. You've chased him all around the playground. And, now you think he's hiding here in my little sandbox," Patricia Peyton said. She turned a few more pages in Norman's file as if this was the first time she'd seen it, said, "There's no active sheet on him, this side of the mountains. Until we actually see him or get some indication of his presence other than your gut instinct it's the same as him not being here in my book."

"He's very good at lying low," Hoot replied, knowing that Peyton was playing him. Being minimally courteous while quietly laying odds on how long it would take him to stub his toe in her part of the so-called playground. "I believe the file mentions that he spent summers during his childhood living with his mother on the Flathead reservation in Montana," Hoot said. "That reservation is only a day's drive from here. If his mother is still alive she's still living there, I'm sure of it – she's the tribal shaman. And if she is there, it's where Norman goes to see her."

"Alright then, Marshal Hooten. The rules are simple; you go snoop around and find your man when you're not working Wilson's case load. And if you find your man in my jurisdiction *I'll* serve as primary on his capture. It'll be a team capture. No one-man grandstanding. No macho gunfights. That's the way we play it around here – period. You don't think you can work with me that way; you should leave now and save us both a whole lot of unpleasantness. Understood?"

"Perfectly."

"Very well. There's a strip joint over in Stateline, Idaho. Goodtime Charlie's," Peyton said, "The place is owned the mob and run by a man named Vincent Petosa, a cousin of the wiseguy who got shot at The Seattle Westin. You might start there. Just don't forget, Marshal Hooten, I expect you to liaise with my office every step of the way. And I mean *every* step. Dead bodies start dropping, yours had better be among the first."

Bosslady flipped the file closed, revealing a glimpse of the one below tagged *E. Hooten, U.S. Marshal's Service, Active, Confidential.*

Saying nothing about Hoot's file on her desk, apparently content for now to let him know that his skeletons were out of the closet and that she would tolerate no gunslinger shenanigans, she said to Hoot and Marcus, "Welcome to

Spokane, gentlemen." Shaking their hands, solemnly, she gave the two marshals one last glance containing a decidedly condescending gleam.

Chapter 13

Angela and Liz spent the afternoon bathing. Making love. Then bathing some more. And finally, napping. Liz's caresses and kisses had aroused more pleasure in Angela than she had ever thought herself capable of experiencing; bringing her to a series of deeply-satisfying spasms curling up from a place she hadn't even known existed. This was something completely new. Something she had never experienced with ol' three-strokes-I'm-done Les.

Waking from her nap sated but embarrassed by her clumsy initial efforts to please her new lover, Angela said, "I want to make magic happen for you like you did for me. But…"

Liz interrupted, laughing, said, "Just relax. Contrary to popular rumor among men, there are no ancient, long-lost secret techniques for fantastic lesbian sex, secrets that make manly men desirable only for their seed and not the planting of it. Trust that anything you think would feel good to you, will feel good to me. I'll let you know if it doesn't."

It turned out that Angela was a quick study once she stopped worrying about doing it right. Stopped comparing Liz's muscular body to her own softer one. Tossed aside her lingering embarrassment about brazen broad daylight nudity. Then, instead of seeing all the differences between them she began to experience their sameness, found that she loved to fondle and kiss Liz's breasts, to suck the hard raspberry nipples and kiss the smooth hot skin underneath, the cooler skin on the sides.

Angela lingered at Liz's breastbone. Listened to her heartbeat. Breathed in her perfume, and nuzzled like a newborn puppy into her cleavage. She reveled in the soft warmth of her lover's flesh on both cheeks at once.

She rolled Liz over on her belly and discovered the silky feel of the skin on her back. The fuzz along the hollow of her spine. The flair of her hips. She ran her hands up both sides of Liz's torso and then back down, kneading the muscles in her buttocks and thighs as she passed. Hard, dancer's muscles; strong beneath smooth warm skin.

Rolling her over on her back again, Angela teased the length of Liz's body with barely the tips of her fingers. Caresses as soft as a baby's breath. Then, drawing her fingertips down both of Liz's legs, along the insides of her thighs and calves to the bottoms of her feet, she found ticklish places in her arches.

Liz laughed and kicked, letting Angela play. Anything she wanted.

Liz's pubic hair was delightful. Fragrant and unbelievably thick. Luxurious. Angela combed her fingers thru it again and again and buried her face in it, seeking out the folds of Liz's sex. Wanting to find that magic place. Needing to find it. She did all this without once wondering how such intimacy with another woman could possibly feel natural. And when she at last discovered the warm slit she was seeking, Liz drew up her knees and opened the way.

Afterward, they lay together, facing, with their foreheads touching and their legs intertwined. Nuzzling and stroking each other. Liz said, "That was good Lover. That was *very* good," and Angela blushed, smiling, said, "Now I know a secret about you."

"Yeah? And what's that?" Liz asked.

"I know that your thick platinum pussy hair has dark roots."

"Oh my! What sharp eyes you have, Little Red said to the she-wolf."

***

Norman put the butane lighter to his water pipe for a long hit and queued-up the saved video once more – Donna's ghost with Liz in Liz's bed. He had seen this clip a dozen times already but he still leaned forward in his chair and watched with riveted interest. This was entirely different from his usual prurient fascination for this sort of thing. He paused the playback near the end, when it came to the part where the

Donna ghost rested her head on Liz's shoulder. This was the sharpest view of her face – *Donna's* face. Then, exhaling the pent-up smoke, he backtracked the vid to the beginning once more, the image speeding backward in a jerky pantomime, arms and legs flying, pixels hurrying in reverse through motions he was already starting to memorize.

"Let me see your breasts again, sweetheart," Norman said in a whisper and the Donna look-alike on his monitor rolled over and complied.

"Perfect...unbelievable," he murmured, taking another hit. They were definitely Donna's breasts. *Had* to be. The teardrop curve. The puffy nipples. He couldn't quite make them out on his monitor but he'd bet even the freckles were exactly the same.

"And now the rest," he said aloud.

The digital image of Liz responded as if to his command and the last of the silken bed sheet was pulled out of the way. A lingering bit of fabric resisted, clinging for a moment to her new lover's torso as if to offer a final tease, but it finally dropped aside with the rest and left Donna's ghost completely naked...exposed.

Exposed to Norman's sneaky eyes.

The lighting in the vid was subdued. Dark and sensuous. The curtains in Liz's bedroom closed. But Norman could clearly see crucial details of a body he had once known. Once possessed. A body that had once driven him into such a rage he couldn't bear it.

Norman leaned in closer, noticing how the ghost image of Donna on his monitor appeared to be looking straight back into his eyes, as if she had discovered his hidden camera and was intentionally mocking him. She would do that, Donna would. Her ghost certainly would. Brazen slut had loved to tease. He remembered how she would dress in semi-sheer tops and flowing tie-dyed skirts to go out. No undergarments. She would flash any guys bold enough to whistle or comment. And she got plenty of whistles and comments.

"Yes...you were a beautiful woman when you were alive – wild in a crazy little girl way," he said aloud. "You were too beautiful for me. Too beautiful for *anyone*."

Now Liz was slithering downward between her new lover's thighs. Norman closed his eyes, remembering doing exactly the same thing so very many years ago. He remembered the texture of her. The smell of her. Her soft skin. Remembered the unbearable pressure of his erection pressing against her. Pressing against the entrance to her innermost place.

Opening his eyes again and watching Liz kissing a pathway down her new lover's belly, Norman clinched his hands into fists, unconsciously resisting, and then suddenly surrendering to a flood of long-dormant memories of Donna. The sound of her laughter. And of her screams. The addictive taste of her. The feel of her small hands on his own naked skin.

Norman remembered Donna under the water, finally still after a thrashing struggle. Under the surface of the ice-cold lake water, but still semi-conscious there at the end with a knot on her head the size of an orange.

He remembered his surprise when she came around the last time. Hitting him and clawing at him with superhuman effort. Scratching at him. Struggling with every ounce of her being before finally going limp and floating away.

Norman had seen Donna's departing spirit fade in the ripples and bubbles – watched it drift away. The rush of potency he inevitably felt at such times so strong that time it almost lifted him off his feet.

The memory of all this was too maddening!

With clenched fists shaking, Norman turned away from his monitor. Disgust mingling with tingles of superstition – with fear – he accidentally knocked his blown-glass bong off the table where it broke into slivers and shards on the floor.

Shit! he thought. That was my favorite piece of California paraphernalia…a souvenir. Fucking woman was never anything but trouble for me. Trouble and pain.

Still is. Her ghost.

Her *skinwalker*.

Bummed, Norman shut his surveillance program down. Set the computer's anti-virus program to scan for spyware and insidious cookies. And then went to his cupboard in search of comfort food.

Chapter 14

Donna was at Hoot's house when Norman got there, that night in the fall of '63, all three of them fourteen-years-old, Donna the oldest.

"They took my old man away again," Norman said. "Said they're gonna keep him a while this time."

"I'm so sorry, Norman," Donna said, offering a consoling hug, tears welled up in the corners of her eyes. "It just isn't fair…"

"Doesn't matter," Norman said, feeling like he was falling. And he was…into Donna's embrace, while turning his head to look Hoot in the eye.

The way Donna's body fit against his…

Aside from her breasts, Donna was smallish and compact, while he was slightly below-average height and lanky. Donna's breasts had exploded into a whole new degree of fullness this past year, and she pressed them against Norman's torso in heartfelt sympathy. If she noticed that her sympathetic attention was causing a stirring in Norman's jeans she kept the knowledge to herself, hugging him even closer before releasing him.

"It's best, really," Norman said, giving Donna an appreciative glance before returning his attention to Hoot. "He's gonna go too far and kill my stepmom one of these days. Wait and see. And who'll have to clean up the fucking mess?...I will. *That's* what's not fair."

"Your real mother know about this yet?" Hoot asked.

"Domestic Unit cop came out. They'll be calling Mom soon enough if they haven't already. Trying to find the best place for me. Funny, isn't it? The way shuffling me around is supposed to help…"

"Bummer. Fuckers will probably send you to live full-time in Montana."

"I know. And it's a stupid idea. Things are no better for me there than they are here," Norman said, looking Donna

107

in the eyes, wanting to tell her that she could wrap her arms around him again, press up against him again if she wanted to. Norman thought that, at fourteen, she already had everything moving in the right direction – he suspected that his imaginations of what she'd look like at eighteen, at twenty, were actually shy of her true potential.

"All my friends are here," Norman said. "In Montana everybody I know is a reservation dog of some sort. My uncle Max Feather who hangs around my mom's place all the time? Supposed to be like a godfather to me – she calls him a *dry well*! He drinks at least as much as my father does. He's a sex fiend to boot. And my mother is a hex-casting witchdoctor. Ordinary people living both on and off the reservation back there think the whole fucking family is nuts."

"You know that if your father does any time in jail they'll probably send you there, regardless," Hoot said.

"I won't go," Norman answered.

"Don't go," Donna echoed, rewarding him with another hug – this one a bit more chaste than the last one, but still satisfying.

Ten days later Norman's father was out of jail on a bail bond and promising to mind his P's and Q's. Norman never learned exactly what happened to his old man, those ten days in jail. It seemed to have something to do with God – or maybe it was only another inmate named Jesus, Joe Carpenter wasn't clear about that. Whatever it was it wasn't enough to stop his drinking, but evidently adequate to curb his enthusiasm for plumbing-up Eileen when he got drunk.

Norman was pleased with the change in the old man, even if his father's new gambit was simply to drink himself into total unconsciousness instead of into arguments. He was doubly pleased that summer to be allowed to stay put in Maine instead of trekking off to Montana. Sure, he'd miss going along on his uncle's escalating excursions to a certain Spokane strip joint, but 1963 had been the summer of Donna's first low-cut, two-piece French bikini, the summer of panty hose and Mary Quant-style skirts…how could he leave?

Both Norman and Hoot spent that summer masturbating with increasing frequency. It was nearly unbearable.

∗∗∗

By the time Liz got involved in the stripping business there was a hell of a lot more than simple blue-collar voyeurism for sale at Goodtime Charlie's. But among all-nude clubs, she knew it was still the most highbrow of the bunch in her opinion – with the exception of The Great Alaskan Bush Club in Anchorage, of course. "I've always wanted to work at The Bush," she confessed to Angela while driving eastward through the homogenized, highly commercialized Spokane Valley, heading for Stateline Idaho, "but I'm nowhere near good-looking enough."

"You're joking."

"No, I'm not. That's where all the really glamorous girls go to work. There and certain clubs in Canada. That's where the really good money is too. But it's a hellava lot easier to nail the centerfold spread in *Penthouse* magazine than it is to get onstage at The Bush. And that whole Canadian scene is…well, you know, *Canadian*." She wheeled the big Caddy into a large parking lot with maybe twenty other cars parked there, many of the flashier ones belonging to dancers. It was 2:45 in the afternoon.

"Looks like a slow day. That's good 'cause I'm late," Liz said as she fumbled around in her purse. Making a serious expedition far into the depths of the behemoth fringed leather bag, she was rummaging for something special, piling chewing gum, breath mints, tissues, tampons, and a can of Mace on the console beside her, and finally pulling out a small velvet pouch containing a tiny brown vial. She asked; "Did you know that Quentin Tarantino discovered Uma Thurman when she was working at The Bush?" tapping the bottom of the tiny vial against the back of her hand and smiling, apparently satisfied.

"Uh…no, I did not know that," Angela said.

"Well. I don't know for sure if it's really true. Doesn't *sound* true…does it? But that's what I've heard. Can you imagine?" Liz said.

She produced a tiny silver spoon, dipped into the brown vial and asked Angela, "Care for a little toot before we go in?"

109

"That the same stuff you had in Seattle?" Angela asked. She remembered being confused on that occasion more that anything else, but recalled that the sensation she had experienced was pleasant to say the least.

"Yeah. This is the real deal…good, old-fashioned, suck-it-up-the-nose *co*-caine. *Coke* – not to be confused with *crack*, or *crank*, or *oxycotton*, or any of that other weird shit all the teenies are doing today. And it's sure as hell not *smack*. It's damned good shit too. I get it from a lawyer customer of mine. Comes in to see me every Wednesday. Likes to play in Sherwood Forest for trade."

A tiny spoonful of the white powder vanished up each nostril, and then Liz said, "I don't heroin at all. And I don't do a lot of this stuff. Can't afford to. But I like a taste now and then for special occasions, or when I'm going to work and need a little help finding my muse."

"Your muse?"

"Yeah. Helps me get my *lewd mood* cranked into overdrive."

"So…it makes you horny?"

Liz laughed, said, "Yeah. Has that effect on some people – myself included. Others aren't so lucky, and I don't know why they would even bother with it. The expense of it."

Liz tapped the precious white powder down to the bottom of the tiny brown bottle. Gauging the remaining quantity to be adequate, she dipped the silver spoon into the vial, lifted it toward Angela's face, said, "Suck in hard when I tell you and don't exhale first or your coat will go way up in value real quick."

Aside from a sudden and persistent post-nasal drip and a slight constriction in the back of her throat which seemed to make the cigarette she was smoking seem awfully appealing, Angela didn't notice any special effect from the cocaine right away. At least not the immediate make-an-addict-out-of-you throw-your-panties-down *lewd mood* high that she had expected. Sitting in the dancer's dressing room with Liz, she said, "Maybe it's just me, but I don't feel a thing. At least not anything like the buzz I get from smoking pot. I think the white stuff's overrated."

Liz snickered, "Sweetie, the candy you just powdered your nose with is as good as it gets these days. Give it a few minutes and see what you think."

Liz was applying makeup…*heavy* makeup…to her face, and the transformation held Angela as spellbound as a kid at the carnival. In ten minutes the woman Angela had walked in with was gone. In her place was a woman who looked harder. Bitchy even. But very exotic. And certainly very beautiful. This new and exotic Liz stood and stripped to her bare skin, hanging her clothes in a locker. She teased her thick pubic hair with a small brush, powdered her breasts and shoulders, and applied a smudge of rouge to each nipple. "Makes 'em show up better under the stage lighting," she explained.

At first Angela simply sat still and watched, soaking up everything. The dressing room fascinated her – it was an inconspicuous den that, once you were inside, was a brightly-lit counterpoint to the rest of the club; cluttered, and trailer-trash tacky with the whorish clutter of Godonlyknows how many women. Then she started to fidget and noticed that she was feeling warmer. Her hearing more acute. There was an underlying noise – either the fluorescent lighting was buzzing in her ears with exceptional persistence or there was a noisy refrigerator in some unseen corner of the room. Her mind went off on a side street remembering the way her refrigerator in Seattle made a noise like that. Had to hit the side of it with her fist to make it stop. Always had to be her that hit it. Les hit it once and knocked off all the refrigerator magnets, the kid's artwork and coupons, so it became her job to beat the fridge. Buying a new one or calling out an appliance repairman was never discussed.

A door opened from time to time and a dancer would exit or enter the dressing room from the main floor of the club, an undulating undercurrent of bass-driven music rolling in and out like thundering waves with her. The door opened again and the wave of music snapped Angela's attention back to the dressing room. Locker doors clanging open and shut. There were three bathroom stalls against the back wall and their doors opened and closed incessantly – dancers coming and going. It seemed the dressing room was a room full of doors. Angela noticed that it took some effort to breathe, the dressing room air heavy with cigarette smoke, the skunky smell of pot, and uncountable traces of lingering perfumes.

In spite of the jumbled aromas, Angela's post-nasal drip had become decidedly pleasant, causing her throat to constrict around the taste. Tonsils and airway tissues seeking the cool numbness. Her newly-aroused nicotine demon was screaming for a cigarette. She lighted one and exhaled the smoke through her nose in a long blue stream that seemed endless. Swirling away, the smoke merged into the thick air.

A compact little man appeared through this dense atmosphere like a genie conjured from a bottle. He walked straight up to Liz, lifted both her breasts appraisingly with his fingertips and said, "It's a damned good thing you're so good-lookin, Barbie Doll, and a double-damned good thing it's slow 'round here today or I'd have to fine you for draggin in so fuckin late."

"But you're not gonna 'cause I'm your best girl, huh, Case?" Liz smoothly took his hands from her breasts. Gave him a no-smudge kiss on his bald forehead and then nodded toward Angela saying, "Besides, I brought you some potential new talent."

This comment caught Angela by surprise. She looked up and saw that both Liz and the man she had called Case were smiling at her. Both of them apparently waiting, as if Angela had forgotten her lines and the dialogue coach was nowhere to be found. She swallowed hard to find her voice, said, "I'm just here to observe."

"Angela, meet Casey Stark," Liz said. "He's the daytime manager here."

Stepping outside herself, Angela observed the odd scene from a safe distance – a completely naked woman introducing a fully clothed woman to a pimplike man, and everyone smiling like a happy huddle of Cheshire cats sharing an inside joke. Angela took a snapshot in her mind, thinking she might want to look at it later, try to figure out what was so amusing to everyone. But her mind couldn't seem to get a good handle on it right now. Maybe the coke was kicking in after all.

112

"Come to work for me an' you can call me *Case*. All my girls do." Casey Stark said, giving Angela a look that burned straight through three layers of clothing – coat, shirt, bra, jeans, panties and all – all the way to her skin. Angela feeling the heat of his glance as if she were standing too close to a campfire. Suddenly she felt hilariously overdressed and suppressed a giggle.

All my girls, he had said. The afternoon girls were all *his* girls.

The way Liz described Case to Angela made him seem like a dinosaur pacing around the rim of a tar pit, the whole nude dancing scene being on the brink of extinction, rapidly pricing itself out of the reach of the blue collar man and too lowbrow for the white collar man, with internet porn so readily available in the privacy of one's own home. But in the meantime, Case was *The Man* every day from 11:00 AM till 6:00 PM. A small man in big man's shoes. He was short, slim, with narrow shoulders and bony hands, his fingers encrusted with heavy gold rings looking like gaudy barnacles. He had a tanned head without a single hair on it aside from pencil-thin eyebrows and thick fluffy tufts sticking out from his ears. Dark brown shiny eyes and a beak of a nose gave him a raven-like appearance. His lips vanished into the walnut tan of his face so that his mouth appeared nonexistent when closed and tight as the pinched opening in a miserly coin purse when it opened. When he smiled it was startling and seemed totally fake. Angela would wager that he dressed the same way every day, in slacks, Italian loafers without socks, dress shirt open at the neck to exhibit a collection of thick gold chains, and a tailored sport coat. She imagined he must own a hundred of those outfits, each identical to the other with only slight variations in cloth and color.

He said to Angela, "Okay, Gorgeous. You go ahead and check it out. Barbie Doll here will show ya the ropes. Then come back later tonight. It's Amateur Night. You'll win. And then we'll get ya all set up on the day shift, *my* shift. You'll like it."

Case retreated to appraise another dancer's breasts and Angela lighted another cigarette to reinforce the one she had still burning but currently sitting ignored in the ashtray. Her hands felt hot. *You'll win*, he'd said, the words still ringing in her ears.

She turned to Liz. "Barbie Doll?" she asked.

"Yeah. That's my stage name. Liz off the stage – Barbie Doll on it. We have a Tiger, two Candy's – one is Can*dee* and the other is Candy *Bar*. We have a whole tribe of Indians – Apache, Cherokee, Suzie Sioux, and Shy Ann. We also have an Asia and a Cookie and a buncha other girls with names that are off the top. You should think up something cool. Use any name you want."

"I told you, I'm only here to watch."

"Sure. I know that. I mean in case you change your mind. Listen, Sweetie, watch out for Case. He's a little bit of a snake – likes to make *special arrangements* with us dancers. And everybody knows he's raking the take. Soon as the owner, Vincent, gets tired of it Case'll be gone and nobody wants to be too close to that."

Liz pulled on a pair of French-cut lace-trimmed tap panties and a matching torsolette, and then she stepped into a pair of white patent-leather spike-heeled platforms with soles three inches thick. This was her starting costume. She would change it three or four times during her shift. "So, how do ya like my Barbie outfit?" she asked.

"I don't remember that one in my collection. Must be the newer, lewder, NSFW version of Malibu Barbie?"

"This is the Goodtime Charlie's Barbie. Not available at Toys-R-Us."

Angela started to giggle so hard she got the hiccups. Looking down, trying to imagine herself with huge breasts, seeing them grow before her eyes from apples to oranges to melons, from water balloons to blimps, she lost her balance and almost fell headlong into Liz's makeup kit.

"*Told* ya to give the coke a few minutes," Liz said in her ear. "Now go find a seat somewhere along the back wall. Get yourself a nice cold Coke – the liquid kind – for your hiccups. And the one-and-only *Barbie Doll* will be along soon to show you what this game is all about."

Chapter 15

College was difficult for Hoot. He was an action kind of guy, not an academic. Not athletic enough to play varsity-level football or other varsity sports, his interests were narrow. Still, Hoot was no weenie; he had worked hard for his young man's muscles. Every chance he got after he turned fifteen, he crewed on his father's commercial fishing boats. Not the long-liners going way out to the Grand Banks. The old man wouldn't allow him on those boats until he turned eighteen. But the seiners and lobster trawlers that stayed closer in. Good money to be made.

Then, the summer before starting at UM, he finally got a bunk on a long-liner for a week and the money was fuckin fantastic. The work was back-breaking but honest. Filling the hold completely full of sailfish on ice weighing up to a quarter-ton apiece or more. It had filled Hoot with pride just to be part of it. College was infernally tedious by comparison. Boring, actually. The freshman classes huge and impersonal, largely taught by graduate student assistants with hardly any input other than lectures from professors, the whole racket designed more to thin out weaker students than to educate anyone. And that pissed Hoot off. To be spending his hard-earned fishing money on a scam.

"I'm failing Sociology," he told Donna six weeks into their second semester.

"*Failing*? You sure?" Donna asked. Having never received a grade below B+ in her life, she could not even imagine how Hoot could be in such dire straits.

"Counselor told me I had to drop the class or it'd bring my whole GPA down. As if I give a fuck."

"You'd better," Donna said.

"Better what?"

"Give a fuck. It's important…"

"Sociology? Important? I don't think so. Knowing how to figure fuel, food, and bait for a crew of six on a forty-foot twin diesel to The Banks and back is important, and I already know how to do that. The demographic breakdown of Boston public schools today compared to 1960 and '64 is not...*important*. Not to me, it isn't."

"You just need better study habits," Donna said.

"Something worthwhile to study is what I need."

Silence followed.

"Maybe we should stop seeing so much of each other," Donna offered in a small voice. "Give you more time."

"Doesn't matter," Hoot confessed. "I've already dropped the class."

"That's three credits! Lose any more and you could lose your draft deferment."

"Big deal. I'm thinking of dropping out of school, anyhow. Go fish full time."

"Ezra! You're not serious..."

"I might be. Fishin's not such a bad gig. My old man has done alright. Owns a half-dozen boats, now. Makes a good living."

"With everyone talking about the draft lottery? The President increasing US troops in Vietnam every other day? You know that the very second you drop out you'll get drafted. End up right in the middle of the war, just like Norman."

"Would that be so awful?" Hoot asked. "I could go do my duty and come straight home again. Buy my own boat, maybe. At least skipper one of my dad's. Get us a nice house on the VA and we'd be set for life. Norm has done alright so far. Says the Army suits him fine. Got a letter from him today saying he was picked for Long Range Patrol training. That's Green Beret stuff – advanced Ranger training."

"Do your *duty*? Do you even realize what you're saying? You actually think that everybody'll suddenly stop fooling around over there if you go and help? That putting yourself in jeopardy will tip the scale and we'll go ahead and win now, 'cause it's our destiny to win? All the guys will come home to big parades?"

"Donna, college suits you. You need it. I don't."

"I can't believe we're even having this conversation," Donna said, disappointment thick in her voice, tears not far behind.

Hoot had always thought that Donna was a smart girl. Every bit as smart as she was beautiful. Certainly smarter than he was. Smarter than anyone else he knew. But it had never mattered. They were perfect for each other and that was all that had ever mattered. So what if he didn't finish college. Big deal. They'd still get married when the time seemed right. Have some kids. He would just be a fisherman instead of an engineer. Donna could still teach if that's what she wanted to do.

But one good look into Donna's eyes told Hoot it wasn't that simple anymore. Told him that he had just reset their compasses on diverging tacks. It was a slap that would sting forever. But later that evening, before the cloth that was *them* had completely ripped in two, they made love with more heartfelt passion than ever before.

Hoot left for boot camp right after spring break, 1968.

***

Norman ordered a double pepperoni pizza from Zack's Pizza and set the elapsed time dial on his watch the instant he put down the phone.

Carryout pizza, the single man's staff of life, he thought.

Sometimes Chinese carryout would crawl to the top of the list, but Norman had been on a pizza kick for the last month – and pizza delivered…Chinese didn't. This week alone he had already scored two freebies for late delivery. Was a real *OhmyGod! What'll I do?* crisis for the last tardy delivery. The guy didn't know how to handle it, acting like an idiot, wanted to come in and use Norman's phone to call in. Norman let the poor bastard use his cell phone at the door. He never let *anyone* uninvited come in, and so far no one had been invited. The guy was weird, anyhow. Old enough to be someone's grandfather, delivering pizzas at his age and fucking up to boot!

117

Norman had felt kind of sorry for him so he gave him twice the usual dollar tip after scoring the pizza for free.

Today he wasn't so lucky. The regular kid was back on duty and made it with two minutes to spare. Norman ate half the pizza with a tall glass of buttermilk, put the rest in the fridge to save and eat cold on the road to Mom's.

He had packing to do tonight. And rigging.

Norman's apartment consisted of the entire upper half-story of the house, a long attic divided into series of *room* areas each behind the other, a pitched ceiling that had a narrow flat strip running along the centerline and sloped downward both ways from there toward the eaves. Gave the place a Quonset hut feeling that Norman found comforting. There were two dormers opposite each other in the middle, adding extra headroom for the bathroom and a sleeping nook. Kitchen at one end, stairs and seating area at the other. Lots of storage crannies under the eaves were accessible behind four-foot-tall curtain walls.

These crannies were where Norman stored the boxes and duffel bags that he brought here from a monthly storage place in Ronan his mother had paid for while he was incarcerated. The boxes full of seldom used but potentially useful trinkets and nostalgic mementos, odds and ends, remembrances and signposts of his life up to now. In one of those boxes were all of his old Pleasanton High School yearbooks – go Beavers! Rummaging around, he found 1967, his senior year, and inside he found Donna Messenger's photograph in at least five places; cheerleader, president of the Thespian Club, Homecoming Queen – in every case looking *exactly* like the girl named Angela now living downstairs.

He found a framed tribal registration certificate that his mother had sent to him certifying his one-quarter direct lineage to the Kootenai tribe. His birth certificate and DD-214 Army discharge papers. His Purple Heart with oak leaf cluster and Vietnam Campaign medals, Sharpshooter's medal. And a sheaf of photographs of Donna along with newspaper clippings regarding her drowning. Nothing regarding the murder case that eventually grew out of it, or his conviction, or his escape from custody.

Norman started pulling stuff out, piling it against the short curtain walls until he had found everything he was looking for. It made a good sized heap, and it wasn't Christmas decorations.

Outstanding among this treasure were two Army-issue duffel bags that had accompanied him all the way from boot camp at Ft. Ord California, to Advanced Infantry Training at Ft. Dix New Jersey, to combat in Vietnam, then back to Ft. Dix for advanced hand-to-hand and Ranger training – not to mention his convalescence in Hawaii after he was wounded when the chopper went down.

The bags had been retired to a long stretch of archival duty in his mother's storage unit after his discharge and during his incarceration, eventually winding up back with Norman in Spokane over forty years later. One of those bags still contained four boxes of unopened C-rations, each complete with the small cellophane bag containing cigarettes, chewing gum, a packet of folded toilet paper, and a chewable piece of bamboo that served as a combination toothpick-toothbrush. That duffel also contained his old field jacket, a wrinkled dress uniform last worn flying to Maine from Hawaii, and a down-filled sleeping bag that didn't smell so fresh anymore.

He reached behind it to grab the other duffel and dumped it on his bed. This bag contained several sets of his old combat fatigues, a pair of jungle boots, a rolled-up jungle hammock, and three live M-67 fragmentary hand grenades that he'd bought a couple of years ago from Glen Trowbridge, a rez buddy who belonged to a group of Flathead County fundamentalists. Norman wondered if he should stop in and visit old Glen on this trip, see if he could pick up something newer and more stable, maybe some C-4 plastic explosive, but these three old frags would do for now.

He set the grenades gently aside, said, "Perfect!" and began to search for a pair of thin leather gloves and an old black watch cap he knew that he had stashed in a box somewhere. Finding these, he put a vintage Jefferson Airplane record album on the turntable and went to work re-stuffing the duffel with clothes, his pillow, a sheet, a blanket. He carefully packed his eBay C-pap machine that didn't quite do the job anymore, Norman a severe snorer and a choker whenever he slept without it thanks to the ventilated cartilage and damaged gag reflex left behind by VC shrapnel. He threw in a couple of towels, too, knowing that Mom always ran a bit skimpy on niceties for unexpected guests and thinking he might be staying a while.

Maybe he'd defrost her refrigerator while he was there. Or maybe not.

But first he had some business to take care of. Vincent P had called. Said he thought of another job he needed done before Norman spooked out for some indefinite amount of time. Said it would be a quickie, on the way out of town. Sort of a low-key thing done right. No bullshit, like his cousin's Everett thing had been, Vincent promised.

"This guy, Casey Stark, is a complete fuckin jerk," Vincent told Norman. "And an idiot. He's gotta go. He's had it comin' for a long time. A petty thief – the worst kind of thief, you ask me, since the reward ain't no way worth the risk. Nobody's gonna miss him."

Norman knew the guy and had to agree.

"Come by the club on your way outta town, you want to," Vincent P said. "I'll have an envelope. Five G's in it and the guy's address. Like t'see it done before the holidays."

Norman didn't mind working for Vincent, doing his dirty work, so to speak. The man had class. Scruples even, considering the sort of company he kept. His money was always welcome. And he would hold the apartment for as long as Norman needed it. No problem.

Still, Norman would take precautions. Everything well-dusted and in its place. This was the largest assembly of Norman Carpenter's history *ever* and he would not have a shred of it getting around. That just wouldn't do at all.

He brought up the surveillance program on his computer one more time to look at the vid of Donna's ghost before archiving everything and taking it all down. Norman didn't know how long he would be away or even if he would return, so he was taking everything with him now that might point a finger at him. Also everything he'd need to keep CatScratch Graphics up and going and that definitely included both of his computers. He could probably make almost everything else fit in his van, too, if he wanted to put a little effort into it. But feeling the heat from the Seattle job the way he did, he didn't want to take the time to deal with it. The rest he could come back for later.

Norman knew it was time to disappear. He could almost *taste* Hoot on his trail. Knew he was in town. Could physically feel his presence in town – a creepy feeling, one not to be ignored. Too bad for Hoot that he didn't feel it. Hoot had always halfheartedly accepted the way they were connected, at best. Didn't embrace it. Didn't *use* it. That's because Hoot had never accepted the most important thing about blood-brothers – *real* blood-brothers – is that they are joined at the heart. On a spiritual level. The way Norman saw it they were like a couple of magnets, always pushing and pulling at each other, they were irresistibly connected. One couldn't live without the other. Or die, either.

Humming along to the lyrics coming from his stereo, he thought; It takes more than one pill to make me larger...

Norman was getting excited, and when he got excited his nervous leg began to twitch so that it seemed he was tapping hyper-time to the music. Soon this would pass, he knew, and he would reach a state of calm that was unattainable by any drug he had ever tried. The calm that always comes before a hit.

"Sure as hell takes more than one pill to make me small," he hummed.

Chapter 16

"I'm not so sure I can go through with this," Angela said, chewing the pathetic stubs that were once her fingernails.

"Think it's easier to finish concrete?"

"It might be. Probably isn't."

"At least it's something I know how to do. But dancing nude...? I'm not even a very good dancer!"

"Maybe it actually is easier to finish concrete." Liz said. "I wouldn't know. But I do know that you don't have to know how to dance for shit to be a hit at Charlie's. We're not talking about The Bush Club here, you know."

"I'm just afraid that I don't have the nerve to go through with it. I'm afraid the customers won't like me. I mean, think about it...my ex had me feeling like a two-legged cow the last few years. Honestly, the man got a boner watching old *I Dream of Jeannie* reruns but it was a struggle for him to get it up for me."

"His loss, you ask me..."

"What if the customers don't like me? Or, God forbid, if they laugh at me, it'll just kill me!"

"Look, you signed up. That took guts, didn't it? Case checking you out the way he did took guts. If you just wanna do the contest and then never come back, that's cool. If you've changed your mind and don't even wanna do the contest, that's okay too. No problem. Believe me, lover, Charlie's is no place for a girl who doesn't wanna be here."

"I don't know what I want."

"If you're just scared about getting up there on stage; don't worry about it. You'll get over that. But if the whole idea of strutting your stuff for a bunch of losers sporting boners turns you off, or if the idea of all those guys going gaga over your tits and ass is repulsive to you. If it's just too whorish and morally disgusting. If it's simply beneath your dignity to make a sexual object out of yourself, to let yourself be looked at, be touched, and touch them back; well then, it's not too late to go finish concrete instead."

"I didn't say I thought it was repulsive or morally disgusting," Angela quipped, thinking that she might have unintentionally demeaned Liz.

"Oh, but it *is* morally disgusting, Sweetie. It can be pretty damned repulsive too," Liz answered. "Trust me – the voice of experience is talking, here, Girlfriend. It's not just the clientele who make it that way. You can pick and choose among them. And you only sell what you're willing to sell – *remember* that. You don't have to make a full-blown whore out of yourself to make it in this business. But the basic nature of the business *is* immoral. Disgusting. And repulsive. And the other girls can be the worst of it."

"The other girls?"

"Yep. They're the ones you really have to watch out for. I mean it. I only work afternoons for a couple of reasons. First of all, the customers usually aren't as rowdy as the evening crowd. They're mostly older retired guys, salesmen, truck drivers on the road, or lonely married guys. A lot of them are my 'regulars' and plan their visits around my schedule. And, secondly; there aren't as many girls competing for the business as there are at night. It's amazing how ruthless women can be to each other, especially dancers. We're jealous. Backstabbing and mean spirited. Scheming and deceitful. And tough as nails.

"At least eight out of ten women in this business were abused as kids, either sexually, emotionally, or physically harmed. Usually all three. So they don't have any idea what respect is. Respect for the customers, for themselves, or especially for each other. Some of these girls will do a thirty-dollar dance for ten bucks to steal a regular customer from you.

"Just remember that there aren't a whole lot of girl-buddies working in this business no matter what it seems like."

"Except us?"

"And a few others. *Very* few others.

"If you stuck around long enough it'd probably break us up, too."

"Then why encourage me?"

123

"You planning on sticking around and making a career out of it?"

"No, of course not."

Liz shrugged, and said, "You need money. You said you needed a place to hang out for a while. You even said you were looking for a guardian angel, sorta fairy godmother-like, and you got me instead. You also said you were movin' on as soon as you could."

"All that's true."

"Like I told you, I'm sure as hell no angel. I've got no magic wand, either. But I do know how to make a buncha money pretty quickly. And as for hangin'…Casa Pervie is your hang-out for as long as you need it to be. That's all the help I have to offer. I promise not to be offended if it isn't the kind of help you had in mind."

Angela thought about it a moment, then asked, "How much money do you make working at Goodtime Charlie's?"

"On a good afternoon, six to eight hundred dollars. On a bad one, maybe twenty bucks. Average, couple-a hundred."

"Wow!" Angela said, thinking that round trip airfare to Joplin Missouri could be made in as little as a single day's work.

"Obviously, the idea is to have a lot of good days."

***

Casey Stark's rental house was a 1930's crackerbox on a side street in Spokane's sprawling East Valley. The whole neighborhood farmland not so many years ago, Norman had no trouble imagining acres of fruit trees, winter wheat and corn. *Drab* seemed to be the neighborhood's common denominator now. It looked to Norman like the 30's crackerboxes had become hemmed in by tracts of cheaply-built FHA splits in the 60's. More recent economic booms had apparently passed the neighborhood by like thunderstorms looking for a trailer park. And now whole blocks of houses were in dire need of dumpsters to clean up the crap. Reminded Norman of his mother's place on the rez in the days before casinos. Stark's house looked as if it had needed paint and shingles for a very long time, his bright red Mitsubishi Spyder parked in the gravel driveway the very definition of oxymoron.

Stark answered the door in designer jeans riding low on his hips. Shiny bald head. No shirt to impede Norman's appraisal of the gold chain collection hanging from the man's neck. Enough to make King Midas weep. Glittery Ringo fingers and Italian loafers, the whole ensemble held together by a big *fuck you* attitude. Heavy eyelids. Sneer. Loose shoulders and cocked hip.

Norman figured the body language was probably learned watching gangster movies on the gigantic flat screen TV that was playing over Stark's shoulder. Was probably practiced daily in front of a mirror until just right. "Do I *know* you?" he asked, looking out the door past Norman with an expression of disgust. Looked back at Norman, said, "Yeah…I know you. I've seen you at Charlie's before."

"That's right, Case. You have," Norman said.

"You with Kevin?" Casey Stark asked, still looking around Norman out toward the street.

"Who's Kevin?" Norman asked.

"*You* know," Casey Stark said. "Fucker was supposed to be here a half hour ago. He has the shit."

Norman stepped over the threshold into the front room of the house. Dining room-kitchen straight ahead. Bathroom and bedroom off to the right.

"Kevin's *supposed* to have it," Stark added.

Closing the door, Norman looked back outside to confirm the situation in the front yard remained stable. No traffic in the street. No conga line of cops forming. No one named Kevin. Nothing.

"I don't think I know who Kevin is," Norman said. "But if he's coming soon we should probably hurry."

"You don't have the shit…do you?" Casey Stark asked, a lingering note of hopefulness rising with his voice.

Norman locked the deadbolt behind him, said, "Actually, Case, I *am* the shit."

Chapter 17

Wednesday night…Amateur Night. It was all a big ruckus, the evening one big roar in Angela's ears from the second she walked through the door with Liz. Liz like a big-bad icebreaker slamming a safe pathway through the man jam, and Angela the little tugboat-that-could in her wake.

Something about the scene reminded Angela of the Mel Gibson and Tina Turner Armageddon thriller *Thunderdome*. She wouldn't have been the least bit surprised to find chainsaws and pikes hanging from the walls for use by the combatants – but *these* combatants were proficient with lingerie and platform high heels. The sound system, painfully loud earlier in the afternoon, had been turned up a few decibels to dominate the surging roar of the patrons.

There were almost two hundred of them packed in the club tonight – mostly men, a few women – crowded around every table, and well-entrenched along the back walls. Late arrivals stood near the bar, waiting like vultures for anyone to leave or attempt a foray into the restroom. More than one scuffle would erupt during the evening over the need to pee versus the right to return to your seat. They hooted and hollered and whistled at the dancers and at each other, screamed profanities, bravado and lewd innuendo. They laughed raucously, and became caught up in the tides of macho wit that swept the room periodically like a *wave* at an NFL game. The whole place seemed to be drunk on sex. And the party was only just beginning.

Angela had expected the contest to be rigged. Was surprised to find out that it wasn't – not exactly. There were only two other girls competing and one of them was the Mississippi Delta waitress who'd served her earlier that afternoon. The only qualification for amateur status being that you weren't currently working as a dancer at Goodtime Charlie's, *waitress* being a fine hair that was easily split. The amateurs competed for the top prize of $200 with a runner-up prize of $100, and a thanks-for-showing-your-titties $50 third prize. The secret was that any girl willing to dance totally naked in the contest was paid the $100 prize, $50 for topless, and they didn't have to pay the usual house fee of $80 for that one night to work the floor between contest rounds. The catch was that the prize money was withheld for a week, and the girls were invited to work on a trial basis as a regular Goodtime Charlie's dancer during that time.

Taking the job was not exactly *required* – Goodtime Charlie's would be happy to mail the check…eventually – but it was expected. Truthfully, the prize money was chump change compared to what the girls could make working the crowd that one evening when they were still fresh meat in the eyes of the customers.

"I'm nervous as hell," Angela confessed to Liz for the umpteenth time, surveying the carnivorous crowd assembled for her debut.

"Of course you are," Liz said. "But just look at you, you're cute as hell too."

During the interim between their afternoon foray into the club and their return for the contest Liz helped pull together the makings of a Catholic schoolgirl outfit for Angela, thus, 'cute as hell' consisted of a short pleated miniskirt, a semi-sheer white cotton blouse with a necktie that matched the skirt, and white knee socks with high-heeled pumps.

They had shopped for the clothes at the East Valley St. Vincent DePaul secondhand store. The saleswoman who helped them was a lively old gal wearing the unbearably loud stench of outdated and overripe perfumes that she had apparently salvaged without discretion from donations to St Vincent's. The poor woman was about as caring and helpful as she could be, but she was impossible to stand near for long without severe risk to the olfactory glands, evidently having ruined her own years ago. She guessed their mission, asking, "Are you looking for a cute stripper's outfit, dearie? Lots of strippers shop here." That statement didn't make sense as most of the girls at Goodtime Charlie's only wore revealing and expensive lingerie, or custom made sequined thongs and bras, certainly not secondhand lingerie or rummage sale sequined thongs and bras, but the woman nonetheless directed them to where she felt the skimpiest, most darling and daring treasures would be found.

Before returning to the club, they shopped at The Lover's Closet for sexy new underwear consisting of an unpadded lace bra that was so thin and tiny it was more decoration than support, and matching thong panties so skimpy and narrow they barely covered Angela's sparse patch of dark blonde pubic hair. They were waited on by another sales clerk who guessed that they were strippers, but this one seemed eager to get them on their way before they tainted the store's reputation for *decent* customers. Racks of dildos, vibrators, and porn videos were displayed along the back shelf along with edible panties, and at least twenty variations of sexual lubricants for the decent customers to choose from.

The amateur contest started at nine, ran to eleven, and Liz and Angela had arrived back at Goodtime Charlie's just after eight. Pausing to survey the madhouse before them, they quickly cut into the dancer's dressing room where another brand of insanity reigned.

Whereas the afternoon shift had featured about a dozen dancers, there must have been thirty of them working tonight, and many of them were just going on shift, so the dressing room was packed. Scantily-clad women thronged in confines that precipitated a degree of intimacy bordering on slapstick comedy as long as the girls were being good girls – a very difficult balance to maintain, the occasional cat-spats sizzling like drops of water in hot grease, the whole place prone to go up in verbal flames without warning. There was often much ado about who had borrowed what from whom, randomly punctuated with strong encouragements to return the items – "Damn! Bitch! I need it back *now!*" Perfume was so thick in the air it stung the eyes, and there was surely enough hairspray being wafted about to render every object in the room both self-adhesive and highly flammable.

In the midst of this din the evening manager, Case's alter ego, Stanley – not *Stan*, mind you, but Stan*ley* – a round, chubby-cheeked man with eyes constantly working in their sockets, words tumbling like crumbs from his busy red lips.

Stanley found Liz and Angela and took them aside, said to Liz, "Lizzy! Good t'see ya Sugar. You seen Case today? Day shift?"

"Yeah," Liz replied. "He was here."

"Well...the fucker's 'sposed t'work Amateur Night second shift with me startin' right fuckin' now. But the lazy fuck ain't here. Ain't the first time, either. Happens all the time. I swear, Vic's gonna have his balls one a-these days. By the way, watch out for Vic, the man's in a shitty mood."

He glanced at Angela, said. "So you're Case's new girl?"

"Well...I'm, uh...you know? The contest?"

"Okay, okay. No problem, Sugar." Eyes constantly surveying the room, never focusing on anything for more than an instant, seeing all, registering only the unfamiliar, "Got a costume?" he asked.

"Uh huh. I'm wearing it."

Stanley gave Angela a series of quick appraising glances. Tongue darting around his mouth in an apparently hopeless effort to keep things moist, he said, "Good 'nuff as long as it comes off. *All* of it...okay?"

Their eyes met for a millisecond, and then his eyes flashed away, returned briefly to Liz. "You here t' work, Lizzy?" he asked, glancing at his wristwatch, scanning the girls, hurrying them along with his glances. "I'm short a coupla girls tonight. You wanna go on?" From the corner of his mouth, very hush-hush, he added, "I'll cover the *house* for ya. Just don't tell anybody. Okay?"

"Sure, Stanley. I'm her momma tonight, anyhow," Liz answered, hooking a thumb at Angela. "I'll go on. Might as well make a buck while I'm babysittin."

A nod sealed the deal and Stanley turned away, clapping his hands; "Okay Sugars! Lets *mooove* it! Got a full house out there tonight. And don't forget those Lady's Drinks...'cause I'll be watching!"

Chapter 18

After completing Boot Camp and Advanced Infantry Training, Hoot went determinedly off to Vietnam. Hooked up with Norman right away. He hadn't specifically volunteered for combat but was hardly surprised when the rosters were posted. Hoot made that sacrifice for his country, for freedom, without having the slightest idea what a *sacrifice*, by definition, really entailed – but certain he was about to find out. He arrived in-country in the middle of a big stink percolating over the so-called 'incident' at My Lai.

"My father says that's what I'm doing. Making a sacrifice for freedom," Hoot told Norman one evening in Chan's, a Saigon go-go bar not known for its cuisine but thick with GIs who would write in their letters home to moms and sweethearts that the food was gourmet, the entertainment *cultural*.

"If your old man says it…it must be true," Norman replied through a big smile, watching three of Chan's go-go girls wriggle and dance like half-nude puppets on a narrow stage behind the bar.

Hoot said, "He says it's something men never want to do, but do when they have to. I think it's his way of telling me he's proud that his boy, Ezra Hooten, young *Hoot*, has officially become a man."

"Exactly!" Norman said, raising his beer bottle. "Let's drink to your manhood…"

Hoot joined in his friend's toast only his heart wasn't in it. His heart was hurting for Donna as it had been since the day he went away to Boot Camp. She'd avoided him the week he was home on leave before reporting in-country. Or maybe he had avoided her. By the time he had a handle on just how much he missed her it was too late to say or do anything that could make it better.

Truthfully, they were on separate paths by then anyhow.

Truth. What a concept! Hoot thought.

130

Shortly after Hoot arrived in-country, every perception he'd previously held of truth, of *life*, became permanently altered. War does that – alters perceptions. Hoot quickly came to appreciate that if a monsoon-season patrol through Viet Cong territory known to be booby-trapped doesn't adequately elevate your pucker factor, a couple of pee-in-your-pants nights spent entrenched under a barrage of heavy mortar fire will change you right down to the core. Bet your sweet ass it will. It'll redefine the meaning of life in a heartbeat, the meaning of death suddenly becoming a buddy's body stuffed into a black bag just because he was unlucky enough to be hunkered down six feet over thataway. It was almost enough to make whatever Lt. Calley's platoon did at My Lai seem like a bunch of ordinary dudes trying to make sense out of senselessness...

Almost.

The entire place, Vietnam, was over-the-top foreign – all of it; the people, the food, the weather, plants, animals, bugs, the very air you breathed so *not* like anything back home.

So what was normal? What was okay behavior in this hot and hostile jungle?

A whole new *truth* was being revealed to Hoot, and he figured if this totally alien place was the stage for that new truth then it was his job to embrace it. "Wallow in it. Grab it by the gills and land it" as his father would say. Hoot's father making a fishing story out of just about everything, even if it tripped him up, even if the entire Vietnam experience for him was summed up in a story he'd read calling the American soldier in 'Nam "a bitter truth walking a narrow and treacherous path between right and wrong." But Hoot's father hadn't paid much attention to stories about My Lai. Where was the honor in *that* kind of truth?

Meanwhile, in-country, Charlie was getting gutsy. The war was escalating like crazy, the mission changing daily. The best shot in his unit, twice recommended for combat commendations in his first three months, Hoot's natural outdoorsy skills worked to his advantage and he quickly advanced in rank. No one was surprised when he was tapped to volunteer for Long-Range Patrol training only six months after arriving. It seems that a certain half-breed LRP scout/sniper

131

known as *Creeper* had hung Hoot's name out on the grapevine. Certain officers had conferred. And now Norman and Hoot, both, were destined to wear the Green Beret. Hoot became known as *Troubleshooter*, building a reputation as a reliable deadeye sniper, while Norman, quick to pick up Vietnamese, excelled at interrogation, infiltration, and hand-to-hand close-quarters work.

The way it worked, a special-ops LRP contingent consisting of up to three or four men, sometimes including Norman and Hoot together, would accompany a routine patrol into enemy territory, the patrol going on by foot after deep insertion by helicopters or swift boats. The special-ops job was to act as scouts for the patrol and handle field interrogation of any captured Viet Cong prior to extraction. After the patrol completed its basic mission, LRP elements would often stay behind and continue on, sometimes staying another week on their own, blending into the jungle, hiding and watching, gaining intel and taking out individual targets with sniper ambushes. It was nervy work.

Then it all started getting weird.

Beginning with the Ho Chi Minh Trail recon mission in '69...

Beginning with the guy in the tree...

***

A half-click before locating Norman's position Hoot encountered a company of Viet Cong. The sun was high, temperature climbing faster than a gibbon climbs up a banana tree, the jungle's morning drizzle quickly turning to steam, and Hoot could see that the VC were agitated, not making the slightest effort whatsoever at stealth, merely holding their position and apparently waiting for either backup or instruction. He gave them a wide berth, eventually closing in on Norman from the flank.

First thing he saw when he finally found his friend was the body – it was hanging upside down in a tree like some kind of hideous ornament. From its clothing Hoot could see that it

132

was the body of a VC soldier and not one of the countless villagers pressed into service on the trail as human mules.

The man's face was a mess, but the awful thing was that both his arms ended in bloody stumps – his hands were missing. And he'd been scalped.

Norman lay hidden under a nearby root. His leg was sporting a tourniquet and blood was seeping from around a punji stake still embedded in his flesh. A big smile on his filthy face, he said, "My favorite blood-brother. You do understand that your job was to wait and cover my path of retreat? You get two demerits for coming here, buddy. But I'm damned glad to see you." He gestured at his leg, "Jungle around here's full of these little nasties. Watch out where you dive for cover when bullets start flying."

Hoot looked at the wood shiv sticking out of Norman's leg, said, "That doesn't look good at all. It needs to come out."

"Tried that already. It's barbed."

"Probably dipped in shit, too. Have you given yourself a stab?"

"Not yet. I've been busy."

Hoot gave the body up in the tree a quick glance, opened Norman's LRP pack and set aside a packet containing a field styrette of morphine, said, "For later. There's a company of VC south of this position. Close. We gotta move before they do. Then you can have the happy stuff."

Another packet contained a styrette of penicillin. Hoot stabbed Norman in the leg with it, Norman saying, "That company is less six that I know of. The flytrap up in the tree is number four."

"What the fuck happened here?" Hoot asked, prepping a fresh compress with sulfa powder and ointment, avoiding a close look at the gristly sight in the tree.

"Soon as I got to this sector I saw signs of activity. Serious hen scratches. Then, come nightfall, they came. *Lots* of them. Wrong side of the river for me to call it in." Norman said. "So I just settled in real quiet-like. It was pitch dark. The VC having a regular goddamned jungle-style parade passing through here all night. Next thing I know an officer sits down on the log I'm hiding behind. I figure he's about to shit on me and I'm gonna let him. Instead, he gets his maps out, a flashlight, and starts jabbering on a radio to his command…"

Hoot cut away the cloth around Norman's wound and swabbed the area with green soap.

"The Gook officer sent his radio man away," Norman said, "but not before I picked up on a few words about Americans in the area – *us*, I presume. I took it as a good opportunity to slit his throat and relive him of the maps." Norman patted a fat pocket, said, "I was departing with these when someone noticed that the officer had slid off his perch. Raised the alarm…"

Norman gritted his teeth and grunted as Hoot loosened the tourniquet and moved it away from the wound. He said, "A running firefight ended just over there with me making a kebob out of my leg. It was still dark, then. I managed to shoot a couple more of 'em. Then that one in the tree got close enough for my knife."

Hoot retightened the tourniquet, eliciting another long grunt from Norman.

Finding a nearby stick, Norman continued, saying, "I tied him up, Sioux fashion, and hoisted him into that tree, still alive…barely. Tossed his hands out on the path for his buddies to find. *That's* what they pulled back to kibitz about. His bloody hands. Seemed to blow their little gook minds." He put the stick between his teeth and bit down, hard.

Doing one hell of a job of blowing my mind, too, Hoot thought as he gripped the punji stake with both hands, put his knee against Norman's thigh and jerked with all his strength, pulling the stake free, a glob of meat attached to the barb, only a gurgle of blood.

Norman's scream was a subdued growl.

Drizzling iodine into the fleshy hole, Hoot applied the compress and tied it off, made a quick splint out of a fairly straight piece of root while Norman seethed, chomping on the stick.

His first aid as complete as possible for now, Hoot eased himself up and surveyed the immediate area. Giving the heinous corpse hanging in the nearby tree a final glance, the words, *the path that brought us here no longer exists,*

134

ominously passing through his mind, he said, "Time to get out of here. Can't call Ma Bell 'til we're across the river."

Norman stood with a wince. "Just waiting on you," he said. "*Di di mau*, motherfucker."

Chapter 19

Hoot and Marcus took two rooms at the Holiday Inn. The accommodations weren't quite on par with the Davenport Hotel where Hoot had stayed the last time Norman's scent brought him to Spokane, but it would do for a few days. Marcus, on the phone to his wife, would hardly notice the Spartan accommodations. New guys never did.

Hoot took a walk, a thinker's stroll around the old World's Fair site. Ten blocks away, at Riverfront Park, he stood beside the upriver rapids portion of the Spokane River. Watching the water rush past, he was reminded of the hard retreat that he and Norman had made out of Laos back in 1968 – it was one of those memories he'd as soon be rid of, but it just wouldn't turn loose. Came to him in dark, nightmarish dreams sometimes.

"Cross the river and we're home free," echoed inside his head. One of his goofy stress jingles taking off. Water rushing past...*cross the river and we're home free* sounding like an indigenous chant, like watery chimes and kettle drums.

Cross the river. Never easy, as you might think. Especially the one on the border between Laos and 'Nam.

***

"Knew you'd come," Norman had said to Hoot that monsoon-season morning in '68, both men wounded and both prepared to go down fighting. It was barely dawn and they were lying in muck on the Vietnam side of a river whose name Hoot forgot long ago. Already sultry, there were bugs and leeches and sweltering heat on the way with the sun. The smell of the river was an aroma that Hoot called *festering green.*

Jungle canopy standing tall and thick behind them. Calling for extraction and waiting for a VC attack from the Laotian side of the river, they had fought an exhausting ambush-and-skirmish then run-like-hell retreat throughout the

136

night to get here. Their ammo and ordnance nearly depleted, this would be their last stand.

A goddamned AK-47 round had grazed Hoot in the side. A flesh wound, missed the vitals, he thought – *hoped* – plugged the hole with a not-too-dirty handkerchief and kept going even though it burned like six kinds of hell. He was exhausted. Norman appeared closer to dead than alive; he had lost a lot of blood in spite of the tourniquet, and his leg was swelling. The punji wound looking bad enough that Hoot was concerned the leg might have to go; he had carried his friend on his back much of the way – heavy bastard with all his skimpy gear and Hoot's. It would be full light soon and they expected the enemy to come in force with the sun. Maybe before.

Norman's speech was slurred, eyes glazed, the two morphine styrettes that Hoot had finally stabbed into him starting to kick in. "Knew youu'd find me," he said.

Hoot ignored him. "Ma Bell. Ma Bell. Alpha-Bravo-One…this is Alpha-Bravo-Three. Troubleshooter," he said again into the portable radio mic. "We are Deep Serious. Repeat, Deep Serious. Requesting Dustoff. Coordinates are…" Hoot had repeated the same call every ten minutes the last half-hour. With a long glance he answered Norman, "How could I not find you? Your blood is my blood…right?"

"Bet your sweet ass it is, Brudder."

***

"The Ghost Dancers were dreamers," Red Coyote had said that time in 1963 when they were holed-up in Wild Horse Canyon in a thunderstorm. "And for a little while it was a good dream. Then it became a nightmare so the People stopped dreaming."

Norman saw a rainbow of colors flowing through the rocky canyon walls; saw the old shaman's face changing shape and color, red and green and purple, a wax face, a peyote face…melting.

The nausea was passing. He was not afraid.

"Wovoka was a Paiute mystic, the prophet of the ghost dance," Red Coyote said. "When he was about your age, his mother died and he was given to live with a White family. He

137

spoke English and knew about Jesus – described him as the messiah who came once to live on earth with the Whites, but was killed by them."

Norman looked into Red Coyote's melting face and could tell that his tired and nearly blind eyes were closed behind the curtain of his dark glasses. He was looking inside, remembering. How deep the well of this man's knowledge must be.

"Tavibo was Wovoka's father," the old shaman continued, "and a Great Shaman though few remember him now. Tavibo prophesied that there would be an enormous earthquake, the earth would swallow all the Whites, and all dead Indians would emerge reborn to live free of their oppressors. He said all the game and crops ravaged by Whites would be restored. Few believed him."

Distracted, Norman stared at the canyon walls' ever-changing colors, the whole place seeming to melt with color. Red Coyote's voice sounded distant, saying; "Many years later Wovoka dreamed that his father's prophecy was becoming imminent, and he directed his followers to prepare for this time by living good lives. He stressed the link between righteous behavior and imminent salvation."

"Sounds like something a White Christian would say," Norman said.

Red Coyote smiled, and he said, "Wovoka also taught that salvation was not to be passively waited for but welcomed by ritual dancing. He told everyone to dance in slow-turning circles while singing spiritual songs. People would dance for four nights and five days. And whenever someone in the dance would experience a vision of a departed loved one, they would go to the center of the turning circle and tell of their vision, the telling becoming part of the song, part of the dance. Food was brought and shared by all, and at the end they would cleanse themselves in the river. This dance became known as the Ghost Dance, and those who practiced it, Ghost Dancers."

Norman, not yet fifteen years old and listening to Red Coyote tell of the Ghost Dancers, began to see it in the theater of his mind. Great circles of Indians dancing and singing and yearning for a vision of their departed loved ones. He could see greater and greater circles, expanding with every drumbeat, Red Coyote's voice becoming the song they sang.

"Algonquin. Arapaho. The Sioux. The Lakota. Many Peoples believed strongly in the power of the ghost dance," Red Coyote said. "The Lakota sent a delegation to visit Wovoka. This group included two members of their reservation at Pine Ridge in South Dakota – they were Kicking Bear and Short Bull and they brought the Ghost Dance back to the reservation. Soon believers there started wearing sacred garments when dancing. These garments became known as Ghost Shirts and were said to have the power to deflect bullets fired by White soldiers."

"Did Ghost Shirts really stop soldier's bullets?" Norman asked.

"At Wounded Knee many were wearing such clothing," Red Coyote said.

"Wounded Knee was a massacre…"

"Yes. It was a terrible massacre. The worst."

***

"Coupla Ghost Shirts would sure be handy about now," Norman said, feeling drowsy, the buzz from the morphine coursing through his blood, a low vibration somewhere behind his eyes, a ringing in his ears. He was still aware of the searing pain in his leg but not exactly *feeling* it, lying in the mud, waiting for Charlie to come streaming across the river from Laos. "'Course, those shirts only work for Ghost Dancers, so maybe we only need one shirt, you being so lily-*white*…"

"I remember that story," Hoot said, smiling at Norman's lopsided attempt at humor. "Shirts didn't work so well for the fuckin Indians, if I recall."

"Not at all!" Norman said, laughing until he hiccupped.

Hoot reached over, said, "Gimme that, you're stoned," and took the Claymore clacker from Norman. Each M18A1 Claymore, with the ominous warning *Front Toward Enemy* molded into the lethal front side, was capable of sending a killer swarm of steel ball bearings at almost four-thousand feet-per-second at said enemy. The last two of those handy devices

139

were daisy-chained together a few meters out, aimed to best cover the fifty meters between them and the far side of the river. He put a smoke grenade in Norman's hand, said, "The shooting starts, pop this after I fire the Claymores. Maybe we'll get lucky."

"You never believed in all that blood-brudder business…did you?" Norman slurred, flopping himself into a new position on his belly to better cover fire zone left.

Hoot turned away, covering fire zone right, said, "No, not really."

"So…how'd you find me, if you don't believe? Explain that. How'd you find your way to me? In the dark. Motherfucking VC watching. Shooting at you the whole way?"

Hoot said, "You got enough morphine in you to make a Friday night junkie happy as a fuckin toad on a lily pad, and you wanna talk spiritual hocus-pocus? Save it for happy hour at Chan's, my friend."

"*How*? Tell me!" Norman insisted.

"You *saw* me in your head…didn't you?"

Hoot checked the clip in his .45 Colt pistol. Chambered a round, and stuck the weapon back in its holster.

"*Didn't* you?" Norman repeated. A liquid grin spreading across his face, Norman was on the verge of zoning-out from the morphine. He tapped his own forehead and said, "Yeah...you *did*…my blood-brother! Youuu *did*…!"

"Just watch your zone. Stay awake. Stay sharp." Hoot said, glancing back over his shoulder at Norman, a hard glance that said *zip it*, a glance interrupted by movement from across the river. VC coming out of the thicket and streaming down the bank like ants at a picnic – Hoot and Norman being the picnic.

"Here we go, Geronimo," Hoot said. Waiting for the right moment. Finally squeezing the clacker to explode the Claymores, **boom-BOOM**! and then training his M-21 on the VC still advancing after the explosions.

"Pop the smoke! Now!" Hoot's words were suddenly lost in the roar of a pair of prop-driven A-1 Skyraiders sweeping in low from upriver, their machine guns and 20-mm cannons chopping the enemy-infested water into a deadly froth. Behind them came the unmistakable music of a .50-Cal Ma

Deuce accompanied by the distinctive *whup-whup-whup* of a Huey rotor.

At last, the taxi was here.

Chapter 20

Hoot came home from 'Nam in the fall of 1972.

One year later, the Wednesday before Thanksgiving, 1973, it was gray and raining in Pleasanton. Some wind in the bay. Not enough bad weather to making docking a problem. Hoot brought The *Annie H* in close, reversed the engines and let her drift sideways to the bumpers. His father waited on the dock in his orange Helly Hansen Narvik suit. Tall, and almost as fair as his son with a permanently sunburned face, he seemed slumped, resigned today. Something was obviously wrong.

"You got bad news. I can tell," Hoot called to his father, cranking the wheel to bring the stern in tight. "I've got a hold full of lobster, so whatever it is, it's just going to have to wait until I'm weighed and paid."

"Donna's dead," Hoot's father said, his voice flat, barely reaching the boat from the dock. Eyes unwilling to lock onto Hoot's eyes. Silence falling. Rain dripping from his elbows. The scraping sound of gunwales rubbing against boat dock fenders.

"*What*?" Hoot responded, that one word breaking the tension. The crew getting busy unloading without the usual hoopla.

"I'm sorry, Son. I thought you'd want to know. But not over the radio."

***

Yes, he had wanted to know. In later years it had seemed to Hoot that what his father told him that day was something he already knew in his heart – part of the supposed *connection* he had with Norman kicking in, most likely.

Now, standing by the Spokane River and listening to the water speak, Hoot wondered about that connection. The one he'd never been quite able to get on board with while Norman always swore by it.

142

Turning his mind toward his old friend; Creeper is here, Hoot thought. Right here in Spokane. I don't understand how it works, but I can actually *feel* him close by. And I'll be damned if I'll let him slip away again. He closed his eyes and listened to the rushing water. Tried to focus his entire mind on Norman. Reaching out to him.

This was as close as Hoot had ever been to embracing their so-called blood-brotherhood. Except for maybe that other time, by that other river...

***

Angela remembered her mother once telling her something about mutton dressed as lamb and that's exactly what she felt like. Or mutton *un*dressed in this case. She stood waiting in the darkness beside the DJ's booth, trying to tell herself she could do this. Alternating with telling herself there was *no way* she could do this. Her feet surely must be superglued to the spot or she would flee.

Was it too late to run away?

The DJ appeared to be chewing at least a half-pack of bubble gum. Only inches from her nose he yelled, "OKAY! WHAT'S YOURS?"

"MY *WHAT*?" Angela replied at the top of her lungs.

"YOUR TWO!"

"TWO *WHAT*?"

"YOU GOTTA PICK TWO SONGS FOR YOUR SET." He surveyed a list that was fastened on a clipboard. "IT'S *ANGEL*, RIGHT?"

"*ANGELA*. I'M ANGELA!"

"SAYS *ANGEL* HERE!"

Didn't matter. He pointed to two lines on the clipboard, said, "WRITE YOUR SONGS HERE! BACK STAGE! FRONT STAGE!" All she could think of was *Feel Like Makin' Love*, by Bad Company, and *Young Lust*, by Pink Floyd. She filled in the blanks, then stumbled away, immediately thinking, No, that's not what I want! Those songs are *ancient*. They're gonna think I'm a grandma... She started to backtrack; then from seemingly nowhere Liz grabbed her and pulled her into the dressing room.

"Been looking for you," Liz said in the relative quiet of this weird haven that Angela was beginning to see as dancer's purgatory. Adjusting her hair, refreshing her makeup. "How ya doin'?" she asked, making eye contact in the mirror.

"Okay, I guess."

"Listen, I've only been on the floor twenty minutes and I'm up ninety bucks! Not bad. You oughta make a killing tonight."

"I don't know…"

"You'll do fine. Just watch the other girls. Ask every guy you see if he wants to buy a dance. Stay if they pay. Move on if they don't. Simple."

Liz ducked into a vacant bathroom stall and pulled Angela in with her. Tiny silver spoon already in hand, two miniature piles of powder disappeared up her nose in two rapid snorts. Two quick spoons for Angela and a passionate kiss on the lips and then she ducked out again. She was here…then poof! She was gone.

Angela leaned against the stall door, her thoughts spinning. From out of the blue she remembered going to the Joplin High Junior-Senior Prom with her best non-McAuley High School friend and confidante, Nancy Nickerson, a neighbor from two streets over. Nancy was a sweet but somewhat unattractive girl who attended Joplin High – thus, the invitation. When they were both juniors Angela's parents wouldn't allow her to car date, always requiring her to ride with them, meet the boy at the dance, and Nancy had yet to have a date of any kind.

Angela remembered ducking into the restroom in the girls' locker room at the prom with Nancy to refresh and intensify their makeup, remembered complaining to Nancy that she didn't think her mom would care overmuch if she sucked her date's cock, as long as she didn't do it in his car. "Doing it in a car makes it…*tacky*," Angela's mother had said.

"I'd gladly suck any cock in the school for a real date. Bring 'em on!" Nancy replied at top volume – in the girl's locker room where they were not alone and sound was known to travel almost magically. "In fact, I might suck three or four and chose the one I like best!"

Thanks, Nancy! All these years later Angela still got a good chuckle remembering that. Somehow it helped to put the current situation in a better light.

What the hell…it's only sex.

"Hey!" an impatient knock rattled the stall door, interrupting Angela's detour down Memory Lane. "We're taking numbers out here!"

***

Norman stopped at Goodtime Charlie's to collect his money. Went directly to the office where Vincent P stood looking out at a full house through his one-way glass wall. They sat down on a leather sofa. Shared a bong. Talked about business and pleasure over Canadian Club on ice. Norman declining the liquor in favor of sparkling water. Vincent P enjoying his all day every day without apparent impairment, Norman sure he'd never actually seen the man stone sober.

"Job's done…and you need a new daytime manager," Norman said.

Vincent P nodded toward a plain envelope on his desk, said, "Done. And done."

"The man's missing some heavy jewelry. And quite a bit of blood. Looks like a robbery occurred at his place."

"Good. You do good work, Mister C. Very efficient. Very timely"

They briefly discussed the three clubs Vincent P had a financial interest in, *Fever* in Vancouver, *The Club* in Seattle, and of course, *Goodtime Charlie's*.

"Maybe you'd like the job. Daytime manager," Vincent P said, fishing.

"Not my sort of thing," Norman said with a mirthless smile, thinking: You actually believe I'd fit in your pocket, do you? He stood and moved over to look out through the one-way glass, saying; "This place is packed tonight."

"Yeah." Vincent P sidestepped to join him, admiring the crowd of paying customers. "It's the last Amateur Night of

145

the year. Mostly regular customers out there in need of a good pussyfix to get 'em through their happy fuckin' holidays."

The DJ could be clearly heard through the thick glass, announcing; "AND NOW, GENTLEMEN, PUT YOUR HANDS TOGETHER FOR AMATEUR NUMBER TWO...FROM SEATTLE...THE VERY LOVELY...*ANGEL!*" and Norman stood completely spellbound by what he was seeing – his very own Donna Messenger walking onto the spotlighted back stage looking exactly as she had in high school. Back when the crush he had on her was undeniable but she was untouchable because she was Hoot's girl.

Hoot's girl...

Hoot...?

Fuck...! There he was, too! Hoot! Right there in the club! He was sitting at a table on the back wall. Watching Donna with the same *she's mine* gleam in his eye he'd had throughout high school and before. Even after they split...

How long had it been since they'd been this close? He and Hoot. And Donna.

Hoot looked old. He looked tired and pale as Death himself. A weathered cardboard cutout of his younger self. Norman could hardly believe it, but the man at the table was definitely Ezra Hooten.

How'd he get this close without me *feeling* him first?

Then Norman knew the answer – I lost him in my thoughts when I first saw the Donna ghost in Wenatchee...

With a little effort Norman knew he should be able to engage his sixth sense and clearly *feel* the old Shooter in the crowd. So close! Instead, Norman took an involuntary step back, instinctively afraid that Hoot's own sixth sense might turn this way and detect him. An errant thought might cause Hoot to look up and sense him even through the one-way glass. The old deadeye could put a bullet between my eyes at this range just for looking at this ghost of Donna...

Not to mention for killing her almost forty years ago.

"You alright?" Vincent P asked.

"Yeah. That dancer looks familiar is all."

"She's a real honey, ain't she? New girl here. Starting tonight. One of the few things that fucker, Case, did that was worth a fuck."

From banks of amped speakers, Paul Rodgers' voice crooned about how thinking about Baby made him think about love... ″

Donna's eyes were closed.

She swayed to the beat. Not seeming to move *to* the music so much as being moved *by* the music. Her pleated miniskirt followed along with her every movement, navy-blue, mesmerizing, and fluid. As if it was being blown by a fresh breeze across clear water – the clear water of a lake in Acadia National Park. Exactly the way Norman remembered another skirt blowing just before his sleever bar came crashing down.

Paul Rodgers kept on singing about thinking about love. And the dancer on stage ran both hands up her torso, raising the hem of the skirt enough to offer her audience a glimpse of lace underneath. Pulled the white tails of her blouse free from her waistband. Her hands continuing on up through her hair, loose strands cascading from her fingers.

Donna's back was turned toward a darkness that she surely had to know was filled with hungry eyes. She writhed against the mirror, pulling at the hem of her skirt, revealing glimpses of her bottom swaying back and forth to the music. She was moving like a snake before a shadowy room full of charmers; all eyes following her every motion. Norman stole a glance through the one-way glass at Hoot and saw that his old friend was mesmerized by the show like everyone else.

Paul Rodgers crooned that he felt like making love while Donna, eyes still closed, hooked her thumbs under the elastic waistband of her panties and pulled them down in a single motion, kicked them aside and turned around, teasing her audience with the swaying miniskirt, glimpses of secrets yet to be fully revealed.

Rodgers insisted that he felt like making love to *you*. And Donna, eyes open now and blazing, unfastened the buttons on the blouse and threw it off, exposing a lace bra as shear as summer rain. She swirled around and flipped up the miniskirt's hem.

Men sitting in the front row growled. Then the bra came off.

That song finished and the house broke into applause and catcalls.

Donna put the blouse back on and carried her lingerie with her to the front stage.

Staying back away from the glass, Norman stood spellbound as Donna stepped onto the nearer platform. From here he could see her clearly, and it almost hurt to look.

Chapter 21

Deciding to keep this first visit casual, Hoot had left Marcus at the hotel. He paid the ten-dollar cover without flashing his Marshal's badge, and entered the foray at Goodtime Charlie's, a muscle-bound doorman giving him a *look* and telling him that he had to have a fresh drink on the table at all times.

"Where is the office," Hoot asked. "I'd like to talk to the man in charge."

"Man's in a meeting," the doorman said, his eyes telling Hoot that he'd already been made as a lawman. "Go sit down somewhere and I'll tell him you're here. And, don't forget the house rule about having a drink on your table at all times."

How could he forget? Two heartbeats later a very pale emo girl dressed in layers of black appeared. One heavily made up eye peeking out from behind a cascade of straight black bangs, a silver barbell through the cartilage between her nostrils and grommets in her earlobes, she took Hoot's order for a Diet Coke, saying; "Dude, I *love* your white skin…"

Burrowing deep into the bowels of the club, Hoot found himself surrounded with living proof that he'd just entered one of the backwater eddies of human evolution. Not the first time he had followed his old blood-brother's tracks deep into the bowels of the adult entertainment industry: here, in this environment, men were little more than *fucksticks* as he remembered Norman used to call guys he perceived to be lower on the food chain than himself – and that was just about everyone except women. Norman had always called women on the low end of the chain *squeeze toys*.

Moving on, Hoot noticed a paunchy middle-aged man getting up to leave and negotiated the darkness to claim his still-warm seat along the back wall. The pale and grommeted emo girl appeared before him like a phantom and placed his drink on the table. "Five dollars," she announced, and Hoot gave her six, said, "Keep it," and she did, disappearing as completely and mysteriously as she had appeared.

Ten minutes later two guys at the table next door decided that maybe they'd better get home for dinner instead of waiting around to find out who won the amateur contest and got up to leave. Three men wearing sweatshirts with logos declaring them to be proud members of the International Association of Bridge, Structural, Ornamental and Reinforcing Iron Workers pounced on the newly vacated spot.

A fourth ironworker attempted to shoehorn in next to Hoot. He leaned hard against Hoot's shoulder, had enough recently-smoked cannabis lingering on his breath to make a strong man's whiskers go limp, and said with a slur, "'Scuse me, Grandpa. You mind I sit here? Share your table?"

"Sit anywhere you want, Dickwad." Hoot answered, flashing him a glimpse of his U.S. Marshal's badge.

The ironworker hopped up like the seat was on fire. Stumbling, he retreated and pried himself in on the other side of his group of buddies. A middle-aged Asian man who sat very upright and ran a nonstop dialogue with himself about each girl's attributes immediately replaced him, politely asking to share Hoot's table.

Hoot sat back to take in the show. He was propositioned at least a dozen times in twenty minutes. Dancers trolling by in ludicrous attire, saying; "Would you like a table dance?" The question was usually asked while his crotch was being fondled, his face buried in perfumed cleavage.

The Asian man was a very amusing tablemate. Hoot decided it was like sitting next to a miniature version of Howard Cosell doing a running play-by-play commentary of nude dancing. "Nice titties. Yes! Yes! Very shapely. Nice moves. Good legs too," the man said with smiling enthusiasm as though he were talking to someone unseen. His gaze remaining fixed on whatever dancer was onstage or nearby, at first Hoot thought the man was trying to converse with him. But no, the commentary was either for the man's own benefit or it was for an invisible buddy. A six-foot-tall rabbit named Harvey, maybe. Or, perhaps he actually was broadcasting; *This is Howard Chin Cosell, Live From Goodtime Charlie's*!

Distracted by a redheaded dancer on stage strutting with practiced movements, Hoot's eye was drawn to a long mirror high up on the wall across the room. One-way glass no doubt, something there nagging at him. He felt agitated. He checked the floor for any sign of management approaching his table. There was none. The redhead reaching her crescendo, the whole place seemed to be overflowing with kinetic energy, so maybe that's what was tickling Hoot's instincts. *Something* sure as hell was…

The redhead crawled like a panther along the mirror, then she rolled and tumbled across the front of the stage while scissoring her legs in the air, finishing by hooking one leg behind her neck, a remarkably lewd maneuver that left her shamelessly exposed and brought the Asian man nearly to his feet;

"Outstanding!" he declared. "Perfect pussy! Perfect!"

Hoot had been nursing the same glass of Coke for a half hour. Was down to mostly ice. Fending off solicitations from dancers until the girls finally got wise and offers were coming less frequently, getting impatient waiting for management acknowledgement, he was becoming annoyed by the whole scene; was about ready to go show his credentials and demand immediate entry to the room behind the glass when a dancer approached with another pitch; "Hiya, Daddy, wanna table dance?"

She was a slender petite blonde with a nice smile. Fantastically soft – possibly even homegrown – breasts were pressed against him. Her hand inside his shirt, her fingers were plowing through his sparse white chest hair like a mink rancher sizing-up a pelt. She had his attention. It felt nice.

"What's your name, sugar?" he asked.

She slid in behind the table to sit beside him without letting go of his chest hair. Breathing into his ear, she said, "I'm Barbie. What's your name, Daddy-O?"

"Call me Hoot."

"Cool name. You're different, Hoot. Kinda vampire-looking. But you've got a nice chest. Mind if I play with it?"

"Help yourself."

"Buy the next dance for twenty-dollars and I'll let you play with *my* chest."

"Thanks. Not right now, Barbie Doll. But it's worth an easy five-dollar tip if you'll go back to the office and remind the man in charge that I'm still waiting to talk to him." He folded a five-spot and slid it into Barbie's soft cleavage, "Okay?"

"As good as done." She said.

Sucking his earlobe like it was a lollipop. Almost taking it with her as she stood and walked away, she said, "I'll come see you again after my set."

Hoot smiled, said aloud, "That was enjoyable," and the Asian man parroted, "That was enjoyable. Very enjoyable. Nice titties!"

"ALRRRIGHT! GENTLEMEN, PUT YOUR HANDS TOGETHER FOR THOSE TWO LOVELY LADIES!" the DJ commanded and got a randomly hearty response including several ear-piercing whistles from the ironworker enclave.

"THAT WAS VIXEN ON THE BACK STAGE AND SHY-ANN ON THE FRONT ! – AND DON'T THAT LITTLE SQUAW JUST MAKE YOUR PEACE PIPE SMOKE?

"NOW, VIXEN AND SHY-ANN WILL BE MOVING ON OUT TO THE FLOOR, AVAILABLE FOR YOUR *PRIVATE* DANCING PLEASURE…SO, INVITE ONE OF THOSE LOVELY LADIES OVER FOR YOUR VERY OWN UP-CLOSE AND PERSONAL TABLE DANCE FOR ONLY *TEN* DOLLARS! ONLY TWENTY DOLLARS FOR A GENUINE TEXAS-STYLE COUCH DANCE!

"REMEMBER GENTLEMEN, WE TAKE VISA AND MASTERCARD AT THE BAR AND WE HAVE AN ATM AT THE DOOR…

"AND NOW, GENTLEMEN, PUT YOUR HANDS TOGETHER FOR AMATEUR NUMBER TWO…FROM SEATTLE …

…The rest of the announcer's hoorah was lost in a rush of blood to Hoot's ears as amateur number two walked past his table on her way to the stage. Could have knocked him over with a feather, he was so taken back by the uncanny similarity between this young woman and Donna Messenger when she was a teenager.

"Yes! Excellent! Very Good!" The Asian gentleman next to Hoot was saying when he regained his senses.

Amazing! Hoot watched the young woman identified as *Angel* taking the stage, wishing for more natural lighting than was provided by the colored stage spots that would make a porcupine look smooth. It had been some time since he'd actually seen a photograph of Donna from those days – his visit home for his mother's funeral was the last time he'd perused the family archives – but he thought of her often. He had noticed plenty of girls from time to time who resembled her, her classic features. But *this* girl – it was unbelievable...

The way she moved like Donna.

The tilt of her head – her lowered eyes reflecting Donna's misleadingly shy demeanor. Her controlled grace. She could almost *be* Donna!

Often, these long years past, Hoot's memory of his first girlfriend had been tinged with regret due to the circumstances of her demise. But in spite of that Donna had forever resided close in his heart.

Close enough that seeing her spitting image so near at hand hit him like a sucker punch to the gut. It took his breath away.

The only dancer thus far to come onstage dressed in anything more than skimpy lingerie, this Donna clone looked for all the world like an actual sixteen-year-old schoolgirl. She was lovely, truly lovely, without a hint of the streetwise aura the other dancers wore like a whore's halo. Hoot knew that Goodtime Charlie's was a far cry from the kind of place where special or unique things are likely to happen, so what was happening on stage right then was about as good as it gets. It was genuine. And, by the change in their behavior, many – certainly not *all* – but many of the other patrons in the audience knew it, too. This was as close to what they were truly looking for as it was ever likely to get without standing in the dark and peeking in the bedroom window of the last virgin in the neighborhood.

Even the ironworker enclave next door simmered down and paid attention.

The Asian man was muttering; "Pretty girl. Oh! Such a *pretty* girl…"

***

The voice of *Pink Floyd's* Roger Waters wailed about how he needed a dirty woman from beyond the one-way glass, and the dancer called *Angel* – who looked more and more like Donna Messenger at age sixteen the longer Norman looked at her – turned and swayed, moving across the nearby stage as if pulled by unseen magnets. She allowed her scant girly outfit to reveal glimpses of the adult body underneath, a bit older than he remembered her, but still very innocent-looking as her nakedness was slowly revealed.

Donna had always been innocent-looking – was actually anything but, Norman remembered. Wild stuff when the mood was right. Damned wild, the games she liked to play. Norman had known the games, but not the rules. Not *her* rules. And he sure as hell didn't like his wife playing those games.

What the hell happened to the shy little sweetheart who couldn't decide between two starry-eyed boys? Within two months of the *I do's* Norman had begun to realize that the liberated version of the pseudo-shy Donna he married would probably be happy to do them both. Him *and* Hoot…at the same time!

Watching Donna's ghost on stage, Norman felt his heart being torn apart by long-forgotten memories.

Yes. He had loved her. As much as he was able to love anyone. As much as he knew how. But love was no simple matter for him. It was not the glue that held things together. Instead, it tore at him like talons. And he bled from it. His whole life he had bled…

The music permeating every crevice in the room insisted that Roger Waters seriously needed a dirty *girl* and the blouse fell away. Angel-Donna struck a coy pose, hiding her breasts with her hands while keeping the beat with her swaying hips.

Eyes closed. Chin held high. Her face was illuminated by the blue and red stage lighting overhead, making her skin

154

look like porcelain, making her look to Norman just like she had that time in the cold water of Eagle Lake.

Slowly drifting away…

No! Norman thought. This is all *wrong!*

The music pleaded with the audience to relate to this rock and roll refugee, and the skirt followed the blouse to the stage floor.

Norman, at the one-way window thought, "Oh, Babe, set me free…"

Save for her earrings, shoes, and white knee socks the ghostly Donna parading herself on stage was as naked as the day she was born. As the day she had died. And, unlike most of the dancers who moved on stage like oversexed zombies, she danced with wild abandon. Then, looking directly toward the place where Norman watched her from behind the one-way glass, she crossed her wrists together, a pantomime of the way he had stripped her and bound her wrists before taking her from his truck to the cold lake thirty-nine years ago.

Her struggle had turned real, Norman remembered. Turned desperate. But too late. To this day he could not remember actually making the *decision* to do it…to kill her. He only wanted her to shut the fuck up – the one thing she wouldn't do.

It just happened. Without any real forethought. His hand found the sleever bar under the front seat…he grabbed it…and, finally, she was quiet.

Norman knew beyond a doubt that the Donna ghost on stage knew perfectly well he was standing there behind the mirror. Watching her. A skinwalker. A shade of the spirit world. She probably *felt* him there.

Of course she did…this whole act was a charade at his expense! She could easily see him there without actually seeing him. The whole time strutting blatantly under the spotlights, showing her ex-boyfriend and the rest of the audience all that she had. All that she had once been. All that he, Norman, her husband if only for a brief time, had taken from her.

155

No matter her stage name, *Angel*. This Donna on stage was no fucking angel. She was a demon. And she was here to reveal him as a demon, too.

Obviously, she had to die…*again*.

And she had to stay dead this time…

Chapter 22

"Oh, *Baby*! You were a total hit! Knew you would be." Liz said, hugging Angela.

Dragging her into a vacant dressing room stall for a quick nose powdering, she looked her in the eyes, said, "You *felt* it, didn't you? I could tell."

"Felt what?"

"Up there. On stage. The energy. When you connect with the audience. The power of it. You felt it...I could see it in your eyes that you did."

Two tiny white mountains of crystalline powder on a miniature silver spoon disappeared one-after-the-other up Liz's nose. She said, "It's the most powerful thing in the world, sex is. Some gals get it. Some don't. Those that do...watch out!"

Two more tiny mountains disappeared up Angela's nose.

"But *you* watch out too. Cause what I'm talkin 'bout is every bit as much a drug as this stuff. Every bit as sweet. And more addictive for some."

"Yeah. I guess did feel it. Never felt anything like that before."

"I know." Another hug followed, and a kiss, Liz saying, "Now's the time to go out there and put it to work. Time to go make yourself some money, honey. Every man out there has pockets full of cash, and they're all just dying to give it to you.

***

It seemed that here in Goodtime Charlie's darkened den of iniquity on Amateur Night there were no possible violations of taboo. From Hoot's vantage place he had witnessed plenty of activity that would make an honest vice cop squirm – and worse – though none of it was unexpected. It all appeared perfectly normal and commonplace in the seedy thick of this environment. Hoot soon figured that if there actually were any undercover vice cops working the house tonight they were either very well paid off or completely unconscious.

The club's owner-manager remaining incognito behind his wall of one-way glass, the only visible icon of authority in the whole place seemed to be a golden-haired middle-age man dressed in silk and leather who watched the dancers interacting with the customers from a place at the end of the bar. The floor manager, Hoot assumed. A shifty-eyed man; his eyes seemed to be operating on a higher frequency than the rest of his head, his eye movement jerky, blinking constantly, as if his eye sockets were filled with grit. His gritty eyes were apparently tuned to see only if the so-called *ladies drinks* were, or were not, moving at a satisfactory pace. No discernable notice was being paid by the to the multitude of handjobs, blowjobs, and other varieties of illegitimate sex being blatantly bartered on his watch. Whenever a girl was called to the bar to be scolded, the reprimand she received seemed exclusively aimed at stimulating the sale of sparkling cider 'champagne' at ten dollars a glass.

And the customers bought it, gladly paying that price for the privilege of sitting a few minutes with the scantily-clad *lady* of their choice. Cut her from the milling herd and rope her in with a lariat of cash was the name of the game. Let the other cowboys chomp and wait their turn. For a few minutes she would sit with him, fondle him and allow him to fondle her. They would laugh at each other's witticisms. Pretend they could understand half of what they were saying to each other over the deafening volume of the surrounding din. Pretend they gave the smallest shit about what they actually did hear.

Hoot witnessed customers buying all the rest, too. The supposedly legitimate offerings from the club menu; lap dances, table dances, and Texas-style couch dances.

Call it by whatever name you like, it was desperation on the barrelhead. Ten dollars buying a desperate customer a few minutes of experiencing a sordid dancer wiggling between his parted knees – the basic lap dance. Hoot could see that limited touching was often allowed. But not too much touching. That cost extra.

It seemed evident to Hoot that twenty dollars paid for some touching. Depending on the dancer, a customer might slip his fingers inside her panties for a second or two, give the offered nipple a couple of quick licks. Maybe get a fleeting cock-rub from outside the trousers.

Thirty dollars might be enough to encourage the dancer to slip her hand inside the customer's trousers – depending on the dancer, some being considerably more uninhibited than others – and from there on is where it often got messy. Some girls would actually pull a guy's personal business out and rub it against her tits in plain view of neighboring customers. Others would whack the guy off inside his pants, the action looking to Hoot like two squirrels were in there were fighting over a walnut.

Forty dollars was a level that seemed to be skipped, the next increment being fifty dollars. For fifty dollars a guy was pretty much guaranteed that he'd experience an orgasm in a public place, sometimes right out in plain sight, often with a gratis condom magically in place, or sometimes with a dancer's lips wrapped around the working end of his agitated pet python.

And a hundred bucks? Hoot had seen no hundred-dollar bills change hands, but he suspected a few had. And he assumed that for a hundred dollars a customer could get whatever he wanted whether he really wanted it or not.

Hoot witnessed at least three quickie blowjobs from where he sat, the recipients left disheveled and scrambling for their billfolds. And he was pretty certain he'd seen one of the ironworkers engaged in a genuine fuckdance, the girl wiggling and bouncing her bare bottom in his lap while he hung on like a bronco rider determined to get his eight seconds in the saddle. The grunts and atta-boys from the ironworker's companions confirming to Hoot that actual barnyard-style copulation was in fact happening at the next table. *That* was probably a hundred-dollar feat. The Asian man seemed completely stunned by this, muttering, "Oh my! Oh my!" several times.

The song ended and the bronco girl took her money, hastily retreating to the dressing room for a pit stop, the details of which Hoot shuddered to imagine. He looked past the Asian man to see the ironworker slumped against his buddies, an

159

inane grin spreading across his mouth so full of oversized teeth it looked as if the mouth of a cartoon carnivore had been drawn on his face.

What kind of cretin would behave in public like this, Hoot wondered. And he immediately knew the answer – a *horny* cretin. He wasn't so far from the edge of that pit, himself, in spite of his age. All hail Viagra! – having never actually used the drug, he nonetheless thought that if there was a vitamin V vending franchise to be had; this was the place to put it. Make a fortune…

Where the hell is the fuckin owner of this whorehouse? Hoot thought. Disgusted. Losing his sense of humor and what little patience he possessed with it. He was about to call it quits and go flash his credentials at the blinky-eyed man, demand an immediate audience behind the one-way glass and threaten repercussions based on what he had witnessed thus far. But, before he could make his move, none other than the *big hit* of the evening, the winner of the amateur contest, *Angel*, the girl who had reminded Hoot of Donna Messenger appeared at his table.

"Mind if I sit with you a bit?" she asked, looking even more like Donna at close range than she had under the lights on stage.

"Gonna cost me twenty bucks?" Hoot replied.

She laughed. "Maybe. Maybe more if I'm lucky." She laughed again, and the welcome sound of her laughter cut through the noise and muddled air in Goodtime Charlie's and took him by surprise. This could, indeed, be Donna Messenger-Carpenter reincarnated. She even had Donna's laugh, ending in a little hiccup, the laugh he had always thought the most pleasant of all laughs – it sounded genuine, refreshing. *Clear as a glacier stream cutting through a mudflat*, Hoot's father had once described it when Hoot and Donna were kids.

"Actually, I wouldn't mind just sitting a few minutes," she said in her glacier-stream voice, offering a handshake. "My name's Angela. What's yours?"

"Ezra. But everyone calls me Hoot."

"*Hoot?*"

"Yes. I'm Hoot," he repeated, his memory flashing back to when he and Donna were eleven years old and she first gave him that name, declaring him to be the most fun boy she knew – a real hoot she'd said, declaring them boyfriend-and-girlfriend for*ever*.

Hoot almost expected a look of recognition in this girl's eyes. There was none, of course, and he said, "I thought the DJ said your name was *Angel*?"

"He did. But it isn't." She slid in to sit on the bench next to him, almost sitting in his lap, said, "I've noticed you looking at me funny, Hoot. How come?"

Hoot gestured at the hubbub all around, said, "You noticed *one* guy looking at you in the middle of all this? How is that possible?"

Angela reached up and ran her fingers through Hoot's white hair, said, "You're different. You stand out."

"So do you."

"There you go…looking at me funny again. I'm a wee bit high right now and when you look at me that way it makes me feel kinda paranoid."

"Sorry. I can't help it." Hoot's voice soft even in this environment, Angela leaned her head close to his until they were almost sitting together like whispering lovers. She smelled nice. Hoot said, "I think that you are beautiful in a way most of these other girls have long forgotten. You also happen to look remarkably like someone I once knew."

"Yeah? They say everybody looks like somebody else to one degree or another."

"Not like this they don't. Even up close. It's eerie."

"Know what? Some of the other girls think you're a cop."

"No shit?"

"Yep." Nodding with exaggerated discretion toward the ironworker enclave, she leaned even closer to confide, "Somebody said somebody at that table over there said you're a cop."

"Somebody'd have to be pretty silly to pay attention to *any*body at that table."

She laughed again. Hoot loved the sound of that laugh. Would gladly part with twenty dollars just to hear it again.

"So...*are* you a cop?"

"I'm a deputy U.S. Marshal. Special assignment-type. And *this*," gesturing at the scene around him, "isn't really my assignment."

"Meaning you're more like *Marshal Dillon* just visiting from Dodge City than *Cops in Spokane* on duty, I guess."

"You could say that, I suppose."

"Ezra...Marshal Hoot. *Mar*shal Hoot..." She seemed to be rolling the names around in her mouth, like choosing an inexpensive but decent wine, saying, "*Hoot*. That's a fun name. I like it. Okay if I call you Marshal Hoot?"

"Sure," Hoot answered. "You can call me that if you like."

"Maybe I'll call you *Ezz*. I like that name too." She laughed again.

It was Donna's laugh to a tee. Her tone of voice. Her mannerisms. Even allowing for a certain amount of projection due to association, Hoot's imagination coloring-in vague and forgotten details of the real Donna with crayons provided by this Donna so to speak, it was still very unnerving to him. After all, a small but sharp-edged nugget of guilt had always remained stuck in his heart, reminding him that Donna Messenger would still be alive today if he'd only had his head on straight all those long years ago. And now, here she was again...or *seemed* to be, leaning against his shoulder and holding one of his hands in both of hers as if offering him another chance to take care of her, to protect her from danger.

A second chance? Could it be, or was this just a slap to take him down another notch? His imagination working overtime, Hoot so fucksure certain he was getting close to nailing Norman at last...

"Either name works for me if it makes you laugh like that," he answered, said, "You have a nice laugh."

"So, Marshal Hoot...Ezz, you wanna lap dance?"

"Actually, I'm just here to observe."

Donna-Angela laughed again, saying, "That's exactly what I said earlier this afternoon. Before I got drafted." She reached across Hoot and touched the Asian man's hand, asked, "How about your little buddy here? Would you like a lap dance, sir?"

Like Hoot, his neighbor had passed on all offers up till now. This time he said nothing, but beaming with a huge smile, he enthusiastically nodded his head yes.

Angela squirmed across Hoot's lap into the space on the bench seat between them and introduced herself to the Asian gent, saying, "Okay, next song. What would you like? A twenty?"

The Asian man promptly replied, "One hundred please," and produced a single bill to pay in advance.

Angela sucked in a breath of surprise, folded the bill and stuffed it into her small bag, saying, "Alright then. My first hundred-dollar dance."

She looked at Hoot, shrugged her shoulders, smiled, and said, "Who would have guessed?" Then she squirmed and wiggled in her seat, removing her thong panties from under her miniskirt. She tucked the flimsy garment into the Asian man's shirt pocket and he started repeating like a stuck record, "Yes. Yes. Very nice…yes."

When the music started anew Angela stood and began to writhe suggestively between the Asian man's parted knees, turning around and pressing her bare behind against him, reaching back between her legs to feel his growing interest through the fabric of his trousers, his hands becoming suddenly busy under the hem of her skirt.

She turned around to face her customer and climbed into his lap. Straddling his legs. His hands staying busy under her skirt. She looked over at Hoot and locked her eyes on his. Unbuttoning her blouse, she was already sans bra underneath, and the Asian man started kissing and sucking her nipples while constantly murmuring something that was indecipherable to Hoot.

The song was quickly over. The Asian man exclaiming, "Excellent! Excellent! Thank you very much!" he gathered himself up and made a hasty departure from the club.

Angela pulled her blouse together and sat down beside Hoot again, tying her shirttails together under her breasts. She put her head against Hoot's shoulder exactly the way Donna used to – Hoot clearly remembered Donna doing that, a flashback, telling him that he was her anchor, saying she wanted to lash herself to him, saying they would weather the tides together. That was a long time ago. A lifetime ago.

His heart in turmoil, Hoot asked, "He get what he paid for?"

"Guess so. I'm not really sure," Angela answered in Donna's voice. "You mind if I sit here for a little while?" she asked.

"You are *not* Donna," Hoot said, his voice firm, trying not to sound as frustrated by this whole encounter as he felt, trying to resist the vertigo feeling of being dragged backward through time.

"Who is Donna?" Angela asked. Thankfully, sounding a bit less like Donna Messenger to Hoot's ears, now.

Hoot looked at her and saw that the resemblance was still there, still undeniable, but it was not as exact as it had seemed only a moment ago. "The Asian man left with your underwear," he said.

"I know."

So did the other customers sitting nearby. They were casting covert glances and open stares in Angela's direction like a pack of hungry wolves waiting for their prey to step away from its protection. Angela took Hoot's hand and placed it on her thigh, snuggling against him, sitting close and waiting out the wolves.

Hoot didn't mind her closeness – even if he suddenly felt a very unofficial stirring inside his trousers.

***

"You have a picture of this man? What did you say his name is...*Nor*man *Car*penter?" Vincent Petosa asked with a patronizing smile, the scruples of a serpent slithering through tall grass evident in his every gesture. So eager to be helpful.

"I do," Hoot replied, distracted, handing over a thirty-year-old mug shot, the most recent image he had of his old friend. Hoot felt distracted because as soon as he walked into

Vincent Petosa's office he'd felt Norman's lingering presence as strongly as if he were hiding behind the open door.

"Nefarious lookin fella, ain't he?" Vincent Petosa said, handing the photograph back. "Not the sort I would normally associate with, I assure you. Gotta be careful in this business, who your friends are."

"Take another look," Hoot insisted. Having little sympathy for the woes of lowlife business management, he tossed the mug shot into the middle of Vincent P's desk. "The doorman and a couple of the ladies downstairs seemed to think he was here tonight. In fact, Mister Petosa, I suspect that he was right here in your office while I was patiently drinking a five-dollar watered-down coke and having my eardrums split while waiting to see you. Is that true?"

Vincent Petosa stood and turned toward the glass behind his desk. "Why'd you say you are looking for this man, marshal?"

"He's an escapee. Federal. Makes it a hard-time felony to harbor him or help him in any way."

Standing there and looking out over his lowbrow little empire, Hoot knew that Vincent Petosa, the Lord of Idaho Panhandle Smut, was also watching him reflected in the glass. A viper on two legs was the image that came to Hoot's mind.

Hoot drew his cell phone out of his pocket as if it were a .45 Peacemaker, said, "FBI and a whole bus full of marshals can be in your parking lot in less than a half-hour. Want me to give em a call? Invite 'em in?"

"Second thought...I believe that man *was* here earlier," Vincent Petosa said. "He was lookin' for a job, but, he wasn't my type. No references. As I said, a man's gotta be careful, so I sent him away. I sure as hell don't know him." He turned back around toward Hoot, tearing his serpentine eyes away from the ongoing bacchanalia behind the glass and locking them on Hoot's pale blues, arms crossed, he said, "In fact, you just missed him. He left a few minutes ago."

Chapter 23

When Hoot first showed up in Norman's unit in Vietnam, Second Battalion, Company C of the 1st Cavalry Division, it seemed like an unbelievable piece of good luck. And luck is precisely what it was. Certainly no one planned it that way. Army command had already demonstrated to Norman that they were incapable of doing anything sensible like putting two friends who would watch each other's backsides together in the same unit.

"This is too good to be true, my blood-brother," Norman said. "And you the best marksman I've ever seen. We have to get you assigned to LRP, make a sniper out of you right away."

"I don't know. I just got here."

"So did half the other Joes in the jungle. More damned newbie's than leeches in the swamp water around here and more coming in every day. By the way, watch out for those leeches. They're unpleasant. Now, let's go get drunk and you can tell me all about what's happening back home."

It was raining. Hard. Raindrops the size of marbles.

"You wanna go out in *this*?" Hoot said.

"Got a better plan?"

"We could wait until it quits raining and then go."

Norman laughed at his friend, so green, said, "Yeah! That'll be in two weeks and two days – count on it. You do that. Wait. Get yourself an umbrella, too, in case it starts to *really* rain." He turned, still laughing, and said, "You coming or not? *Di di mau* motherfucker! That means hurry the fuck up in the local lingo."

"I wrote you that Donna and I split up," Hoot said at Chan's Place. Cocktails so strong the local rumor was that they caused facial hair to grow between swallows. Guys shooting up heroin in the back room behind a bamboo curtain. Whores smoking opium with GI's.

"Yeah. What's up with that? I thought you and Donna were *it*. Forever."

"So did I. But college just kind of…you know…found us drifting apart."

"*Drifting*?" Norman chided. "Just like a fucking fisherman to talk about *drift*ing away from the best-looking girl in Pleasanton. Hell, in all of Maine, I suspect, if not the entire fucking world. Talking like it was some riptide that did it. Forces beyond your control. Nothing the Hooter could do to stop it."

"That's right…a fisherman drifts…"

"You know what it takes to find an *ugly* girlfriend around here?" Norman sucker-punched his old friend in the gut, holding back, said, "I'll tell you what it takes. Tell you straight – twenty bucks and a penicillin shot."

"I know it's all fucked up," Hoot said. "I'm the one who fucked up. It's weird – I'm still crazy about her. But it wasn't working anymore. College wasn't either. I dropped out."

"So," Norman said behind a knowing smirk, "to get over blowing it with Donna you joined the Army? Came here to be jungle buddies with your trusty old blood-brother? And I always thought you were smart. Man…was I ever wrong – you're a fucking idiot!"

"For joining up? Far as that goes, they were gonna draft me anyhow. Quit school and you lose your deferment – you go to the top of the list. That's how it works."

"I know about all that," Norman said. "This man's army is full of idiots like you. Ask around. Enough heartbroken college dropouts here, you fuckers should form a fraternity of lost boys. Weep into each other's monogrammed hankies."

Norman took a long gulp of *Ba-Moi-Ba* – Tiger Piss '33' beer – and added, "You should have stayed in college, man. Should have got yourself a degree in something – *any*thing. Underwater Basket Weaving magnets-cum-loudly. *Any*thing! Should have found another girlfriend. Should have found two so you'd have a backup."

167

"Thanks," Hoot said sarcastically. "Subtle understanding of the problems of others is evidently not your strong suit…Butthole."

They stayed at Chan's, drinking and talking, pitching bitches the way only two close friends can, while just outside the drafty bamboo walls and ill-fitting windows the monsoon sky kept on dumping bucketfuls.

Somewhere in the middle of all that drinking and talking the pictures rampant in Norman's head started to become three-dimensional. More real than real. And for the first time in his life he felt truly and unconditionally thankful for what he'd had.

The love of good friends. The good times they had shared.

Hoot talking about the love for Donna that he had wasted only encouraged Norman to remember the love he had also felt for her, feeling it more sharply than ever before – the three-way game of cutthroat romance they'd been playing from the start seeming for the first time to have been for keeps rather than merely a tease.

Hoot would talk of Donna and Norman would see her in his mind. Maddening details of her. The way her laugh always ended on an up-note. The way she loved Dr. Pepper and would get the hiccups after drinking one, need to drink another to make them go away. The way her eyebrows changed from light brown at the bridge of her nose to blonde through the arches to clear at the sides. The way her fingers held a pen. Her long legs. The blush in her cheeks…

And then it suddenly quit raining as if someone had shut off the tap.

A breeze came up as they were leaving Chan's, the fresh salty air slicing the fetid air into ribbons and blowing the everyday stink away. It was late, just before curfew, and the breeze suddenly smelled of flowers and spice, jasmine and water-lily.

It smelled clean. Smelled like Donna.

The wind ruffled Norman's hair and he turned his face into it, thinking how much it felt like Donna mussing her fingers through his hair like she had done once before at a spring break picnic – just Donna and him hanging around, Hoot off crewing on a long-liner fishing boat; nothing came of it, but the opportunity had clearly been there. It's just that she was Hoot's girl...then. Norman turned into that breeze, finally accepting that he really did love her. Without holding back, as much as he knew how, Norman Carpenter loved Donna Messenger. After all the years Norman had known Donna and loved her as a friend; finally, without her even being present, only her spirit floating to him on a breath of air coming from the other side of the world, only now did he realize that he truly did *love* her. He always had.

Oh shit, he thought, walking a weaving path between puddles with Hoot, his best friend. Hoot, whose unhappy pale face clearly showed that he knew he'd fucked up when he let her go.

***

Forty-four years later Hoot had not exactly planned for retirement, yet it was coming. It was almost here. In truth, after 'Nam Hoot never really believed he would live long enough to retire. He didn't seem the retiring type.

Hoot was convinced the fact that he didn't die in those sweltering bug-infested jungles was not because of skill, training, simple good luck, or even *fate*. It had been a colossal mistake; one that kept repeating itself – Hoot staying alive against all odds. It seemed that God shook and shook the pan but only fool's gold sparkled in the slurry. Hoot accepted that a mistake of this magnitude was either because of, or likely to cause, some sort of slippage in the fabric of the universe. Possibly a rip. He was pretty sure that his so-called blood-brother, Norman, had played a part in engineering it – he just didn't know exactly how he'd accomplished it.

Bunch of sweat lodge hocus-pocus at work, no doubt, Hoot thought. Probably involving Norman's mother – the one person Hoot was convinced actually did have some influence in the spirit world, this conviction a result of the summer vacation that he spent with Norman and his mother on the rez when they were impressionable boys.

169

Hoot remembered Norman's incessant talk about reality being relative back in their High School days when they would talk endlessly about shit like that. In Vietnam, twisted arguments to support Norman's version of facts would drive Hoot crazy, but after that one sweat lodge experience when they were kids, sitting around as naked as peeled bananas in the sweat lodge with Norman's mom beating her drum, nothing Norman said or did really surprised him. He'd chalk it up to all the pot, opium, acid, and booze that Norman routinely consumed doing the talking, drawing conclusions from coincidental circumstances. But it was nonetheless unnerving when similar incidents happened again and again. It got Hoot to wondering if maybe Norman had inherited something from his mom, after all.

"I spend an awful lot of my chi keeping your backside out of hock," Norman once told Hoot in all seriousness. "Don't be afraid to spend a little extra of yours on mine." This after Norman had been transferred to 4th Air Cav/Medevac. Just before he got shot down – making Hoot feel uncomfortably responsible afterward.

"There is no way we can ever be entirely apart if we're anywhere near each other. So, let's stay near," Norman said, pressing his fist to his own heart and then to Hoot's and adding, "Each beats for both."

Hoot didn't pretend to actually understand how any of Norman's spiritual protection bullshit worked. His was a credo requiring more blind faith than Hoot could muster. But he had to admit that for the most part it seemed both he and Norman were privy to some kind of unreal Twilight Zone existence where enemy bullets didn't fly straight. Didn't keep them from shooting at you – or even hitting you – but made you a slippery target to hit. This wasn't the sort of insurance that Hoot figured a man could bank on, but after living a life where dodging bullets and other potentially fatal calamities had become routine, it was something that inevitably left him curious after the fact.

After 'Nam, after Donna's murder and Norman's conviction, Hoot took it for granted that his run of freakish good luck via *guides* from Norman's spiritual world would peter out through lack of association with his old friend and luck charm. But it didn't. Hoot lost his first partner in a courtroom shootout a year after Norman was sentenced. Didn't suffer so much as a scratch, himself, even though witnesses claimed the shooter had taken aim and fired directly at him. Norman called from Leavenworth the next day to ask if Hoot was okay and said, "Knew you would be." End of conversation.

Hoot and Norman – blood-brothers forever.

Hoot later asked Norman why the infamous *Creeper* had allowed himself to be captured alive. Norman had looked surprised and said; "For *you*, my blood-brother – for us, really.

"*For each and for both. Always.* Remember?

"Don't you get it?" Norman said. "We're connected. I die – you die. And vice-versa. I thought you knew that."

What Hoot knew was that his number had come up plenty of times and somehow he'd stayed in the game, stayed alive.

It seemed that ever since that time in Laos – when he and Norman had truly been up the legendary Shit Creek without a paddle or a prayer of a chance – Hoot had been cashing-in the same Lotto ticket over and over. Winning, for the most part. He had long suspected there was a hidden cost attached to his good fortune. A karmic service fee keeping the account open. Only one way to close it.

But how would he know if it worked?

Chapter 24

Norman's apnea-tormented mind wandered. He was feeling off his kilter from seeing Hoot and the ghost of his dead wife Donna together at Goodtime Charlie's. That just *couldn't* be good...

Twenty-minutes into his drive to his mom's place he pulled the Wonder Wand van off the Interstate and checked in at a motel in the woods of the Idaho panhandle called Pistol City Motor Court. Located on a dead-end service road, it was a throwback to the days before Interstate Highways. Musty individual one-room cabins with tiny bathrooms and unforgiving mattresses. Threadbare carpet and cracked linoleum. Filthy, basically, by Norman's usual finicky standards. But he had been falling asleep at the wheel and didn't think he could drive another mile without driving off the road and killing himself.

Fully-clothed, Norman kicked off his shoes and lay back on the bed, plugged in his C-pap, and strapped the mask on his face. He immediately fell into a fitful sleep, dark images running laps inside his skull without his active participation or permission. Dried scalps pinned to a board in the back of the Wonder Wand van including some fresh ones that had been scraped and cleaned but hadn't quite turned to leather yet. Casey Stark made no appearance, but Donna was in his dreams like she hadn't been in a very long time, running around on exposed nerves wearing nine-inch spikes.

Norman slept late the following morning. He awoke feeling headachy, and was back on the road by midday. His lower back stiff, he soon turned the van off the Interstate, snaking his way north on Highway 200 at Saint Regis after crossing into Montana. The air was clear and crisp, the landscape sharp in every detail. No map was necessary. Norman had driven this route so many times with his uncle Max Feather he could make the trip blindfolded. Passing through Paradise Montana at seventy miles-per-hour with barely a blink, he wondered like he always did when passing through here just who'd been so unbelievably optimistic to name a God-forsaken wide spot in the road like this *Paradise*? He had never bothered to find out. Norman figured his old man would have done something like that. Optimistic son of a bitch that Joseph Carpenter was. Idiot that he was.

Norman remembered how Dad had remained convinced that Mom would forgive him and take him back right up to the day the divorce was final. Then he threw up his hands, packed a duffel bag and an old Samsonite suitcase and headed east. Got as far as he could go without getting wet – as he told it – met Eileen working the register at a convenience store in Pleasanton Maine, and that was that. Said he was happy.

Norman figured his dad's proclamation of happiness had actually pissed Mom off more than his many indiscretions had in the first place. She had wanted him to suffer, and he simply wasn't the suffering kind.

"Never make pain for yourself. There are plenty of others who will do that for you," Joe was fond of saying. "Happiness is your own responsibility," was another favorite.

Come to think of it, the day she found out about Eileen – *the bitch* – and her ex-husband's newfound happiness was the same day that Norman's mother began to consistently call his father by the moniker, *your-father-the-rotten-bastard* as if it were all one word, his true name, and couldn't be said otherwise. "Your-father-the-rotten-bastard can't be bothered to spare a second thought for anyone but himself. Doesn't care *who* he hurts. Treats people like snot rags;" she would say when the venom was in her. Another time she would say; "Your-father-the-rotten-bastard wasn't a *bad* man for the most part. Except, of course, he thought he was such a hot hotdog, couldn't keep his weenie in one bun."

More than I needed to know, Mom, Norman thought.

"And he wasn't cut out for reservation life, either;" she would say when in a forgiving mood, as if those few twisted statements summed up his father's life and somehow made it all make sense.

It didn't – the woman was her own compass.

173

Norman knew that his father hadn't been an especially *bad* man, or a *good* man either, and that was all he needed to know. He turned off Highway 200 onto 28 and headed north toward Camas-Hot Springs. Then, leaving the pavement and putting the hammer all the way down, he cut across the reservation toward Ronan from the west, taking the unpaved caliche road at speeds over seventy miles-per-hour on the downhill and leaving a powdery dust plume hanging for a half-mile behind him.

Driving like a banshee set loose on the high plains, Norman's white van looking like it hadn't seen a carwash in at least two years; he could have been a local – *loco*, anyhow, he chuckled to himself. He cranked up Robbie Robertson on the stereo and let go with two big whoops and an ululating yell that he thought was particularly savage. Even though he'd spent a relatively small portion of his youth around here, he was back home again for whatever that was worth, this wide-open land always having a way of making him feel…free.

At Wild Horse Flats, Norman cut off the main road and drove up a familiar rutted and winding box canyon road all the way to the end. There he parked the van and walked the last quarter-mile to a boxed-in clearing.

A budding naturalist and geology geek long before he became something of a computer geek/professional hit man, Norman had been fascinated by the surrounding hills since he was a kid. Heaved-up slabs of rock cut a jagged silhouette against the indifferent sky. All of it unchanged since long before Norman's time and likely to remain unchanged long after. But forever in flux as well, the land always on the cusp of some dramatic metamorphosis. Forests, rivers, mountains. Ice floes and great seas. All having their influence over time. And mankind having very little.

Standing here, a chill wind blowing up the canyon, Norman reflected on how there were some – mostly older Whites and some Mexicans – who knew about this place and thought it was cursed. They thought it harbored malefic spirits from the ancient world. Most Indians knew better. Norman knew better.

He knew that ancient ancestors of The People had lived on the high plateau more than ten thousand years ago. No doubt that's how old some of the spirits lingering here were, but they were only a few, their presence detected only by the more powerful shamans. Whether these spirits were actually prone to malice or not was debatable.

Norman doubted they were. His mother had often said that she doubted the dead gave much of a shit about the living and Norman shared that sentiment. The living, wrapped up in their superstitions, simply misunderstood the apathy of the dead, thinking they were malicious because how could they *not* care?

Any legitimate shaman was generally uninterested in attempting to contact the truly ancient spirits that loitered in this area. It would be difficult anyhow as the ancients had not lived as *Se'lictcen*, Salish-speaking people.

Those known as *Stlqetkomstcint* people, People of the Wide Water, of Flathead Lake, came much later. Flathead Lake did not even exist in the truly ancient world. That landscape had been a far different one from the landscape of the Se'lictcen, the present-day world that Norman and those of his bloodline knew. His mother had taught him that much, at least. From her he knew about the game that the ancients hunted, the plants and roots that had fed and healed them and the totems that had protected them even though they were long extinct by the Se'lictcen's time, all gone with the Great Ice.

And then the whole face of the land was carved anew. Flathead Lake was left behind by lumbering glaciers and was called by another name then, in its beginning. So those spirits would have little empathy or interest in the ways of the world today.

The spirits you really had to watch out for weren't as old as all that, Norman knew. Mostly they were spirits from the time of trouble with the Whites, and the Crow, and the Blackfoot – and these spirits had lived miserable and bitter lives when they walked the land in their living skins.

There were, of course, more recent spirits having reason to linger and meddle, but even those spirits were not necessarily malefic – they were just restless – with the possible exception of his dead wife, who had never even set foot in this place. Norman had had some experience with a number of those. Enough that he was wary of the spirit of Donna showing up in Spokane like she had. Too close…

Norman's mother had often claimed that he was well protected by his spirit guides. Especially during the time when he was in Vietnam. But Norman's faith in that protection, thin to start with, had grown even more tenuous in those sweltering jungles, his longstanding belief that his father was not actually his father taking ever-firmer root the more he considered it.

Norman was more Sioux than Se'lictcen. He knew this in his heart – it was all the proof he needed that he was not his father's son. Let the bones fall where they will, he thought. This, his new credo.

Norman shivered. It was very cold and still in this ancient box canyon. He was alone but not afraid. The only spirit he might have cause to fear had already manifested herself in the flesh in Spokane, and there she could wait until he was ready to deal with her. He remembered one April nearly fifty years ago, remembered how he, his father, his uncle Max Feather, and a curious old Shaman from the Spokane tribe had sheltered cattle from a freak thunderstorm in this canyon. He had eaten the old shaman's dried peyote and went looking for the entrance to the spirit world that time. Often, during summer forays back here to satisfy his mother's custody rights and responsibilities Uncle Max would bring Norman here, and he always felt himself polarized by the power of these canyon rocks, by the power of the memories that dwelled here.
Norman had seen his first man killed here on one of those long ago visits when he was thirteen-years-old – Charley Allard had pulled a gun and shot James Sparrow dead during a poker game. Allard said Sparrow was cheating, and that was the end of it. There was no police investigation and no one spoke of James Sparrow any more.

Afterward, Norman remembered Uncle Max telling him almost like it was a catechism to be memorized; "You see somebody killed…you kill somebody…you don't talk about it…*ever*. Nobody else needs t' know. Nobody else wants t' know. Take that secret to the grave. Talk about it in the afterlife, if you still feel the urge."

In addition to the peyote, Norman had smoked his first cigarette, his first bowl of weed, and had his first taste of corn-mash moonshine right here in this canyon. He'd helped himself to Candice Mann's virginity here, two other girls before her and one after. All these and countless other rites had occurred in this canyon. He often dreamed of this place. It was the only place on the rez where he felt that he actually belonged.

At the back end of the canyon was a familiar dolmen-like formation consisting of a large flat rock perched atop three smaller rocks. Norman climbed up on top and sat down, rolled a joint and smoked it. Sucking in the smoke, he felt like he was sucking in the whole place – dirt, sky, rock…and memories. The air had a flat metallic whiff to it like snow was coming. Snow was late this year, and when it finally did come he knew it would be in blizzards out of the north and the east. In the old days this place would be crowded with cattle driven here for protection from storms whenever they came, a few cowboys watching over them just in case, watching out for wolves. Times had changed. The wolves had gone away near extinct and then came back again. The cowboys were not coming back.

Finally ready to drive on to his mom's place, Norman walked the path back to the Wonder Wand van, his native spirit lingering a while atop the dolmen after his body had walked away. There are many places in the world where body and spirit may travel by different paths, and for Norman this was one of them.

Driving into town he drove by the old Carpenter homestead only to find that it was gone. It had evidently burned as nothing but the charred foundation remained. Norman slammed on the brakes and skidded to a halt, stared out the van window in disbelief. His first thought was that his mother must have done it. She had always hated that place, couldn't get out of it fast enough after the divorce even though she made a big stink of claiming it in the settlement, another fiery bolt of spite aimed at his father that had missed the mark.

Of course, Norman's father-the-rotten-bastard had already left the house long before his mother did, left it as if it were a ship sinking into the prairie and he'd drown in dirt if he didn't escape as quickly as possible. He left behind virtually everything he owned that wouldn't cram into a single load in his trusty Oldsmobile Eighty-eight, never once looking back, remorse a foreign concept to him.

That's a good trick, Dad, Norman thought. Works for me…

Hell, Norman had nearly burned the place down himself when he was nine years old and set the straw in the barn afire. He had been hiding up in the loft, spying on the neighbor girl in her shower when he burned his fingers and then dropped the match while trying to light a pilfered cigarette. Dad had guessed what was happening and came running out of the kitchen door when he saw Norman sneaking at a trot toward the smoking barn with the garden hose drizzling. Norman's mom came racing out of the house right behind his dad, and while Dad fumbled with the gate latch, Mom cleared it in a single stride like an Olympic high-hurdler and grabbed Norman away from the smoldering building. Later, no one including her could believe she had done it. She was a short woman after all.

Dad saved the horses but lost the barn. Afterward, he took Norman up to Wild Horse Canyon where the spirit guides witnessed him getting the belt lashing of his life followed by his first non-pilfered cigarette. "You see your mother clear that gate?" Norman's father asked, chuckling, flipped open his lighter with his thumb and sparked a flame, held it to the trembling cigarette in Norman's lips. "Goddamned gate's five feet tall and she cleared it by a foot! I swear, she didn't touch that gate…fucking incredible!"

He gave Norman a handkerchief to wipe his tears and blow his nose and showed him how to inhale. Gave him half a pack of Lucky Strikes and his old Zippo lighter to keep for his own.

As if they were old buddies.

As if Norman hadn't just burned down the barn.

It was forgotten. His old man was weird like that.

Much as his mom had hated the old homestead, Norman had liked it. His childhood there had been as good as anyone could expect, especially a quarter-breed Indian kid growing up on the res. Sure, Dad would come home drunk and find an excuse to beat him now and then. But he had usually deserved it. And Mom was always there to make it better.

Mom could make anything better back then, he thought. Except Dad.

Norman walked thru the ruins of the house he'd grown up in until he was twelve years old. Hands in his pockets, hair blowing in the cold breeze, eyeglasses crooked on his face, he looked for what he couldn't see. Looked for what he could only feel. Closed his eyes and could see certain things better than with them open, spirits of things that existed on a plane somewhere beyond static reality. Reality told him nothing was left but a blackened foundation and a few charred timbers, some ash and rubble. Everything else was gone. Still, he looked.

He stood where the long narrow living room had been with the oil-burning furnace that never quite made the house toasty in the wintertime, the black-and-white linoleum floor always ice cold in the tiny kitchen where Mom had cooked meals for twenty or more guests. Four people had lived here; Norman, his mom and dad, and his grandpa before he died.

How did we all fit in such a little place?

It all seemed so small now. As a kid, that house had been the center of his world. And now it was just another ghost. He closed his eyes again and tried to remember how it had looked, where his cluttered room had been, Mom and Dad in the front bedroom, grandpa in the added-on room off the kitchen, the single bathroom in the middle next to his room where he could hear every groan and fart.

He stood where his closet had been. He'd kept his comic book collection here along with a few *Sun Lover* nudist magazines mixed in that he'd sneaked out of his dad's collection. Dad would sneak them back now and then, and then Norman would steal them from his dad again, a little game with unspoken rules they'd played.

The images in his mind blurred together, some were unfocused, and others were easily damaged like pages in an old album, the paper brittle with time. The only image he could make stick was the way the living room had looked for Grandpa's wake. All dark and beautiful and trimmed in black crepe with everyone in the world crowding in to drink and eat and rave about what a good man Grandpa had been…

Liars! Norman thought. His grandfather had been a certified rotten bastard. Everyone knew it, and they said so to Grandpa's face as well as behind his back when he was alive. So, what had all that *he was a good man* shit been about?

Grandpa Colin Carpenter wasn't your everyday, mundane, born-out-of-wedlock bastard. He was a smooth talking, generally untrustworthy, quick tempered, hard drinking, hard fighting, Irish-Catholic asshole of a human being who was genuinely handicapped by his inclination towards blunder, a local character of minor renown who screwed-up just about everything he touched and had a fondness for indigenous women based on the ludicrous notion that they took better care of their men than white women did. Not surprising that his son and grandson were cast in the same mold, Norman thought. A notoriously fractious bunch, the Carpenter men.

They'll tell lies at my funeral, too, Norman thought. Assuming I even have one.

Norman's life had been an especially selfish and secular and violent life. My passing will not come easily, he knew. Nor will it be well marked.

Mostly he didn't care. But sometimes…

Chapter 25

Norman spoke to his mother in softened tones that he reserved for her alone; "Hi, Mom," he said from the last working pay phone he knew of before leaving the main roads, always suspecting cellular to be a direct feed to *The Man*. "I'll see you for dinner."

"Good. I'll make beans and rice with ham hocks. Some fry-bread. I'll invite Susan Klennert, if you like," his mother said.

"No, Mom. Please don't. I'd prefer just us two."

"She still asks about you…you know? She's a nice girl, Norman. *Really* nice."

"She's not a girl. She's past fifty, Mom."

"She's still a girl, and you're still a boy."

"Yeah, Mom," Norman said, thinking: I'm a fucking fugitive. *That's* what I am. I do not have the luxury of an ordinary life like everyone else in your cozy television-addled Reservation world. And the fact that you can't get that simple truth through your thick skull makes you the most dangerous threat I live with. Shouldn't even be talking on the phone to you. In fact, if you weren't my mother I'm sure I would have killed you years ago.

Norman looked out the skuzzy phone booth window at an unfocused panorama. The Reservation, the Bitterroot Mountains like cardboard cutouts on the distant horizon.

"Some other time, maybe," he said.

"Why don't you call Susan while you're here? She hasn't been out with anybody in particular since you took her out. And I can't even remember how long ago that was."

"I just don't want to, Mom."

Norman considered his mother's age – eighty-two – and considered again that the woman's encroaching senility was an incalculable liability. She amused herself with it and thought everyone should go along with the joke. He said, "You know the drill. Anyone asks – and I mean *anyone* – you haven't heard from me…okay?"

The phone was silent in his hand a long second. Could have been an eternity, who was counting? Then his mother, back on her soapbox, asked, "You seeing anyone else, Normie?"

"No, Mom. Did you hear what I just said?"

The phone went silent again, then; "I s'pose you've heard…Carl Blackwater had a stroke last month an 'bout died from it. He's out of the hospital, now. Back home. But he ain't lookin' any better. His speech is slurred and he drools."

"Sorry to hear that," Norman lied. He didn't give the smallest imaginable shit about Carl's stroke. The nutless wonder had it coming far as Norman was concerned. He had known Carl all his life and the man had never once actually admitted the link between them. Just hinted around that he and Norman's mother were *close* – usually dropping hints when under the influence of liquor. Would look at Norman in a funny way as if looking for some resemblance. There was none. Still, he would hang around Norman's mother's place like a raven on a roadside fence post. Carl, ten years younger than Norman's mother, with his wide spaced corn-cob teeth, his bad complexion, and his one eye that didn't look quite straight ahead so you were never sure if he was paying attention to you or catching a glimpse of something else. Carl, as full-blooded a Sioux as could be found in the modern world, *not* Kootenai nor any other tribal branch of the Flathead nation; the man didn't have one drop of Se'lictcen blood in him but played it to the hilt anyhow – living on the Kootenai reservation simply because the Kootenai would take in anyfuckingbody and call them their own. The son of a bitch sat on the Tribal Council for Christsakes!

In his mind Norman could see his mother sitting in her recliner facing the TV. Television always tuned to the weather channel as if a step outside wouldn't tell her everything she needed to know. She would worry about him. Wringing her hands that were becoming more blotchy and wrinkled than ever. Wringing the stubborn gray cells of her shaman's mind until she hit upon some notion about her only child that would

182

put her at ease. And then she would remember some long-forgotten hex that would untangle all the knots.

Norman remembered how *Inez* always said she wanted to be laid to rest with her people in Beaverhead – the Ruby River country. "Let's take a drive while I'm here, Mom," he said.

"Where to?"

"Down to Yellowstone. To Beaverhead."

"Back to my old homestead? Good idea! Wanna invite Carl to come along?"

The drooler? So the two of you can carp on me all the way there about shit I don't care to hear anymore? Norman thought.

"No," he answered, politely. "I think just the two of us would be better."

***

Spring 1963. A man of uncertain age somewhere well into the *old* category told young Norman, "You must say your name and the name of your father. Say it loudly and clearly so the underworld spirit guides will hear you. It's important. Then you can enter The Cave."

Norman was about to turn fourteen years old. He was sitting atop the flat stone dolmen in Wild Horse Flats' Big Butte Canyon with his uncle Max Feather and an old man who was called Red Coyote; they were keeping watch on a small herd of cattle and waiting for a sudden storm that had closed the distant passes to blow over, waiting for the spirits in the canyon to come forth. The old man, dressed in black from head to foot including a big black fedora pulled down over eyes that were shaded by black sunglasses, said he was only passing through. Temporarily delayed. And would not be coming back this way again. He burned sweet-smelling tobacco in his pipe, musky-smelling incense in a clay dish sitting on the rock.

"Spirits living in the rocks told you that you won't be coming back?" Norman asked with a hint of derision in his dubious young voice.

"No. My ticket to Chicago is one-way. That's how I know. People don't seem to like the train too much nowadays – I dunno why. I don't like t'fly – it's unnatural."

"Red Coyote is one of the few male Salish-speaking shamans alive," Max Feather had told Norman's mother before setting off on this impromptu quest with his nephew. "It's our good luck that his train got delayed in Kalispell until the track is cleared. A day, maybe. He'll stay with me and catch the next train. Meantime, he can help with Norman's initiation to the spirit guides," and Norman's mother agreed. Sent them off to the canyon roundup with her blessing. She said she would go into her sweat lodge and beat her drum. Said it was all she could do.

And now the old man sat next to Norman on the dolmen, motionless, perfectly upright and straight-backed, with his ancient hands like Methuselah's neatly folded in his lap. Norman looked him over, trying not to be too obvious, wondering if he was blind.

"No," Red Coyote said.

"Pardon me?"

"No," he repeated. "I'm not blind. You were wondering. I have glaucoma."

Norman glanced over at his uncle who seemed pleased by this small exchange.

"My eyes are sensitive to light," the old shaman said, working his mouth around the words. "It's true that I can't see too well anymore – not with my eyes anyhow – but I'm not entirely blind yet." Leathery lips. Nothing else about him moving, he could have been a Disneyesque animated puppet reciting a fable. "Doesn't matter," he continued. "What you see with your eyes is only half the picture. Know what I mean?"

The canyon floor was dusted with snow. Beyond the protection of the canyon walls the ground was smoothly blanketed in white stretching off to the dark north where chiseled mountains defied the gathering storm. It was 8:30 in the evening, early in April at the dark of the moon. Only halfway through his fasting and Norman was hungry.

There was a flash in the north. A deep rumble in the sky was answered by one in Norman's belly. Rain was coming to wash the thin snow cover away. Or, maybe not. Here on this high plateau the spirits have been known to change their minds in half a heartbeat just because they could – not to fuck with the living; they couldn't care less about the living. Maybe they'd send sleet and hail. Maybe more snow.

"There is no cave here," Norman said, feeling moody, feeling his hunger, feeling *exposed* atop this big flat rock with bad weather coming.

"When you are ready to see the cave, you will," Uncle Max Feather said, tending to their fire, strategically placing green wood on the blaze to make it smoky and add to the mix of heavy aromas already staking a claim in the crisp night air. "Now, pay attention. Red Coyote is a great shaman and you can learn a lot from him."

"My mother is supposedly a great shaman, too," Norman said, feeling like the only doubter in a coven of hocus-pocus drum-pounding true believers. Not to say he didn't believe – he just didn't *believe* like they did. "Why haven't I heard her speak of these things?"

"Your mother is a great *female* shaman. She casts hexes and reads earthsigns. She reads moonsigns. Starsigns. She performs blessings. Drums up curses with the best of 'em," Uncle Max Feather said. "She makes tasty fry bread. Spins yarn. And knits real well.

"*This*" – he opened his arms to encompass the canyon walls, the dolmen, the fire, the milling cattle, the darkening sky and the coming storm – "is *men's* business."

"What if I don't actually know the name of my true father?" Norman asked, shrugging off a hard glance from his mother's brother.

"Then your passage will be difficult," Red Coyote answered. "The way may even be closed to you."

Norman looked at the old man more closely and realized Red Coyote possessed the most *Indian* features he'd ever seen. A massive wedge of nose dominated his face and held the dark sunglasses securely in place above a broad, thin slice of a mouth that looked as if it had been carved with a single chop from a tomahawk. His skin seemed to be all wrinkles laid over more wrinkles, as if he had once been enormous in size and was now deflated.

"I'm a *Spokane*," he said, his voice raspy. "The *tribe*, not the city." He turned his head half toward Norman, smiled broadly with a mouthful of teeth that looked worn down with age but were as white as the nearby snow, and said "My name is Red Coyote, and I've never been to a dentist in my life."

"Glad to meet you, Mister Coyote," Norman said behind the hint of a play-along smile that he was struggling to keep hidden.

"Call me Red," the old shaman said. "Matthew Hole is my given name, but I think *Red Coyote* has a better ring to it for an old Indian shaman. Don't you agree?"

Norman nodded his head, unconcerned if Red could see his reply or not.

"Actually, *Red Coyote* was the name of my grandfather on my mother's side," the old man continued. "Lived to be one-hundred and four years old. Now...that's *old* for an Indian in those days."

Norman thought the man sitting beside him might be that old, himself. It was impossible to guess.

"I'm not three digits yet, but getting closer every year," Red Coyote said, answering Norman's unstated observation. "I'm going to Chicago so some doctors can cut my eyes with a laser beam and try to fix them. Tribe's paying for what the US government won't cover. They want me to go and do this because I'm the tribal shaman. Last of the line on my mother's side. And they want to keep my vision in this world as sharp as in the other for as long as they can."

"Sounds wonderful," Norman said, his stomach growling.

"Got a cave bear inside ya?" Red Coyote asked in a joking tone.

Only thunder answered from the north.

"Don't know if it's such a good idea, sending an old man who's already seen too much in this world to have his eyes fixed," Red Coyote said. "I do know that eyes are unnecessary for seeing dreams, anyhow. And dreams are a shaman's stock-

186

in-trade. I also know that dreams don't lie and reality does. My mother taught me that when I was too little to clean my own damned fish."

"Your mother was a shaman?" Norman asked.

"Yes. As yours is. My mother was a healer and a tribal shaman with knowledge of the spirit realm, just as her father, the *real* Red Coyote, had been a tribal shaman. It passes like that you know – the *gift* – from male to female and back again."

Of course, Norman thought with a pang of long-implanted guilt. He knew all about the *unbroken chain* as his mother called it. The *succession*. His presumed role as her sole heir…

The old man sitting across the smoke from Norman said, "Red Coyote was one of the last of the Great Shamans who learned the ways of the *Puha* before the coming of the Whites. Now, much of the Puha – what most people call God – is confusing to the younger generation. That's because the old stories are always being challenged and changed by those who preach too much about things they don't understand.

"Do *you* understand what I'm telling you? This is all part of your pathway."

The fire smoldered, and Red Coyote drew the smoke to him with his hands, drew it to his face, to his hair, cleansing himself of this world. "Look over there," he said, nodding in the direction of the high peaks to the north. "Beautiful, isn't it? I can't see it so well anymore, but I know it's beautiful."

"I can't see anything. It's dark."

"Yes. That's true. But the sky is purple behind the darkness. The stars burn. Don't look so hard with your eyes and you will see."

Lightning lit the sky again, and rolling thunder followed.

Still looking northward as if seeing into some great far-away distance, Red Coyote said, "There. That direction…other side of those mountains is the place where General Howard's troops finally caught up with the Nez Perces. Where *Hin-mah-too-yah-lat-kekt* – Thunder-Traveling-to-Loftier-Mountain-Heights – the man who was known among the Whites as Chief

Joseph, finally surrendered and brought the Indian Wars in these parts to an end."

He sighed deeply. "That was in 1877."

"Was there a big battle?" Norman asked, his young warrior's blood always ready to boil.

"No. It was a long and terrible campaign, but no battle at the end. Chief Joseph had led his people for thousands of miles, winning skirmishes and evading capture against the best the US Army could send. In the end his people were freezing and hungry, and they thought they were safely across the border in Canada when General Howard's men came upon their camp in those mountains. There was no fight – just sadness."

"I would have put up a fight," Norman said. "A great last stand."

"Big warrior, you betcha," Uncle Max Feather mumbled.

"Cleanse yourself with smoke," Red Coyote said. "Your mother is a great shaman to her people. The Puha is strong in her. That means it's strong in you."

"I get it," Norman said, derisively. "I've heard all this before. The father-to-daughter, mother-to-son business. You're saying I'm in line to be a *shaman*. Great. I've noticed how well Mom has done in that line of work."

Red Coyote turned his weathered face to the fire, said with answering derision in his tone, "I think you may not find your way this night…we will see," his voice seeming to fade as if he were much farther away than just across the fire. From a battered pouch he produced a few coin-size buttons looking like wrinkly dried mushrooms, placed two in Norman's hand, said, "This is peyote. Not a local thing, but shamans everywhere use it.

"Eat the small one first. Then, after you throw it up, eat the larger one.

"These are keys to the cave."

Chapter 26

Thursday morning. God…how Hoot hated to fly! Especially on puddle-jumpers.

Early and still dark, he was at the Spokane airport waiting for a Horner-mandated commuter flight back to Seattle to personally update the senior deputy on his progress and direction. Also to take another firsthand look at the body that was found in the dumpster at his apartment complex, now at the morgue and patiently waiting for him.

Hoot figured he would take another good look at the crime scene while he was there – the one at his apartment complex; even though almost two days old it would still be cordoned-off. He knew the likelihood that anything new would turn up was slim. Slim, but still worth a stop. He could pop into the apartment for a fresh shirt while he was there. A trip to The Westin would be a wasted trip, he knew. As far as Hoot was concerned this whole facetime trip to Seattle at Horner's insistence was a waste of time. Hoot already knew who did it, and where to pick up his trail. What more was there to report? He also knew that even if he got business taken care of and made it back to Spokane by 4:00 PM, Norman's trail would be getting colder while he was away – no criticism of his new partner Leon Marcus intended.

His thoughts interrupted by his cell phone, Hoot answered on the second ring and Agent Peyton's voice was crisp and curt; "We found him," she said. "Your Creeper. If you want to help us apprehend him you'd better tear yourself away from your buttkissing trip and get over here, quick."

Okay…he got the buttkissing jibe, but he wasn't sure he quite got the first part of what Peyton had said. "What do you mean you *found* him?" he asked, his surprise turning profound as her meaning began to come clear. Peyton actually knew where Norman was.

"A task force is assembling at the Holiday Inn, South Hill, and I just got off the phone with your boss, Horner, in

189

Seattle. You can unpucker your lips and thank me later. I sent a car to pick you up."

***

Deputy Leon Marcus was already on site with the Ford Five-hundred when Hoot arrived. Hoot and Marcus exchanged glances as Marcus threw open the trunk of the Ford and handed a standard-issue Kevlar vest to Hoot, then grabbed the weapons case.

Loud enough for the agent who'd driven him from the airport to overhear, Hoot said, "G'morning, partner. How was racquetball with the B-I pussies last night?"

"I killed 'em."

"Glad to hear it."

"How were the titties at Goodtime Charlie's?" Marcus asked in a droll tone, also loud enough for Carlisle, the agent-driver, to overhear.

"Plentiful."

A smile crossed Carlisle's face as he turned and walked away as if giving the two U.S. Marshals extra space to stroke each other's gonads.

"You talked to the club owner?" Marcus said. "Did he mention that he has been renting an apartment to Norman Carpenter, aka *Nathan Cook*? It's in a converted house. Three blocks up the street. Northwest Talent and Entertainment, the club owner's business name, is on the deed."

"No. Matter of fact, he didn't mention it." Hoot said, fastening his bulletproof vest. "Peyton found all this out? How?"

"Lucky break. She put out a routine FBI's Most Wanted flash. Local part-time security cop, who delivers pizza when not pulling security detail, picked up on it and called. Peyton's across the street with him now," Marcus said, nodding toward a pizza joint on the corner where a big turned-off neon sign proclaimed, *Zack's* in a scribbled font. "He's confirming the ID."

"I'll take a lucky break any day I can get one," Hoot said, "But remember…never take good luck for granted. If Creeper actually is there, he'll be dangerous as hell."

"And if he's not there, he'll *still* be dangerous?" Marcus offered.

"You got it…"

***

They reassembled at a forward staging area on Arthur Street. The neighborhood was quiet. Agent Peyton said to Hoot, "I invited you because I'm a generous person, but this is my bust. We do it my way."

"And what way is that?"

"By the book."

"That's reassuring."

Agent Peyton flashed Hoot a hard glance, said, "The pizza-delivering security cop said he delivers to our guy all the time. The way he describes the front stairwell, it's a duck shoot. But he says it's the only entrance to the guy's apartment on the upper floor. Back entrance only goes to the lower floor.

"SWAT has the lead," she said. "They'll take video surveys, then gas the place and go in the front, more SWAT and city police covering the fire escape and the back window just in case. Two plainclothes agents are going door-to-door up the street posing as Jehovah's Witnesses. They'll check out the lower floor and basement and get any civilians out. Then SWAT goes up the stairs…"

Marcus asked, "Where do you want us?"

"Anywhere out of the way," Donna Peyton said.

"You take a position in the front," Hoot told Marcus after the Bosslady was out of earshot. Chambering rounds in his Baretta and the Glock 19; he looked up the street, a fragile scene of peace and quiet. "I'm going around back. Keep one eye on those dormers, the casement windows, too. The fucker used to be pretty spry back in the day. Not shy about close work. If you see Creeper come out…you shoot him. Don't warn him or even attempt to Miranda him. Just shoot him.

191

Assume he has body armor, so shoot him in the ass or leg if possible, in the head if he won't show his ass."

An hour later Hoot was thinking this bust was on the verge of taking forever. Must be lots of paperwork and union-mandated coffee breaks to deal with when you do it *by the book*, he thought.

Time had always seemed to grind along for him whenever someone else was calling the shots. Hoot had always been one to nudge things along. He forced himself to relax, stayed focused on the back of the house, a single window up under the eave, fire escape ladder fastened next to it. Below was a huge hulking boat propped on a rusting trailer and a pink Caddy almost as large as the boat.

SWAT and police taking positions, the show was finally beginning when, with a tingling sensation up his spine, it occurred to Hoot that something was wrong…very wrong. He heard Point One's whispered report on his headset, "Vid snake showing nobody inside. I see lots of low doors under the eaves – possible hiding places. Bed's made. I see part of the kitchen. Doesn't look like anyone's home," and Hoot realized that he already knew all this. He knew that if Norman had been this close he would have *felt* his presence. He would have known without a doubt that Norman was there, would have seen him in his mind's eye the same way he saw him in the Laotian jungle – in that creepy, spiritually-connected corner of his mind that he and Norman had shared ever since they pressed their freshly-sliced teenaged palms together and pledged themselves to be blood-brothers for the rest of their lives.

"See if you can pick the lock," SWAT Leader replied.
"Copy that. We're on it…"
Don't, Hoot thought.
Norman had never been fond of booby traps. But something simple…
A string tied to a stick?
There was *some*thing.
It was just a feeling he had.
But it was getting stronger. Something Hoot could almost see…

"The lock is a no-go," Point One said. "Bringing up the doorbuster."

There was definitely *something*…

"Wait!" Hoot said, but his mic wasn't keyed.

"*WAIT!!*" he repeated.

And then, ***BLAM-BLAM!***

The sound of exploding grenades filled the whole neighborhood.

WOOSH-BLAM! A larger secondary explosion caused by the natural gas line to the house knocked Hoot off his feet with a deafening concussion, and in the space of a few heartbeats the whole house burst into a total inferno.

Everything…gone.

Chapter 27

The day was growing colder. Snowflakes were starting to fall and they were sticking.

Angela stood amidst a veritable lightshow of emergency vehicles. Red and blue lights flashing, reflecting off nearby window glass and looking almost merry in the falling snow. Two-way radios were jabbering. Men wearing serious expressions were moving with serious intent. She overheard that two SWAT members had been killed in the explosion. Others were hurt.

SWAT, she thought. Killed? Why were SWAT members in our house?

Shocked and wondering if the two plainclothes agents who'd rushed Liz and her away from the house were among those hurt, Angela was bundled in her trench coat, sneakers on her feet, and wrapped in a blanket provided by the paramedic who'd pronounced her unharmed. She watched from behind a barricade up the block as what was left of the house on Arthur Street collapsed in flames halfway up the block. A billowing cloud of smoke, rising, was absorbed into lowering clouds.

Liz stood next to Angela in a borrowed policeman's coat. She was rigid except for shivering, her stance awkwardly unnatural, as if she had been impaled through the gut and would retch if she only could. Her lower lip was trembling, and twin rivers of tears ran down her cheeks.

"How can they be so sure Emilio wasn't in there," Liz asked, her voice cracking. "Everything happened so fast. He could've been in there."

"The police said everyone was out. Said they got everyone out," Angela replied.

Several moments of cold silence ensued, and then Liz said, "Everything I owned was in that house." Turning away. Looking as if she was ready to go ahead and retch, and then turning back. Her bloodshot eyes practically glowing.

"Everything worth a fuck since I was twelve years old. Everything that made me feel...*good*. All gone in a single freak explosion. Gone! I can't *believe* it!"

She dug the fingers of her free hand through her short blonde hair as if searching the surface of her skull for a nonexistent spot that didn't ache. A switch that would turn the nightmare off.

"How? *Why*?" she said. Repeating, "How? *Why*?"

Hoot saw them standing there and walked over to Angela. "I recognize you and your friend. From Goodtime Charlie's. Amateur Night," he said. "You were the big winner."

His white hair singed, his pale nose and cheeks looking scorched and sporting an assortment of small scrapes and cuts, she realized he must have been very close to the blast. She answered, "Yeah...I remember you. You had me confused with someone else."

"You *do* look an awful lot like her," Hoot said. "Maybe a little less so in these circumstances. Are either of you hurt?"

Angela shook her head. Returning her attention to Liz, her heart was torn with ache for her friend's loss. They were obviously lucky to have escaped with their lives. Lucky that Emilio must've left town early for the holidays, but still...

"You ladies lived in the house where Norman Carpenter lived?" Hoot asked.

"Who?"

"Norman Carpenter. How about *Nathan Cook*? Does that name ring a bell? Your upstairs neighbor. It seems apparent that he booby trapped his apartment."

Liz jerked as if she'd just received a static shock. "Are you suggesting that Nathan Cook is the one who blew up our house? That fucking *freak* living upstairs?"

Her breath was steaming. The collar was up on the policeman's coat she wore.

"So it wasn't like the cops *accidently* did this – blew the gas main chasing some nosey neighbor's *Drug Hotspot* tip," she muttered, and then said. "You're telling me it was Nathan fucking Cook who torched my entire life...lousy as it was?"

195

"I'd appreciate it if you didn't tell anyone you heard this from me, but, yes…I'm afraid it does appear that Mister *Cook* booby trapped his own apartment," Hoot said.

"I'll kill him!" Liz announced. "I swear I will – I'll castrate him and pour lye up the bloody hole where his nuts used to hang!"

A twinkle of amusement in his eye at the imagery contained in Liz's statement, Hoot said in a soft and soothing tone; "I'm very sorry. Please, let me introduce myself. I'm Deputy U.S. Marshal Ezra Hooten, and I need to ask both of you a few questions." He showed his marshal's badge and said, "The FBI will also have questions. And the local police. Perhaps we could do this in the FBI office downtown where it's much warmer?"

***

Norman slept in fits when he slept at all, and his dreams had become surreal. Good dreams where he lived a different life and was a good man. And bad dreams where very bad things happened. Pervasive, Norman's dreams had become tactile and all-enveloping since his return stateside from 'Nam. Sometimes it seemed to him that much of his life was actually lived there in an alternate dreamworld reality – a place possessing every bit as much substance as the physical world. Smells. Tastes. Heat and Cold. Good and Bad.

He even had dreams there in that alternate dreamworld – these were dreams *inside* his dreams – and those dreams were often nightmarish. Most of Norman's scary dreams were just irritating, closet-variety nightmares, being chased by something, or chasing something. Ordinary stuff. Other times they were much more obtuse. Frightening and real in the extreme.

But, bad as they often were, the dreams usually didn't bother Norman too much. Not really. He was accustomed to nightmares – had been having them all his life. But those awful dreams inside of dreams were more disturbing than the others because they seemed to contain important messages that he couldn't quite understand. And he would continue to be bothered by them long after waking, kicking his own ass trying to figure them out.

They were premonitions, he knew. Signs and warnings from the spiritual realm.

Long ago, when Norman was too young to sport a single pubic hair – much less have a meaningful opinion of his own – his mother and her whole damned tribe of drum-pounding kin had made him very aware of the pertinence of premonitions. And the ones he'd been getting recently were sure as hell not good ones; he was on fire in many of them, burning to death. Eaten alive in some. More recently they were full of grisly details of the life that he had actually lived – and would sooner forget if he could.

But he couldn't. Forgetting was a blessing long beyond his reach.

Used to be that Donna would soothe him. At first, when they were still new. She'd never been able to make him forget, but she could distract him. Keep him from surrendering too easily to the dark side.

This was before he wore her down, as she put it. Before she decided the fix was too short-lived, and exposure to Norman's dark side too unsettling.

He was not making the effort necessary to "work through this," she complained.

What the fuck did she know about the effort he was making?

These ominous nightmares haunted a new and shiny alter-ego Norman that was an entirely different personality from the tarnished original-issue Norman. This new version was an unscarred Norman. Confident. Happy. Eloquent. And most importantly, a *good* man – someone he truly yearned to be.

But, in spite of the appealing attributes possessed by the new and shiny Norman, the original issue Norman remained untrusting of the way this new manifestation would slip away without warning into a dreamworld reality. Original Norman didn't care for all that unannounced departure business one bit. He found the experience infuriating even if it did tickle his curiosity from time to time. Even if he suspected this new

197

alter-ego was an organic sweat lodge Trojan planted by Inez Feather or her cohort Red Coyote, some kind of benign Other World fail-safe mechanism protecting him from himself.

The Norman Carpenter who rode the chopper away from the Laotian border with Hoot in 1969 was the first fully-realized manifestation of this new alter-ego Norman that he could remember, the *good* man nudging the *tainted* man aside – aided more than a little, perhaps, by a raging fever from infection and a couple good stabs of morphine.

What Hoot and the chopper crew did not realize was that the original-issue Norman had lingered behind. Blood on his hands, fire in his eyes, watching the VC advance and waiting for the kill. Original Norman staying to count coup, he would catch up later.

It was almost a year later that Norman got fragged and burned during a dustoff in a hot zone. And it was during his recuperation from those injuries that he truly crossed the line into the realm of severe sleep apnea, although it wasn't commonly called that back then.

Hypersomnolent Syndrome what the Army doctors labeled it; Norman's troublesome dreams an unfortunate side effect – linked, he knew, to his mother's sweat lodge and the Other World beyond the cave. This was knowledge best not shared with his doctors, he figured. They'd toss it aside, anyhow, doctors saying that nothing could be done and then moving on to the next patient.

Surgeons eventually – in the course of three separate surgeries – picked enough shrapnel bits from Norman's face, neck, and chest to fill a candy dish, leaving behind a clusterfuck of internal scar tissue and perforated cartilage. Messed up his airway. So, in addition to losing some teeth and gaining scars both inside and out from his adventures in US Army Huey gunships – officially labeled HU *Iroquois*. Appropriately, Norman thought, the Iroquois tribe being almost as big a bunch of pussies as the Kootenai – he developed a world-class snore, something else that Donna quickly lost patience with.

As for Norman's feelings about his ever-increasing sleep apnea and the sideshow of bothersome dreams that came with it…it sucked – *except* one interesting side-effect was that it seemed to be holding the entrance to the Other World open. Impossible to control, but always open. The Other World was a compelling oasis to him. With an always open door it was irresistible, yet potentially very frightening.

He grew especially wary of the *waking* experiences that started happening more and more frequently just before the wedding, his and Donna's. These were the not-asleep non-dreams, when – while in an otherwise perfectly normal waking state – he would feel his heart skip a beat or two, feel a python-like constriction welling up from somewhere deep inside. Unable to take a breath, his pulse would gradually become suspended, his whole head feeling like a cauldron full of hot blood with nowhere to go.

That's when he would sometimes find himself playing a role in an alternate reality – a waking phenomenon that was theatrical as all hell, he would feel as if he'd just burst forth onto a stage already set with a scene that had begun without him and he had to improvise to find his place in a mad rush.

It was especially unsettling to Norman that he could spend hours or even days in this other reality and return to find that only a few moments had passed in the physical plane – in the actual real world. Any nearby witness in the real world when one of these events occurred would inevitably be gawking at him like he might explode, Norman not even realizing what had happened until after he snapped with a jolt back into his own true self.

He would be momentarily confused. Angry to realize the experience he'd just had was not real. That there was nothing he could do to make it real.

Donna was worried about him, obviously and vociferously, but she seemed to accept this new development as expected in his case, setting up yet another appointment for him with yet another specialist at Togus VA hospital near Augusta Maine. Togus, the oldest veterans' facility in the country, where everyone seemed content to label Norman's condition a manifestation of 'shell shock,' Norman keeping the likelihood of Other World influences to himself – secret, even from Donna.

Poor Donna. If she ever did truly love him, Norman had never honestly understood why. But he knew that she couldn't help him. Not really. And that frustrated her. It quickly became clear to him that she loved the new version, the alter-ego Norman, far more than she loved the original real deal, even if the real deal appealed to her wilder, more uninhibited side.

The wedge between Norman's obviously split personalities growing ever wider, Donna was confused. Norman didn't blame her for that. How could she even know which version of her husband she was dealing with at any given moment?

She couldn't. He seldom knew himself.

What Norman knew deep down was that Donna shouldn't have let Hoot go. He'd always known this. They were perfect for each other, Donna and Hoot. And Norman knew that Donna was no quitter. Just look at how she has put up with me these last months, he thought. But she had let Hoot go, anyhow. Maybe it was because she'd been so quick to turn Hoot loose that she seemed so determined to stick by Norman.

Donna, always the good girl, meeting him in Hawaii when the Army sent him there for surgery and convalescence.

Donna, driving him all the way from Pleasanton to Togus every six weeks after his medical discharge. Waiting for him, and driving him back to Togus. Again and again.

Donna, leading him upstairs to her bedroom, her parents away for the weekend. He remembered turning out the light and she turned it back on, saying she wanted to see his scars, saying she wanted to *relate*.

Donna, so full of shit. So wound up in romance. She went to Acadia National Park with him. Camping out. Helping him launch the canoe. Saying yes to his marriage proposal their first trip there.

She hadn't helped him launch the canoe that last time, though.

She was tied up that time. And unconscious. And still beautiful.

Until she started to struggle.

Donna once told Norman that it seemed she had known him her whole life and yet hardly knew him at all.

That much was true. She didn't *know* him.

***

It was the spring of 1972. Norman, still struggling with life in the Real World, observed that '72 was turning into The Year of Plentiful Dope for everyone living anywhere near a college campus or a truck stop – cocaine and smack creeping into every neighborhood on the cheap. Donna, wearing her new mantle of marriage like a cloak that dragged in the dirt a bit but looked great on her anyhow, was also quickly turning into the quintessential tagalong hippy. She read *Rolling Stone* as if every word was gospel, and enjoyed portraying herself as a freethinking peacenik high on having a handle on the politics of the day.

Norman didn't think she really gave a big shit about politics. The war had turned boring to her but made for good conversation as long as the accompanying music was pertinent and loud.

Norman understood that Donna was possessed by a demon – one thing they had in common. But unlike his bloodlustful alter-ego, Donna's inner demon was a playful devil and a bit perverted, ever-eager to ensure she purged her guilt for being born white and middle-class, a privileged American female. She did this by debasing herself with sexual extravagance.

She seemed to think Norman was the perfect hubby for that side of her. Norman a half-breed ethnic from a broken home, an emotionally and physically scarred victim of Imperialist hostility, he had a big dick and an insatiable appetite. A veteran of the *Conflict*, he had genuine scars to prove it.

Submissive slave girl was Donna's favorite game.

Norman's too. As long as they were the only two playing.

They say war changes people. In Norman's case it had created a whole other personality, a doppelganger of sorts, a smiling puppet always happy to put on a benign act while the real Norman slithered around backstage, wrecking havoc. Turned out that this was a useful trick. Donna seemed to love it – what she knew of it in the beginning; loved the way one version of him was perfectly geeky in mixed company while the other version was ever ready to tie her up and choke her when she started to climax.

Rough enough with her to excite her secret demon.

Rough enough to add a dash of real fear to the mix.

Play it to the hilt in private and on special occasions away from home – and take pictures to boot.

This was a side of Donna that Norman had not known existed before he came home from Vietnam. A side that he was certain Hoot knew nothing about.

No one knew about it at first – only Norman. And then, later, those lucky bastards she started picking up in art bars, art galleries, at concerts and poetry readings, right off the fucking street. Bringing them home to introduce them to her master and goading them into asking his permission to use her.

Use her? Now there's an oxymoron for you…

"You've changed," Donna told Norman when she came to see him in Hawaii, and he thought, how's that for overstating the obvious? "Don't worry. I understand," she said. "It's inevitable, after what you've been through." *Understanding Your Burden* a role she loved to play almost as much as her newfound uninhibited sex games. "I've changed, too."

"Yes. You've changed, alright," he agreed after she brought him home to Maine.

Told her again the day he set her free in the waters of Eagle Lake.

No changing back once the beast was loose. Not for either of them.

Chapter 28

Hoot was grouchy because he had yet to find the perfect breakfast spot in Spokane. Ideally, it would be a long-established joint possessing a dignified degree of balance between greasy-spoon hole-in-the-wall and fine cuisine. Anything better or lesser gave him gas. He was doubly grouchy because it was 4:30 AM and he was back at the Spokane airport for another earlybird hop to Seattle that he didn't have the time for, Horner's facetime caveat quickly turning into a regular gig.

"We work in a cesspool, Marcus," Hoot said to his partner over runny grits, limp bacon, and overcooked eggs at The Landing Strip, the only airport eatery open at this ungodly hour. A significant bout of indigestion was on a flight path to land shortly after Hoot's commuter hop touched down at SeaTac, no doubt. "And we get some on us," he said. "Can't help it. Every time we move around we stir it up. And we sink a little deeper into it. The bosses constantly stir it up, and we sink even deeper into it. The bad guys stir it up, and down we go again. Suffocating in filth, that's what we're doing..."

Marcus, apparently content with his biscuit and dab of jam and ignoring Hoot's rant, said, "You don't think splitting up is a good idea?"

"No, I don't. But under the circumstances it's not a bad one, either. Divide and conquer. Might as well since it looks like we're the only two marshals available to hound-dog this case – unofficially in our spare time, no less – local marshals spread so thin. I have no choice but to spend another half day back in Seattle at the senior marshal's request – reporting on our unofficial progress – while Creeper's trail turns cold under our noses right here. I've already asked Horner for more help and he told me to take it up with Bosslady Peyton. Said he's keeping his nose out of it until we have a confirmed sighting of 'my old buddy' as he put it. I told him we need *marshals* and reminded him that Peyton shot her wad already at the Arthur

Street house. I'll ask again while I'm in Seattle. Meanwhile, Peyton will give us Carlisle to help with surveillance for a few days."

"Is Carlisle supposed to be a token gesture to the U.S. Marshals Service? We get a *token* from Peyton?"

"Doesn't matter. I know Norman and we'll get him. In the end he'll come to us."

What Hoot wanted to do was return to Goodtime Charlie's. Hoot knew that Angela would be irresistible to Norman, as she was to Hoot, and that would put her in danger. He recalled she told him that she planned to work the rest of the week for the money, then move on to…where? At the very least, Hoot knew that he would need to keep an eye on her. Maybe she could be encouraged to move on sooner instead of later. That would be best as Hoot knew it was too late to set up a ruse suggesting that she'd perished in the blast and fire at the apartment house.

Hoot didn't believe in coincidences. Certainly not the coincidence of Angela showing up and looking like Donna the way she did. Ethereal forces at work? One of Hoot's nearly-invisible eyebrows shot up at the very idea. He was no more a believer in sweat lodge magic than he was the New Testament. But I'm not precisely a *disbeliever*, either, he thought. I do believe that life is essentially self-leveling; I've just never been one to give spiritual entities all the credit for it. A follower of instinct; a hound dog, that's what I am. And it was because of Angela that Hoot's instinct was telling him Spokane was the place where Norman would stick his head up again. With her unreal resemblance to Donna, she just about guaranteed it.

The best ambushes are the ones the target willingly enters into – as every sniper knows, and Hoot knew that Goodtime Charlie's was exactly the place where he should be waiting and ready. But for how long? His resources were limited, so adequate surveillance of the situation was impossible. First and foremost, he had to somehow protect Angela while using her as bait to attract Norman – a thought that clenched his gut enough to send him diving for antacid tablets just like in the old days.

His grits turned more and more unappealing as they turned cold. Hoot turned away from the food, thinking that he knew exactly where Norman had gone. To his mother's place in Montana, if he had gone anywhere at all. If that was true, there was no telling how long he might stay there or where he may go next. Norman *could* vanish without a trace in ten different directions from the reservation, across endless backcountry he had traversed every which way since he was a toddler. Hoot didn't think Norman *would* vanish – not this time. Nonetheless, that angle needed to be covered as soon as possible; hence Marcus was heading to Montana on the next flight after Hoot's.

Marcus on horseback? Watching his plane taxi toward the terminal, Hoot was having trouble wrapping his imagination around that image.

***

It was big country, Montana. Too damned big to stake out. And Hoot's visit a year ago to question Norman's mother on the Flathead reservation had proven fruitless and frustrating. The woman was as stubborn as stone, insisting that he sit naked with her in her sweat lodge.

Yeah…*sure*, he thought, remembering her toothy smile when she said, "You wanna talk 'bout my boy, Norman? Come sweat with me an we'll talk."

"I'm afraid this is more of an official visit," Hoot had said.

"Don't worry. I already seen your weenie. That time when you an Normie was boys. Remember? Normie's was a lot bigger 'n yours."

"Thank you for remembering," Hoot recalled replying.

He had no problem passing a visit to Inez Feather off to Marcus. Spend a day. Two if necessary. Talk to the old woman and look for any sign of Norman. Marcus volunteered to go alone.

Hoot didn't mention the sweat lodge to Marcus. Sent him off, saying; "The old lady may seem senile, but don't believe it. Call her a backstabbing Injun and she'll think you're

205

flirting with her. Last time I saw her I left thinking that I was a little too *white* for her taste." He smiled, said, "You shouldn't have that problem."

"Don't worry. I'll keep my guard up."

"You can trust the tribal police," Hoot said. "They're good. And don't forget, Creeper was a sniper – just because he prefers to count coup doesn't mean he won't take you down from a quarter-mile away, you give him the chance. You see any sign of him, even a hint...*call* me."

***

Using Angela as bait was distasteful. Nevertheless, Hoot knew she would be a powerful magnet, his best shot to nab the Creeper. Assuming Norman saw the resemblance Angela had to Donna Messenger – and he *must* see it – he would feel every bit as drawn to her as Hoot was. Probably feel it even more since he had killed Donna with his bare hands, clubbing and drowning and choking the life out of an innocent young woman who'd treated him far better than he deserved.

That close, in the heat of the moment, Norman would certainly believe that a good-size piece of her life force would've become caught up in his – *the soul's last effort to save itself,* he called it. The whole point behind counting coup was to increase your life force. If Norman didn't take certain hexing measures right away – measures that his mother would've taught him but he might not have wholly embraced – then a bit of Donna's essence would live in him, and it might be his undoing.

It doesn't matter that I have doubts about Angela being Donna's ghost, her *skinwalker* as Norman would call her. Doesn't matter that I have doubts about Inez Feather's brand of Kootenai hocus-pocus, Hoot thought. It only matters that Norman believes. And he does. He always has...

"We become the fears we conquer," Hoot remembered Norman telling him when he was half delirious with fever from a punji stake infection, loss of blood, and a mild overdose of morphine.

He'd had a feral look in his eyes then.

That was the beginning, Hoot thought. Right there.

If I had only paid attention. I could have easily left him there – the VC would've had themselves a grand ol' time with the infamous *Creeper*.

Or *could* I have?

Hoot knew Norman's superstitious mind well enough to know that he would see Angela as some kind of messenger from the spirit world, a rebuke from disapproving ancestors, a rebuke that he would have to deal with or risk being haunted for the rest of this life *and* the next. That's why Hoot knew Norman would come.

And he would come to kill.

***

It was because Hoot had not been there for Donna when she needed him most that he didn't dare leave Angela unprotected for a minute while Norman's whereabouts were unknown. So here he was at eight o'clock in the evening after a damned long day to Seattle and back, entering Goodtime Charlie's den of iniquity once more, taking a couple of shots of Glenlivet before getting out of the car to steady the hand. Peyton's man, Carlisle, on stakeout across the street, said there had been no sign of Creeper since he came on duty before noon when the place opened.

A quick chat with the doorman confirmed Hoot's suspicion that Vincent P was long gone. "Away from Spokane until after the holidays," the muscular lump had confided.

The slimy fucker, Hoot thought. Vincent P had lied to him about Norman and Hoot was eager to set that little faux pas straight. Maybe next time.

Hoot wondered how much hurt he would have to put on Vincent P to compel him to reveal where Norman was hiding now that his apartment building was a smudge in the snow. Find out if Vincent owned or knew of other convenient apartment houses where his pal could hole up. Maybe he could use Mister P to reel Norman in instead of putting the girl at risk.

Sure. And maybe Hoot was hoping Norman would simply show up here, walk in, walk over, and say; "Take me away old friend. Arrest me…you win."

Hoot knew better. Knew that the girl, Angela, was going to need some close surveillance. Some genuine protection…

And there she was, now, just going on stage. Dancing to an older song that Hoot recognized; *Emotional Landslide*, by Garbage, Shirley Manson urging her on in her sex-fueled voice.

Yes. Angela definitely needed some close surveillance.

And Hoot was just the man for the job.

Good work, Marshal Hooten, keep it up! Hoot's imagination chided him in Special Agent in Charge Peyton's testosterone-challenged voice.

Keeping it up just fine, Bosslady, he thought, settling into a seat along Goodtime Charlie's back wall. He ordered a Coke, looking around the waitress at the living apparition up on the stage. "Go, baby go!" he whispered.

Watching Angela on stage was like watching a sweet dream unfold. Dancing in the spotlight, she was soon to be completely naked – that was the promise. And soon enough, it was fulfilled – Angela…naked. She was very touchable-looking. She was even barefoot this time. No platform ho-heels for her. Very little makeup. She was perfect. And she looked more like Donna Messenger at age eighteen than would even seem possible.

Hoot caught his mind thinking how perfect it would be to take Angela home. How easy. Let her curl up and take a nap in his arms. Turn the clock back to 1968 and dream that he'd stayed at U of M with Donna instead of going off to Vietnam.

She had been so touchable, Donna. He had been completely insane to leave her.

Touchable. Yeah, that's the key, Hoot thought, tearing his eyes off the naked young woman on stage and bringing himself back to the here and now. The problem with most entertainment of the *adult* type – other than the criminal expense of it – was that the girls just didn't look touchable. At

208

least not in a way that wouldn't give you the heebie-jeebies if you got right down to the reality of it.

The club was nearly empty, fifteen customers and eight girls that he had seen including Angela and her roomie, Liz. Angela came over to his table after her set on stage," said, "Back again, Marshal Hoot?"

Dancers were only using the back stage tonight. Each girl would do two songs on the back stage and then work the floor – some of them obviously bored, others resentful at having to work such a slim house. Very few lap dances being bought. Hoot knew these women paid a house fee and didn't turn a profit until they sold their third or fourth dance. He wondered why they stayed when there were so many empty seats.

"Have to," Angela told him. "If you miss your assigned shift you pay *double* the house fee as a fine. That girl just going on stage, Missy, told me she usually lets her fines hit three-twenty – that's only a couple of misses – then she gives the manager a blowjob to negotiate the bill. Said she was thinking about skipping out tonight, but Stanley already had one blowjob this morning and he wouldn't barter, so she has to stay and work. That's why she looks so pissed. I bet she won't even take off her top."

Angela slid her hand under Hoot's shirt. "How about you, marshal? Wanna dance?"

"Wanna sit?"

"Sure. For a minute. But you've got to buy at least one dance."

"I'm sorry about what happened at the house on Arthur Street. How is your roommate doing?"

"Better…I guess. I honestly don't know her well enough to tell for sure. It's horrible, what happened. And Liz was devastated by the loss of all her artwork. But she's tough. She'll bounce back. Right now she's mad instead of sad. If Nathan Cook walked in the door this minute she'd kill him with her bare hands, I'm sure."

"I understand. In fact, that's what I want to talk to you about. You remember I told you Nathan's real name is

Norman…Norman Carpenter, and I've been chasing him for a long time?"

"Yeah. You said he's a bad guy. But we told you everything we know about him yesterday. At least Liz did. I don't know him at all."

"Be glad that you don't. He's a very bad person." Hoot pushed a note pad toward her, said, "Write the address where you and Liz are staying and I'll do what I can to keep an eye out the next few days. Just in case."

"In case he comes back? Why would he?"

Hoot glanced over the top of his polarized glasses and said with some concern; "You're a sweet girl, Angela. I'm surprised you've hung in here at the club the way you have."

"Maybe I'm not really so sweet. I'm not really a *girl*, anyhow – I'm a mother of two. It's all in the report we gave."

"I know. You said you left your kids with your sister-in-law?"

"That's true. I call them every day."

"Why don't you just go home to them?"

Angela scowled.

"Has your husband been…*aggressive*, Miz Hunter?" Hoot asked.

Blushing, Angela said, "Soon as I can, I'll be back for my kids. We'll work it out. But right now I'm a stripper and that's not what they need."

"You recall how I told you that you resemble someone I used to know? Norman Carpenter used to know her too. In fact, he was married to her."

All this was much harder for Hoot to put into words than he expected. This girl, Angela Hunter, looking so very much like Donna Messenger. Looking at him with Donna's trusting eyes. The same trusting eyes that would have looked at Norman, unwilling to believe he was killing her.

"Her name was Donna," Hoot said, "and Norman murdered her."

Startled, Angela said nothing for a moment, and then she said, "You really think she looked a lot like me, his wife that he murdered?"

"She looked *exactly* like you. Moved the way you move. Sounded like you sound. Even laughed the way you laugh. It's…unsettling."

"You knew her?"

Hoot nodded and looked away. "Yes. I did."

"So what are trying to tell me, Marshal Hoot?"

"I'm telling you that Norman Carpenter is a very superstitious man as well as a very violent one. I'm afraid he may see you as some sort of…manifestation."

"Do you mean a *ghost*?" Angela said with a short laugh. "He thinks I'm a ghost…"

"Yes. I think he believes exactly that," Hoot said, the serious tone of his voice snuffing out her laugh. "I suspect that he left this area when he booby trapped his apartment, but he may come back. He may come looking for you. Just watch out for him, okay?"

Hoot handed Angela one of his cards with his cell phone number and the number of the phone in his motel room scrawled on the back, said, "Let me know right away if you see him. Anytime. Night or day."

Another song started and Angela jumped up, scooted the table aside and wiggled in between Hoot's legs. She said, "Time for that dance you promised," and before he could protest, she had him pinned to the bench. Rubbing her soft breasts against his cheeks. Hoot smiled, he was *up to his gills in titties* as his father would've said, and nowhere to turn.

This girl – this Donna clone, Angela – was a natural tease and had learned the business side of lowbrow male seduction quickly and remarkably well. Angela was doing things that the real Donna Hoot had known and loved would've never even considered. And yet here she was, inconceivably wearing the guise of Donna Messenger to a tee and evoking long-lost intimate memories, deliberately arousing Hoot to a threshold that was nearly painful to resist.

He decided the agony of this ecstasy would be over soon enough so he should just relax and enjoy it – and that he did, quickly sporting a very unofficial erection that was screaming for attention, the Glenlivet shouting encouragement as well, Go, Big Boy! Go!

Shut up down there! Hoot thought, but it was too late, she had already found the one-eyed crybaby and was stroking it through the fabric of his trousers like a well-loved puppy.

"You'll never make it behave that way," he mumbled, feeling the scotch flowing nice and warm through his veins, feeling an inane Cheshire cat grin crawling across his face. Mesmerized by the magic of illicit sex, someone could have performed a root canal on any one of Hoot's smiling teeth right then as long as you didn't disturb Angela or otherwise cause her to stop doing what she was doing.

Wouldn't Marcus just love to see him now? Would never let him live it down…

Marcus…Fuck! Hoot sat up straight and gathered his wits.

The song was over and Angela sat down beside him, said, "I think you liked that, Marshal Hoot, at least I'm pretty sure your deputy down there did."

She laughed.

God, he loved the sound of her laugh. She almost had his complete attention again, but he was embarrassed by his reaction to her attentions. Now he was definitely irritated at himself.

He jumped to his feet. "How much?" he snapped.

"Twenty."

He tossed a bill on the table and gathered up his cigarettes and lighter, said, "I gotta go."

Hoot's abrupt change of attitude seemed to throw Angela off balance.

She said, "Did I do something wrong, marshal?"

Turning back, Hoot saw that she was actually upset and it surprised him. Stopped in his tracks by a non-callous stripper…Hoot would've given anything to sit back down, be anything but a U.S. Marshal knowing what he knew about Norman Carpenter.

He said, "No. You didn't. In fact, you were perfect – I just gotta go is all. Don't forget to call me if you see any sign of Norman Carpenter."

Chapter 29

"We should take my car," Norman's mother said, serving him fry bread and link sausages for breakfast. Overcooked scrambled eggs. "That old van of yours is too much a rattletrap to take on a nice drive."

"Your car is too small," Norman answered. This was New Norman talking, keeping calm. Old Norman waiting and watching, ready to step in. "Don't worry. I'm taking the van out back of the shed to change the oil and tune it up. Thought I'd even give it a quick spray-bomb paint job so you won't be too embarrassed to ride in it."

"You're just afraid you'll be seen. Be recognized. *That's* why you're gonna paint it," Norman's mother said through pursed lips, working her jaw as if chewing her cud. "I know that. The way you're always sneaking around. You've always been a sly one."

She tossed a couple more slices of bread on the griddle, said, "Burned down the barn with your sneaking. I remember that. Do you?"

It was a prod, and Old Norman stirred at it but held back.

"You just get ready to go, Mom," New Norman said. "Pick out a nice outfit. Make some more bread. Make some sandwiches to take along. We'll leave first thing in the morning."

"Look at this…my phone is dead again!" Norman's mother said when Norman came in for supper. "I'm sure I had it plugged it in. Did you sneak in here and unplug it?"

"Is there any supper, Mom?"

"Swanson's chicken pot's are in the freezer."

"Anything to drink? Some tea or coffee?"

"Do you have your cell phone, Normie?"

"It's in the van."

"Can you get it? I need to call Freda Sue. Tell her I'll be out of town. Ask her to watch for my mail."

"You pick up your mail at the post office, Mom. You don't get delivery."

"I know that."

"The mail will wait till you get back. They'll hold it a few days."

"I still wanna call Freda Sue."

"How many chicken pots you want me to fix?"

"Just fix for yourself. I'm not hungry. I'm going to the sweat lodge."

Good place for you, Old Norman thought. Beat on your drum like a banshee and sweat like a hog on a stick. See if it helps. Twenty minutes later he walked around the shed and saw his mother in her sweat lodge robe leaning in the passenger-side door of his van. She was rooting around in the glove box, her spindly pale legs sticking out below the threadbare garment.

"Done sweating already?" he said.

"Can't find that doggone cell phone of yours," she said.

"Here it is. I forgot that I had it right here in my pocket the whole time."

"I need to use it."

"Come on, Mom. Let's go."

"I need to call Freda Sue."

"I know, Mom. Chicken pots are about done. Let's go call Carl Blackwater, the drooler. See if he wants some supper…"

Old Norman helped his mother down from the passenger door step.

Putting his arm around her bony shoulders, he pulled her robe aside and deftly slipped the blade of his knife underneath her flaccid breast, between her ribs, pushing the weapon up and into her heart, saying, "We need to get you dressed, Mom, before Carl gets here."

Norman's mom released her last breath with a brief but valiant struggle.

***

214

From Ronan south the drive was uneventful in the extreme, the road one of those monotonous Montana highways that tempts drivers to lay a brick on the accelerator and crawl into the back for a little snooze. Norman speeding along in the same old Wonder Wand van now painted as flat black as VC pajamas. It would only do about ninety, top end, without wheezing with vehicular asthma – granny speed for this stretch of highway. Norman held it down to eighty thinking it simply would not do to bust a gasket or get pulled over, risk someone of authority taking a look in the back and finding Mom out for a drive, dead as a fencepost.

Norman was thinking how peaceful it was with her being like this. Looking nice in her best dress. No bitches or opinions offered or listened to. Carl was being nice and quiet, too. Not drooling. His crooked eyes closed.

Norman couldn't remember ever before being around the old blowhard Injun without having to listen to his constant gum-flapping. It was a welcome change.

"What do you think, Carl?" Norman said aloud. "Are we making damned good time today or what? Speak up there, Carl...don't be shy!"

Given its age and condition, the Wonder Wand van was far preferable to his mother's ancient and tiny Pinto. There was simply not enough room for the three of them in the Pinto.

Norman's anonymous van was being passed now and then by other vehicles doing three digits; their drivers laid back and speeding belly-first across the landscape. One arm over the back of the passenger seat, the other propped on the driver's door armrest and steering with two fingers, everyone playing rancher or chief.

That was okay with Norman. He was in no hurry.

"You two are being awfully quiet back there," Norman said. "Quiet as the dead, in fact."

Eyes steady on the highway ahead. Stifling a snicker.

"I just want you to know how much I appreciate it," he said.

Chuckling to himself. Stealing a glance up at the rearview mirror after a few more miles and seeing a pair of ghosts looking back at him. Mum was still the word from both of them regarding his true heritage. Fuckit. He didn't care anymore.

The reservation stretched to the horizon, the same mostly treeless plain it had always been, with low flat-topped buttes in the foreground, tall snow-covered peaks of the high Rockies hunkering beyond them in the east, the Bitterroots in the west. Broad acres of sagebrush and dust rolled into square miles of nothingness. High country, dusted with snow. All of it pinned down by relentless wind. Clouds soared past overhead, unfolding in endless billows and wisps, dragging their heavy shadows across the frozen ground. Deep blue sky lurked behind the clouds. Montana's famous big sky.

This was lonely country. Huge and spread out. You had to love it here to bear being here for very long. And Norman didn't anymore. Maybe he never had.

These were stressful thoughts. Norman could ordinarily put common nervous aberrations like stress and anxiety away in one of the back rooms of his mind. Lock the door and turn away. But recently…

Have to stay sharp, he thought. Have to take care.

Meanwhile, Norman's mother had deserved a better end that the one she'd been giving herself, wasting away in front of her television with a plate of Pop Tart crumbs in her lap. And Norman felt a certain morbid satisfaction that he'd been able to help with that. It wasn't just that she was a nosy old witch who couldn't resist gossiping, calling people up all the time, calling Freda Sue, Susan Klennert, Carl Blackwater, and God knows how many others to hint that her son was home for a visit. She was a venerated tribal shaman and deserved a death with dignity. Norman sincerely hoped that his blade had given it to her.

If she had only died a little easier, if she had just let go without so much kicking and struggling it would have been better. But Norman respected her spunk. She had lived a hard life, too. And now, before he did anything else, he would take the time to lay her body to rest with her own people on the Beaverhead River near Yellowstone – it was the least he could do. With luck he should reach there by tonight.

Norman had only one small errand to run on the way – Nicholas Trowbridge, purveyor of all things lethal.

Norman kept at least one of his pistols with him at all times – it only made sense, a man in his situation. At the cost of an hour's detour, he'd pick up a rifle from Nicholas just in case he needed it. A fully-automatic AR-15 would be handy. Or better yet for true long-range sniper work, a Remington 700 or a 308 caliber Savage 10FP, bolt-action, with a decent scope. A 12-guage streetsweeper shotgun for close work. Maybe a couple of Italian grenades to replace the M-67's he had left behind in Spokane – all part of the plan.

Of course, he'd have to retire old Nicholas Trowbridge. A shame. He had known the Trowbridges for fifteen years – since a couple of years before Maggie Trowbridge died – and Norman figured that Nick, lonely as he was, was bound to tell someone about his visit. A good plan leaves no loose ends, Norman thought. And nothing soothes a fevered mind like a good plan.

The landscape seemed to be growing more distant and intangible as Norman drove south through it. He was a stranger here, his place lost in the overriding puzzle of it, as if he were passing through without actually being part of it. This was a feeling that Norman had had for a very long time – in context; he thought it explained a lot about his actions.

Passing a hungry-looking hawk on a fencepost, Norman decided that if he had ever loved this place once he certainly didn't love it anymore. And the absence of affection had left a vacancy inside of him aching to be filled, a malignancy growing in its place. It was his misfortune that this was a feeling he'd been familiar with since childhood, its tangled roots growing forever deeper, threadlike feelers finding the cracks and crevices, probing all the fractures of his life, taking hold and breaking it all apart.

Driving away from his mother's small house on the rez, away from the burnt-out foundation in Ronan, Norman was driving away from the last place he had ever called *home*. Ahead, the highway seemed to be floating skyward – it was an ordinary optical illusion and Norman's eyes became locked on it. He had to tear them away now and then to keep from dozing at the wheel.

Too tired! he told himself.

Norman had felt tired for most of his adult life, but he seemed to be feeling more fatigued recently than ever before. After all his exploits and all his close calls. All the missed appointments with his maker. A deathcheater extraordinaire, would Norman Wayne Carpenter finally give in to simple fatigue? Crash head-on into a loaded eighteen-wheeler driven by an agent of fate?

He chuckled. What fine evidence of God's sense of humor that would be!

Still, it was a far better death than old age, Norman thought with a shudder.

Norman had assumed for so long that his life would end in either hot anger or cold blood that he had grown quite comfortable with the idea. To think that he might succumb to old age was a totally loathsome concept to him. Made him relish his singular lifestyle. One that was guaranteed to end with a flourish at a youngish age. And stubbornly, in spite of six decades of survival, Norman remained convinced that he would die young; the definition of *young* being revised from time to time as the years passed.

His mother's dignity these last few years had become as withered and arthritic as her hands. Norman would not share that fate. No one would have to come and put him out of his misery. There was nobody who would do it, anyhow.

Except, maybe…Hoot.

Yes…*that* would be the way of it when the time came. Him and Hoot going together. It had to be…

"Getting old sucks!" he shouted at a passing Cadillac full of blue-hairs. Men up front. Women in back. Looking for a casino, no doubt.

He reached for his thermos and, steering with his knees, poured a steaming cup of coffee that was, as usual, strong and bitter and black. Drained it in three deep gulps and imagined the black brew splashing with little effect against the bottom of the cavernous void that was his otherwise empty stomach.

What he needed was a good stiff drink. Something with some kick to it. Rocket fuel for the rocket man.

But not while I'm driving, he thought.

Norman didn't approve of drinking while driving.

But driving stoned…now, *that* was a different matter. He fumbled in the ashtray for his roach clip and lighted a little taster. Changed the CD in the stereo to Led Zeppelin.

The song, *Black Dog*, began playing, and Norman cranked the music up beyond loud. He increased his speed – pedal to the metal, the van wheezing and complaining but charging recklessly ahead. The music was little more than a pulsing noise, so distorted by battered speakers and muted by road roar that no individual rhythm melody or instrument could be discerned, only beat. But the beat was all Norman really needed, an incessant pulse passing through him like a thick infusion, rearranging his DNA.

The beat…

It could be the beating drums of a thousand gathered shamans. It could be his mother's drum, alone. Drumming the door open. Passing through…

Spirit guides showing the way, the great Kootenai shaman, Inez Feather, was going home.

Chapter 30

Leon Marcus had just returned to Spokane from Montana. He sat with Hoot at Luigi's Authentic Italian Restaurant on East Sprague, waiting for their complimentary spumoni dessert. Their table had a plastic tablecloth with a red gingham imprint and one leg was shimmed with a flattened matchbook cover to take some of the wobble out of it.

Marcus said, "All the places in this town to eat and you choose the greasiest spoon in the Spokane Valley?"

"It's not the *greasiest*. Not by a long shot. I know the difference."

"All I know is I'm suddenly worried about my bowels," Marcus said. "It's not normal for a black man in the prime of life to worry about that sort of thing."

"Buck-up, partner. A little olive oil and garlic is good for you."

"You should taste my wife's shrimp étouffée," Marcus said.

"Alright," Hoot said, making eye contact, then added, "Horner still won't approve our transfer off Warrants and back to fulltime Fugitive Apprehension. Only if another positive ID pops up on Creeper."

"You mean an informant? Or another dead body?"

"Unfortunately, we've already got another one of those right here under our noses," Hoot said. "Druggie daytime manager at Goodtime Charlie's was found stinking up his own living room right here in the East Valley area earlier today. I just came from the scene. I'm sure it was Creeper's work, but there was no hard evidence so I kept my mouth shut – the sorry fucker had a shaved head or I'd have all the positive ID we need. Knife wounds looked familiar. Flays and genital mutilation. Prints and DNA will be confirmed in a day or two. Probably won't tell us anything if it actually is Norman's work."

"Shaved head?"

"I told you that Norman's Creeper personality likes to take scalps. A scalp without hair would offend the aesthetics of his collection. Norman has very delicate artistic sensibilities."

Marcus, appearing to be stricken with barely suppressible distaste, changed the subject, saying, "You were right about the reservation police. Sheriff Essmeyer's guys were good. Didn't take them long to ask around and establish that Norman Carpenter *has* been there. Recently – someone noticed a guy matching his description poking around a burned-out house where he used to live when he was a kid. That was yesterday. Someone else who personally knows him saw him buy gas in town – but he didn't stay. Apparently he left again almost as soon as he got there. Maybe late last night or early this morning. I had phone conversation with the sheriff about an hour ago and there's still no additional trace of our guy on the rez, but Essmeyer says he'll keep looking."

"And Norman's mother?"

"She's gone too."

"Gone?" Hoot said. "I remember Norman saying that she never goes anywhere. Won't set a foot off the reservation. Thinks others may tamper with her spirit guides if she leaves them unattended."

"So I gathered from the sheriff. We went out to her place this morning. Nobody home. Everything locked up, which Essmeyer thought was odd since she never goes anywhere. Didn't know she even had locks. So tribal guys are putting together a warrant to go in and look around. I reminded them that Norman likes to set deadly booby traps, then came back here rather than wait around for the warrant. If they find anything, I'll get a call."

"There won't be anything to find. Norman only leaves tracks when he wants to. Mostly to fuck with me."

"Seems that way. Meanwhile, how's the titty recon going?"

Hoot smiled thinly. "No sign of Norman there, either. I managed to get a little help from Bob Wilson, even Peyton choked up a spare agent, barely enough to post continuous one-man surveillance on the club for a couple of days."

"Now that I'm back, where do you want me?"

"Outside of Goodtime Charlie's in a few hours. I've got a feeling it's gonna be tonight or never. Relieve Peyton's man, Carlisle, at eleven. I'll be inside."

***

Early winter, 1968. Norman took three weeks of convalescent time in Hawaii to recover from the punji stake infection, and then he was sent to Ft. Dix for advanced hand-to-hand combat and Ranger training prior to returning in-country. Almost three months had passed before Hoot saw him again in Vietnam. By then the chain of command had awarded Hoot the Bronze Star with Valor for throwing Norman over his shoulder and packing him eleven clicks out of harm's way while under hostile fire.

Without regard for personal safety, the citation read.

"Bullshit," Hoot said. "I had plenty of regard for numero uno. They were behind us. Remember? I was using you as a shield."

"They pumped me full of new blood," Norman said. "You got the Star...I got the blood. New blood – new man. But we're *still* blood-brothers...even if mine is new."

New?

There was no doubt in Hoot's mind that Norman was a *different* man when he returned to his unit in-country. For one thing, in a conversation his eyes couldn't seem to hold on Hoot's eyes like they used to; for another, his sense of humor, macabre before, now sported a truly wicked edge. He said he was eager to get back to it, eager to try out some of his newly-acquired hand-to-hand skills. "You think I was dangerous up close before...just wait. I'm a fucking jungle menace, now. Don't even need a weapon. I *am* a weapon."

Norman had taken a few days' leave and spent the time in Pleasanton instead of Montana. Said he saw Donna. Said, with a distinct twinkle in his eye, that she looked damned good. Said that she told him she didn't blame Hoot for the breakup. Said she'd been studying her ass off to keep those straight-A's rolling in. Said she told him that she'd been out on a couple of dates, but nothing serious. Said she hopes we're both smart enough to stay out of trouble over here. Told me to bring you back alive." And that was all Norman had to share with Hoot on the subject of Donna Messenger even though Hoot knew there was much more that could have been said.

Maybe more should have been said, but it wasn't. They went about their assigned patrols and ambushes – sometimes together, sometimes not. Off duty, they drank beer at Chan's, Hoot often seeing the reflection of Donna in Norman's eyes, knowing without having to be told what had happened between his girlfriend and best friend while Norman was on leave for R&R.

It wasn't as if any trespassing had occurred. After all, Hoot had given Donna up. But he still cared about her. Wanted the best for her. And something about recently-promoted-to-corporal Norman Carpenter, the *Creeper* who returned to combat duty, was very bothersome.

Hoot had no previous experience with so-called split personalities. Wasn't sure he actually believed in the concept any more than he believed in werewolves. But it was becoming abundantly clear to him that there were two opposing personas inside Norman, both fighting for dominance – a new, thoughtful and considerate Norman who seemed to possess a moral compass and obviously cherished Donna, and the old Sioux warrior Norman, grown more crass and hateful, driven by some malice unworthy of Donna or any other decent woman.

This Norman was evolving into a hard-drinking, opium and pot-smoking whoremonger – and a Charlie killer beyond reckoning. If Norman hadn't insisted otherwise, Hoot would have assumed all this was the result of a recent visit to Inez Feather's sweat lodge, her fiddling with the spirit world beyond.

"Didn't even go there this trip," Norman said, sitting with Hoot at Chan's bar, a sizeable collection of empty bottles in front of them.

A Vietnamese go-go girl somewhere between sixteen and thirty-six years-old hovered on the bamboo catwalk above the bar, her brown nipples scanning the joint like eavesdropping owl eyes, a dancing whore with a dirty nooky, Hoot figured – and a calculating heart, no doubt. Norman stood to slide a dollar bill under the band of her sequined gee. Sitting back down, he said, "My mother's crappy little sweat lodge isn't the front parlor to the Other World, no matter what she might have you believe."

"She certainly had me fooled…remember?"

"No, brother. The spirit world is everywhere. I don't need Inez Feather or some blind old Coyote coot to show me the way. The key is right here," Norman said, tapping the center of his chest. "Not that you actually believe in any of it, anyhow."

"I believe in the difference between right and wrong," Hoot said. "Do you?"

"All those little motherfuckers running around the jungle in black pajamas shooting at us…you think they believe in right and wrong, too?"

"What's this? Are you turning pink on me?"

"Thinkaboutit. It was Donna that got me thinking about it."

"Donna," Hoot said. "She has a way…doesn't she?"

"You know, Brother, a soldier over here's gotta be careful not to think too much about whose jungle it is we're fighting in. What it is we're fighting for. Get his head all screwed loose real quick."

"I think you're drunk."

"Well, that's good news…"

"Gotta go kill some bad guys," Norman would say, then set out on a mission and come back with blood, literally, on his hands, a hard but weirdly-vacant look in his eyes. This at the same time that Hoot was having a bitch of a time wrestling with the moral ambiguity of what they were accomplishing: LRP mission after LRP mission into Laos and Cambodia with no evidence they were making any lasting disruptions to the supply trails there; repeated sniper assaults on hard targets with other key VC seeming to be right there to take up the slack before their predecessors hit the ground. It was a damned difficult war in which to measure victory, made harder by stories in the press about what was going on in the youth movement stateside, anti-war sentiment back home making much ado about the distinction between those who were running the war and those who were fighting it.

Once Norman let it slip that Donna had expressed some anxiety about the possibility of his and Hoot's involvement in attacks on civilians. "She said she didn't understand how we could be anywhere near the atrocities soldiers routinely committed on innocent civilians over here and still live with ourselves. She said the soldiers always claim they were only following orders. All that shit on the news every night. I told her LRP was different. Told her all our targets were confirmed enemy, genuine bad guys. Didn't seem to help. Might've even made it worse – the way that girl can get wound up so tight."

Atrocities? Hoot thought, his heart aching at the very idea that Donna would believe he could be part of any of that. He was only too aware of isolated atrocities committed by American soldiers that had produced torrents of outrage in the stateside news media. But he also knew similar VC atrocities were commonplace and receiving hardly any media attention at all. Anyone on the ground in-country with open eyes knew that the Viet Cong made attacks on civilians a strategic centerpiece of their war effort. Happened all the time. The rat's ass rub for U.S. soldiers was that Americans who killed Vietnamese civilians received prison sentences and dishonorable discharges, while Communists who did so received commendations. It was all wrong...*everything* in this war was wrong, and he and Norman were smack in the middle of it.

Hoot's quandary was that he was growing weary of it all while Norman seemed to be in his element since his return to LRP. Norman having fun in a twisted way, he even started taking scalps – little ones to be sure, bloody patches of flesh the size of quarters with hair growing from them hanging from his kit after missions. Officers refused to see them. Norman racking up his kills as if he were moving tokens on a board game. It freaked out other soldiers, even hard-ass Delta Company tunnel rats. It made Hoot feel sick. He began to see Norman as fucked up – seriously fucked up. And he began to wonder if he was, too. After all, they'd both been subjected to the same kind of madness, perhaps it was inevitable that part of it would stick.

***

It was four days before Christmas and Goodtime Charlie's seemed to have assumed a seedier air than usual with all the remotely decent customers staying close to home, spending their money on tangibles. What was left was man-chaff, the club half full of sullen, redneck man-chaff. It was Amateur Night again, and Hoot took a seat in the far back corner where he could watch both the front entrance and the side exit. Wishing he had more backup posted outside, he wasn't going to let Norman walk in unnoticed.

He offered to buy Angela a Lady's Drink as soon as she came over to his table.

"Guess what? I'm an *amateur* again tonight," she said, sitting beside Hoot.

"Get fired from your regular gig?" Hoot asked.

"Only two contestants signed up, so I got drafted."

"I won't whistle or catcall, but I'll applaud extra loudly for you."

"You do that," Angela said with a laugh. Her laughter sounded like candy and there was no denying Hoot had a sweet tooth, made him think of Crackerjacks and Dr Pepper – two of Donna's favorite sweet-fixes – Angela saying, "You're getting to be a regular customer here, Marshal Hoot."

"Any sign of Norman Carpenter since we last talked?"

"Nope. But I've never actually seen him, anyhow, that I know of. Just the pictures you showed me. He could be sitting two tables over and I probably wouldn't notice."

"Has Liz seen him?"

"Don't think so. You should ask her."

"I will," he answered, his expression dour.

"Why the serious look?"

"You and Liz found a place to live?"

"Yeah. We're staying with one of Liz's artist friends until after the holidays."

"I'm thinking maybe the two of you should lie low for a while. You know, don't accept any invitations to parties if you

226

don't know who's going to be there. Or, better yet, just don't go."

"You're trying to scare me, talking like that. What's up?"

"It's just a gut feeling I have. But I think Norman Carpenter may show up here again. Soon."

"Here? At Goodtime Charlie's?" Angela said in a tone of disbelief. "All he wants for Christmas is a bunch of naked boobies?"

"What he wants is *you*, I'm afraid. And I simply don't have the resources to keep you under surveillance the way I'd like to."

If these words were scaring Angela she shrugged it off, saying, "So I'm the bait and you think you can catch your escaped killer by keeping an eye on me. I think I've seen this show on TV – don't remember that it worked out well for the bait."

"Might be better if you didn't think of yourself as *bait*."

"Thanks for worrying about me, Marshal Hoot. But I'm thinking about leaving town pretty soon, anyhow."

"You'll be spending your holiday back in Seattle?" Hoot asked, glad to change the subject but not willing to be blown off. Be cool and warn her, he'd told himself before coming here and he'd done that. No need to scare her any more than he already had.

"No," she said, turning her eyes away. "Liz is going to Seattle – not me. I really do miss my kids. And hate missing Christmas with them. But I can't go back yet. Actually, I'm traveling to Joplin Missouri soon as Liz leaves. I've got family in Joplin. Stuff I need to do there."

"You don't *sound* like you're from Missouri," Hoot said, struggling with the thought that her accent sounded *Maine*ish; Angela Hunter from Joplin Missouri sounding exactly like Donna Messenger from Pleasanton, Maine – *that's* how she sounded.

It was increasingly disturbing, the way this woman, Angela Hunter, kept turning into Donna Messenger in Hoot's mind, dragging him back through time and planting him nose-to-nose with his greatest failure.

"I've lived in Seattle the last nine years," Angela said. "But I was born and raised in Missouri. I'll probably get my drawl back after about two minutes at my mother's house. How 'bout you? You got someplace to go for Christmas, family to be with?"

"Not anymore. I'm a single old fart," Hoot said with a flat snicker. He felt deflated, was thinking he might need to slip outside soon. Check-up on the outside surveillance. Maybe visit the dregs of Glenlivet waiting for him in the car. "I'm divorced. My kids are all grown up, living back east. I've moved around a lot, only lived in Seattle since September. I have an apartment near the airport – no pets allowed. That's about it."

"What happened? You said you're divorced."

"That's not unusual for law enforcement people."

Angela looked unwilling to accept the usual flippant answer so Hoot said, "Life happened. I got busy and let life get in the way of living. Spent an awful lot of it chasing Norman Carpenter. It's a bit too late to catch up on the fun stuff now, I'm afraid."

"Bad deal, but I think I know how you feel," Angela said. "We're a pair of oddballs, aren't we? And we seem to be caught-up in something. You and your outlaw friend both thinking I'm someone else's ghost. I wanna tell you something weird about that: I actually have walked around most of my life thinking I'm the wrong person trapped in a stranger's body, like I'm *possessed*, or something. Crazy coincidence, huh, meeting you now? Couple of weeks ago I felt so lost in my own life that I sorta panicked and ended up here. I've never done anything like this before."

"Maybe you should stay at the hotel with me until you leave for Missouri," Hoot said. "I have an adjoining room."

"Are you an exorcist?"

"I really don't think you need one."

Angela laughed a nervous laugh, said, "Hope you're right. I gotta go on stage. Buy a dance when I come back and we'll talk some more."

A reverberating downbeat took her away. *"All rrright, gentlemen! And now, for your enjoyment! Put your hands* *together for Goodtime Charlie's next lovely amateur – the one and only **Angel**!"*

It was uncanny how much Angela looked like Donna Messenger up on that stage, unsettling to Hoot that she said those things about feeling possessed. Since he met her he'd been having frequent hairs-on-the-back-of-the-neck impulses toward believing she actually *was* the ghost of Donna reincarnated.

Yeah. Sure. If only that were true then it might also be true that he really could have a second chance to do right by her somehow – first by keeping Norman as far away from her as possible.

This woman, Angela, bore an uncanny resemblance to Donna – that's all this was, all it could possibly be, Hoot told himself yet again. The woman on stage was doing things up there that Hoot had never seen Donna even approximate – though there was a nugget deep inside him wanting to argue that the Donna he'd known had indeed possessed a wild side that he'd simply not appreciated at the time.

Angela finished her first song, gathered her costume and moved to the back stage.

Ezra Hooten was one of the conspicuous few who bothered to applaud.

Right in the middle of applauding Angela's performance a familiar feeling washed over Hoot. A wave of dread, the undertow from it dragging at his subconscious until it suddenly became clear to him – Norman is *here*!

Tearing his attention away from Angela, Hoot looked wildly through the darkness, focusing for a brief instant on every face he saw until his eyes were finally drawn to movement near the side exit and he looked there just in time to see the door closing. He jumped up, ran the gamut of chairs tables and customers in a quick second, and was out the door into the dimly-lit parking lot with his Glock 19 drawn and cocked.

Hoot ran over to where Marcus was parked. "Where did he go?" he demanded.

"Who? *Creeper*?" Marcus said.

"Yes! Which way did he go?"

Haven't seen him," Marcus said, exiting the Ford with a 12-gauge Browning pump in hand.

"Shit! He came out the side door not two seconds ago."

"I'll take the front lot," Marcus said, racking the shotgun to chamber a round.

"I'll take the side," Hoot answered. "Call it in to Peyton. And remember, no warning shots."

"Meet you in the back lot."

Norman, sitting in the spray-bomb-black Wonder Wand van with secondhand Montana plates, watched all this from a dark parking place down the street, thinking: You're losing your touch, my blood-brother. Getting too old for the game. But at least you're entertaining – you and your new partner running around the parking lot like kids playing paintball!

Still, Norman knew Hoot to be a dangerous adversary. Determined as all hell.

That made him a worthy adversary.

And good for a laugh.

Chapter 31

Only three shopping days left until Christmas. Angela took the day off. So did Liz and they stayed in bed for hours and talked. Made love, too, but mostly they talked.

"So, what're you gonna do with yourself?" Liz asked.

"Don't know yet."

"You won't be stripping anymore, right?"

"No, I won't."

"Good."

"Why'd you bring me to Goodtime Charlie's if you suddenly think it's so bad for me?"

"*Suddenly*? I distinctly remember warning you up front that it was bad. Or didn't I make that clear? Regardless, it is. And don't you forget it." She passed the Ritz crackers and peanut butter to Angela. "Tell me, Sweetheart, you still think you were such a bigtime sinner when we met?"

The tops of Liz's breasts were littered with cracker crumbs. Angela loved that, wanted to nibble them clean, she answered, "Guess not. But I'm catching up fast."

Liz said, "Allow me to share one of my favorite sayings. It's by Graham Greene; he wrote that 'an army of women live on the lust of men.' And it's so right-on for strippers. Your dancing career barely scratched the surface of that little truism. Be glad you're getting out as quickly as you got in. You made some money. Experienced the rush. Call it a win."

More crackers. More peanut butter. Crumbs everywhere. "That 'army of women' business," Liz said – "I've often wondered about his use of the word, *army*. There weren't very many of us drafted or otherwise pressed into service except by our own desperation, and that includes you. Makes it a *volunteer* army – more of a *militia* than an army. So, in theory, what it means is you can leave whenever you want, desert the ranks anytime…doesn't it?"

"Yeah…so?"

"So the problem is if it really is like an army that's not so easy to do. A soldier I once knew – a friend, not a customer – called it the *gruesome factor*, soldiers re-upping for combat. He said the more action you see; the harder it is to leave it behind. So don't renege and stay in just because you've had a taste and felt the power…okay? A lifer in this woman's army isn't a pretty thing for very long."

The crackers and peanut butter screamed for milk. Angela went barefoot and naked to the kitchen and returned with a half-gallon carton of two-percent, no glasses.

Crawling back into bed, she asked; "Why'd you quit art school?"

"Simple. I couldn't afford it anymore. It was too much of a burden on Mom, even though she tried. Then I got busy, joined that army of women, and never got around to going back.

"And you know what? It doesn't really matter. I didn't learn anything in college that I've used in the real world. Except for reading. Reading is the one skill that all the others are built on, it lets you go where you want to go and do what you need to do. Whatever else you do – *read*."

"My Seattle library card was my best friend."

More crackers. More talk. Milk moustaches. Kisses licking them away.

Liz was fascinated by stories Angela told. Stuff that Angela was surprised a street-savvy stripper would care about; about teaching her kids to read; about checking out old Keystone Cops and Charlie Chaplin movies along with a clunky sixteen-millimeter projector from the library and playing the films afternoons after school on the front room wall before Les got home from work.

Angela learned that Liz's mom was very ill and this was difficult for her to talk about because, unlike Angela and her mother, Liz had always been very close to her mom. The weird thing was that Liz's mom had also been a stripper in her time, when Liz was little. She had never married, and put Liz through high school and two years of art school by working at a plastic injection plant in Kent, south of Seattle. Angela sincerely wished that she could meet her, thought she sounded like an altogether different kind of mom from her own, but her immediate path lay in the other direction – *far* in the other direction, toward her own mom.

Maybe another time, she thought.

Would there be another time? Neither woman daring an honest guess, both of them blew the question off with: "Yeah, sure there will!"

***

After Liz left, after all the goodbye tears had dried up and the hiccups that accompanied them had subsided, Angela felt empty, so dead inside that she figured that she would soon start to stink from the inside out and didn't care, felt herself sinking deeper and deeper into a pit of lassitude, too melancholy to get dressed, go out, take a nap, or fix dinner for herself. She couldn't seem to hold onto a thought long enough to do anything with it, but eventually forced herself to plan her trip to Joplin. Started making a *to do* list that was endless, then put it aside. She found the small bag and book Liz had given her as a going away gift and drew a Rune for guidance. She drew *Teiwaz*, the Rune of the Spiritual Warrior, suggesting that you can only get out of your own way and let the will of Heaven flow through you.

Yep! Time to get on with it, kiddo, Angela thought. She grabbed an actual paper phone book from under the phone and called Amtrak. Found out that if she left on the 1:40 AM train tonight instead of waiting until tomorrow she could still be in Joplin in time to see Mom for Christmas. Two days by train and six hours by bus. Hell of a trip, but she wouldn't fly – she was scared to death of flying.

Deciding that she would use the time between here and there to get her head straight, Angela refreshed her tea and worried over details of the idea. She had a wad of cash in her backpack that she figured was big enough to get her down the road quite a ways if she Scrooged it. Maybe enough to get all the way there and back home again...

There was nothing to pack. Angela wore clothing she had acquired since the fire, a new unbleached white cable-knit sweater, a new pair of blue jeans – the most expensive blue jeans she'd ever owned, a new pair of Harley-Davidson boots like Liz's, and her trench coat, with a pair of Liz's knitted silk gloves that Liz had insisted she keep stashed in the pocket.

Angela saw Hoot drive up and sit waiting for her in his government-issue Ford Five-hundred. It was snowing. From the dark front room window of the apartment she could see flakes falling in the headlights of Hoot's car, but it was still too warm for much to stick. The temperature was dropping. By morning she knew that it might be piled butt-cheek high and rising. Light and fluffy flakes, each unique but still all the same, erratically dancing around in the wind, melting away and vanishing when they hit the ground. She watched them fall, taking special note of how some fell faster than others, rushing ahead to their doom. Less than two weeks ago she had longed to be such a snowflake – melting away and vanishing – but now she wasn't so sure that she didn't want to stick.

If not in Seattle with Les, then somewhere else.

Where? She didn't know.

She didn't know anything except that it was time to move on.

***

"You like motor homes?" Hoot asked. "Fifth wheels? A person could pick one up pretty cheaply this time of year. If I did that, you might not have to twist my arm too hard to talk me into driving you all the way back to Missouri."

Angela laughed, said, "Thanks for the offer, Marshal Hoot. And thanks for the ride to the train station."

"We're a little early. I don't know if Norman expects that you're taking the train, but I have a strong feeling he's close by, so I want to walk in with you, watch you get on the train. And I'd appreciate a call when you get safely to Joplin."

"I'll be fine."

"I have to tell you, I'm glad you're getting out of the adult entertainment business."

"Me too. And I gotta tell you, you weren't my best customer."

Angela laughed again.

Hoot knew he would miss that laugh. He asked, "You have a plan?"

"Nope."

"You need a plan – even if it's a bad one. That's personal experience talking. Can't be living your life like the whole thing is a big unpremeditated accident and expect anything good to come of it."

"So what's *your* plan, Marshal?"

"I'm going to retire and hit the road. Buy a fifth wheel or a motor home big as a palace on wheels and see everything like it's never been seen before. All I need is a beautiful young naked lady to come along and keep me company."

"Shouldn't be too hard to find. They're everywhere, you know."

***

Yes! From a low rooftop half a block away, Norman could see Hoot's uncertainty in pantomime through his rifle scope. Hoot could obviously sense him nearby but couldn't pinpoint exactly where he was…Hoot's instinct keeping him in position to screen any clear shot at the woman beside him wearing Donna's skin.

Norman thought, If you were only a true believer you'd finally have me, my blood-brother. You'd have had me when I first followed you and your pretty girlfriend here. When I first took this position. So, what are you going to do, knowing I'm here but not trusting what you know?

Norman watched Hoot walk *Donna* out of sight back toward the ticketing area. He would take his shot when they returned. A good flat trajectory, only about a hundred meters, open promenade. No glass between him and the kill zone. But after a while his old friend reappeared alone.

Shit! Good move, leaving her there, Norman thought.

Hoot turned and went down the aisle marked *Restrooms*.

That was a mistake, my brother, Norman thought, happy to feel in charge of the situation again, he grabbed his gear and went to a secondary position where he'd have a better view of the loading platform.

The ticket window was in an alcove at the rear of the promenade, across from the big central waiting area. "I'm going to leave you here," Hoot said after looking around the immediate vicinity. "Don't go into the waiting area. Promise me you'll stay right here out of sight until the conductor makes his last call. Then walk straight to the train and get on, find your car and seat after you're on board the train. No stops or side trips to the lady's room. Nothing."

"Got it, Marshal. I hide here until the train is ready to leave, then straight to it."

"Exactly."

Hoot turned to go but Angela touched his arm, turned him back around, kissed him, and said, "Thank you, Marshal Hoot. I hope I see you again someday."

"Have a safe trip," Hoot replied. "And have a nice holiday with your family."

***

Norman had a good view of the full length of the loading platform from this new angle – a much better location even if it was farther from his van and escape route than he would have preferred.

It was after midnight and it was snowing, small flakes. The air was crisp.

He lay prone in a fresh dusting of snow behind rooftop signage at the corner of a one-story warehouse. Straight down the mainline from the Amtrak station. The Savage .308 resting on a folded towel atop a short parapet wall, the Leupold Mark 4 scope fastened to the rifle was recalibrated to zero-in on the center of the kill zone. Norman adjusted another click for elevation, estimated crosswind and adjusted for it, and then waited. This would be his best long shot. A 500-meter shot. He would not miss.

Passengers started filing out of the station and boarding the train in two's and three's, a few larger groups. He knew she would come along soon, the skinwalker. If Hoot was still shielding her then he could die, too…

Come on, Donna-girl, Norman thought, all his concentration bearing down on the group of people milling around trackside…I'm ready.

"You've already killed her once," Hoot said, his quiet voice carrying across the chilled rooftop behind Norman. "Isn't that enough?"

Norman froze, a faint smile spreading over his face. He had not heard his old friend's voice so nearby in a very long time. Through the lens of the Leupold he could see that more people were filing out of the station and boarding the train. No sign of Donna yet. Norman had been concentrating so completely on acquiring his target that he had not felt Hoot closing in on his position. His finger remained on the trigger, glove off, getting cold. "She didn't stay dead," he said.

"The young woman down there. She isn't Donna," Hoot said.

"You sure of that?" Norman answered.

"I am."

"I'll have you know, my old friend, that I'm wearing a Ghost Shirt," Norman said without taking his eye from the Leupold scope or his finger from the Savage Sharpshooter trigger adjusted down to less than three pounds of pressure, people still filing out of the terminal below, still no Donna. "Kicking Bear himself promised our people that this garment will deflect your white man's bullets."

"I remember that story. Wanna see if it works?" Hoot said, cocking the Glock 19.

With an exaggerated sigh, Norman removed his hands from the rifle and slowly rolled over onto his back. "Neither of us will have another day's peace if she lives," he said.

"I recall you told me that once before," Hoot said, holding steady aim on the center of Norman's forehead with the Glock. "You were right – I haven't. Have you?"

"I don't know what the fuck are you talking about?"

237

"Think back. Waay back. And if you tell me you've forgotten about that girl, I swear I'll put you out of your miserable existence in the next heartbeat."

"That girl? *That* girl…are you talking about that VC girl and her mama-san? The ones we interrogated on the Laotian side of the A Shau that time?"

"Move away from the weapon," Hoot said. "And *we* didn't interrogate anybody. *You* did."

"Ohmygod, you *are*…aren't you?" Norman said, sitting up and scooting over a few inches. "Talking about that girl and her mama-san? My God, man…that was forty fucking years ago! It was a *war*!"

"You told me to hand the girl over to you and I did – to my lifelong shame," Hoot said. "Then you made her watch while you stuck your knife up that woman's…"

"And the girl told us everything we needed to know, didn't she?" Norman interrupted.

"*That* does not make what you did right. Bleeding that woman to death like an animal in front of her daughter."

"You should've let me kill the girl, too. I told you so at the time," Norman said. "Yeah. I remember warning you that neither of us would have another day's peace if she lived."

"You did. In fact, those were the last words we spoke to each other in-country."

"You always were a grudge-holder," Norman said. "I was right about that, by the way. The way some of those people would get stuck in your head. Better to kill them and move on. But *nooo*! Your guilty fucking conscience wouldn't allow it. *You* were the one insisted we turn her loose!"

"We had to. We were so fuckin far off the reservation, we couldn't bring her in."

"And then it was what…" Norman said with derision, slowly standing, "only three weeks later the very same girl blew up a barfull of GI's in Hanoi? Blew her own bony butt to hell doing it. Are you still beating yourself up over that? I can see that you are."

Hoot answered with cold silence and Norman said, "The whole fucking war was dinky dau, Brother. They always are – you said it, yourself. We did what we had to do."

238

"*Had* to do?" Hoot mimicked. "Since when do we *have* to bleed people to death? I've relived that whole scene countless times in my head trying to get a handle on what I should have done. As I recall you got an Article 15 for what you thought you *had* to do; rape a woman to death with your fuckin combat knife! You should have been court-martialed and put away for life right then and there. If I hadn't kept my cowardly mouth shut, you would have been, and Donna would be alive today. Who knows how many others? God damn me to hell for that awful sin!"

"That one and plenty more," Norman said.

"No shit. Standing mute and letting Donna marry you in the first place was the worst – I'll burn for sure for that one because I *knew* what you had become and did nothing. And now you believe you have to kill a young woman because she happens to look like Donna? *You're* the one's dinky dau."

Norman grinned, said, "Did you miss me, all these years? I've missed you. Tried to stay in touch."

"Get down on your knees and put your hands behind your back," Hoot said.

Hoot didn't even see the knife before it nicked his arm, getting stuck in his coat sleeve, Norman was that fast, throwing the knife and turning away, saying, "*Xin loi*, blood-brother…excuse me!"

Hoot's first shot with the Glock hit the corner of the sign Norman had been standing next to. His second shot hit the ground somewhere a thousand feet or so down the Amtrak mainline. Norman was returning fire, now. Hoot stood his ground and his third shot hit Norman as he ran, somewhere non-lethal, in the leg or the ass Hoot thought, saw him stagger before darting into the roof access stairwell and slamming the metal door closed behind him. Hoot's last shot hit the door as he heard the inside bar drop into place.

"He's coming to you, partner," Hoot barked into his two-way, heading for the exterior fire escape. "He's armed. With a .38 snubbie, I think."

Seconds later, shots were being fired down in the street.

239

Chapter 32

Norman drove west on Highway 2 headed toward Belvedere on the Colville Indian Reservation. His ass hurt like a motherfucker on fire. Other than that he felt remarkably refreshed and alert. The excitement of being so close to his old buddy, Troubleshooter, ratcheting up his adrenaline drip to a full flow. The close call. The escape.

And then there was that stupid spook deputy in the street hollering at him, "Halt!" Hoot should have taught him better. Norman, raising his hands in surrender, turned and shot three times. It was comical, the blackest man he'd ever seen, going down in gleaming white snow with a look of disbelief still stuck on his face. He'd wanted so badly to go back for a sure killshot and a quick scalp just to fuck with Hoot's mind, but Hoot had his knife, and he had a bullet in the ass slowing him down.

All in all it was a very exciting and satisfying day – even if he got shot, even if Donna got away…for now. If he could only stay awake, not fall asleep at the wheel from exhaustion and kill himself after so much excitement all would be well. He turned on the radio and found a Country-and-Western station. Norman hated C&W music, but the old Volvo that he'd jacked at the Spokane Amtrak station only had an AM radio and it was the only station he found that didn't drift. He was in a good mood, so it didn't matter.

Over two hours later he crossed the Columbia just downstream of Grand Coulee Dam. Still dark. The road slick in places with black ice. He turned north, heading for sanctuary at Debbie-Sue's. Debbie-Sue was the best damned cook within a hundred miles in any direction and would be happy to tell you so. Her truck stop establishment on Highway 155 was so ramshackle and ill-imposing with its mounted Canadian moose lurking over the entrance that only those few regulars who knew what a secret little culinary oasis it was dared to venture inside.

Norman knew. He also knew that Debbie-Sue had been a veterinarian and a taxidermist before becoming a cook and a wife, and she knew a thing or two about gunshot wounds. By the time he got there the sun was giving some thought to rising in the east.

Sliding home, Norman was stuck to the Volvo's driver's seat in a puddle of his own blood and he was starting to feel faint. He parked the car and leaned on the horn.

***

Marcus lay sprawled in the snow, a red blood stain near his head. Hoot ran to him with his jaw clenched. A stream of expletives backing up behind his teeth, he slid to a stop and knelt, ripped open Marcus' jacket and shirt and felt for a pulse. He found it as Marcus groaned and opened his eyes. There were two slugs in the vest over Marcus' heart, another in his shoulder, hence the blood.

"Lucky fuckin bastard," Hoot said, a breath of relief following the words from his mouth. He holstered the Glock and helped his partner sit up.

"Jeezus, that hurts!" Marcus said, ripping his vest loose with his one good arm. Sirens were getting closer. The blare of the Amtrak's horn was growing more distant.

"Impact knocked you down," Hoot said. "The fall knocked you out. You get hit anywhere else?"

Shaking his head, Marcus said, "No. I don't think so. How about Norman?"

There was a trail of blood leading down the street but Hoot knew it would soon disappear. He said, "He got away."

"Angela?"

The Amtrak horn blew again.

"She did too," Hoot said.

***

The train arrived in Chicago with a screech of rail-car brakes and, finally, a halting jolt. Angela disliked the hulking city instantly. The sky was dark and menacing. Clouds heavy with

241

unfallen snow drew close down the sides of towering skyscrapers to lie atop the rooftops of lesser buildings, searched for places to dump what was left of their loads, adding to the ugly mounds of plowed frozen mush already on the ground. A bone-chilling wind occasionally blew up the ship canal from Lake Michigan so that Angela had to walk with her head down, looking at the toes of her new Harley-Davidson boots and missing Liz desperately. Tears that might have been primed by the icy wind, by her longing for Liz, or both, froze on her cheeks like stinging nettles.

She would find a phone and call immediately. Tell Liz that she missed her. Tell her that she needed her. Tell her *something*. For a moment she wondered if Liz had actually been there at all – her time with her so dream-like, all of her time since leaving home, everything in Spokane so completely unreal.

But Liz surely had been real, Angela knew because her absence left such a vacuum.

***

The Greyhound to Joplin could have just as well been a circus bus, so many out-of-costume clowns on board. It was packed with low-end travelers of all ages, from newborn and pissed off to be there, to long retired and equally pissed off to be there, and scattered throughout were every kind of freak and weirdo the holiday season could produce…including Angela. Many of them sat with eyes riveted straight ahead, looking semi-nauseous, clutching wrapped gifts too precious to be regulated to the luggage compartment in the belly of the bus. Others brimmed-over with gregarious spirit, and seemed determined to bring a little holiday cheer to everyone else on the bus. Angela only prayed that no one would start a chorus of *The Ant Song* or a medley of Christmas favorites.

Charging down Highway 71 from Kansas City. Passing through a town honest-to-God named Peculiar Missouri, and heading for points south. The Hispanic girl across the aisle from Angela, unbuttoned her blouse, produced a heavy tit capped with a swollen nipple half the size of Rhode Island, and proceeded to nurse the infant in her lap.

The old geezer seated in front of Angela cranked his head around well past the normal human range of motion to watch. "Nursin's good for 'em," he said, smacking his lips as he spoke as if barely holding himself back from joining the infant on the other tit. "Makes 'em strong!"

Angela wondered if he was referring to making babies strong, or making tits strong. The Hispanic girl didn't seem to understand him. After a while she put the show away and burped the baby. Soon it would shit its diaper and everyone on the bus would know it.

Meanwhile, the bus was afflicted with the oily stench of heavy diesel fumes invisibly clinging to the floorboards down the center aisle and getting stirred-up whenever it was walked through. A small bathroom in the rear of the bus was situated directly above the source of those fumes – the engine compartment. This was the doorway to the Dark Side as far as Angela was concerned, and she wouldn't even consider going there short of a dire emergency, but practically everyone else on the bus seemed to feel it was a feature not to be missed and they formed a constant ebb and flow to the rear until the Hispanic girl took the baby back there to change its diaper. Might as well have hung an *out of order* sign on the door afterward, the other passengers' interest waned so quickly.

Angela wondered if there might be some kind of direct connection between the toilet and the engine directly below it. And then it occurred to her that a certain amount of human waste might be required to keep the bus running. If so, could they possibly become stranded along Highway 71 on Christmas Eve for a lack of shit? Someone may have to brave the baby poop and diesel fumes and take care of business back there just to keep them moving, and it wasn't going to be her.

***

Christmas Eve. Arriving in Joplin at last; Angela got off the bus murmuring to herself, "*Never* take the bus. Never. *Ever.* Again."

243

It was early evening, dark and cold. Bold Merry Christmas lights twinkled from festive swags spanning Main Street a block over. Only two other passengers got off the Greyhound – the rest of those annoying, stinking, greasy-food-eating people were evidently going to destinations farther down the highway. Angela was pretty sure that Hell itself must be the last stop at the end of the line. She wondered how many of them were going all the way to Hell.

The bus station was located on 2nd between Joplin Street and Wall Street in a block of old brick structures that could do with some renovation, the neighborhood past its prime but left unscathed by the massive octopus of a tornado that had flattened much of the rest of the town in the spring of 2011. The station was in a squat building that took up the back half of the block and looked more like an automobile service garage from the days of Bonnie and Clyde than a bus depot. The waiting area inside was a rectangular room somewhat smaller than the lady's restroom had been in the Amtrak station in Chicago.

It was a drab place. Along one wall stood a row of vending machines looking as if regular refill service occurred somewhat less frequently than it should. The machines bore a sign advising that nickels should be used in the machines – *agents will not make change for nickels or pennies!* it warned.

The agent who was parked behind the ticket counter looked like it damned well better be worth his time to bother him – and you sure as hell shouldn't bother him to make change for the goddamned vending machines. A sparse collection of indestructible-looking molded plastic chairs were set in two rows down the middle of the room, ostensibly to make waiting comfortable; they were ugly and ergonomically ill-designed to cause severe spinal misalignment if used for any length of time. A skimpy row of coin-op lockers lined the other wall, their locking doors removed per Homeland Security doctrine. Angela noticed that the colorless tile floor seemed to be stained with blotches of grief. Looked as if it had soaked up whole rivers of despair in its time. Looked like you might stir some up if you trod too heavily across it, so Angela walked as softly as her new boots allowed over to a pair of pay phones and swiped her credit card. Relieved to see that the card was accepted, she punched in her sister's number.

A half hour later Nikki drove up in a Chrysler minivan with a festive holiday wreath fastened to the grill. Angela's sister was all hugs and howareya's at the curbside – she had come alone.

"We've been worried to death about you!" Nikki said as soon as they were driving away.

Seeing her long-lost sister made Angela miss Liz all over again. Made her anxious. She'd call her again as soon as she could.

"I told you not to worry," she answered her sister. "First time I called. Told you I was coming."

Bogus cheerful silence filled the van while Nikki turned left onto Main, heading north past the bible college and onward.

A wide highway. 45MPH speed limit. Individual businesses here and there. Long distances between driveways. Very little had changed during Angela's absence. "Who's been worrying?" she asked.

"Everyone! Mother. Me and Jeffrey, of course. And Kenneth, even though he can't be here – our brother the big-city Texas nurse. Very busy. *On call* you know. And God knows how Les and the kids have managed without you! They're just worried sick."

"You talked to Les?"

"I called."

"He wouldn't talk to you, would he?"

"I left a message. Your sister-in-law was there. I spoke to her and she was very concerned. I can't imagine how awful this must be for the children."

"Stop it, Nikki. You've never figured out how to make me feel half as bad as you always thought I should, so why don't you just assume I already feel as bad as I'm able to feel...okay?"

They drove in silence awhile, and then, Nikki, all cheerful and bright, said, "Mom can hardly wait to see you!"

"I can hardly wait to see her, too."

245

"Hope you're hungry. We have lots of leftovers from dinner – a big baked ham, my own secret recipe sweet potatoes, hot rolls, the usual feast. Turkey tomorrow. Everyone's waiting for us."

"Except Kenny, you said."

Angela wondered about her out-of-the-closet brother. Wondered what he would have to say about Liz. Probably not much. They hadn't been close even when they were kids.

"He was here for Daddy's funeral," Nikki said. "Then he had to go right back to Dallas."

"Was it a nice funeral?"

"It was. Half the town came."

Silence again. The streets of Joplin drifted past as if Angela and Nikki were passengers on a small-town carnival ride with no destination in mind. They passed the Bible College, the big electronic sign out by the street proclaiming joy and highlighting the schedule for Christmas day worship in the campus chapel. They stopped at a local Wal Mart the big hand-of-God tornado had spared for a few things, and in the parking lot Angela was assaulted by the smell emanating from McDonald's and KFC deep fryers nearby. Mainstream Midwest cuisine for the holidays and any other day.

Ah…nothing quite like hick civilization! Angela thought. The fast-food aroma lay on her like a breath of warm canola oil, making her feel half nauseous and half hungry. First, the stinking bus. And now this. She just knew she was going to throw up before the day was over.

At Nikki's house the joyous holiday festivities were almost too joyous for Angela to bear. But the food really was excellent and plentiful, and it did feel good to be among family again after so many years. Mom, two nieces Angela had never met before, Aunt Elsa and Uncle Ralph, and even Nikki's hubby Jeffrey the pudd – all seemed happy to welcome her home. But between Angela and Nikki, it only took a couple of hours for their sibling affection to wear thin. By then all the bland reminiscences had been played out, all the horrifying stories about the tornado had been told, and it was time to start adding a little spice.

"Bet you miss *your* kids tonight," Nikki said.

"Yeah. I do," Angela said.

"I don't know how you can stand it. Don't know how you just leave them. Bet they miss you too, poor things!"

"Probably. But how would you know? You've never even met my kids, Nichole. You especially never wanted to meet the *illegitimate* one...remember?"

Nikki blushed. "That's not fair. You're the one who went away."

Angela looked ready to punch her sister.

"Angela!" Mom interceded, "Nichole, please!"

"We've never met them either, Aunt Angela," said one of Nikki's daughters, Stephanie or Catherine – who could tell? "We want to meet them!" the other added.

"I was only thinking of how awful it must be for them. Not knowing where their mother is at Christmas," Nikki said, still picking at it like a fresh scab. "How could you just up and leave them alone at Christmastime?"

"They aren't alone. They're not *abandoned* children. They've got their father and his sister's family looking after them. They'll be okay without me this one time," Angela said, standing and pacing. "In fact, I'm sure everything back there is just hunky-fucking-dory without me this one fucking time!"

"Angela, *please!*" her mother exclaimed. "The children!"

"I'm sorry. Really I am. Please forgive me girls. Aunt Angela is very tired."

Angela refused to be goaded into crying. She said, "Mom, Sis, I apologize. If you don't mind...I think I'd like to use your phone and then just call it a night."

Nikki, the perfect hostess now, asked if Angela needed anything before she retired, showed her sister to the phone and then hovered nearby wearing a disingenuous smile until the awkward silence between them encouraged her to move along.

Saved by the answering machine from having to talk to her children – or thank God, Les! – Angela left them a message wishing them a merry Christmas and promised to call again soon. Les and the kids were probably attending the annual bacchanalia at his sister's house, drinking eggnog and playing

Risk. Les played Risk as if one of his testicles were in jeopardy so he seldom lost.

Angela called Hoot, told his voicemail that she was in Joplin and okay. Then she made another call and the same tireless mechanical voice from before informed her that Liz's Nextel number was still not in service. Suggested she try again at another time. It worried her, but she was too exhausted to dwell on it. She needed sleep. She slept like a woman in a coma that night.

*** *** ***

Norman was slowly and thoroughly enjoying every bite of a crab-and-artichoke omelet and chasing it down with strong black coffee perked – not *dripped* – in a percolator that looked as if it had not been cleaned beyond a simple rinse-out since Reagan was president. He soaked it up with biscuits that only Debbie-Sue knew how to make. Honey from beehives that he could see from where he was sitting.

Debbie-Sue said, "Curtis'll be back from Banks with some of the guys pretty soon. I'll bake a couple of fresh-caught silvers with butter'n onions, fry some squash, bake a couple of pies, and we'll have us a little party tonight. You get to feelin' better you can be Father Not-Christmas and roll the Boxing Day joints."

Curtis was Debbie-Sue's husband. He was a horticulturalist and ecologist. Worked the Banks Lake area for the EPA. And was the only tree-hugging dirt worshipper Norman knew that wasn't completely full of shit. He had developed a strain of hybrid sativa cannabis for the medical marijuana coalition that Norman had profited from for the last few years, in his travels becoming a very low-key but successful seller of some of the most potent bud grown anywhere in the world.

"You say I was unconscious for two days?" Norman asked, still feeling a little groggy and weak. A growing pain was centered behind his eyes, settling-in for the long haul. The fork was shaking in his hand.

248

"Three, counting the day you got here. You remember that?"

"Not exactly."

"Curtis thought you were the ATF trying to pull some stunt, slidin' into the parking lot an' leanin' on the horn," Debbie-Sue said. "He was just gonna shoot ya but I said let's see who it is, first. Good thing I did, too, you passed out with your bloody ass glued to the seat of a hot Volvo."

"So, how is my ass?" Norman asked.

"I've seen better. You'll live. The bullet passed through without hittin' the bone. Lucky. If it had mushroomed, you'd be just about buttless right now. That diaper you're wearin' is a poultice for infection, so don't be getting' any macho ideas about takin' it off 'less I say so."

Norman looked out at the empty parking lot, said, "Where's the car?"

"Up the river. Or down," Debbie-Sue said. "I don't know for sure. Curtis thought it best to make it disappear right away seein' as how the registration in the glove box said *stolen* all over it."

Norman turned back to admire in fullness the most hospitable place he knew, said, "Thanks, Deb. I'm looking forward to partying with you guys. Want to sample Curtis's latest. Want to talk to him about the lay of the land up north. Discuss some new business arrangements. Connections he may have with a few legit medical outlets."

"Up north? You thinkin' about crossin'?"

Norman, understanding that she meant crossing the US/Canadian border, said, "Yeah. I am."

"I thought you stayed *this* side of the border."

"Normally. But it seems that I may have just killed a U.S. Marshal in Spokane," Norman said. "So I need to get real invisible for awhile. Maybe a long while."

"A marshal? That ain't good…but you said *may have* – so maybe he ain't dead. I haven't heard anything about it on the po-lice band or the internet, so, dead or alive, you're ahead of the shitstorm so far. Still, I guess it's a good thing the bloody Volvo went fishin' before anyone saw it here. As for goin' north, I think the old dirt road near Molson was still passable last week. Curtis'll know."

"You mind if I go back to the room?" Norman asked, a killer headache starting to team up with his ass on fire to sap his strength. "Even after your wake-the-dead coffee I feel like I could use some more sleep."

Curtis and Debbie-Sue's place was actually an old motel that she and Curtis had bought and remodeled into their residence and Debbie-Sue's restaurant. Three of the old motel rooms were still attached and not yet remodeled. One of them was not completely filled with junk. "Good idea," Debbie-Sue said. "You're still about a quart low on blood. Curtis will come fetch ya when he gets home."

Thankful, Norman gave Debbie-Sue a hug and excused himself, walked along the sheltered verandah to the door at the end and almost fell inside. His capacity for exhaustion, while remarkable, was not limitless, and he was miles past the limit. He sat down carefully in an ancient recliner in the middle of a cluttered motel room that hadn't seen a paying guest in over twenty years and fell into a fitful sleep, one where he was haunted by dreams of children picking dead flowers in fields where jets had dropped napalm, where bloody water flowed from faucets and showerheads, and where his old friend, Hoot, repeatedly opened the back of the Wonder Wand van, thus discovering the third M-67 grenade.

Norman had lost his secondhand C-pap when he abandoned the van in Spokane, so he woke up several times from choking. It was a poor excuse for *sleep*. But that was as good as it was going to get.

***

Christmas day, Santa was rewarding all the good boys and girls.

Angela knew she had definitely not been a good girl, but felt rewarded nonetheless, felt a quiet joy spreading through her like honey on a warm biscuit. It was a sweet temptation to relax and soak it up, but she dared not relax too much. Thoughts of her kids might steal up from behind and grab her as they were prone to do from time to time. Concern about Emilio's sudden disappearance or Liz's silent absence might reach in and stir things up in her stomach. Or a glance from Nikki might stab her in the back without warning. Things had already been a little dicey in the kitchen over coffee while they waited for Mom and the girls to wake up, Nikki saying; "So you met this vampire-looking bounty hunter in a *top*less bar?"

"He's a U.S. Marshal. And it was actually an all-nude club. And, yes, I worked there. By the way, *topless* went extinct centuries ago."

"What in the world were you doing working in an all-nude club? Don't tell me you've become a...*whore*." Nikki said, dropping her voice to a whisper saying the word.

"For Christsakes, Nikki! I worked there because a friend of mine worked there," Angela said, obfuscating. "Don't worry. I kept my panties on most of the time."

"*Angie*! Don't even joke about that! How was I to know?"

Nikki couldn't know, of course. But Angela knew that if her sister had even the slightest inkling of her recent experiences she'd probably toss her out into the street, Christmas or not.

She was sorely tempted to tell her. Tell her and Mom both in excruciating detail. Mom would be stunned, of course, and then she'd start working out some vague connection to her own responsibility for her daughter's fall into the low life, into prostitution. Nikki would probably faint and crack her own skull, then recover well enough to toss her sister out.

"What difference does it make why I was there?" Angela said. "I was only trying to share a minor detail of my life. About a psychopath wanting to kill me because I look like someone else. We can turn the conversation back to your kids' grade-point averages and Mom's advancing forgetfulness if you prefer."

"Sorry. I just meant...you know...we've been so worried about you. Didn't know where you were. What you were doing."

"Forget it."

Oven preheating. Ingredients on the counter. It was time to bake something. Time for the fifty-thousand-dollar question; "What *happened*, Angela?"

"I just told you, nothing happened!"

"I meant between you and Les." Nikki said.

"Nothing happened there, either."

"Did you simply quit loving him *with all your heart* the way you swore you always would? Remember how Daddy thought that was the silliest notion ever invented?"

"Maybe I do still love him and don't know it. Maybe I love my kids, too."

"*Maybe* you love your kids! How can you even say that?"

"I don't know – I didn't mean it that way. I *do* love them. I just know there's no going back. No starting over. Whatever is next will be something entirely new."

Nikki, in a huff, said, "Life is all a big movie to you, isn't it? You think you can just keep rewriting the script until the ending comes out right…"

"I *wish*."

Nikki's mouth clamped in a tight pucker, she tried a new tack; "Listen, if you're going to leave Les and start over, why don't you just stay here in Joplin. Send for your kids, and help me with Mom?"

"Help you with Mom? What kind of help do you need?"

More coffee. More cream and sugar. Bread-hook mixer grunting, Nikki was grinding nuts, mixing brown sugar and butter as if she was preparing the very Staff of Life and she could only get it right with concentrated effort.

"It would never work," Angela said, "trying to make our family whole again."

"Isn't that what you're already trying to do?" Nikki countered. "Coming here at Christmas. Stirring things up?"

Brown sugar and butter and flour were as well mixed as they could be. Nuts were folded in. Rolling out the dough, Nikki, the quintessential Libra always wanting to fix things, was calmer now but still couldn't let it go; "So *that's* your plan? You're going to start all over. Just like that…throw

252

everything away, and start all over? What makes you think you can do that all by yourself? Don't be such a fool, Angela."

"A fool? Being made a fool is nothing to be afraid of. As you know, I've been one for a long time. But I've been thinking about it, and I think I see now why Daddy couldn't bring himself to forgive me when I left home with Les. It was because he'd tried so hard to teach me to stand on my own two feet and build something for myself. He thought I had gumption. And then he thought that I threw all those lessons away when I threw in with Les."

Tears were standing by, waiting for their cue. Angela washed them down with a big swig of hot coffee and refilled her cup. Then she added, "Daddy was right. Then, two weeks ago, I did something for myself for the first time since I was seventeen and ran away from a *quiet* abortion."

"Angie! *Please* don't…"

"So maybe I'm a late bloomer. And maybe I jumped into the dirty end of the pool. But at least I'm swimming."

Silence fell between Angela and her sister like an opera curtain at intermission – end of Act Two, Kitchen Drama. They sipped coffee and baked cinnamon rolls until the girls and Jeffery made their enthusiastic entrances. Served them orange juice and fresh-baked treats and catered to their needs while they flocked around the table; a rooster, two hens, and two chicks. They were waiting for Mom to join them, knowing that she would feel entitled to impose recent details of her ailments upon them with no consideration for the burden of that knowledge. They were her daughters, and it was high on any list of daughterly duties to listen to the daily manifest of their mother's suffering, then respond with deep concern for her well being. Bite the tongue for Mom.

It occurred to Angela that Nikki was raising her own little brood of required listeners. She went to the phone. She would call again and tell Les to hug the kids for her. She would tell him that she'd see them, soon.

Chapter 33

Norman was thankful for the beat-up old Land Rover that
Curtis had found even if three thousand cash for it had been a
rip. It burned oil like a sheik and had a heater that didn't work
for shit. But it had good tires. It had a clean title and legal
British Columbia plates. And it could climb a near-vertical
mountain face all the way to the moon if need be. The bloody
Volvo would have never made it through the rugged winter
hills northwest of Molson.

Norman was traveling with one hundred kilos of cured
bud vacuum-packed in Seal-A-Meal pouches in the back of the
Land Rover, part of a revised business arrangement with Curtis.
He also had a couple hundred dollars in cash left after paying
for the Volvo, a bogus driver's license and American Express
card, and a few secondhand clothes in a plastic trash bag. And
he had his S&W .38 snub-nose.

He was as tired as he knew how to be. Norman hadn't
slept worth a fuck in over a week. Figured he would get used
to it…eventually. Thanks to Debbie-Sue, at least his ass felt a
little better, even after the merciless beating the road had given
it.

Molson had once been a thriving mining town. Was
now an uninhabited ghost town made into a state park at the
end of a dead end road. Norman left the paved main road about
a mile before Molson, took a forest service dirt road, which
soon turned into a backcountry road, which eventually became
a steep trail barely wider than the Land Rover, and then not
even that. There was snow everywhere deep enough to hide
both the car and the frozen body of the fool driving it until
springtime…

But luck was with him. He came through on the
Canadian side a few miles east of Osoyoos. Opened his packed
lunch and enjoyed two of Debbie-Sue's pesto salmon
sandwiches and some homemade potato salad with leeks and
dill. Damn, that woman could cook! Ugly, and a bossy bitch

to boot, he thought, but one hell of a cook. Knew her way around gunshot wounds, too. A man could do a lot worse.

The snowcapped panorama of the Canadian Rockies was breathtaking. After lunch, Norman turned west and then north again and kept on going a few hours until he came at last to an apple and peach orchard on the banks of the Thompson River just outside Spences Bridge. It was well after dark. A lighted sign near town proclaimed that the fishing here was the best in the world.

Norman was known by certain people here – at least by reputation – and he was expected. He took his trash bag luggage and the hundred kilos into one of several small pickers' cabins set close above the river, and threw himself down on the built-in cot.

He was home. At least for the time being.

***

There is something especially depressing about a hospital parking lot during the holidays, a few cars being there far too long.

Parked in the Triangle Parking garage at the University of Washington Medical Center in Seattle, there was a dusty-pink Cadillac with *Slutmobile* written in the back window and a wad of trinkets hanging from the rearview mirror. Inside the car, inside the glove box, a cell phone with a dying battery rang and rang and rang with no one to answer it. The automated voice kicked in, suggesting with its usual inanimate lack of empathy that the caller try again later.

Christmas Day and a phone is ringing.

Isn't someone going to answer that phone?

Maybe some gonif will steal it. The silence would be a blessing.

Angela dropped the receiver back on the hook. She had to stop worrying. She had plenty to deal with right here…

Things with Mom had started out a little gummy. It had actually been that way between them for years before Angela left Joplin, so really, they took up where they'd left off. This wasn't the way either one of them wanted it to be, but it wasn't until they found themselves alone together that the fog parted. After all the Christmas hoorah, after the big family brunch, the verbal fisticuffs between sisters, Mom asked, "Would you like to go for a ride out to your father's grave, Angela?" Then after a sharp glance from Nikki, Mom continued, "You can drive. I don't drive much anymore. But I could use some fresh air."

They drove first out to the old McClelland/Park Ridge neighborhood where Angela had grown up to check on the house. Park Ridge was a stoic upscale neighborhood that Angela's mom said had been "spared God's wrath vis-à-vis the big tornado." The house she had grown up in appeared surprisingly foreign to Angela's memory of it. The ancient elm trees that she had loved as a kid were gone. The oaks still stood, weathered and bare, forlorn-looking in the broad front yard. Angela and her mother sat in the car in the driveway and looked at the house as if waiting for an invitation from a ghost. The house was empty and appeared unlived-in though well kept up. There was no house-for-sale sign in the yard, but a realtor's key caddy hung on the front door. A flyer available from the realtor or over the Internet proclaimed: *Custom designer house. Excellent condition. Very solid and well placed. Large beautifully landscaped yard with many trees. View. A bargain at this price.*

"Why're you selling it?" Angela asked.

"I don't want to live here anymore," Mom answered. "I'm staying with Nikki and Jeff and the kids until it sells. They've asked me if I want to make it a permanent arrangement – living with them – and I just can't decide. Nikki has such hooks, as you well know. Wouldn't take us long to start hating each other."

Mom sat surveying the carpet of fallen leaves in the front yard as if she could still see her girls helping their father and brother rake them up in the fall, the way they'd run and jump in the piles, have to do it all over. "It was too lonely here without your father. And too big," she said. "He was a big man. It didn't seem like such a large house with him in it. But the living room. The kitchen. Dining room. Den. The whole house – *especially* the bedroom – was empty without him. So I moved into your old bedroom for awhile, hardly venturing out of it until Nikki insisted."

"You think you'll be happier living out at Briarbrook with Nikki instead of in your own place?"

"Happier? Honey, I haven't had a happy day in my life. Why would I start now?"

Liar, Angela thought. Her mother had been deliriously happy. She just didn't know what happiness was – it was a condition that didn't come with adequate sympathy to suit her.

Yeah. Angela could see her mother fitting right in with the *grande dames* at the Briarbrook Country Club. Cozy in Nikki's five-bedroom Tudor backed up on the fourteenth fairway at the far end of the community, where the homes were newer and the streets were named Green and Tee and Par; where you could always tell which of the stay-at-home gals was hosting the weekly bridge club luncheon by the jam of golf carts in the driveway at eleven sharp. Icons of the community, they would gather at one place or another and digress endlessly on their current pet provocations, the shuffles and rubbers a byproduct of their insatiable need for chitchat.

The old Park Ridge neighborhood was rustic and quaint by comparison – it had been her father's house and her mother had only lived there.

"Wanna go inside, Mom?"

"Not really. You?"

"I'll pass."

Both of them were strangers here now. Home is always underfoot, never over your shoulder, and it suddenly occurred to Angela that she was presently homeless.

They drove on. Passed a big new Harley Davidson dealership standing near the entrance to Wildcat Park on the banks of Shoal Creek, a familiar place where she had lost her oral virginity. Turning north they drove past Freeman Hospital, the first and largest major structure to suffer the tornado's wrath last year. Cranes and heavy equipment busy, it was still being rebuilt. Beyond the hospital, they entered a broad expanse of utter devastation nearly a year old. With a whispered gasp, Angela realized what God's wrath actually looked like.

"This was the path of the storm," Angela's mother said, solemnly. "You should have seen it before it was cleaned up. Unbelievable!"

Circling back toward the east end of the tornado's path, they passed a standing sign from a once-popular fast food joint with no fast food joint attached only a few blocks from Angela's alma mater, McAuley high school – the shrine of her shame. Staff and students heroic after the tornado, the old school was finally adding a new wing that had been excitedly planned while she was still in attendance there.

Being raised a good Catholic girl was handicap that Angela had had a natural motivation to overcome. It was hard not to feel a little outcast out in the heathen world of small-town Protestants, but at McAuley you were safely gathered into the flock. And the penguin sisters were forever coaxing the strays from out of harm's way. It had distressed them intensely to find that they'd dropped their guard long enough to allow Angela's unfortunate lapse, as if she had thrown down her panties right there in the school gymnasium virtually under their cloistered noses and not in the back seat of Les's Chevy at the drive-in theater. Angela had never forgotten what the movie playing, unwatched, on the screen had been – she realized with a shrug that she still hadn't seen it.

It was a short drive to St. Mary's, where Angela instinctively hunkered across the vestibule. She looked all around as if she'd never seen the place before, all familiar but all strange, the inside vast and imposing just as it had been when she was a girl. She accompanied her mother to the small side chapel, genuflected, and lit a votive candle for her father, then she sat down in one of the pews near the back while her mother busied herself with prayer.

New, soft benches…Angela had forgotten how cold and hard those old benches had been. But now she remembered how she usually half-dozed through the liturgy and how her mind periodically leapt with wild abandon to thoughts that were sexual in the extreme – she'd be sound asleep in no time on these cushy seats, having who knows what sort of erotic fantasy! Over to one side were the cramped confession cubicles, except that nowadays many younger church members prefer to do it face-to-face. Her mother said, "They like to call it reconciliation, now, *confession* being so blameworthy."

Is that my problem? Angela wondered. Am I blameworthy?

If I had stayed in Joplin would I be wondering if that monster tornado had come for me? Would it have got me?

She remembered the sacraments:

Bless me, Father, for I have sinned.

How long has it been since your last confession?

Forever.

***

Ten months later…

"Why'd you choose this place, *Paddy O'Flannigan's*?" Marcus asked.

"I'm Irish," Hoot answered, smiling. "Didn't I ever tell you that? *Hooten* is Irish for '*Big Pile o' Crap.*'"

"Can't argue with that," Marcus said. "How's retirement treating you so far?"

They were sitting at a window seat in a bar at Pike Place Market in Seattle, the pale white man and the dark black man. The view was of Elliott Bay. It was wet outside, October, raining and gray, and Hoot was drinking a smoky martini, coffee for Marcus.

"Retired? Bite your tongue. I'm just enjoying a bit of medical disability," Hoot said. "Besides, nobody wants to hear an old fart complain so I won't bother. You still keeping an eye open for Creeper?"

"As much as possible. FBI still thinks he's in Canada. But no confirmation."

"Been almost a year."

A hefty waitress wearing lace-up purple boots, fishnets, and a tight skirt brought a large bucket of steamer clams and topped off Marcus' coffee. Hoot said, "Thank you, dear. Would you please bring another of these?" holding up his nearly-empty martini glass. "And also tell the cook I'd like to have a word when he has a moment to spare."

259

A few minutes later a very nervous-looking Hispanic man approached their table wearing a guilty smile.

"Relax, Emilio," Hoot said. "Have a seat. He's not INS. We just need to ask you a few questions. Like you and I talked yesterday, okay?"

"This is *Emilio*?" Marcus said, casting a sidelong glance toward his ex-partner. "The same guy who was staying with the two gals in Norman's Spokane rental house?"

"In the flesh," Hoot answered.

"He vanished, I remember," Marcus said. "FBI had him listed as *missing*. They were looking for him like crazy after the explosion that blew the house to smithereens. How the hell did you find him?"

"I have more time for this sort of diversion now that I'm *retired*," Hoot said. Cracking a smile, he added. "A certain titty-bar manager was helpful. And, between you and me, this is strictly off the record – INS especially doesn't need to know. If Emilio here tells us what he knows about Creeper, that is."

"You remember us, Emilio?" Marcus said. "In Spokane?"

"Si. Not you so much, senior – but him," Emilio said, gesturing at Hoot. "I see you both at the fire. But I don't know any *Creeper*."

"Where were you during the fire," Marcus asked.

"House after next door house. Mister Cook tole me to go there," Emilio said. "Tole me to stay with old Missus CasCopio. Said she would be scared. She was."

"*Nathan* Cook told you to go stay with a neighbor?"

"Si."

"When?"

"Soon as I get home. Early. On the day of the fire. Maybe one o'clock in the morning. Mister Cook said INS was snooping 'round, an tole me to get lost. He tole me to go to Missus CasCopio."

"So where is all this leading?" Marcus asked Hoot. "You know Horner will be pissed if he finds out you're still digging around in the Carpenter case. It's an open case and you aren't an active marshal anymore. He'll have your ass."

"Want to recommend a wine that would go with my ass? Something red?"

"None of this is any sort of evidence we can use. Come on…coerced testimony from an illegal – Horner'll have *my* butt on a platter if he finds out I'm talking to you about this!"

"May as well get used to it, Marshal Marcus. Horner has a fondness for fresh ass, time to time. Tell him the rest, Emilio," Hoot said. "Tell him what you told me."

"Mister Cook comes back later. To Missus CasCopio's house. Tole me he's looking for Liz an her friend. Tole me I owe him a favor. Tole me he have a friend can get me this job in Seattle, an I owe him *two* favors."

"What did Mister Cook want?" Hoot asked.

"He want me to find Liz in Seattle. He give me her mother's address an tole me to watch out for Liz. Tole me to tell him right away if I see her with her friend, Angela."

"Tell him? How?" Marcus asked.

"A place on the internet," Emilio said.

"What else?" Hoot asked with a wicked smile.

"He tole me to watch out for *you*, senor. Said to tell him if I see the pale lawman with either of these women…"

Chapter 34

Late in October, Angela was working late again. She could certainly use the money, but the extra hours cut into the precious little time she had with her kids. She had promised to take them trick-or-treating. And they talked about Christmas almost constantly. She understood, they were no doubt apprehensive that Mom might pull a goner again if not regularly reminded of the importance that particular holiday had for them. Maternal guilt was such a tidy black hole, Angela had learned, able to hold vast amounts and still have plenty of room for more.

She gulped the last of her coffee, tossed her limp banana peal in the dumpster, and screwed the cap on her Thermos. Her hair largely hidden under a black Harley bandanna printed with smiley white skulls, she was dressed in cement slurry-splattered Carhartt coveralls, a flannel shirt, a sweatshirt, and Red Wing boots. She stood aside with others waiting for the manlift to take them up.

It said *Angie* in yellow letters on the red hardhat that Angela wore backwards. Took some effort to find her name among all the stickers plastered there – at least four different contractors' stickers, Brundage Bone and Olympic Concrete Pumping stickers, EFCO, Symons, Patent, and Wacker equipment suppliers' stickers, Coast Crane and Morrow Crane stickers, MasterBuilders, Raeco, and Davis product stickers, along with two project name stickers, all crowding for space on the hat, earplugs in a plastic case dangled from the adjustment knob. She got off the manlift on the twelfth floor, strapped on her knee pads, and went to work.

Angela was an apprentice concrete finisher, part of a crew working overtime to get the floors of a new twenty-eight story mixed-use building ready for carpet and tile. There were four of them working late tonight, spread out over three floors where they were pouring thin layers of self-leveling underlayment, or grout, in selected areas to smooth out any irregularities in the structural concrete slabs that might create problems under the finished floors – tile and carpet. It was specialized work that had to be done quickly with painstaking attention to detail, and she loved it. She was good at it, and it had the added benefit of being *indoor* work, a worthwhile perk for a cement mason in the wintertime.

She had been working in construction and attending apprenticeship classes since returning to Seattle after her little escapade to Spokane and Joplin last Christmas. It had taken almost three months for her back to quit aching ass-to-earlobes 24-7 when she first started working as a full-time finisher, but she was tougher now. Only thing was the cold and wet in the wintertime, and in Seattle that meant from October to June so the winter work season was just beginning. She didn't know if she would ever get used to that part of it – being so *close* to the weather day in and day out – but she took whatever they gave her without bitching.

Sometimes she couldn't help remembering what Liz had said about spending less time on her knees and making more money. Now *there* was a sage little tidbit of truth!

If only her co-workers knew...

They didn't. And she was planning on keeping it that way.

Not a word about that part of her past had leaked from Angela's lips since returning to Seattle. And even though she missed Liz desperately sometimes, she had wiped Spokane and Goodtime Charlie's off her resume for good. Her working life was all about concrete now. Poured and vibrated, screeded, floated, troweled, stamped, colored or stained – if it was about finishing concrete she was learning how to do it right, and she was getting more proficient at it every day.

Angela took some comfort believing that her daddy would be proud if he'd lived to see her now. And it didn't make her sad to think about it anymore, her daddy's untimely passing – it's just the way it was. She would find herself remembering what her mother had said. Maybe Mom was right and he actually wasn't so disappointed in her when he died as she had thought; a comforting idea, but she still had to earn it – Daddy had always given generously...when it was earned.

One day she would own her own contracting outfit. That was the plan – Marshal Hoot would be proud that she had one. She missed Hoot, too.

In the meantime she got to see her kids every other weekend and in-between once in awhile, and was hoping for joint custody by the time school was out. That was what the rest of her life was about.

So much depended on convincing others of what she knew to be true…that she was okay now. That she'd be okay tomorrow too. No more running off on wild tangents. For that reason she didn't dare even try to contact Liz. A *stripper* would not look favorable in the eyes of people who were judgmental as part of their job description. They knew about Angela's brief career at Goodtime Charlie's, looked on it with a combination of pity and disgust, and would see a current association with a working stripper as a deviation back to the dark side.

The batch of underlayment that Angela's hod carrier had just brought up in the manlift needed a few more minutes to take its initial set.

Waiting, her mind returned to the visit she and her mother made last Christmas to her daddy's grave in Fairview cemetery on Maiden Lane. A derelict old concrete products manufacturing site standing like a wraith across Jung Boulevard, A supermarket distribution warehouse that had once been a major-brand cookie and cracker bakery hunkering across the street the other way.

"Why couldn't the tornado have torn down these old eyesores instead of the high school and Wal-Mart?" her mother had said, and the sentiment seemed a bit less ludicrous to Angela, now, compared to how it seemed then. Familiarity tipping the scale.

The family plot was in an older corner of the cemetery, where rows of the more ancient headstone monuments to the dearly departed leaned this way and that, captured in the slow-motion act of falling over.

Her father's marker was a simple marble headstone that said; Charles David Blackstone, Husband, Father, Builder, 1940-2011. Remembering that visit with her mother, Angela considered how hundreds of families cozily celebrated Christmas every year in *Blackstone Polestar* homes all over the tri-state area and all but a tiny few would remain unaware that the builder of their homes rested here. The *Blackstone Polestar* trademark survived under Jeffery's stewardship, but the heart of it had died and was now retired to the family plot.

The sun shone through lowering clouds while they stood at Daddy's headstone and Angela saw her mother gazing across the cemetery into another time. "There's a nice park right over there where your daddy used to take us to hear whatever group was playing in the gazebo on Saturday evenings in the summer.

"Do you remember that park, dear?" Mom asked, cocking her ear as if listening for the long-ago music. "Schifferdecker Park. It had all those amusement rides? You loved to ride the little train."

The little girl who loved that train was gone. A grown up Angela had stood next to Mom in her place, the same grown up Angela struggling to keep her kids now that her wits seemed to have returned.

"The old gazebo still stands but the amusement rides are long gone," Angela's mom had said.

"I don't know how to miss him like you do," Angela remembered answering. "It was all so long ago."

"Not really," her mother replied.

"I was too impatient to leave here," Angela had confessed. "I'm sorry I hurt him. Sorry I hurt you both."

"I know that. He did, too," her mother said. "You got it from him, you know. Your daddy never had any patience, either. Drove like a bat out of hell everywhere he went. The amazing thing is that the cancer got him before he killed himself in a car accident. Never left to go somewhere on time, but was never late for anything in his life."

She had focused on Angela as if seeing her anew and said, "You're impatient to leave here again, aren't you?"

Angela had only nodded her head. A formation of geese flew over right then, squawking like a herd of flying jackasses laughing at dirty donkey jokes.

Her mother looked up, tilting her head as if to hear the joke.

"And where will you go next?" she asked.

"Follow those geese, maybe," Angela said

"Was Les...*abusive*?" Angela's mother asked, saying the word as if she had just learned it that morning.

"Some, I guess. Depends," Angela answered. "Depends on what you would call abusive...it's one of those words that isn't sure what it means. It keeps changing."

"Your father made the mistake of trying to hit me once," her mother said, the first Angela had ever heard of it. "Sometimes men just can't seem to hold it in," she added, "Especially impatient men."

"What happened?" Angela asked.

"He backed off. Went out for a few drinks instead. Drank for almost thirty-five years. But he never tried to hit me again."

"I remember him drinking," Angela said. I remember him mowing the lawn on his riding mower with a beer in one hand, but I didn't realize he was an *alcoholic*."

"I guess you could say that he was," her mother replied. "Could even say that I drove him to it. But he was a *good* drunk – if there is such a thing. Didn't drink around you kids too much. It kept him in a happier mood. Kept him from dwelling on things."

"What kinds of things?"

"Things," Angela's mother said. "Recently...his shame I think."

"Because of me and Kenny?"

"He was easily hurt."

"He was ashamed of me, wasn't he?" Angela had asked, feeling her back and shoulders physically shift as if she'd just dropped a load carried for so long that the weight had settled in and become a part of her.

"Your daddy had a lot of pride," Angela's mother said. "Pride is one of the seven deadlies – you remember? And prideful men are usually full of shame as well. But shame can be a motivator, too. Countless men have succeeded in their endeavors only out of fear of the shame they'd have to bear if

266

they failed. Your daddy was that way. Our marriage was testimony to that. So was his business. But I don't think he was ashamed of you. Or Kenneth. He simply couldn't understand your brother. A manly man, he couldn't relate. And he was hurt by you. He lost his authority over you, and that fed his shame – shame he felt for his failure to do better by both of you but too obstinate to call you up and tell you so. Actually, I think he was kind of proud that you had the backbone to go out and make your own mistakes."

"Oh. I've made plenty of those," Angela said.

Silence had blessed them for a few minutes, and then Angela's mother asked, "Will you be flying back to Seattle soon?"

"I don't really want to fly. I've still never been on an airplane in my life. Can you believe that? And I don't want to start now, not with all the airport hassle anymore. I'll probably take the train again. Starting out from here on the bus, of course, the only part of riding the train that I hate."

"Take my car instead," Angela's mother had said.

"Do *what*?"

"Take my car. I don't drive it anymore. Your daddy bought it and it's too big for me."

"I can't," Angela had answered, stunned. "Nikki will hate me forever if I do."

"She already hates you because you were your daddy's favorite," Angela's mother said. "She'll get over this easier than that."

Angela had looked at the waiting silver Chrysler Concorde and said, "I don't know…"

"Go on," her mother prompted. "Go now. You have your backpack. I have my cell phone. I'll call Nikki to come get me when I'm ready to leave your daddy. I'll tell her you said goodbye and thank you and all that business."

Angela's tears refused to stay put any longer. Twin rivers of them racing down her cheeks were only the headwaters of an emotional flood that had been building for years.

"Just don't forget to call once in awhile," her mother had said.

"And come for visits when you can. Bring my grandchildren…please."

***

For the second time in her life, Angela drove away from her hometown – a Midwest ghost town that just wouldn't give up the ghost, a town full of neighborhoods smashed by the hand of God, ringed by truck stops and fast food joints, and filled to the brim with faded memories built around a family she had disowned on her way out of town the first time ten years ago. But, for better or worse, she had them with her this time.

And now, back in Seattle with Halloween just around the corner, she was using a fresno float to touch-up some underlayment just out of reach of her mag trowel, she set the fresno aside and grabbed a margin trowel, a tool shaped like a butter knife or an artist's palette knife, but bigger, with a thin two-inch-wide steel blade about eight inches long. She needed it to work the area around the doorway where the kitchen joined the dining area, but the only margin trowel she had with her was an older one that was worn down to such a thin and sharp edge it was hard not to slice the surface of the grout. She decided she would run downstairs to the toolbox and replace it with a new one before she started the next unit.

Fiona Apple was playing on a crusty-looking old boombox-style CD player in the room behind her. Sullen music. Angela liked it. She alternated Fiona with Sinead O'Connor and Pink Martini; no stripper's heavy down-beat on the job for her. If she went down one floor to where Reggie was working it would be Pink Floyd, no doubt, which was fine except that The Floyd got old when it was all you heard over and over. Go up two floors to where Ralph and George were prepping the floors and shot blasting and there'd be no noticeable music; hip hop and gangsta rap on their iPods turned up real loud to hear it over the noise of the shot blaster, as if that were possible.

This kind of spread-out detail work was perfect for Angela. Made her feel independent. On a big pouring crew everything was all hurry up-and wait. Hurry to get the mud placed and screeded. Wait for the mud to take its set. Then hurry up and get all over it to finish it. Working around the other trades she was constantly aware that someone was looking at her ass, trying to figure her out, wondering if she could cut it. And there was always a risk that she'd get dispatched out to a job and find out Les was also on that job. But Les was an ironworker, and ironworkers and finishers seldom worked side-by-side. Still, she avoided it. Was something she just wasn't ready for.

She wasn't sure she'd ever be ready for that. A part of her wanted to believe him when he said he still loved her. He probably did in his own way. Another part of her wanted to believe she could love him again. But she probably couldn't.

Whatever. There would be time for all that later.

Angela had had exactly two *dates* in the last nine months and both had been disastrous. They had only served to convince her that she was certifiably addicted to sex as she was sure she'd scared the holy crap out of both of the lucky men, both men calling her the next day hoping for seconds, neither scoring. So she'd decided to fly strictly solo for a while. Other priorities, specifically her divorce and custody hearing, needed her attention first and she didn't need the risk of a loose reputation in the meantime.

She had also worked with special diligence to cultivate a distinct chill between herself and the lesbians working in the trades who would inevitably check her out from time to time. Guys and the occasional gal would flirt with her and she'd toss it right back at them. She'd stop after work for a beer on Friday sometimes when the whole crew was going to be there, and then go home…alone. Not that she was particularly content with the single life, but it was best that way. For now.

Angela didn't hear him slip into the room behind her, so, when she glimpsed Norman standing in the doorway she nearly jumped out of her skin. Sucked in a quick breath – she had never learned how to scream – and stepped back into the work she'd just finished. She dropped the margin trowel and stood frozen and mute in place.

"Shitty music," Norman said. "Depressing. Didn't mean to scare you."

Angela found her voice, said, "I know who you are. I thought you were *dead*. In Spokane. There were shots. The police."

"You mean the old *Troubleshooter*, Hoot, didn't tell you that he missed me?"

Norman appeared calm. He was talking slowly and wearing a big oversized grin in the middle of a scarred face that didn't look like it should be sporting a grin at all. In spite of the grin, his expression was as cold and dark as the rainy weather outside, and it made her feel a chill. He was wearing crooked taped-up glasses and his eyes behind them were scanning the room. He glanced down at the mess Angela had stepped into and said, "You'd better fix that."

"Why are you here?"

"That's exactly the same thing I've been wondering about you since I first saw you. You probably don't remember – it was at a truck stop in Wenatchee. And then…presto! Imagine my surprise when, all of a sudden, we were housemates! I just stopped in to say hi, Donnagirl. Haven't seen you in a long time. Hardly at all with your clothes on."

His gaze locked on her a moment and he said, "And that outfit! It just isn't you. You hardly look like…your*self*…at all."

Norman's eyes were busy, taking in the room, sizing up every detail, barely glancing up at Angela. With hardly any eye contact at all, he said, "Really. Go ahead and fix that. I'll wait." It sounded more like an order that a request.

Stepping out of the mess, Angela picked up the margin trowel and scraped her boots clean, said, "I can fix it later."

Norman's eyes locked on hers for a second, a look so hard that she felt burned.

He said, "No. Do it now, before it sets up."

It definitely sounded like an order. He was scaring her.

Angela knelt down and went to work, deftly applying the last of the mixed-up material, and smoothing out her footprints with the margin trowel. It was the wrong tool for this application, but she didn't want to reach too close to where Norman was standing behind her to get the fresno.

"If you don't think I look like myself, Nathan, who do you think I look like?" Angela said over her shoulder.

"*Nathan*?" Norman said. "Oh, yeah, my Spokane name, *Donna*. You mind if I call you Donna? You *are* her, aren't you?"

"Hoot told me about Donna," Angela said. "He told me you killed her."

"Good old Hoot, the U.S. Marshal," Norman said. "Did you hear that he put his guns away? Hung up his hat and spurs?"

"He did?"

"Hoot and I have been friends for a long time. He tell you that? He was crazy about Donna. Fucked him up in the head when she died."

"You mean when you killed her?"

Norman smiled that creepy smile again, his eyes taking on a compassionate look, he said, "Of course, pardon me... *You* would know."

"I don't know anything," Angela said, standing up. "You're confused. I'm *not* this person named Donna from your past. I'm not her ghost."

"Would you take that off your head please," Norman squinted up his eyes through his glasses to read her hardhat, "*Angie*?"

It didn't sound like a request. Norman's hand was in his coat pocket and Angela was sure it held some kind of weapon.

"The other thing, too," he said after she set the hardhat aside.

She removed the bandanna and shook her hair free. Not so blonde now that she had quit using a rinse on it.

"That's better," Norman said.

Looking at her Carhartt's he said, "Those are the baggiest pants I've ever seen on a woman."

Glancing up, he added, "You ought to loose the sweatshirt too."

Defiantly, Angela said, "I'm not going to strip for you, Nathan. I don't do that anymore."

"Of course not," Norman said. "Why don't you just call me *Norman...?*"

"And you can call me *Angela*, okay"

Norman laughed, said "What a feisty little skinwalker you are, Donnagirl."

"So, what happened to Emilio? You kill him, too?"

"No. I didn't. I heard he had to leave Spokane in a hurry – green card problems. I'm surprised you haven't seen him around here in Seattle. Try dining in some of the better establishments."

Norman stepped closer, observed her work, said, "Nicely done, but you missed a spot over there." He pointed at a small area near the jamb and then stepped back.

"That Emilio. He was a faggot. Did you know that?" Norman said.

"No. I didn't."

"Yes. You did." Norman looked at Angela like she'd failed a test. "You seen Liz?" he asked.

She stiffened. "You want to kill Liz?"

Laughing as if that was the funniest damned joke he'd ever heard, Norman said, "*Liz*? No! Of course not! I *like* Liz. Only slut I've ever known who isn't really a slut at all."

"I haven't seen her."

"You've probably been too busy to look very hard."

"What do you mean?" Angela said. "Do you know where she is?"

"I can find her easily enough if I want to," Norman said. "I found you, didn't I?"

Angela looked at Norman and was suddenly very afraid. She glanced at the door, wanting to make a run for it.

There was a clicking sound and a knife suddenly appeared in Norman's hand. He said, "I'm looking for a simple answer, *Donna*...who'd you come back to haunt? Me? Or Hoot?"

Another voice from the hallway said, "She's not Donna, asshole!"

Ezra Hooten stepped into the room. He had a gun in his hand and it was pointed at Norman. He said, "She's been trying to hammer it through your thick skull. She *isn't* Donna's ghost. She doesn't know anything about Donna. Doesn't give the tiniest bugfuck that you killed her or that I abandoned her. Now, drop the knife…"

Norman felt deranged, his eyes darted from Angela to Hoot and back and he couldn't stop them. Hoot had slipped up on him again! Either he was loosing his connection or Hoot had found his. Either way…

He was having trouble holding on to thoughts that seemed to have elsewhere to go. This sensation not a foreign one – Norman recognized that it was a manifestation of his sleep apnea, a result of not getting a moment's deep REM sleep since he left his C-pap machine behind in Spokane – goddamn that Troubleshooter, sneaking up on him like that. The van had been parked too far away for him to get to it with Hoot's bullet in his butt.

Norman was feeling so goddamned tired! And a little dizzy, he felt like he was riding backward on an escalator. The music from the other room. Hoot's voice – he hadn't thought his old blood-brother had it in him, and that was a mistake. Everything sounded hollow. He felt his pulse becoming erratic. A sheen of sweat appeared on his brow in spite of the chilled air. There was a constriction working its way up from inside him.

Not *now*! Norman thought, feeling himself sliding away. Bad timing!

"*This* woman is a mother and a cement finisher," Hoot was saying, sounding far away. "Her name is *Angela*. She is not Donna…"

Norman became very still. His eyes were focused on a tiny spot on the floor near Angela's feet. He could feel his face turning dark red and getting darker. His ears buzzed. He didn't seem to be breathing, and he was pretty sure it had been a long time since his last heartbeat. "You sure of that?" he said, his voice seeming…disconnected.

"I happen to like the baggypants look on you, Angela," Hoot said as if they had last spoken a couple of weeks ago and not nearly a year ago.

273

"Where did *you* come from?" Angela answered.

"Same place he did. Ground floor," Hoot answered, folding his shades into a pocket even though it was dark as pitch outside. "And it's a long goddamned hike up the stairs for an old retired fart."

"There's a manlift." Angela said.

"Too noisy. And I didn't think the guy at the bottom would let me on without a hardhat," Hoot answered.

Norman was redder in the face than seemed humanly possible. His eyes were dilated until his pupils looked the size of saucers. He stood as still as a department store mannequin. He still wasn't breathing.

Hoot pulled a cell phone out of a pocket punched a speed dial numeral, said, "Marcus, he was here alright. Call it in to Horner. Looks like he's having some kind of seizure. We need a paramedic unit. Twelfth floor."

Angela looked at Hoot as if he were an apparition and could vanish as mysteriously as he had appeared.

"I've been waiting for your old housemate here to show up again since he left Spokane," Hoot said, cocking his head a bit to look into Norman's eyes. "Been keeping an occasional eye on you as well, just in case."

"Still using me as bait?"

Hoot smiled, said, "You shouldn't think of yourself that way." He gestured toward Norman with the gun, saying, "I *said*, drop the knife!"

Nothing. Not a movement, a flicker of the eye, or change of expression from Norman. He could have been frozen, a freaksicle on a stick. Didn't drop the knife. His complexion was turning from red to ashen pale now.

"Move away from him, Angela," Hoot said.

Norman suddenly jerked to life as if his heart had been jump-started from an ethereal place, his head snapping, his hands jerking, he sucked in air that hissed through his dentures and said, "You know that's not her real name?"

"Close enough for me," Hoot answered. "Now lose the fuckin knife."

Still nothing. Norman looked confused, as if he had just been dropped into the room from another planet and needed a

274

moment to assess the situation. He asked, "You got no partner, lawman? No backup? Wait a minute…I shot your partner, and you're not even a lawman anymore, are you? I heard you turned in your star. You're only my blood-brother, now."

"Partner's right behind me."

"I don't think so, blood-brother. I think you came charging up here all hero-like, all alone, thinking that you could save sweet Donna this time."

Angela sidestepped away. When she was safely off to the side Hoot glanced at her, asked, "You okay?"

Angela answered, "Yeah…"

And in the time it took the sound of her voice to reach his ears and register, the knife flew from Norman's hand to the center of Hoot's belly.

Hoot stumbled back a step. Squeezed off one round before dropping the gun.

The bullet missed its intended target and ricocheted a couple of times off concrete walls before burying itself, harmless, in a patch of fresh self-leveling underlayment. He looked down, and there was Norman's knife buried to the hilt in his abdomen. The sight of it was surprising. It felt cold. It felt as if it went all the way through him. He sank to his knees, and then fell backward against the wall.

Norman walked over to Hoot, said, "It's a good thing you retired when you did. You're getting too old for the street. Your reflexes are pathetic!" He kicked the gun away and then leaned down close to Hoot's ear, running his fingers through his old friend's white hair, he whispered, "Stay right here my blood-brother. I'll be back for my prize." He squatted down, jerked the knife from Hoot's belly, and Hoot felt his guts racing out the bleeding hole after it.

There was pain! *Lots* of pain!

The sound of scrambling footsteps behind panicked voices came from the stairwell. "Angie! Angie! You okay?"

"Tell them you're okay," Norman commanded without looking at her, still staring down at his old friend.

"Do it!"

"I'm fine!" Angela cried out.

275

A face appeared in the doorway, saying, "I thought I heard a gunshot."

"Get back, Reggie! Please! Keep everyone back. I'm okay."

"What the fuck? Who're these guys?"

"Old friends. It's okay. Just get back!"

Norman stood and said over his shoulder, "Very good, Sweetheart." He listened to the voices receding down the stairwell, then turned around and there she was, Donna reincarnated, standing right behind him. She was looking down at Hoot with an expression that looked like anger on her face and Norman thought he liked it. A little anger was better than a bunch of makeup for some women. It convinced him that he'd been right about her all along – she was a malefic spirit, a skinwalker, here for Hoot as much as for him, and was disappointed that he had failed her again.

Oh yes…there was disappointment in her eyes.

He glanced down at Hoot slumped against the wall, saw that a dark red stain was rapidly spreading from his middle, said, "Looks like he's going to make a mess on your nice new concrete floor."

When he turned back to Angela he was wearing another one of his disingenuous denture-perfect grins pasted across his face. The grin quickly turned sour when, without any warning or the slightest indication that might have made him wary, she jabbed with unexpected speed and strength and sank the razor-sharp margin trowel into his neck, slicing through the middle of his larynx and cutting his jugular.

"That's for Marshal Hoot!" she hissed, and spat on him as he fell backward. *And* for your Donna…"

Blood poured from Norman's neck and down the front of his chest like hot lava from Mt. Vesuvius. He dropped his knife and stumbled back until he slumped down against the wall next to his old friend.

Shit! he thought. She *got* me!

Norman struggled once to get up, and then surrendered the effort. Seemed his legs didn't want to work just now.

Something was hurting like hell.

Norman's glasses lay half-crooked across his nose. He looked up at his assailant. She stood there in her baggy and dirty work jeans and flannel shirt, blonde hair all askew; there were kneepads on her knees. He liked the kneepads. He remembered the last time he saw her dance at Goodtime Charlie's. She'd been so naked and lewd up on the stage. He thought she looked sexier now than she had then. She was kinda dirty and tough-looking with the kneepads on. His attention kept going back to those kneepads.

To Angela he tried to say, "You should have worn those kneepads at Goodtime Charlie's," but all that came out was a series of gurgles sounding in his head a little like a Harley-Davidson running under water. The margin trowel, its handle sticking out of his neck, wiggled when he tried to talk. Norman wanted to pull it out but couldn't seem to lift his arm.

Both of his arms had turned to lead and his legs were getting cold. His breathing wasn't working right either, lungs aching for air that couldn't seem to get through like the worst apnea attack of his life. He thought, I'm all fucked-up here. And then he realized that he was probably dying.

I think I went and got myself killed.

Killed by a goddamned ghost!

It figures. My mother is probably turning over in her grave...

Norman could see Hoot propped against the wall and bleeding next to him, both of them dying together. He smiled, and thought, Yes, this is the way it had to be.

Donna was looking down at him. Except she didn't look so much like Donna to Norman now – maybe she was only Angela after all. She was looking down at him with a quizzical expression, like she was trying to understand something. People had been looking at him with that same expression his whole life.

She knelt beside him and whispered something familiar in his ear.

She said, "The path that brought us here no longer exists."

Chapter 35

Ezra Hooten lay in the hospital with IVs and monitor probes stuck in places only a sadist would think to stick them. He didn't look too good, but better than when they had hauled him in here.

The 911 guys always come quickly to construction sites; they'd had a slight head start in this case because Marcus had set it up, and it was a good thing because Hoot would have run out of blood in a couple more minutes.

They were not quick enough for Norman. What blood he hadn't spewed all over the floor, he'd sucked into his lungs and drowned in it. There was no reviving him even though they had tried.

"What now, Angela...*Hunter*?" Hoot asked.

"Or maybe Blackstone," Angela answered. "I can keep my married name if I want, or switch back. I haven't decided yet. Still got some rough ground to cover with my kids and want to do whatever is easiest for them. My divorce will be final in a couple of months, and I think maybe I have a pretty good shot at getting joint custody. Les called and said he'd decided not to fight it. I'll keep up my apprenticeship classes and become a journeyman, for sure. Whatever it takes. Have a life that's my own."

"Sounds like a very good plan."

"Yeah? Well, it's a *plan*, at least. Remember, you told me once that I needed one?"

"I guess this means you won't be hitting the road with old Hoot?"

She laughed, said, "'Fraid not. Send me postcards?"

"Sure. Maybe I'll call next time I'm cruising through this part of the country. In case you change your mind."

"Yeah. You do that." She stood to leave, said, "You still think I look like a girl from Maine?"

"Not so much anymore. Still good lookin, though, in a Midwest sort of way."

Angela fished in her purse and produced a plastic evidence bag containing the margin trowel that had been the death of Norman. She laid it in Hoot's hand, said, "Don't tell anyone...Deputy Marcus gave it to me. I think you should have it. Something to remember me by."

"You won't be needing it?"

"I have a new one. They wear out. Get real sharp on the end."

"I've noticed."

Hoot admired the razor-sharp trowel, said, "I've got something for you too." He nodded toward the side table where there was an envelope that had *Angela Hunter* written on it in neat block letters.

"Should I open it now?"

"No. It's not from me."

"A mutual friend trusted me with it."

Angela ruffed-up his halo of white, said, "Bye, Marshal Hoot," and then she went out through the door and was gone.

The room seemed exceptionally empty without her.

"That would be *ex*-marshal, Angel," Hoot said to a lingering memory that he hoped would take a long time to fade.

He took the margin trowel out of its bag and looked at it more closely. Noticed the manufacturer's name branded into the wood handle – *Marshalltown*.

He had to laugh.

It was still early. The morning fog lay in a thick blanket over Elliott Bay, cloaking West Seattle and creeping around in low spots all the way down to Federal Way. It would burn off by mid-morning. A good day to pour concrete as long as it didn't decide to rain.

Angela bought a hot coffee on the way out of the hospital, amazed at how good the coffee was in certain hospital cafeterias nowadays.

She stopped at her car and pulled out the envelope Hoot had given her. Inside was a folded page from an old *Far Side* desk calendar. Written on the back was the name and address of an assisted care nursing facility nearby in Burien where a short, spiky-blonde woman with dark roots sat at her mother's bedside. At the bottom of the note was a familiar-looking scrawl that said only, *Liz*.

Chapter 36

"Ezz! Happy t' see ya," Hoot's younger brother, Eric, said with a big muscular hug. At fifty-four years old, Hoot figured Eric was probably at the physical peak of his entire life. Two kids. Three stepchildren. Five grandkids. And the man looked like he could still singlehandedly gaff a half-ton swordfish into the hold with the best of 'em – as truly he could. "Been too long, Brother."

"I know," Hoot said, looking out over the manicured rolling landscape that was Forest Lawn Cemetery, a few sunrays making one last effort to burn through an all-day blanket of fog before calling it quits and setting. He carried a basketful of flowers in one hand, a rising sense of purpose in his heart.

"Have a good flight?" Eric asked.

"There's no such thing," Hoot said. "Got me here alive and on time. That's all I can ask."

Hoot's other hand rested on an aluminum cane. He didn't really think he needed the cane – but using it these past couple of months seemed to keep his gut from hurting so much at the end of the day. Plus, it was handy for pointing and poking at things. And for garnering sympathetic glances from the opposite sex.

He saw a growing crowd milling about in the direction they were heading, toward Donna's gravesite – his mom and dad's site three rows up. More folks joining them, the crowd began to sing. Hoot stopped and listened, leaning on the cane and hearing the lyrics drifting up the hill: *Amazing Grace, how sweet the sound, that saved a wretch like me.*

"What are all these people doing here?" Hoot asked Eric. Annoyed that a nearby interment could jeopardize the privacy he sought for what he was about to do.

I once was lost but now am found, was blind, but now I see...

"I don't know, Ezz," Eric answered. "But I think they're here for you."

"*Me…why me?*"

"Word's out about you killing Norman Carpenter in Seattle. Lots of people around here have been following that case since the beginning. Most of us were 'fraid the bastard got away with it. Somebody musta leaked it that you were coming here today."

Hoot started to argue it wasn't him who killed Norman, but looked at the gathering crowd, instead. It looked as if half the town was here. And he knew they weren't here for him – they were here for Donna, just as he was.

He heard them singing: *Through many dangers, toils and snares, I have already come;*

He looked at the flowers in his basket – one colorful bouquet each for his mother and father, a spray of white roses for Donna – and considered turning back, doing this tomorrow or the next day; privately placing the roses on Donna's grave and saying, *It's done.*

'Tis Grace that brought me safe thus far and Grace will lead me home…

Hoot yearned to be away from so many eyes. But that was impossible.

The crowd was looking back at him, holding his gaze.

Even from three rows away he could see several tearful faces in the midst of many familiar ones, all of them singing out: *Yea, when this flesh and heart shall fail, And mortal life shall cease, I shall possess within the veil, A life of joy and peace…*

Hoot turned to his brother, said, "Alright. Let's take care of Mom and Dad, first."

The End